*Also by Jenny Bayliss*

*A Season for Second Chances*
*The Twelve Dates of Christmas*

## Praise for *A Season for Second Chances*

"[An] inspiring tale of strength, integrity, and self-respect . . . Readers will be enchanted." —*Publishers Weekly*

"Bayliss's fans and readers who enjoy laugh-out-loud rom-coms will want to spend a cozy winter evening by the fire with Annie and the residents of Willow Bay." —*Library Journal*

"There's so much to love about this enchanting story. Readers will want their own seat at the café Annie opens and to attend every quirky holiday party the townspeople dream up. This lovely, cozy read is perfect for winter." —*BookPage* (starred review)

"Enormously entertaining, this manages to be escapism of the highest order." —Minneapolis *Star Tribune*

"A gorgeous, cozy winter read that will transport you to the coast on a windswept day. Full of quirky characters and a refreshingly mature leading lady, this book will restore anyone's faith that it's never too late for a second chance at love, or indeed, life."

—Sophie Cousens, author of *This Time Next Year*
and *Just Haven't Met You Yet*

# Praise for *The Twelve Dates of Christmas*

"With its cozy, small-town setting and adorable premise, *The Twelve Dates of Christmas* is the perfect book for anyone looking for a charming holiday romance."             —*PopSugar*

"We can't get enough of this twist on the '12 Days of Christmas'!"             —*Country Living*

"Bayliss delivers delightful holiday atmosphere and believable romantic tension in her cute and cozy debut . . . By turns tender and hilarious, this adorable rom-com is sure to satisfy."             —*Publishers Weekly*

"Charming . . . This slow-burn rom-com set in a small British village at Christmas will be the perfect cup of tea for fans of Marian Keyes or Helen Fielding."             —*Library Journal*

"Fans of the best-friends-to-lovers and second chance tropes will savor this."             —*Booklist*

"[A] nice cozy rom-com novel, one with a bit of an edge, a larger meaning, and a satisfying ending."             —Minneapolis *Star Tribune*

# Meet Me Under the Mistletoe

*A novel*

## JENNY BAYLISS

G. P. PUTNAM'S SONS
New York

**PUTNAM**
— EST. 1838 —

G. P. PUTNAM'S SONS
*Publishers Since 1838*
An imprint of Penguin Random House LLC
penguinrandomhouse.com

Library of Congress Cataloging-in-Publication Data
Names: Bayliss, Jenny, author.
Title: Meet me under the mistletoe / Jenny Bayliss.
Description: New York: G. P. Putnam's Sons, [2022] |
Identifiers: LCCN 2022027443 | ISBN 9780593422229 (trade paperback) |
ISBN 9780593422236 (ebook)
Subjects: LCGFT: Romance fiction. | Christmas fiction. | Novels.
Classification: LCC PR6102.A975 M44 2022 |
DDC 823/.92—dc23/eng/20220613
LC record available at https://lccn.loc.gov/2022027443

Printed in the United States of America
1st Printing

Book design by Tiffany Estreicher

For Bev, Jayne, and Helen.
Friends for thirty years and counting,
with love xxx

# Meet Me
## Under
### the Mistletoe

## One

Shepherd Market is old London. Two small squares of ye olde quaint shop fronts and pubs, some dating back to the 1700s, nestle unconcerned among the steel and glass monoliths of their descendants. A peculiar vibe of village camaraderie and tourism pulses through the tiny neighborhood; doors open with tinkling bells into welcomingly dark shops, and people mingle in the street, strangers and friends passing the time. And it is here, sandwiched between a tailor and a bistro, that Elinor Noel—Nory to those who know her best—runs her secondhand bookshop, Serendipitous Seconds, with her right-hand man, Andrew.

The woman in the long blue floral coat with curly gray hair flowing to her waist had been leafing through a book of prints by the Dutch Old Masters for nearly twenty minutes, and Nory was beginning to twitch. One of the only downsides, so far as Nory could see, to spending your life surrounded by beautiful books was that people kept wanting to buy your favorites.

Andrew pushed a mug of coffee into her hand.

"Stop staring," he hissed. "You'll put her off the sale."

Nory narrowed her eyes and stared harder. "That is one of the most comprehensive books we have on the Old Masters' still lifes," she whispered. "The quality of the prints is exquisite. They don't print books on that kind of paper anymore."

"Which is reflected in the price tag, which is why we need this sale. Now stop intimidating our only customer and help me decipher this inventory."

She allowed herself to be led away to the large mahogany desk at the back of the shop. Andrew was on an eternal quest to try to keep track of the vast and eclectic jumble of books for which they had long since run out of shelf and stacking space. Nory didn't feel that the alchemy of bringing books together with readers could be contained in a spreadsheet.

Face-to-face sales may not have been her strong suit, but Nory had a gift for finding rare and beautiful books and matching them with owners who would treasure them forever. It was like she could feel the books calling to her. She could sift through a box of dime-a-dozen titles and find the hidden gem. Not only that, but she would instantly know who the book was destined for. Andrew called her the book whisperer. And it was this talent that kept people coming back for more. In her desk drawer, she had a small leatherbound book with the names of all her repeat customers and the books they had purchased. When a fresh consignment of titles arrived at the shop, she would reach for the book of names, fingers tingling with the promise of matches to be made; book love was a magical thing.

Matilda murmured in her papoose, which was attached to Andrew's front. Matilda was four months old now and Nory wondered how long Andrew could continue to carry her around for hours at a time without developing a stoop. Matilda spent two days in the shop with Andrew and three days at home with his husband, Seb, who worked in graphic design. In January, Matilda would start at nursery and Andrew was already fretting.

The woman in the floral coat began to walk toward the desk, zigzagging slightly as she negotiated the piles of books on tables and footstools, organized in an order known only to Nory, and Nory felt herself tense. Andrew rested a steadying hand on her shoulder.

It wasn't that she was against selling books—this was, after all, her chosen profession—it was that she felt a particular affinity with anything botanical, in particular botanical art, and she had collected some rather fabulous books on the subject, which she was loath to part with. She guessed that's what you got for growing up in a family-run nursery business; her whole family was plant obsessed.

The woman placed the tome—a collection of the works of Rachel Ruysch—with due reverence on the desk, and Nory thawed slightly; perhaps she was the right owner for this book after all.

"Can you do anything on the price?" she asked.

Nory made a face like she was thinking about it. "It's a very rare reproduction. I think it's priced more than fairly."

You did not, in Nory's opinion, haggle where the Old Masters were concerned. The woman eyed her.

Andrew, with Matilda snuffling contentedly into his chest, leaned over and asked, "I wonder if this book could be the first in our ten percent discount Christmas offer?" in a terribly polite voice that only Nory knew actually meant *Make the goddamned sale!*

The woman's eyes widened briefly, and she raised one eyebrow expectantly at Nory. Nory smiled.

"Of course, how silly of me to forget the Christmas discount! Let's round it down to three hundred and twenty-five pounds exactly."

"Wonderful!" exclaimed the woman. She began immediately to rummage around in her handbag, while Andrew whisked the book—which Nory had been wistfully stroking—out of Nory's reach to wrap it.

Andrew handed the book, enveloped in thick brown parchment paper and secured with string, to Nory, and Nory held it out to the woman. The woman took it, but Nory held on. Suddenly she couldn't seem to make her hands unclench. The woman tugged and Nory resisted. The woman smiled uncertainly and tugged again. Reluctantly Nory let go, and the woman hurried out of the shop, apparently fearing Nory might give chase. In fairness, if Ameerah hadn't ambled in at that moment and flung herself into one of the old chesterfield armchairs in the reading corner, she might have.

Ameerah was wearing a black floor-length military coat, undone to reveal a tailored black skirt suit that nipped in at the waist and a brilliant white shirt with a ruffle down either side of the buttons. Her knee-high, stilettoed black boots squeaked as she crossed her legs elegantly and settled her gaze first on Nory and then Andrew.

"Hello, my darlings. Coffee's on the way." She smiled.

Where Ameerah was tall and Marlene Dietrich sleek, Nory was five foot five at a pinch with decidedly Rubenesque proportions. Nory had a heart-shaped face with high cheekbones, emphasized by almost permanently rosy cheeks; if she were an actress she would surely be typecast as a buxom wench. Her shoulder-length hair, like her eyes, was a mixture of browns, golds, and ambers that caught the light. Her friend Jenna had once said that Nory had the coloring of a tortoiseshell cat. Nory had decided there were far worse animals to be likened to.

Nory checked her watch. "Shouldn't you be in court, defending the defenseless?" she asked.

"The case was adjourned until the morning."

"Lucky us," said Andrew slyly.

"Don't pretend you're not delighted to see me," said Ameerah. "Now, bring my goddaughter over here so that I can coo over her."

"Actually, Ameerah, Matilda is *my* goddaughter."

"Yes, but we're best friends, so she's my goddaughter by proxy."

Nory couldn't argue with that.

The bell jingled, and Hannah, the owner of Delizioso Coffee, came in bearing three cardboard cups, steaming in the cold air.

"Thank you, Hannah," said Nory, taking the cups. "You didn't need to bring them over, I would have come and got them."

"It's no bother. We're quiet at the moment. The lull before the lunch rush. Lots of people are talking about your window display. It's quite a hit."

Andrew beamed. This year's Christmas window design had been his idea: a three-foot plump and jolly Father Christmas sat in a rocking chair, reading, his half-moon glasses slipped to the end of his nose. Around him were piles of well-loved books and vintage Christmas titles propped up, covers facing outward. This morning they had sold a particularly crusty-looking copy of *The Little Match Girl* from the display.

"Let's hope it brings the customers in," said Nory.

"If she can bear to actually part with the books," added Andrew. He was kneeling at Ameerah's feet, the papoose still attached to him while Ameerah poured adoration upon his daughter. Having men at her feet, even gay men, was something Ameerah was used to.

Hannah left, and Nory began searching for a book to fill the hole on the shelf left by the one just purchased—an unfilled bookshelf was a sad shelf indeed. She wandered over to a pile of leatherbound tomes sitting on an antique dining chair with a frayed red velvet seat. She knew exactly what she was looking for and gave a little hum of satisfaction when she found it: a book celebrating paintings by Maria Sibylla Merian. Nory carefully extricated it from the stack and stroked the cover. The antique chair creaked in gratitude at having some weight lifted from it. She gently opened the book and began to turn the pages, feeling a sense of deep contentment as her eyes roamed over paintings that were as familiar to her as her own face. Nory had studied literature and art history at university and had written her final dissertation on the forgotten female artists of the golden age; Merian's work had featured heavily.

"Stop fawning over that tatty old book and drink your coffee," called Ameerah.

"Don't listen to her," Nory comedy-whispered to the book, closing it and slipping it into the space left by the latest sale. Ameerah had very little appreciation for anything that came before the 1990s, and that included her boyfriends. Nory sat down on an old wooden milking stool she'd found in the basement when she'd taken over the shop, and sipped her coffee.

Serendipitous Seconds had more than its fair share of cozy nooks and each was filled with a comfortable old chair of some description. In Nory's opinion, book buying should never be rushed; she wanted her customers to feel they could sit and get to know a book before they purchased.

"Andrew, I've had another email from Jenna to say that Nory is dragging her heels about the house party. We're supposed to arrive on the twenty-ninth of November—that's this Sunday! Your employer is being unconscionably difficult. Talk to her."

"I've tried, believe me. She's being very resistant."

"I am here, you know! And I'm not being difficult, I'm going to the wedding, and I've offered to help with prep in any way I can. I just don't know if I ought to go to the house party first."

"But it won't be the same without you. The whole point is that we have the old gang together again, just us, before all the other guests arrive. When was the last time we were all properly together?"

"You know when," said Nory.

A familiar pang of sorrow coiled around her ribs, making her chest tighten. They had been such a tight group at school. It had seemed unthinkable they could ever drift apart. But of course they did. Until Tristan's death had brought them back together in the worst possible way.

"Exactly," said Ameerah more softly. "And we said we wouldn't drift apart again."

"We haven't. I keep in contact with everyone . . . well, almost everyone." Nory frowned as a memory of her and Guy, in flagrante, flashed into her mind.

"Yes, but not all together at the same time! Come on, Nory, we're the *shits and giggles gang*, remember? You have to come, or we'll be another member down." She pulled a sad face and then said: "Don't make me benzodiazepine your tea."

"For someone who works in law, you have a decidedly squiffy moral compass," Andrew noted.

"My client list is long and varied and each one brings its own education." Ameerah winked.

"Christmas is our busiest time of year; I can't just go galivanting off for a jolly in a castle," Nory reasoned.

"It's not just *any old castle*, it's Robinwood Castle, the playground of our youth. And it's not just any old jolly either. It's a week spent with our oldest and dearest friends."

Ameerah made a compelling case. It wasn't that Nory didn't desperately want to spend time with her friends, but it was complicated, and these days she tried to avoid complicated where possible. Still, she was running out of excuses.

"Also, I've had sex with the groom," she countered.

Ameerah threw her head back and laughed. "We've all had sex with the groom, Nory!"

This was probably true. The very exclusive private school to which Nory had won a scholarship had been somewhat isolated, and as such provided a rather small pool in which its horny teenage students could experiment sexually; so, the girls and boys of Braddon-Hartmead made sure they swam every inch of it. Charles, the groom, had been generally known to be an absolute hound in the sixth form. Beneath his yearbook picture, the quote read: *Most likely to become a porn star.* He'd become an investment banker.

"Are you bringing Dev?" Nory asked.

"Yes. Man-Barbie will be accompanying me for the purposes of being eye candy and heroically good in the sack."

Dev Chakrabarti was Ameerah's latest boyfriend, a model who was the darling of *British Vogue* photographers and a well-known figure on the catwalk at the Milan, Paris, London, and New York Fashion Weeks. Ameerah was fond of saying she had neither the time nor the space in her life for men who had *something to say*, she merely wanted them to look good and fuck better.

"It doesn't seem fair that he should be a nice person and attractive *and* good in bed. There must be something wrong with him," said Nory, screwing up her button nose.

Nory had met Dev several times now and found him to

be very good company, quite different from the vacuous men Ameerah usually dated.

"There is," Ameerah said, stretching and yawning. "He's a man-Barbie."

"I think Dev has hidden depths. You simply won't give him the chance to show you. Did you know he has a degree in politics and international relations?"

"What?" Ameerah was taken aback. "Who? Dev?"

"Are you objectifying a man, Ameerah? I'm shocked." Andrew smiled wickedly.

Ameerah pulled a face at him. "Andrew, darling, I have been objectified since the day I grew these." She paused to poke out her boobs and prod them in turn. "Do you think men see me in my barrister getup and think 'Gosh, she looks like a clever well-read woman'? No, they look at me and think, 'What's she got under those robes,' and assume I must have slept my way to the top. That is, if they don't first mistake me for a defendant."

"Cynical much?" asked Andrew.

"Tell me I'm wrong," said Ameerah fiercely.

Andrew put his hands up in surrender.

"Does that mean we ought to behave as badly as men?" Nory queried.

"Oh, I'm sick of having to be the better person. Why is it always down to women to act like grown-ups and lead by example? I want equal rights to objectification."

"Well, objectification aside, if hypothetically I do come to the house party, I'll be the only person without a plus-one. I'll be the proverbial third wheel."

"Are you not enough as you are?" asked Andrew, one eyebrow raised archly. "Do you need a man by your side in order to feel complete?"

"Certainly not!" Nory was indignant.

"Then you should be perfectly happy to attend as a one." He smiled triumphantly.

"I'm worried about the shop." This was a small lie.

Andrew, who had left his position beside Ameerah's throne and begun to re-alphabetize the middle-grade children's section, turned with his hands on hips.

"And what am I?" he asked. "Chopped liver?"

"Andrew, you know what Christmas is like here. I can't leave you to cope on your own."

"I'll get Seb to come in. He's helped out before."

"And what about Matilda?"

"Well, naturally she'll come too. We can take turns to carry her in the papoose. She'll love having both her parents with her all day."

"As if that baby isn't spoiled enough," said Ameerah.

"How can you spoil a four-month-old baby?" asked Andrew. "All they want is cuddles, love, and food: pretty basic requirements for any human, really."

"I only saw my parents at weddings and funerals; didn't do me any harm," said Ameerah mirthlessly.

"I rest my case," Andrew remarked, giving Ameerah a side-eye.

Ameerah had been a boarder at Braddon-Hartmead from age eleven and had been raised by a nanny before that; she was only slightly exaggerating how little of her childhood she had spent with her parents. Nory's family lived in the village down the hill from the school, so she only boarded Monday to Friday.

"What about Mugwort?" asked Nory.

Mugwort was her cat. He was seventeen years old and only

had three legs, since he'd lost one during an altercation with a Deliveroo bike two years ago. Mugwort had decided, rather wisely, that he would become a house cat after that.

Andrew crossed the room and laid his hand on Nory's arm. "Nory," he said. "We'll have Mugwort, he's no bother and he knows his way around our place. Go and have some fun! Your shop and your feline will be fine."

"Andrew, that's really very sweet of you, but you've got enough going on, you really don't need an elderly, disabled cat moving in."

"We've got Seb's mother coming to stay for the whole of December. What's one more cantankerous cat into the mix?"

Ameerah stretched out her long legs and her boots creaked.

"There we are," she said. "All your stupid protestations have been quashed. You're coming!" As a barrister, Ameerah was not used to losing cases.

"And what about Guy?" Nory asked.

"What about him?"

"You know what."

Ameerah puffed out exasperatedly and looked at her perfectly manicured nails. "Well, obviously he'll be there. Like it or not, he's one of us. I'll be on hand as your human shield, but honestly, Nory, he's not going to be making sleazy jokes about it with his wife there."

"How can I face Camille? I'll just burn up with shame every time I see her."

"You didn't know he was married, so the shame isn't yours. If anyone should be burning, it's Guy. And anyway, that was five years ago!" said Ameerah.

"I don't see how that's relevant, Ameerah, it doesn't become less adulterous the longer ago it happened."

"All I'm saying is, it's water under the bridge, done and dusted. It's not like anyone's going to remember. And even if they do, they're hardly going to mention it with his wife there."

Nory knew full well that her old friends remembered just as well as she did.

It had happened after Tristan's funeral. The old gang had booked a farmhouse for a long weekend after the wake. They had spent the time drinking and reminiscing and swearing their allegiances to one another. There had been tears and reflections but there had been laughter too. In the early hours of Sunday morning, after far too much wine and hearts heavy with old memories, Guy and Nory had stumbled into her bedroom and the inevitable had happened, multiple times. It wasn't until they'd come down for breakfast, looking sheepish and beaming in the afterglow of having been shagging for the last six hours, that Charles had informed Nory that Guy was in fact married with two children under five. They'd had another child since.

"I still can't believe no one stopped me." Nory was filled with fresh mortification every time she thought about it.

"Nobody knew you two were going to embark on a marathon fuck-fest. Anyway, I didn't know he was married either. And by the time Pippa filled me in, the sounds of the headboard smacking against the wall suggested that Guy was already very much filling *you* in!"

Andrew spluttered a laugh, which made Matilda jump.

Nory buried her head in her hands. "You are so crude," she mumbled.

Ameerah continued. "I could hardly knock on your door while you were mid-coitus to let you know, could I? I planned to take you to one side the next day and tell you, but Charles got in first. He always was the biggest gossip."

Nory and Guy weren't the only friends to pair off that weekend. Jenna and Charles had also reconnected with each other and now they were about to be married. It was strange to think that their happiness was born out of such a tragedy. Would they have found their way back to each other if it weren't for Tristan's death? It made Nory sad to think about it, and she knew Jenna struggled with it too. Jenna said she felt guilty sometimes that her life had been transformed because of Tristan's death. Before that weekend, she'd been boomeranging hopelessly among men, trying to blot out their failings and make one of them stick. And then she'd seen Charles again and suddenly it all seemed to fall into place, as though she'd been trying to force her previous boyfriends to fit into a Charles-shaped hole.

Nory would be lying if she said she hadn't entertained similar thoughts about Guy during their brief encounter; she had fantasized between orgasms that the Fates had thrown them back into each other's paths for a reason. But of course, the Fates had had nothing to do with it, although Nory suspected Guy may have been channeling Priapus, the Greek god with the permanent erection.

"Oh, say you'll come, Nory, please! I can ask Dev to bring along another man-Barbie to play with you." Ameerah waggled her eyebrows and winked.

"No thank you. I am sworn off meaningless sex with mindless men."

"Good! That leaves more for me. Now stop playing hard to get and tell Jenna you'll come to the house party."

"You know she won't give up," said Andrew. "And besides, you haven't had a proper break this year, and really, why are you letting this hack Guy stop you from spending a week living in the lap of luxury with your oldest friends? Why are you making his life easier?"

"Yes!" said Ameerah, clapping her hands together. "Andrew is spot-on. This is about fighting against the patriarchy. Women have spent too long making apologies for men's bad behavior. If you don't come to this house party, you are allowing the cycle of systemic misogyny to continue. Don't be part of the problem, Elinor Noel, be part of the solution. Break down the walls of patriarchal mind control!"

Nory gave in. She was no match for Ameerah's courtroom arguments. And why should she be relegated to hide in the shadows because Guy couldn't keep his penis in his pants? She hadn't cheated on anyone! With Ameerah looking over her shoulder, she messaged Jenna, apologizing for "dragging her heels" and confirming that she would be coming on Sunday for the whole week.

Nory felt indignantly roused by Ameerah's speech for a full hour before she came down off the high and remembered she was a compulsive worrier and had just agreed to spend a week in a castle avoiding Guy's wife.

It was dark when Nory locked the door to Serendipitous Seconds. She stood for a few moments looking in at their festive display through the thick leaded windows. They had left the fairy lights on and Father Christmas rocking in his chair. The Christmas titles stared out at her: a 1930s reproduction of *A Christmas Carol*, a particularly battered copy of M. R. James ghost stories, an illustrated copy of *The Nutcracker and the Mouse King* by E. T. A. Hoffmann, and Tolkien's *Letters from Father Christmas*. And her favorite of all, a vintage edition of *The Night Before Christmas* illustrated by Arthur Rackham—she wasn't sure she could bear to part with that one; she had fought Andrew on having it in the window and he had won. He was right, of course, it looked beautiful, laid open to a page of Father Christmas in his sleigh among the snowy rooftops. Maybe she would pop a little red "sold" sticker in the bottom corner to put off potential buyers.

She was slowly becoming resigned to, even a little excited by, the idea of spending seven days in a drafty castle with her old school friends. Ameerah had messaged to say they would leave on the morning of Sunday the twenty-ninth, stopping for a leisurely pub lunch somewhere. Jenna had insisted that no one should arrive before 3:00 p.m. because she wanted to get acquainted with the place first. This was Jenna code for wanting to make it absolutely clear to the staff that she was the bride aka number one guest aka in charge.

Nory shivered as the cold evening eked in through her coat. Shepherd Market was picture perfect; lights twinkled from every window, and people spilled out from the pubs wrapped in scarves and clutching cold pints of ale. Nory walked the short distance to the Italian restaurant, waving and calling goodbyes to fellow shopkeepers closing up for the night.

As she pushed open the door to Pepe's, the scent of garlic and vine tomatoes washed over her.

"Elinor!" Anthony called across the crowded restaurant.

Anthony was the owner of Pepe's and Nory never failed to marvel at how sensual his strong Italian accent managed to make her name sound. She smiled warmly at him, and her stomach growled as she made her way through the candlelit tables to the small bar area at the back.

"Hi, Anthony," she said as he dramatically kissed both her cheeks.

"When are you going to marry one of my sons so that you can start calling me Papa, hmm?"

Nory laughed. This was a familiar routine. Anthony ran the restaurant with his two sons: Anthony Jr., who managed the kitchen, and Paul, who worked the bar. They were both in their late fifties. Anthony Jr. had been divorced twice and Paul was gay, but Anthony Sr. saw none of these things as an obstacle for their "making an honest woman" out of Nory.

Anthony Jr. came out of the kitchen holding a brown paper bag, which he handed to Nory before also kissing her on both cheeks.

"Lasagna," he said in his broad London accent. "And a decent helping of Mama's tiramisu."

"Mmm, thanks, Anthony. I put the money in your account earlier."

Anthony Jr. waved his hand as if money was the furthest thing from his mind.

"Leetle Elinor, always eating alone!" exclaimed Anthony Sr., loud enough for all the patrons to hear. He brought his voice down to a loud whisper and winked. "You know I would give you our best table for two if you ever want to bring a man in for dinner." He said the word *man* like it was some exotic creature, which Nory supposed it was for her; at thirty-four, she was beginning to feel like a Jane Austen spinster.

She left the restaurant, calling her goodbyes, and hurried between two buildings down a skinny alleyway that broadened out into a dead end filled with wheelie bins, giant flattened-out cardboard boxes, and other detritus from the businesses and private lets that inhabited the premises. Iron fire escapes clung to the walls and the smell of clean washing blew up through fans from the communal laundry rooms in the basements. Hidden in an alcove was a door, colored deep purple with chips revealing the navy blues and dark reds of paint coats past. An ornate Christmas wreath hung from the door knocker, incongruous against the tatty alley.

Nory let herself in and began to climb the stairs. The carpet was worn, but the walls were painted sage green and Etienne and Ross—art lecturers at UCL—had painted trailing flowers and climbing wisteria in the hallway. Nory lived on the fifth floor and there was no lift, but she didn't mind; working so close to home, sometimes these stairs were the only exercise she got.

She passed several doors on the semi landings as she climbed. She liked hearing the sounds and soaking in the smells of the lives happening behind the doors; always meaty smells and soap operas from the Greek couple in flat 7, the starchy scent of boiling rice and the sound of classical music from Anna and her Russian girlfriend in flat 10. Farther up the building, Kia, the newest addition to Neela and Jonas's brood, was making herself heard above the saccharine soundtrack of Disney tunes.

Nory turned the key in the lock and pushed open the door to find Mugwort waiting for her. No one could describe Mugwort as a looker, but that was what had attracted her to him in the rescue center; she had always been a sucker for an underdog, or in this case, undercat. Mugwort followed her into the kitchen, which saw far less cooking than she would ever admit to her mum. She fed Mugwort and slid her lasagna out of its foil dish onto a plate, then, emptying the last of a bottle of red into a wineglass, she settled onto the sofa and switched on the TV. This was her nightly routine. Later she would attempt some bookkeeping—which Andrew would correct tomorrow—and then she would scour the online auction houses for estate content sales and check to see if any of her house clearance contacts had any new book acquisitions.

In the last two years, she hadn't dated anyone for longer than three months. She wasn't sure if she had changed or if the men on the dating apps had changed, but lately she hadn't been clicking with anyone. She was supposed to be in her flirty thirties, but all the guys her age and older seemed to be wanting someone younger and she was finding precious little opportunity to do any flirting at all. Why were all the thirty-five-to-forty-year-old professional men wanting to date twenty-two-year-olds straight out of university? She was a catch, a dammed fine catch! She had her own business; staff (one member, but it still counted); a studio flat in central London; she was well-read, intelligent, curvy, reasonably attractive, a non-smoker (except after three shots of Sambuca), and she liked sex—not only that, but she was rather good at it too. How was that not getting her all the likes?

Her mobile rang.

"Hi, Mum."

"Hello, love, what are you up to?"

"Eating dinner and watching TV."

"That's nice. What are you having?"

"Lasagna."

"Homemade?"

"Mmhmm."

"Lovely. You'll have to make one for us when you're next down."

"Um, yeah sure, why not."

"Thomas said there's a big house party staying at the castle next week. Is that your friend's thing?"

"Yes, it is. How does Thomas know?"

"They've ordered all sorts of flower garlands for the staircases and arrangements for the tables, hundreds of loose blooms and greenery too. Shelley's doing extra shifts, but you know it's hard for her with the boys as well. I remember trying to manage you two and the business, especially at Christmas with all the castle displays. I was going to cut my hours back before Christmas, but there's not a chance with all this going on as well as our usual orders. Thomas thought he recognized the name on the order sheet—Pippa something, I think. You used to be friends with a Pippa, didn't you?"

"Yes, that is my friend Pippa."

Pippa had the kind of job that would send Nory's dad into a

tailspin: She was a house stylist. People with excessive amounts of money paid her to go into their houses and create floral arrangements in every room and garnish their sideboards with the correct objet d'art to make them look effortlessly stylish. It didn't surprise Nory that Jenna would have hired their friend to "dress" the castle. In her real life, Jenna didn't have quite enough money to have a house stylist on the payroll—though she had aspirations for the future—but she would be pushing the boat out for the wedding.

"Will you be there? At the castle for the week? I know you're going to the wedding, but I didn't realize there was a holiday first."

"I wasn't sure I was going to be able to make the house party. But as it turns out, I will be there, yes."

"Oh, how lovely! Make sure you come and see us. You can't be so close and not come to say hello, I couldn't stand it. Will Ameerah be coming too?"

Ameerah had been "adopted" by Nory's parents in Nory's first year at Braddon-Hartmead when they discovered that Ameerah's parents wouldn't be in the country for Christmas and Ameerah would be staying at school over the holidays. That was to be the first holiday of many for which Ameerah's parents wouldn't be around, so she had been assimilated into the Noel household. Ameerah's relationship with Nory's family was far less complicated than her own.

"Yes, Ameerah will be there."

Her mum squealed over the phone and then began to talk to her dad, while Nory hung on the phone, half listening, half watching an old episode of *Midsomer Murders*.

"Jake! Jake! . . . Guess what? . . . Nory and Ameerah are going to be at that house party Thomas was talking about . . . I

know . . . Yes, I told her they have to come down to see us . . .
Hang on, I'll ask . . . Dad says will you be bringing one of your
Tory capitalist boyfriends with you?"

Nory rolled her eyes. As far as her dad was concerned, any
man earning a living in London must be a Tory capitalist.

"No, tell him not to worry, no boyfriends this time."

Nory had given up introducing boyfriends to her dad. He
was a fiercely proud working-class man, originally from York-
shire, and no matter how left leaning Nory's boyfriends were,
somehow, they never measured up to her dad's standards. Even
if their politics aligned with her dad's own views, the dinner
table discussions would soon become a competition of who was
more working class. (Her dad always won.) Unless Nory could
produce a man who strode into the kitchen with a pickax over
one shoulder and hands callused to the point they resembled
tree bark, they were unlikely to impress her dad.

"Do you want Thomas to pick you and Ameerah up from the
station?"

"No thanks, Mum, we'll make our own way."

Ameerah had a brand-new Mini Countryman sitting in the
garage below her apartment block in Mayfair that saw very little
use, since parking in central London was horrific and you could
get everywhere you needed to faster by Tube.

"Okay, love. It'll be lovely to see you. And then it'll only be a
few weeks till Christmas, and we'll see you again! What a nice
treat."

London was less than two hours by train from the small village of Hartmead, but it might have been another country as far
as her mum was concerned. Her parents rarely visited Nory, and
each time they did, her mum marveled anew at how tiny her flat
was and the enormity of her rent.

"It'll be lovely to see you too, Mum."

"I'll tell Thomas he was right about that Pippa. Jackson lost a tooth last week, did Thomas tell you?"

"Erm, no he didn't, Shelley sent me a photo."

Shelley was her sister-in-law and the only person with the power to make her sullen brother smile, or maybe he smiled at everyone and reserved his scowls for his kid sister.

"Bless him, you can see the new tooth already, it looks like a big one, I think he might have buckteeth like you did before your braces. Do you remember Thomas used to call you Bugs Bunny?"

"Yes, Mum, I remember."

Occasionally he still called her Bugs even now. Nory and her brother's relationship was equal parts affection and low-level resentment. There were times when she just couldn't be arsed to deal with the latter.

"Won't it be lovely to be together with all your old friends again, love?" her mum said. "Well, not all of them, but you know what I mean," she added. Nory did know.

Her eyes wandered over to a framed photograph on the windowsill. A picture of the leavers picnic on the very last day of sixth form. Eight smiling young faces, excited to be moving on to the next chapter of their lives. Tristan sat between Nory and Pippa on the picnic blanket, an arm casually slung over each of their shoulders. He was laughing. Happy. Nory waited for the familiar ache to settle and smiled back at the image.

"Well anyway," her mum carried on, "I'd better leave you to it. Vera's about to start on ITV3. Say hello to Andrew for me. Love you!"

"Love you too, Mum. Bye."

∽

Tristan had been everyone's friend. At school he'd fallen into the role of peacemaker; there were some big characters in the group and some even bigger egos, but Tristan had a way of calming down heated situations. It was no surprise to anyone that he aspired to be a doctor; his mum was a surgeon, and his dad was a fertility specialist, so it was in his DNA.

He had his ups and downs, but that just seemed to be the way he ticked; he'd have months of being okay and then the cloud would fall, and it would take a while for him to come back out from underneath it. None of them had ever expected that one day he wouldn't be able to.

Tristan used to say he was his therapist's favorite client because he was a guaranteed repeat customer. He'd not long come back from a stint working in a hospital in Nairobi when Nory had last seen him. They'd bumped into each other quite by chance in Soho when they'd both wandered into a vinyl record shop. They went for coffee, which became lunch, which ended with both canceling their evening plans and going to dinner together near Leicester Square. Tristan seemed okay—better than okay; he'd said the therapy was really helping.

In fact, he'd been more worried about *her*. She'd been struggling since moving to London. School and university had felt like a safety net; in those places, she'd always been surrounded by people. Now her friends had scattered, busy building their careers, and the big wide world was lonelier than she'd expected. She felt like she was failing at adulthood while, through the lens of social media, her old friends were adulting like bosses.

Nory had landed a good job with an advertising company,

and she was constantly out of her depth. There was a lot of schmoozing involved, a lot of afternoon and evening drinking with clients, and Nory found it easier to be the person she was expected to be after a couple of drinks. It gave her the confidence she needed to close the deals; it took the edge off. Shy, nervous, sober Nory was less efficient than Nory after three glasses of wine. But this only conspired to make her feel even more of a fraud: If she was only good at her job after a dose of Pinot Grigio, did it even count?

"What's going on with you? Where's the old Nory?" Tristan had asked, after she'd necked another shot. "This isn't you."

"I'm trying to be more dynamic."

"I liked you as you were before."

"I just needed a change, you know? I've always been so small-town country bumpkin compared to the rest of you."

"Why are you comparing yourself to anybody else? It was never a competition."

"Not to you lot, no, but you didn't have anything to compete with, you already had it all!"

"There were plenty of things that you had that we didn't."

"Are you giving me the 'more to life than money' speech?"

Tristan had laughed. "I think I am, yes."

"Okay, that's fair. But it isn't a money thing. Which is just as well, as I still don't have any. You've all got your shit together and I'm still doing the doggy paddle."

Tristan laughed again. "Is that what it looks like to you? I'll let you into a secret: We're all just making it up as we go along. We're just better at faking it."

"But you were born to it."

"What?"

"Success!" said Nory. "It's in your genes. You're all children of super-high achievers, trained from birth to one day yourselves become high achievers. I'm just not up to it."

She downed another shot.

"We just had a head start, that's all. Nory, are you happy?" He was looking at her in that earnest way he had, which instantly dissolved all bullshit. Tristan had these big brown eyes that saw everything, even the stuff you didn't want him to, and a smile so reassuring you would trust him with your life. That probably made him a good doctor. He had thick brown hair that looked as though it had been cut with a knife and fork, and a frame so long and gangly he rarely found shirtsleeves that reached his wrists. But somehow these things added to his easy charm.

"I hate my job, and my job hates me," Nory said, and laughed mirthlessly. "It takes a lot of Dutch courage for me to be the person they think they hired."

"Are you drinking on the job?"

"Not in the office."

"If you need to be hammered to make a sale, you're in the wrong career."

"Tell me about it! So, what about you, what's next?"

"I've got a job at St. Thomas's. I'll spend a couple of years getting more experience, save some money, and then I'll head back out to Africa. I feel like I'm really needed there."

Nory smiled. "You always were the best of us," she said, meaning it.

"You need to give yourself a break," said Tristan. "Seriously. You're better than you know."

"Oh, you don't need to worry about me. I am on a voyage of self-discovery!" She laughed.

"Overrated." Tristan laughed. And then he said more seriously, "You won't like this, Nory, but you don't need to find yourself, you already know exactly who you are. Of all of us, you always had the strongest sense of self."

"Jeez, is that how I came across?"

"You always knew your own mind; your moral compass was immovable!"

"What if I don't like the person I am?"

"Then you need to learn to love her, because like it or not, you're stuck with yourself."

"Are you taking your own advice?" she asked, knowing that Tristan would understand she was referring to his battle with depression.

"I'm trying," he said, smiling. "Every day's a school day!"

They'd had a great night, laughing over old times and talking about the future. In that moment, it never would have crossed Nory's mind that Tristan might not have a future.

At the end of the evening, they promised they wouldn't leave it so long again and they both said they'd call. But they didn't. It wasn't purposeful, it was simply that life got in the way. They were busy people. It wasn't like she hadn't thought about Tristan; she did, often, in between needing to text her gran and changing the bedsheets, one of those things you determine to do tomorrow.

Almost a year later, Charles called to tell her Tristan had taken his own life. At first, she felt winded. Then came disbelief, that terrible feeling like you're stuck in a bad dream and you can't wake up, it can't possibly be true. Hot on the tail of disbelief came regret; why hadn't she made that call? Was she really so busy? What had been so important that in a year she hadn't had the time to call up her old friend?

During those first few weeks after Tristan's death, the group had pinged back together like they'd been on elastic and she realized they all felt the same. Each of them felt horribly guilty. Pippa hadn't seen him for a couple of years and Guy even longer. Jeremy had met Tristan for a drink a few months after Nory had. Ameerah had bumped into him on the tube, and they'd promised to get together, never did; they all had a similar story. It wasn't only with Tristan; they'd all lost touch, aside from Nory and Ameerah. Before the funeral, Nory hadn't seen Guy since their post-graduation reunion weekend. She'd not seen Jenna or Charles for almost five years, aside from seeing Jenna on the TV. Occasionally she'd meet with Pippa but not regularly enough. She'd met Jeremy at a book festival maybe three years before Tristan's death.

It seemed unreal that they had been so close, so tight with one another at school and even through university, and then suddenly they'd blown away in different directions, like dandelion seeds in a stiff breeze.

The worst part of all, the part that Nory couldn't get her head around, was that Tristan wasn't in the world anymore. It hadn't mattered that they hadn't seen each other from one year to the next because she'd known he was in the world somewhere. And suddenly he wasn't. She would never see him again; that option had been removed from the universe. It was almost unbearable. How could anything be so very final? Had Nory told him how much she loved him the last time she'd seen him? She couldn't remember. She wished she had. She knew it was selfish of her to want a neat ending, one that left her conscience unburdened. Tristan had been unable to cope with his own demons, she didn't need to palm hers off on him as well.

Aside from the inevitable grief, Tristan's death had reconfigured time for all of them. Suddenly there was no such thing as "all the time in the world." They weren't all running around in a hedonistic state of carpe diem—although Nory's brief encounter with Guy was certainly a knee-jerk reaction to the fleetingness of life—but they each in their own way became more aware of time and its importance. Jenna and Charles stopped their decade-long dance of flirt and denial and made a commitment. Ameerah bought an apartment. Pippa started her own business. And Nory left the well-paid job that she hated and opened Serendipitous Seconds. They all vowed not to lose contact again. Apart from Guy, Nory had seen or been in contact with all of them pretty regularly ever since the funeral.

Nory lay in bed that night, waiting for sleep to rescue her from the maze of shoulda, coulda, woulda tangents into which her mind kept disappearing. It had been a while since she'd been plagued by these thoughts, but knowing she would soon be back with everyone again had brought them back with a vengeance.

She wondered if Jenna was feeling the same. Of all of them, Jenna was the one with the most complex feelings around Tristan's death. Jenna and Tristan had been each other's first loves. Throughout school, those two were always breaking up and getting back together. By the time they went to their separate universities, things were properly over between them, and Jenna and Charles were showing sparks that would eventually come to be a flame. But you never forget your first love. You leave a tiny piece of your heart with them, always, and hope that they keep it safe.

A few weeks after the funeral, just the girls had gotten together for drinks. Jenna confessed that she felt as though she had lost a piece of herself. She'd said she hadn't even known there was such a piece until it was gone; Tristan had taken it with him.

And now here she was, five years later, marrying Charles. Nory supposed all actions begin with a catalyst of some kind.

Her phone vibrated with a message; clearly someone else

couldn't sleep either. Nory reached beside the bed to where her phone rested on a pile of books, which had become a kind of makeshift nightstand. She'd once had a date claim it was unnecessary to have so many books in such a small flat; he hadn't made the cut, obviously. The screen glowed green in the darkness. It was a message from Jenna. She should have known.

> Hello! I'm so pleased you're coming for the house party. I understand why you were holding back but it really wouldn't be the same without you. Here's to shits and giggles! Xx

Nory's fingers hovered over the keypad.

> Sorry for my dithering. I'm looking forward to it, it'll be lovely to catch up with everyone. To shits and giggles! Xx

If it wasn't for stupid cheaty-face Guy and his poor unsuspecting wife, she would have had no qualms at all about being there. Argghh! How could she have been so stupid! Her cheeks burned in the darkness.

> Don't forget to pack evening wear. We're going full 1920s castle glamour in the evenings! Xx

Nory huffed loudly at the ceiling. She was not a woman who possessed *evening wear*, at least not the kind Jenna was talking about. The kinds of parties Nory attended were those for which a good Primark dress with some bold accessories was perfectly adequate. It wasn't like she could raid Ameerah's extensive dress collection either, since Ameerah was three sizes smaller than Nory. She would have to ask Andrew; his sister, Scarlett, had a vintage clothing shop and she rented out some pieces as well as selling.

**Sounds wonderful!** Nory typed back, hoping her reluctance wouldn't translate over the ether. **Don't worry, I'm on it. It'll be nice to get dressed up. Are you nervous yet? Xx**

**Not yet. Too busy to be nervous. OK Magazine are sending a photographer on the day!! Xx**

*Of course they are*, thought Nory, smiling.

**Oh My God!! That's awesome Jen, you'll be the bride of the year! Xx**

**Ha I don't think so! Xx**

Nory laughed silently to herself: Jenna definitely did think so.

Jenna played a country vet in the soap opera *Days and Nights* set in rural Surrey, and she pretended as best she could to hate being recognized and asked for selfies wherever she went. She read for audiobooks and radio plays, and she'd had a few bit parts in films, but she hadn't yet made it properly onto the big screen. As a thirty-four-year-old woman, she knew her chances to play the leading lady in a blockbuster movie were dwindling by the day.

"Before too long," she'd complained at their last lunch date, "I'll start being offered mother roles. I don't want to be the mother; I want to be the lead!"

With the likelihood of Hollywood calling looking increasingly slim, Jenna had turned her attentions toward the theater, claiming, "An actress has more longevity in the theater. The theater doesn't cap women at the first hint of crow's-feet!" Not that Jenna needed to worry about crow's-feet; she'd been pumping her face full of Botox since her twenty-seventh birthday. Sometimes Nory found herself missing the things Jenna said because she was entranced by her paralyzed forehead.

Nory laid her phone back on her book pile and turned over, pulling the duvet over her head. The messages from Jenna had hauled her out of her thoughts maze and at last she knew she would be able to sleep.

It would be good to be all together again. They were—for the most part—as dear to her as family. Since opening the bookshop, Nory felt more comfortable in her own skin. She had found her calling, and that brought with it the inner peace that she had so craved in her twenties. And even though she still wasn't sure she was adulting at full capacity (Would that come with age? Children? A mortgage? Fat chance.) she no longer felt like she was being left behind.

# Three

"Fancy a nightcap?" Ameerah asked as they reached the point when they would have to part ways to get home. They'd just left Andrew's sister's secondhand boutique, having scored a couple of reasonably priced evening dresses for Nory.

"Sure." All that was waiting for Nory was a grumpy feline (she'd already nipped back after work to feed him) and packing decisions; what did one wear to a castle in the middle of winter?

They ended up in O'Malley's, an ancient, crooked little pub near Kensington Gardens they'd discovered when they first moved to London, and which had become their favorite hideaway ever since. They sat up at the bar, sharing a tub of peanuts and taking bets on what song the drunks hogging the jukebox would choose next.

"'Piano Man,'" said Ameerah.

"No way. They've got 'Fairytale of New York' written all over them."

They waited. Sure enough, after a moment the sounds of violins filled the dimly lit pub, and the drunks began dancing and singing a terrible tribute to Kirsty MacColl and Shane Mac-Gowan. Ameerah shook her head laughing. "All right, you win. What'll it be?"

"I'll have a small glass of Chateauneuf, please."

"A small?"

"It's only Wednesday!"

"Lightweight."

"Alcoholic."

"Celibate."

"Ooh," Nory cried. "Low blow!"

"You need to stop holding out for Mr. Perfect and loosen up a bit. Have some fun. Have a one-night stand."

"If you remember, my last one-night stand didn't exactly end well."

"Guy doesn't count. A one-nighter should be anonymous."

"I don't want anonymous. I want . . . well, I don't know what I want." The barman rested her wine down on a coaster, and Nory took a sip.

"Don't take it all so seriously. Look at me. I'm not going to fall in love with the man-Barbies; they're simply a delightful way to pass the time."

"What happened to man-Barbie Allan?"

"He was a flat-earther."

"Really?"

"I mean, I know I'm not with them for their cerebral faculties, but if they must occasionally speak, I require them not to spout bullshit."

"Fair enough. Have you checked man-Barbie Dev's opinions on the whole flat-earth thing?"

"Yes. He's firmly in the spherical camp."

"Well, that's something. Maybe Jenna's got a hot poetry-writing cousin who plays jazz and whittles woodland animals in his spare time. Our eyes will meet at the wedding over the hot buffet in the evening, as we both make a play for the last tempura-battered king prawn, and we'll fall madly in love," Nory said dreamily.

"Those are quite specific requirements. That is, in fact, the opposite of loosening up."

"It doesn't have to be tempura king prawns. It could be chicken wings or mini pancake rolls."

"Not really what I was referring to," said Ameerah, frowning.

⁓

Mugwort was already asleep on the end of the bed when Nory climbed into it. She wondered how he would take to playing second fiddle to a baby while she was away. Matilda hadn't been born the last time Andrew and Seb cat-sat, and Mugwort had grown rather used to their chicken terrines and nightly grooming; he'd been an absolute prima donna for a week after his return.

Nory sighed, pulled her laptop onto the bed, and balanced it on her knees. She had been putting this off for weeks, but she couldn't avoid it any longer. She clicked on the wedding invitation and opened the dreaded wedding gift list.

It was as she had expected: tailored to the wallets of the well-heeled. She scanned down the list. *Ooh spaghetti tongs! That's more like it. How pricey could they be? £95??? What are they made of, gold? Okay, a spoon rest—£125 for a place to rest a spoon?* This went on for some time.

Eventually, sandwiched between a bespoke hand-whittled garden arbor and a reproduction Art Deco–style drinks cabinet in solid walnut, she found a scented candle for £80. She winced as she pressed Purchase Now. She was glad to see that all gifts would be delivered to the bride and groom's home address, so that she wouldn't have the embarrassment of placing her gift next to the bronze statuette of Eros or the chaise longue upholstered in Chinese painted silk. Nory imagined her dad launching into a rant about the abominable elite.

⮑

Nory dropped Mugwort off at Andrew and Seb's after work on Saturday. The elderly cat had sniffed Matilda suspiciously before deciding she was acceptable company and allowing her to tug on his ears as he curled up next to her and Seb on the sofa.

"When's your mum arriving?" Nory asked.

"Monday evening," Seb replied. "I was going to pick her up from the airport, but she's insisting on getting a taxi. She doesn't want to be a *burden*." Seb cringed as he said this. Seb's mum made Mariah Carey look low maintenance.

"I've almost finished hand stitching the red carpet for her arrival," said Andrew.

Seb's mother lived in Boston, where Seb had grown up. She adored Serendipitous Seconds; the first time she'd seen it she had actually screamed, "Oh my sweet lord, did you ever see a more adorable store in your life?" which had instantly endeared her to Nory. She had also likened Nory to a brunette Marilyn Monroe, and this too had gone in her favor. Besides, Nory was used to *tricky* characters; she had grown up with her dad.

"Are you sure you don't mind having Mugwort?"

"My mother adores babies and cats, she can't get enough of them. So the longer she's lavishing her attention on them, the less time she has to focus on all the things that are wrong with me."

"She's still not keen on Seb's decision to work for himself," said Andrew. "She had him pegged for climbing to the top of the corporate ladder."

"You want my dad to explain to her the error of her desires?" Nory smiled.

"I'm not sure my mother and your father should *ever* be in the same room together!"

Mugwort seemed to have remembered that this was the household that fed him poached chicken breast and didn't so much as look up as Nory said her goodbyes.

"Now I wouldn't normally suggest this to anyone," said Andrew, pulling her into a hug on the doorstep. "But since your man-bar is set so impossibly high, I feel it's justified: Lower your expectations and increase your chances of finding true love!"

"What kind of advice is that? I thought you were a feminist!"

"I am a feminist. I am also a realist. Seriously, Nory, no human man is ever going to be able to climb the pedestal you've created in your mind. So, give mankind a break and be open to possibility."

"You're telling me to sweep the gutters for men?"

"Elinor Noel, your notion of gutter sweeping is most people's aiming for the stars. Now get your game face on. It is a truth universally acknowledged that many people meet their soul mates at weddings, and this is going to be a big wedding. Spend the week leading up to it doing your homework on Charles's and Jenna's eligible relatives, and by the time the big day arrives you'll have a plan of action!"

"You really don't get out much, do you?"

"Almost never. Last week I got excited when I had to do a nine p.m. co-op visit for Calpol and nappies. It was the closest I've been to being out-out in months."

∽

Back at the flat, Nory packed the last of her clothes for the house party/wedding at Robinwood Castle. Nory was no stranger to Robinwood or the grounds surrounding it. It had been a part of her life in one way or another for as long as she could remember. Her parents couldn't afford holiday clubs when she was little, so Nory would shadow them while they worked through the school holidays.

She had fond memories of helping with the weeding and watering in the polytunnels at the nursery and handing long-stemmed flowers to her mum for floral displays up at Robin-wood Castle. Sometimes she played in the castle gardens or read books while sitting on the big window ledges in the library. The marquis—also known as Lord Abercrombie—was very kind to her. He'd lived in the castle proper in those days; she understood he lived mostly in the east wing now.

Then, of course, she had attended the private school on the other side of Robins Wood, when the adjoining castle grounds became a place in which to hide out and bunk off. If they were caught by the head gardener, they'd been sent packing.

There had been a long-standing private war between her friends and the head gardener's kid, Isaac; mud flinging usually, occasionally moldy windfall apples, sometimes manure. He'd started it by chucking a clod of manure at the back of Nory's head one day when she and her friends were truanting in the castle grounds. It had sailed right over the wall from the gardener's cottage and smacked into her ponytail. The prefects in her dorm had called her shithead for months, and the ensuing aggressions between the gardener's kid and her gang had been named "Turd Wars."

She wondered if the old head gardener was still there; he was always nice to her when he'd visited the nursery and he'd never let on to her parents about the things she got up to at school, for which she was eternally grateful. Her mind drifted back to the gardener's son. Issac had been a gangly, scowling sort of youth—on whom she'd had a top-secret crush. He had dark skin like his father and the potential to be handsome, if he'd ever decided to cut the hair that fell in thick, greasy curtains across his face and stopped dressing like a Nirvana reject. He was older than her, the same age as her brother. Had he said his goodbyes to the castle and disappeared off to some far-flung destination, or was he, like her, bound by invisible threads that kept pulling him back into its orbit?

Her family still living and working down in the village of Hartmead meant Nory was a fairly frequent visitor to the area, unlike her friends, for whom this house party would be a trip down memory lane. But she hadn't ventured up to the castle for a couple of years, and despite her initial reticence, she had to admit that she was looking forward to seeing it again.

To be staying as a guest was the kind of thing that child Nory had always dreamed about. She would get to sleep in one of the four-poster beds she used to sneak peeks at when the house-keepers were changing the sheets. And spend a week eating food that didn't come in a foil tray. She would have access to the library! All those musty books without pictures she hadn't appreciated when she was a kid were calling to her now. She bet there were some cracking first editions hiding in those shelves. And then there were the gardens, a world unto themselves, hidden gates in high walls which led to fanciful spaces where plants ruled and every season was allowed to shine. Yes, she was looking forward to going back.

## Four

Ameerah pulled off the country lane they had been driving down for some half an hour—ten minutes of which was spent crawling behind a bouquet of pheasants running panicked along the center of the road—and passed the old gate house that marked the beginning of the castle's drive.

After several twists and turns, which led them through a varied landscape of orchards and large open spaces with heavy-coated sheep roaming freely, they emerged from beneath the skeleton canopy of an avenue of lime trees. Robinwood Castle rose up before them like a mirage. Nory's heart skipped a beat at the sight of it, and the sharp intakes of breath from both Ameerah and Dev showed that the feeling was unanimous.

"I'd forgotten how beautiful it was," said Ameerah.

"I hadn't," replied Nory.

Her eyes roamed lovingly over the sand-colored stone, which was mottled with age and scarred by the many climbing plants that had tried to claim its walls through the decades. Chimneys cluttered the roof and the smoke spiraling out from them spoke of fires roaring in hearths within.

"I think I've been here before," said Dev, squinting out of the back window.

"Wouldn't you know if you'd been here before?" Nory asked. To her mind, Robinwood Castle was a place that, once visited, was never to be forgotten.

"I've been on a lot of photoshoots in places like this. After a while they begin to meld into each other. But I thought the landscaping looked familiar as we drove through. The glossies like an old building as a juxtaposition to the cutting-edge modernity of fashion."

Each time Dev opened his mouth, he said something that endeared him to Nory a little bit more. He was impressive in such an unassuming way that she imagined he was constantly underrated. Nory eyed Ameerah, to find Ameerah's expression mirroring her own curiosity, with something else mixed in. Concern? This man-Barbie was turning out to be dangerously insightful. He clearly had brains and wasn't afraid to use them—not at all in keeping with Ameerah's usual type. Earlier in the journey he'd let slip that he was starting an MA in environmental politics and Ameerah had almost lost control of the wheel.

The front walls of the castle were constructed around three square turrets, each containing large leaded casement windows, which glittered black and silver as the winter sun glinted off them. A row of gabled windows ran along the top of the building, once housing the many live-in staff.

They drove slowly down the last stretch of drive, taking in the splendor of the building. The oldest parts of the castle hailed from the medieval period, which were then added to and modified over the centuries as each owner made their mark for posterity. Wings were added and removed, either by design or natural disaster. The structure that greeted them now had not been touched, other than for preservation purposes, since the eighteenth century.

Ameerah pulled up outside the castle, and they climbed out of the car and stretched their legs. A man in a black suit—a butler no less—came out to greet them and told Ameerah that someone would be out in a moment to park her car and bring in their luggage. Nory had to tell her mouth to close itself; already, she was understanding that being a guest at Robinwood was going to be a very different experience from being an honorary staff member.

As they followed the butler through the iron-studded wooden doors, the sound of Jenna's laugh drifted down into the entrance like an overexcited ghost.

The hall was as Nory remembered it. Above the pale gray wood paneling, rococo-style plasterworks curled along the tops of the walls and up into the ceiling. Chalky white clematis, honeysuckle, and impossibly rambling roses snaked round to form a frame for the semi-naked winged men and women painted in the clouds at the center. Back on the ground, the eye was drawn to the writhing Baroque staircase, which seemed to grow up out of the stone floor and sweep sinuously away, forking left and right at the first landing—Nory knew that each fork would split three times more before it reached the old servants' quarters. For a relatively small castle, it packed a punch.

Fresh flowers had been woven between the balustrades—white and pale pink lisianthus, held in place by dark trailing ivy—and at the bottom of the staircase two plinths showcased enormous floral displays, which cascaded down to the smooth, gently undulated stone floor. *No wonder Shelley was pulling extra shifts to get all this lot done*, Nory thought. An enormous Christmas tree stood to one side of the staircase, reaching up through the stairwell to the floor above. It was decorated in a riot of red and gold baubles that glittered in the tree lights. A whole log spluttered in the giant fireplace as the flames slowly licked it clean, the warmth from it was like an embrace after the cold outside. The air was redolent with fresh pine and woodsmoke.

On either side of the staircase, two long corridors led down toward large stained-glass windows at the far ends, before turning left and right and continuing out of sight. Through several open doors along the passage, light spilled into the hall. It was from one of these open doors that Jenna's laugh came again.

"If you would like to follow me, some of your friends are taking afternoon tea in the garden room," said the butler with due sobriety.

They entered a sumptuously decorated room with three enormous bay windows looking out onto the formal gardens. Tiered cake stands brimming with scones and triangle sandwiches sat on round coffee tables beside china teapots. And beside them, Jenna and Pippa looked as though they were being gradually consumed by an enormous velvet sofa. The indentations of two further bottoms on the opposite sofa indicated that Charles and someone else—Nory hoped it wasn't Guy, she hadn't quite steeled herself for that meeting yet—had recently left the room.

"You're here!" screeched Jenna, extricating herself from the voluminous cushions and hurling herself first at Ameerah and then at Nory, before holding out a slender hand to Dev and purring, "I don't believe we've met."

Pippa raised her eyebrows and rose gracefully out of the sofa as though pushed by invisible hydraulics. She air-kissed each of them in turn and nodded a hello at Dev. After a spell apart, it always took Pippa a little while to ease back into being relaxed around them. Pippa Harrington wasn't gushing or romantic by nature and liked to introduce herself by saying "I'm not a hugger." It took her a long time to feel comfortable around people, but once she chose you as a friend, you had a friend for life. Nory was one of the few people to have ever seen Pippa vulnerable, and Pippa was one of the few people Nory would call in a crisis.

Through a set of French doors, Nory could see the backs of Charles and Jeremy; they were leaning against a wall that overlooked the gardens, the smoke from Charles's cigarette curling above his head, while the cloud from Jeremy's vape covered them both like a rolling fog. Jeremy was on his phone.

"Charles hasn't given up smoking, then?" Nory observed.

Jenna huffed. "He keeps pushing his end date back. Now he's saying he'll stop after the honeymoon. But of course that's a cop-out too because we aren't actually going on honeymoon until next year because of my filming commitments."

"I can't imagine Charles not smoking," said Ameerah.

"Neither can he, that's the problem."

"Are you not going away at all after the wedding?" asked Nory.

"We've got a couple of days off afterward, but then it's back to work till Christmas. Even Christmas won't be restful since we've got to split ourselves between Charles's family in Cornwall and mine in York."

"That sounds like hell," drawled Pippa.

"What will you be doing for Christmas, Queen Pip?" asked Ameerah.

"I'll be with my father, in his suite at the Savoy. He's coming up to town on the twenty-third. We have four days planned of eating and drinking to excess."

"You won't be going home?" asked Jenna.

"No, my mother is back from wherever she was, and it's her turn to host Christmas. She'll be inviting all her god-awful cronies, so Dad and I thought we'd make ourselves scarce."

Pippa's was an unusual family setup. Her parents had never divorced but had separated years ago, each to their own wing of the seventy-two-room house they shared in Dorset. Her mother seemed to drift from one private-island rehab to the next, and Pippa's relationship with her siblings was often cool. Her father was another matter; she worshipped him. As the eldest child, Pippa was in line to inherit the responsibility of the familial home and her dad had been scrupulous in training her for the task.

"So, what's the plan for the week?" Nory asked.

"I have a full itinerary," said Jenna.

"Of course you have." Ameerah half-smiled.

Jenna ignored her. "It's just Guy and his wife left to arrive. We invited their children too, but Guy said they needed some time on their own. Fair enough, I suppose. Who would have ever thought Guy would be the first one of us to have kids? He's always been so selfish."

At the mention of Guy's name, Nory's stomach churned, and she felt her cheeks redden. She saw Ameerah give her a sideways look, which was instantly pounced upon by Pippa.

"Of course." Pippa nodded knowingly. "This is the first time you've seen Guy since your sex marathon."

Nory tried to think of something clever to say. Nothing came.

"Well at least if his wife's here, he's less likely to try for a repeat performance," said Ameerah helpfully.

Nory didn't know if the presence of his wife would make her feel better or worse. Worse probably. She wondered again how she'd been talked into this. At that moment, Charles turned and saw them, and the greetings began anew.

"Cocktails!" called Jenna shrilly, jumping up and pulling an ornate brass bell lever on the wall near the door. Nory imagined the staff ruing the day their predecessors ever installed the bell system. Jenna would be sure to make full use of it for the duration of their stay.

～

Later, slightly woozy from the two cocktails warming her blood, Nory followed Ameerah and Dev, who followed Jenna up the grand staircase to be shown to their rooms. From the way Jenna spoke, you would have thought she had chosen the decor and made the beds up herself.

"This is you, Ameerah," she said, opening the door wide and waiting for Ameerah's response. Dev threw himself straight onto the four-poster bed and said, "Awesome!" Jenna sometimes forgot that Ameerah's family boasted mansions in several countries, and she was therefore not often inclined to be overwhelmed by luxury. But Ameerah made all the correct noises of pleasure. Besides, many of her familial properties were too modern for the kind of run-down grandeur that only history can bring.

Before Nory had attended the private school, she had assumed that there were simply people who had money and people who did not—her family fell into the latter category. But she had quickly realized that being wealthy was more nuanced than that; there was old money and new money, and there was a healthy snobbery on both sides toward the other camp. Many of the students at Braddon-Hartmead had come from old money—Charles, Pippa, Jeremy, and Guy included. Ameerah, Jenna, and Tristan were new money, although Jenna's family tried to pass themselves off as old money; her dad had purchased titles for himself and his wife, which had scandalized the school governors at the time.

In the simplest terms, Nory learned, the old money tended to be history rich but cash poor (relatively speaking) and new money, the opposite (though they had a far nicer time in Nory's opinion). After too much wine, Charles used to tease his wife-to-be by describing her family as "flash with the cash but mostly trash." However, Jenna had the last laugh when her stepmother graciously stepped in to bail out Charles's family business when it was threatened with receivership; he no longer teased his fiancée with that particular joke.

Nory's room was down the hall.

"I chose this one for you because it looks over the formal gardens and I thought you'd appreciate it more than anyone else here." Jenna smiled as Nory crossed straight to the window and let out a sigh of ecstasy.

The summer flowers had long since passed, and even the autumnal colors were starting to fade. But a garden like this had to cater for every season, and though the borders were understated at this time of year, the patterns of the garden design were picked out by lines of evergreens, gravel paths, and stone columns showcasing bulbous urns and shapely Greek statues.

"Thank you, Jenna, it's perfect."

Jenna smiled wider.

"What's it like for you being back in this neck of the woods?" Nory asked. "How long's it been?"

"I've not been back to Hartmead since the day we left school," said Jenna. "Sixteen years ago! It feels weird. Even just driving past the school to get here. It's like it's put me right back where I was, in that mindset. I'm not sure if . . . Oh, just ignore me, I'm being dramatic."

"No, you're not. I mean, I come to Hartmead quite often because of my family, but it feels a bit weird even for me. I certainly haven't been up to the castle for years. And with all of us together . . ." Nory let the last sentence hang, realizing that they weren't *all* together. She only needed to glance at Jenna's face to see she was thinking the same thing. Nory cleared her throat and carried on brightly, "But it'll be great to reminisce about the old days . . . I can't wait for Charles to bring up my year-ten fringe!"

Jenna burst out a laugh, and the melancholy slipped back into the shadows. "Shit! I'd forgotten about your cringe-fringe!"

"The very one."

"What *were* you thinking?"

"I was trying to look like Hilary Duff."

"It didn't work. So, what's with Ameerah and the model?"

Nory shrugged. "Who knows! Maybe he's her Christmas gift to herself?"

"I wouldn't mind finding him in my stocking."

"Jenna! You're almost a married woman."

"I know." Jenna smiled like she had no control over it, a big wide smile that stretched across her whole face. "Can you believe it?"

"Actually, I can," said Nory. "You two always had a spark."

A shout from downstairs echoed through the house: "Oy, oy, let's get this party started!"

Nory and Jenna looked at each other.

"Guy," they said in unison.

Nory must have grimaced, because Jenna pulled a sympathetic face.

"Don't worry about it, you didn't know."

"Everyone else did."

"Not everyone. I didn't."

"I'm going to spend the whole time feeling like everyone's watching how I react around them."

"Relax, darling, no one will be watching you at all, they'll all be watching me. I'm on TV, you know!" She winked and pulled Nory into a hug, kissing her cheek. "Come on, you might as well get the hellos out of the way." And linking her arm through Nory's, Jenna pulled her from her nice quiet bedroom, down the stairs toward the noises of three grown men reverting to their seventeen-year-old selves.

# Five

Everyone was instructed to meet in the drawing room for cocktails and canapés before dinner.

Guy hadn't looked at all sheepish when he greeted her in the entrance hall earlier and introduced her to his wife, Camille—who seemed shy and unassuming, unlike her husband. Nory wished she was as shallow as he was, then she wouldn't feel like a conniving harlot every time she spoke to Camille. It would be impossible to avoid her for the next six days, and she would look as guilty as she felt if she tried.

"Look," said Ameerah, her voice a mite strained as she zipped Nory into a gold evening dress centimeter by centimeter. "If Guy's pretending it didn't happen, then just follow his lead. I know you're cursed with an inflated sense of *doing the right thing*, but in this instance, honesty is definitely not the best policy. Let Guy fuck up his marriage on his own, you don't want it on your conscience."

Ameerah was wearing a square-necked, long-sleeved evening dress, with a side slit that almost met her knickers, in her signature black.

"It's already on my conscience," Nory said, sucking in her stomach as the zipper squeezed her torso. She reasoned that if they were to be dining like kings for the next week, it would be better to wear the tightest dress first, before the calories began to take their toll. She pulled the accidentally-escaped-on-purpose tendrils of hair that weren't tied up in the loose chignon out of the way.

"Believe me, if you relieve your conscience by telling her, and the result is the end of their marriage, your conscience will be a hundred times heavier."

"If it was me, I would want to know."

"But it's not you. And you don't get to decide what's best for Camille when you don't even know her."

"What if I get to know her and we become friends? What then?"

"Let's leave the hypotheticals alone for now. At the moment, your only job is to smile and be friendly and not rip this dress. "Gaahh!" she exclaimed as the final inch of the zip came together.

Ameerah let out an exhausted puff, and Nory found herself jealous of her friend's ability to breathe easily; there would be no more easy breathing for her till bedtime. But when she looked at herself in the full-length mirror, she decided this dress was worth a little asphyxiation.

It was floor-length satin with a fishtail bottom, which complemented her curvy figure, and a chaste Audrey Hepburn neckline. The rich honey-gold color was warm against her pale skin and pink cheeks and picked out the gold streaks in her hair.

She'd brought a choice of evening dresses with her: a teal velvet number that pushed her boobs up impressively high, a navy-blue A-line chiffon gown with long lace sleeves, and an emerald-green dress with a brocade bodice. It would be a miracle if she made it through the week without spilling gravy down the front of at least one of them. She wondered why no one had invented a glamourous socially acceptable bib for eating dinner in evening wear.

Dev knocked on the door to escort Nory and Ameerah down to the drawing room. He looked ethereal in his tuxedo, but then he *was* a model.

"You're so good-looking, it's like you're not real," Nory said as she took his other arm and the three of them descended the stairs. Nory paid particular attention to not tumble down ahead of them in her inadvisably high-heeled shoes. For some people a stiletto heel added a level of grace to the way they moved. In Nory's case they made her walk as though she had a bike between her legs.

"I don't know whether to be flattered or offended," said Dev, smiling.

"Oh, be flattered, I meant it in the best way." She stumbled slightly, but Dev steadied her. He'd probably had lots of practice with stilted shoes on the catwalk. "I've never seen a person look quite so perfect without a filter."

∽

The tinkle of music and the hum of voices behind the heavy door met them on the last few stairs, and Nory felt her stomach twist with nerves. She tried to take a steadying breath, but her dress seams creaked under the strain.

As they entered the drawing room, Nory had the sense that she was stepping into a bygone era. The drawing room walls were covered in a repeating pattern of baroque flowers in blue and white. Family portraits hung from the picture rails in ornate golden frames. The dark autumnal hues favored by seventeenth-century painters looked especially moody against the bright walls and the two pale marble fireplaces at either end of the room.

Charles was seated at the grand piano in the corner, idly playing "I Can Give You the Starlight" by Ivor Novello—he always was annoyingly musical—while chatting with Pippa, who was leaning one bony hip against the shiny black wood. She looked chic in a black bias-cut evening dress that showcased her pale skin and ginger hair.

Jenna was sitting with her feet tucked under her on a gold brocade sofa, her red velvet dress so low cut that Nory felt sure she had sticky tape holding her boobs in place. Guy was on the sofa talking animatedly with Jenna, while leaving his hand territorially on Camille's knee, as she sat beside him looking starstruck in Jenna's direction.

Ameerah and Dev wandered toward the piano, and Charles smiled and called hello without missing a single note. Jeremy was standing beside a sideboard that showcased various military-themed statuettes in bronze. He was looking intently at his phone, but when he looked up and saw Nory, he pocketed it and crossed the room.

"You look lovely," he said, smiling, and handed her a glass of something bright green off a tray.

"Thanks, Jez. You scrub up well yourself. I'm used to seeing you in camel cargo trousers and baseball caps on Instagram."

He laughed. "Yeah, it's a bit of a change-up from being in a rainforest."

Nory saw his hand unconsciously touch the phone in his pocket. "How's Katie?"

"Am I that transparent?"

"It's understandable."

"I wouldn't mind so much if she was in a city at least. I just worry about her and the baby. I mean, we've got medical insurance and all that sort of thing, but I'm counting the hours until she's back in the UK instead of being on an eighty-mile trek along dirt roads to the nearest hospital."

"How does your mum feel about being a grandma?"

Jeremy's family owned an estate in the Scottish Borders, not quite as big as the Robinwood Castle lands, although the manor house that he had grown up in was almost as grand as the castle itself. Nory had visited on several occasions during school holidays, and most recently at his wedding to Katie four years ago—Guy had thankfully been on assignment in Mexico at the time and hadn't been able to attend. Jeremy's mother was a formidable woman, mostly to be found wearing head-to-toe tweed with a shotgun resting open across her right forearm. His father, Michael McIntosh III, by contrast, was a naturalist and often joked that it was his life's mission to preserve the local wildlife from being shot at by his wife.

"My mother is beside herself with joy and relief that one of her children is finally giving them a grandchild." Jeremy smiled. "She's already bought the baby a pony, and it's not even born yet. She wants us to hurry up and put our name down at a good school, but Katie and I have decided our child is going state school all the way."

"What will your mum say to that?"

"I'll tell her it's all Katie's idea; she worships the ground Katie walks on. I think she's grateful to her for marrying her weird bug-loving son."

"That's sweet."

"What about you? Have you met anyone you love more than books yet?"

Nory laughed. "Not yet. But I remain vigilant."

Nory and Jeremy had had a very brief thing when they were sixteen, and finishing off their GCSEs. In truth, they were pushed together by a matchmaking Pippa and Ameerah, who thought they'd be perfect for each other: two book nerds together. But the reality was that they were too similar for sparks to properly fly; they'd always been mates, it felt unnatural to try and think of each other as otherwise, and after some unsatisfying fumblings, they'd decided to go back to being homework buddies.

Jeremy's phone began to ring, and he looked pleadingly at Nory. "It's Katie. I'm sorry, I've got to take this . . ."

"Go!" Nory laughed. "Go, speak to your lovely pregnant wife and send her my love."

"I will."

Jeremy gave her the briefest smile and disappeared out the door. Nory made her way over to Pippa and Ameerah, who had left Charles and Dev playing a duet—Dev was a surprisingly good pianist. Jenna was still being stared at by Camille and grilled for celebrity gossip by Guy.

"Thank god there's only an hour's time difference," Pippa said, nodding toward the door left ajar by Jeremy's exit. "I'm not sure he would cope if they were living in completely opposite time zones. Poor chap."

Jeremy was an entomologist and had worked with universities all over the world. His wife, Katie, was six months pregnant with their first child and currently working in a chimpanzee sanctuary in Sierra Leone. Katie was due to fly back for the wedding and would then remain in England for the rest of her pregnancy; it was clear that for Jeremy it couldn't come soon enough.

"It's sweet, isn't it?" said Ameerah. "But then Jez always was an absolute darling."

"I don't think I'll ever have the energy to worry about another person so intensely," said Pippa.

"Wait till you have children of your own," said Nory, smiling mischievously, waiting for Pippa to bite.

"Nory, you're making my smoked salmon blinis repeat on me," Pippa replied.

"Just because you hate babies . . ." Ameerah winked at Nory as she said this.

"I don't hate babies!" Pippa exclaimed, right on cue. "I fucking love babies. I fucking love all small people. I simply don't want one of my own. I don't want a fish either, it doesn't mean I hate all fish."

Ameerah laughed. "Wow, Pip, your baby antenna gets more sensitive every year!"

Pippa screwed her face up and narrowed her eyes, but she was smiling. "Biatch," she said. "Anyway, what about you? Are you going to get your man-Barbie to impregnate you?"

"No," Ameerah mused. "He's purely for my personal pleasure. I'll be taking him back to the store after the wedding."

"You two sound so jaded," said Nory.

"I'm not jaded," said Pippa. "I've just spent the last ten years explaining on an almost daily basis why I don't want children. I'm tired of having to excuse myself. I shouldn't have to. And it's only getting worse the older I get because now every bugger seems to think they can hear my biological clock ticking. Someone asked me the other day if I'd considered freezing my eggs because I might change my mind! I don't know what makes everyone feel, A: that they have shares in my uterus; and B: that I don't know my own mind."

"I'll tell you this much: If I do end up having kids, I won't be packing them off to boarding school for the entirety of their childhood," said Ameerah. "They'll go to private school, obviously, but they won't board."

"Somehow I can't picture you as a stay-at-home mummy," said Pippa.

"I didn't say I'd give up work; I'll have a nanny, or a stay-at-home husband. But my children and I will always share the same postcode."

"How very new-age hippie of you," said Pippa dryly.

Jenna extracted herself from Guy's probing conversation and came over. "Doesn't everyone look lovely," she said. "I'm so pleased everyone made the effort to dress up."

"I feel like a tightly packed sausage," Nory complained. "If I get any hotter someone better prick me so that I don't burst."

"She's not getting on with the Spanx," Ameerah stage-whispered.

"It's all right for you, you don't need to wear them," Nory hissed back.

"Everyone wears them, darling," said Jenna. "If you gathered up all the hidden spandex on the red carpet you could make a trampoline the size of the Shetland Islands. I should know."

"They make them for men too, you know. My father wears them for formal occasions," Pippa added.

Nory tried and failed to imagine Pippa's dad in hold-you-in pants.

"Speaking of formal occasions," Jenna began. "One of my cousins is getting a divorce . . . and he'll be at the wedding!"

She beamed at Nory as she said this, and Nory recognized the glint in her eye.

"Your poor cousin," she replied, ignoring the inference. "I expect he'll need time to recover from his marriage breakdown."

Jenna completely ignored her. "He's forty, very fit, always at the gym. No children. Works in finance."

"Is he attractive?" asked Ameerah. "Nory won't go for just any old soon-to-be-divorced cousin, you know."

"Of course he's attractive!" said Jenna. "That goes without saying. My family have very good genes."

"This is excellent news!" Pippa clapped. "Bring on Operation Get Nory Laid."

"Oh my god!" Nory laughed. "Really?"

"Darling, you've had so little action lately, the love police have sent out a search party to find your sex life," Pippa teased.

They laughed, clinking their cocktail glasses together, and the years fell away like no time had passed at all.

*Six*

The bell rang for dinner, and the group made their way through a door disguised as a bookcase into an opulent dining room with a table that could easily seat twenty. Flowers ran down the center of the table, punctuated by glittering candelabras set at just the right points so that no one's view of the person opposite was blocked. There were place cards beside each setting, and as Nory began to look for hers, Pippa leaned in and whispered in her ear, "I've got you covered," before gliding off to take her own seat. Nory found her place—at the other end of the table from Guy and his wife. She leaned forward and mouthed *thank you* to Pippa, seated opposite, who winked in return. To her right was Dev and to her left, with a place made up, was an empty space and a place card that read *Tristan*. Next to the space, at the head of the table, sat Jenna. She caught Nory's eye and gave her a wistful smile.

Pippa stood and clinked her soup spoon to her glass. The table quieted.

"When I started planning the seating arrangements, you can imagine how horrified I was to discover that we were an odd number."

Everyone laughed.

"Ever the control freak!" heckled Charles.

Pippa nodded her agreement. "But then I realized we weren't really an odd number at all. Because one of us isn't here, one of us who should be here."

All eyes fell upon the empty place beside Nory.

"But he is here in our hearts. And we will never forget him." Pippa raised her glass, and the rest of the table stood and raised their glasses with her. "To Tristan, wherever you are, know that you are loved and that we miss you."

"To Tristan!" came the chorus.

Everyone resumed their seats. Nory looked at Jenna, who was doing her best to smile, but her eyes were glassy with tears. Nory reached out and laid her hand palm up on Tristan's place setting, and Jenna laid her own palm on top of Nory's and squeezed.

The meal started with spiced pear and parsnip soup, sourced from the kitchen garden, and homemade sourdough bread. Nory had once harbored a fancy that she might be the sort of person who made sourdough bread after work; she often fantasized about being a domestic goddess. Anthony Jr. had given her a sourdough starter in a glass jam jar with instructions. If she was honest, it frightened her a bit, bubbling and growing on the worktop. She'd seen *Little Shop of Horrors*, she knew how these things could escalate. But she needn't have worried; within a week she had managed to kill her starter without ever having made a single loaf. Nory decided to leave sourdough to the professionals and went back to buying it from Pepe's.

Conversation around the table was lively, and of course much of it inevitably reverted to "back in the day" stories. These shared histories were like comfort blankets, drawing them together, safe against the tide of time and the outside world. Nory was pleased to see Dev and Camille enjoying the tales as much as those who remembered them by heart.

As the main course was served, the talk moved on to relations with the local kids who went to the comprehensive school. Nory reflected that her own brother had been one of them, seething with mockery and disdain for his counterparts up in "toff towers." At the mention of the many and varied altercations between the two schools, there was some general chest puffing on the part of the men around the table. Nory wondered if the red meat was having an effect.

"You seem to be remembering this like you were the T-Birds and they were the Scorpions." Pippa laughed.

Jenna joined her. "The reality was somewhat less cool," she added.

"It's hard to look threatening in a maroon blazer and boater." Ameerah giggled.

"I think they were definitely threatened by us," said Jeremy. "We were the toffs on the hill and generally feared and loathed by the kids from the village."

"I don't think any of you were *feared*, Jez," Nory butted in. "I know you fellas liked to think you were a cut above, but most of the kids *I* knew thought you were a bunch of preppy weaklings."

Jenna laughed and clapped her hands. Charles in particular looked peeved.

"You've got to remember most of them were farm kids, they'd been working almost since they could walk. They were driving tractors and lifting hay bales before and after school. You were playing lacrosse and croquet!"

"And rugger!" added Guy defensively. "You can't be a weakling if you play rugby."

"Well, Nory's implying we were sissies for playing lacrosse and croquet," Charles griped.

"Actually, I think Nory is implying that you were mollycoddled by privilege and burdened with an inflated sense of power," said Dev, and all eyes swung in the handsome model's direction.

"Thank you, Dev," said Nory. "I couldn't have and indeed didn't put it better myself."

Ameerah eyed Dev with suspicion.

"Brilliant!" shouted Guy rambunctiously. "First night here and already we're being emasculated."

"Just like the old days!" quipped Charles.

"Well, it's all shits and giggles, isn't it?" Nory winked, and a roar of agreement rolled along the table.

"To shits and giggles!" said Pippa, raising her glass.

And the dinner guests joined her, shouting, "To shits and giggles!"

⁓

Dessert continued in the same rowdy manner, until eventually the butler invited them to go back into the drawing room for after-dinner cocktails, presumably so that the waiting staff could clear down and go home.

Nory had become aware of Guy trying to catch her eye. At first, she had thought she was being overly sensitive, what with her being hyperaware of his wife, but when he began to lean across the table to smile at her each time Camille's head was turned the other way, she knew it wasn't simply her imagination.

When the group meandered back into the drawing room, Nory moved quickly away from him. She deposited herself across the room, where Charles had reclaimed his seat at the piano and

Jenna was looking dreamily at her fiancé as he began to sing "The Way You Look Tonight."

Guy had always been someone whose Off button malfunctioned after one too many drinks. He'd become more audacious, and his self-belief swelled to narcissistic proportions. It was his daring and his cavalier attitude toward other people's privacy that often got him the big scoops and center spreads in the paper; it had also earned him a few black eyes in the past, which he claimed was "the price of good journalism."

Ever the eagle eye, Pippa caught Guy's arm as he made his way to where Nory was standing and talked at him until Camille arrived back from the bathroom. Nory found reasons to move out of his orbit two or three times more, but she could still feel his eyes on her. She really rather wished he'd either pass out or bugger off.

Nory was breaking out in a sweat. Whose idea was it to insist on formal wear? She could barely breathe inside her cocktail dress before dinner, but now, after a three-course meal, her so-called shapewear had become pants of iron clamping her middle.

Ameerah was smooching with Dev on the chaise longue. Even if Nory had wanted to interrupt the lovers, she wasn't sure her Spanx would allow her to sit down.

Nory wiggled out into the hall and along to the downstairs bathrooms; something was going to have to give, and it was going to be her Spanx. She had just reached the door when a warm hand touched her shoulder. She spun around to find Guy smiling down at her. His face was relaxed by excessive amounts of alcohol, and he looked puffy around the eyes, as if the champagne had nowhere left to go and had decided to fill up his eye bags.

"Hey," he said, in what Nory assumed was his smooth jazz voice. "Sorry, I didn't mean to startle you."

Nory craned her neck to look around him.

"Relax," he said, rubbing his hand up and down her arm.

"Where's your *wife*?" asked Nory, shaking his hand off.

"She's talking renovations with Pippa; Christ knows how much that's going to cost me."

"I doubt it'll cost *you* anything; from what I understand, Camille outearns you by quite a bit. I don't know why you keep trying to pass her off as the *little woman*."

Guy smiled sheepishly. One of his eyelids was drooping. "You always could see through my bullshit, Nory."

"Not always," Nory hissed pointedly through gritted teeth.

"Hey, I never lied to you," he said.

"No, you just omitted the teeny fact that you were married with children!"

"You can't deny that we were hot together," he whispered, moving closer.

"Your wife is here, you pig!"

"Thrilling, isn't it?"

Nory's indignation was making her Spanx feel even tighter. She suddenly knew exactly how Augustus Gloop felt when he was stuck in the tube in Willy Wonka's chocolate factory. She pushed past Guy, shoving him hard as she did so, the alcohol making his reflexes slow, so that he stumbled into the wall, then slid down it to the floor.

But Nory wasn't taking any chances; she didn't want him catching up with her. She walked, as fast as she reasonably could in a dress that prevented her legs from moving, toward the French doors at the other end of the hall, then pushed through them onto a veranda, down the steps, and out into the night.

# Seven

The frigid air hit her at once, and she imagined the sweat on her skin instantly turning to a sheen of ice. She shivered and considered turning back, but she wasn't ready for another run-in with Guy. The lights from the castle spilled out across the lawn, crisp underfoot with frost, and where their reach ended, little lights tucked into the earth illuminated the flower beds.

This was Nory's old stomping ground. She knew that beyond the main gardens was the old folly, always unlocked when guests were in residence, and generously stocked with blankets, wingback armchairs, and brandy. Shaking quite vigorously now with the bitter cold, Nory hugged herself and headed through the archway in the Victorian wall, which led into the formal gardens. Here the beds were organized in smart rows, many of them almost bare, only shorn stumps to hint at what might be sleeping beneath, waiting for spring to warm the earth and reawaken them. She moved through here with the ease of someone who knows the lie of the land of old, and through another arch that led to the Winter Garden.

The Winter Garden had always been her favorite growing up, and despite the cold by now having almost completely numbed her limbs, she walked more slowly. Any plant could dazzle when the sun shone warm and the days were long, but to Nory's mind, it took a special kind of flower to be able to bloom when the weather was freezing and the days were bleak.

The little footlights in the flower beds highlighted purple heathers, bright pink sedums—or "ice plants" as her dad had always referred to them—and winter jasmine, with its showers of yellow stars. But it was the hellebores that Nory loved the best. Their dark leaves with sharp serrated edges, so in contrast with the soft powdery bells and bonnets of its flowers; heavy blooms nodding bashfully toward the earth.

Her joy at being back in her favorite part of the castle grounds was hampered only by the notion that she might develop hypothermia. She was about to hurry toward her final destination when something at the back of a border caught her eye. It was a hellebore, but not one she'd seen before—and if any girl was going to know her hellebores, it was her. Maybe it was the dark playing tricks on her. But still . . . she bent down, as best she could in her silk sausage-skin dress, to take a look, and she could feel the thin wire that ran the perimeter of the bed cutting into her calves.

"What are you doing?"

Nory jumped, her actions jerky from shock and partially frozen limbs. Unfortunately, her movements were limited by her very tight dress, and she stumbled forward. With gravity pulling her down toward the bed of hellebores, which she would undoubtedly pulverize, she began windmilling her arms wildly to propel herself backward. She tried to shuffle back, but her dress had snagged on the wire. She yanked one leg back hard, and the fabric gave way with a rip that seemed to echo off the garden walls. The force of it sent her off along the path like a spinning top. She came to rest abruptly in a wheelbarrow, the manure in it breaking her fall and preventing any major injury other than the crushing blow dealt to her dignity.

For a moment she sat dazed, but the sweet, punchy aroma of cow shit soon punctured any discombobulation. She tried to heave herself out of the wheelbarrow, but she had never been gifted with upper body strength, and her bottom half was practically a mermaid tail due to her stupid dress. She was about to resort to some incarnation of the Worm Dance to wiggle her way to freedom when a man—presumably belonging to the voice that had gotten her into this mess—in a parka zipped up to the top loomed over her, and said, "I'm not going to hurt you. I work here. Take my hands."

Nory had very little choice. As she reached out her own rather grubby hands, she hoped that he was a security guard and not an armed robber come to burglarize the toffs playing house in the castle . . . She decided that the latter would probably have left her in the barrow.

With a most unladylike "Ooof!" Nory was lifted out of the wheelbarrow and was relieved to find her feet back on the ground—not that she could feel them anymore, or any other part of her anatomy for that matter. As if reading her thoughts, the man unzipped his coat and held it out to her.

"I'll make it smell," she half protested; even from this distance she could feel the warmth he'd left behind in the fabric, tempting her in like a warm bath.

"It'll wash," he said simply.

She didn't need telling twice. She slipped her arms into the sleeves and pulled the heavy coat tightly around her, little moans of ecstasy escaping her lips as the heat enveloped her. She looked up at him then.

"Isaac?" she said incredulously. He had changed, of course, but there was no mistaking him.

The man stared at her for a long moment, a frown causing a crease between his brows, and then recognition dawned.

"Elinor Noel," he said in a tone that wasn't exactly friendly.

"Oh my god!" She laughed. "You're still here!"

She saw Isaac bristle.

"'Still here' would imply I never left. Which is not the case."

"Oh." Nory was a little taken aback. *Touchy! I guess some people hang on to their grudges for life.* "Sorry, I didn't mean anything . . ." She trailed off. *Excellent start, Nory!*

His frown softened, one eyebrow raised as he regarded her. Isaac. Isaac Malik the head gardener's son, all grown up and standing before her like a dark-skinned Adonis in green Wellington boots and a cable-knit fisherman's jumper. And she'd already managed to piss him off. Some things never changed.

"You used to throw mud at my head" was all Nory could think to say.

"I could say the same about you," said Isaac. "Can I ask why you're out here in the dark, in the freezing cold, with no coat on, trying to sabotage my hellebores?"

"That's a lot of questions. Would you like my national insurance number and date of birth as well while we're at it?"

The corners of Isaac's mouth twitched.

"No," he replied, "that won't be necessary, unless I decide to press charges."

"Charges?"

"For trespassing," Isaac explained with a completely straight face. "After all, you've got form for that."

"I'm not trespassing, I'm a guest."

"A guest?"

"Why is that so shocking?" she asked.

"I suppose it's not really, if you run in *those* kinds of circles. I saw some of your fellow *guests* smoking out on the lawn earlier."

"Is smoking on lawns illegal now?" she asked exasperatedly. "And what do you mean *those kinds of circles?*"

"People with more money than sense."

"You don't know anything about them, so stop being so judgy," she said, affronted. "And for your information almost all of them have more sense than money, which amounts to a lot of sense indeed!"

He smiled, his peevishness replaced by amusement. "Sorry," he said. "Ignore me. I'm not usually such an arse. But smoking *is* bad for you."

"Okay."

Nory was having trouble keeping up; this guy was capricious.

"You still haven't told me what you were doing in my flower beds. Were you burying something incriminating?"

Nory narrowed her eyes at him. "I wanted a closer look at the hellebores near the back of the bed. I don't recognize the cultivar."

Isaac seemed unable to hide his surprise.

"But then a big oaf scared me half to death, and well, you know the rest," she continued. She shivered despite the warm coat. Her teeth had begun to chatter loudly, and her feet were stiff with cold to the point of painful.

"Shall I escort you back to the castle?" Isaac asked. His voice was deeper than she remembered it, much deeper, but it had a soft edge to it.

Nory groaned. She didn't really want to go back to the castle wearing a ripped cocktail dress infused with eau de heifer. No doubt they'd all still be drinking and reminiscing, and if they saw her now, she would be the butt of their jokes for the rest of the stay and all reunions thereafter. The expression *mud sticks* would in this case be both idiom and literal.

"No thank you, I'm going to the folly."

"The folly is closed for maintenance."

"Oh." *Dammit!* "Is there another option? Couldn't I maybe hide in a barn for a while, just until my friends have all gone to bed? Snuggle up with a nice warm sheep maybe? I'm already covered in crap, so I don't think things can get much worse on the dress front, really."

"Didn't you only just arrive this afternoon?"

"So?"

"So, isn't it a bit soon to have already pissed off your house-mates?"

"I haven't pissed anyone off! I'm just . . . Oh, don't bother!" She harrumphed, yanked off his coat, and shoved it at him. She began to hobble away on frozen feet, the cold biting deeper into her skin after the respite of a warm coat.

Isaac came after her. "What are you doing? Don't be stupid. Put the coat back on."

"Wow, I'm stupid too?" she stuttered through chattering teeth.

"I'm sorry, okay? Now put the coat on. Please. I can't afford to have a guest get frostbite on my watch."

Nory realized she must look pretty pathetic because she saw his concerned expression. He held the coat out and she shrugged back into it, muttering a thank-you.

"Look, if you really don't want to go back to the castle right now, I could maybe rustle you up some clean clothes. You can warm up by the fire in my cottage," he said. "I'm not a weirdo, I promise. And then I'll drive you back round later; you can sneak in through the servants' quarters."

She looked up and found him smiling at her. Suddenly she was sixteen again, the kid sister, bumping into her brother's mate on the stairs as he made to leave the house, his rare smile making her flush.

"That is the best offer I've had all night!" she said, and she meant it.

# Eight

The gardener's cottage was reached via a wooden door set into the wall at the farthest point of the Winter Garden, flanked by two long Victorian glass cold frames. To the casual observer, the door looked as though it would lead to a potting shed or something equally banal. But the reality was quite different.

A thin, winding path led through a densely wooded area, which Nory knew to be bright with bluebells in the spring and liberally strewn with pink rhododendron flowers until early summer. Now, lit by the yellow gleam of Isaac's torch, she could see clumps of ruby-red holly berries, glittering like jewels in the frosty air.

"So, what finds you out prowling the grounds at this time of night?" Nory asked, trying to make conversation.

"I always do a lap, last thing, to make sure everything's in order." And then he added, "You never know when you're going to find some DFL wandering lost around the grounds half-drunk and half-dressed."

"DFL?"

"Down From London."

Nory balked. "I hardly count as a DFL, and I was not lost!" she said indignantly.

"Why were you going to the folly anyway? A clandestine meeting?"

"If you must know, I was trying to avoid someone. I thought I could hole up in the folly for a while and go back to the castle when he'd gone to bed . . . or passed out."

Isaac didn't answer.

"And also, I am not half-drunk. At the very most, I am a quarter-drunk; the cold is very sobering. And this is a whole dress! Or at least it was, before you made me rip it."

Isaac laughed quietly. "You're still as mouthy as I remember," he said.

Nory couldn't argue with that.

The path opened out into a perfect English country garden, complete with a carved stone birdfeeder and wrought iron picnic set on the patio. An arbor was wound around with the skeleton of a rambling rose. Wisteria climbed the stone walls of the cottage. In the center of the lawn stood an ancient yew tree, its trunk twisted with age, arthritic branches stretched beseechingly toward the stars while keeping a tight hold of its needles. The fruit trees that ran along the garden walls had long since shed their leaves, their frames shivering in the breeze.

At the back of the house, the wall was lower on one side, and it was from here that Isaac's dad used to shout at them to "get back to school!" as Nory and her friends crept out from Robins Wood in search of adventure. Robins Wood marked the boundary between the school grounds and the castle and served as a perfect cut-through for truanting students.

One of the leaded windows of the house glowed golden, as did the little stained-glass panes above the front door. Nory felt the thrill of anticipation. All those years of wondering what the inside of the enchanted cottage at the edge of the woods would look like were about to be satisfied.

Inside the front door was a small hallway, with rooms going off left and right and a staircase in the middle. Isaac pulled off his boots and Nory bent down to undo her very muddy—and one and only pair—of stilettos; she smiled inwardly that she now had the excuse to downgrade to her more sensibly heeled Mary Jane shoes—of which she had two pairs—for the duration of the week.

As she shrugged out of Isaac's thick coat, the warmth of the cozy cottage seemed to enliven the scent of cow pats clinging to her dress.

"Would you mind waiting in the hall while I get you some fresh clothes?" Isaac asked. "I don't want to sound precious, but you kind of stink and I'd rather we kept it contained."

"I think that is absolutely fair," Nory replied.

From the room to her left there was a snuffling sound, and a long nose squeezed through the gap in the door and nudged it open. An elderly lurcher padded into the hall and proceeded to give Nory a good sniffing.

"Oh, hello. You're lovely." Nory cooed, despite the hound nosing around her bottom rather enthusiastically.

"Come on, Lettuce, leave our guest alone," said Isaac. Lettuce looked up at Nory with big soft eyes before turning to follow her master through the door to the right.

Left alone in the hallway, Nory glanced around. Beneath her own powerful aroma, she could smell woodsmoke and oud. The uneven walls were roughly plastered and whitewashed. A barometer hung below a bookshelf. She checked his books—she always checked the books—a nature almanac, an encyclopedia of trees, and several pocket handbooks on foraging and woodland plants. Her bookish self approved.

Isaac came back into the hall with Lettuce at his side, holding a pair of tracksuit bottoms—she quietly gave thanks for the generous elastic waist—and an oversized hoody with a thick fleece lining.

"I'd offer you the use of my shower, but is that too weird? I don't know. It's too weird, right? I'm not sure what the etiquette is for dealing with women you've rescued from a wheelbarrow full of cow crap." He said all this without giving her a chance to speak, and then seemed to have made his decision because he handed her the clothes and said, "I'll just"—he pushed open the door to a small sitting room with a large fireplace and a fire crackling within it—"give you some privacy," he said, going through the door and closing it.

The clothes smelled newly washed and warm from the radiator; too bad she was about to stink them up. Checking that the sitting room door was firmly closed, Nory began the process of peeling herself out of her silly cocktail dress. She had expected to have Ameerah on hand for tugging and yanking duties. She reasoned that if things got too desperate, she'd just rip herself out of the damn thing, but as it turned out, being frozen into a human ice pop meant the satin slipped off easily. She would have liked to keep her bra on, but it had suffered the same level of manure marinading as her dress and was therefore discarded along with her Spanx—oh, the sweet relief—and finally her tights, before she immersed herself into the soft leisure wear. She felt instantly refreshed. Nory pulled her clothes into a bundle, opened the front door, and left them in a pathetic pile on the doorstep, next to a potted bay tree.

Nory hesitated outside the sitting room door. Then she

knocked and gingerly crept in. Lettuce was sprawled out on a rug in front of the fire; she looked briefly up at Nory and then let her head drop back onto the thick rug. Isaac was seated on one of the two sofas on either side of the fire, a book in his hand: *The War of the Worlds*, she noted, and added another mental tick beside his name. He smiled when he saw her.

"Better?" he asked.

"Much," she said. "Thank you."

"I took the liberty of making you a mug of cocoa."

Nory clocked the two steaming mugs on the coffee table and almost purred. Next to one of the mugs was a pair of knitted socks.

"For me?" she asked.

Isaac nodded. "I figured your feet would be cold after those stupid shoes."

"Thank you." She beamed, pulling them on gratefully. "They are very stupid shoes. I shan't be at all sad to see the back of them." Nory took her mug of cocoa and settled on the opposite sofa, tucking her feet underneath her. "How long have you had Lettuce?"

"Four years. I took her on when my dad died."

"Oh god, Isaac, I'm so sorry!"

She hadn't considered his dad might be dead, she'd assumed he'd gone off to retire somewhere. Why hadn't her family mentioned it? Then again, why would they?

"Thanks," said Isaac.

"Your dad was always nice to me."

Isaac raised his eyebrows.

"When I was at the nursery with my parents, I mean," she clarified. "Not when we were trespassing."

Isaac smiled at that. "His bark was always worse than his

bite. He told me once he didn't like shouting at the kids from the school, but he had to, or the castle grounds would be overrun with truants."

Nory laughed. "That's probably true," she admitted. "He was young, though. Your dad. Sorry, I don't mean to pry, it's just that I remember he and my dad were around the same age."

"Cancer," said Isaac simply. "It's a bastard disease."

Nory nodded. "So, you took over as head gardener."

"I was a horticulture lecturer in Cornwall. But I'd been getting itchy feet for a while; I missed getting my hands dirty, wanted to get back to practicing what I'd been preaching. When Dad knew he wasn't going to be able to work anymore, he suggested to Lord Abercrombie that I take over his role. Been here ever since."

"Do you miss it? The teaching?"

"I miss the learning atmosphere, the hopeful vibe at the university. But I'm not a natural academic, I need to be doing. So, when I came here, I had a meeting with Lord Abercrombie and we created a partnership with Hart's College, so that kids taking vocational courses like horticulture and environmental studies can come up here for their practicals and fieldwork."

"The best of both worlds."

"Exactly. How about you? Corporate banking? Or CEO?"

"Sorry to disappoint you. None of the above, I'm afraid. I own a secondhand bookshop in Shepherd Market, London."

Isaac smiled. "That's unexpected. You've taken me by surprise there. It sounds wonderful."

"Are you teasing me?" she asked.

"No! Genuinely, that sounds wonderful. I have a thing for old books. I dunno, something about the smell of them or the binding . . ."

"Yes! There is no smell like book smell." She nodded like a woman who'd sniffed a lot of books.

They were quiet for a moment, each sipping their cocoa while contemplating the other. This was not how Nory had envisaged her evening turning out, but it was a welcome surprise. She looked around the room. It was peaceful and comfortable, just the sort of space you want to relax in after a hard day's work. The sofas were particularly sumptuous. A painting in one of the alcoves caught her eye.

"Is that . . . ?" She crossed the room, still hugging her cocoa, and stared at the small botanical study of wild garlic, from bulb to flower, in a dark wood frame. "Is this an original Serena De-Veer?" she asked a little breathlessly.

Isaac was contemplative for a moment. "Yes."

"Oh my goodness, do you know how rare these are?"

She couldn't quite believe she was looking at an original De-Veer; she'd only ever seen them in museums or books. And here was one just casually hanging in Isaac's front room.

"I have an idea," he said.

"You are very lucky. I've got books of De-Veer's prints, a couple of first editions. I've been offered a small fortune for them, but I'd never part with them. I keep them under glass in the shop; they're so rare. I love her work. Where did you get it?"

"I inherited it. It's been in the family for some time."

"Gosh, don't be tempted to part with it, will you? Or if you do, make sure you speak to an actual art dealer first."

When Isaac didn't answer, she turned to find him gazing into the fire. Perhaps he was worried she might offer to buy it from him. Fat chance.

"This is a lovely room," she said, sitting back down opposite Isaac.

"Thanks. I changed a lot of things when I moved in. My parents were sentimental souls, which was great, but it meant they could never throw anything away. When Mum married Dad, she brought her parents' old furniture with her because she couldn't bear to part with it, and then when Mum died, Dad couldn't bear to part with it either. I swear the old sofas were only held together by dust and memories."

Nory smiled. "That's kind of sweet, though," she said.

"And kind of gross," he joked.

"And there's no Mrs. Head Gardener? Or Mr.?" She didn't like to make assumptions.

Isaac laughed. "No, no Mrs. It's just me and Lettuce."

Nory couldn't help feeling a little twinge of pleasure.

"So, you're here for the big wedding," he said.

"Yup."

"Coincidence? Or does the wedding party know the area?"

Nory shifted on the sofa. "The happy couple used to go to Braddon-Hartmead. You'd probably recognize them if you saw them."

Isaac's expression darkened, just for a second. "I thought I recognized the smokers on the lawn. So, you're having a bit of a school reunion before the big day." His tone, if not unfriendly exactly, was less congenial than it had been a moment ago. Nory decided to ignore it.

"Yes," she said brightly. "The rest of the guests arrive on Saturday."

"And how's the reunion working out so far?" Isaac asked.

"Well, I'm hiding out here drinking cocoa instead of sipping cocktails at the castle, so . . ."

Isaac nodded. "Will you be going down to see your family while you're here?"

"Yes. I couldn't not, really, being this close to home. I plan to go down tomorrow."

"I've got a few things to pick up from the nursery, so I can give you a lift down if you like?"

"Thank you. That's very kind of you."

Isaac shrugged it off.

"So, you noticed my hellebores. That's pretty impressive in the dark."

"Hellebores are my favorites. I mean, I'm not a flower nerd or anything . . ." She was a total flower nerd.

"Unlike me," Isaac teased.

"Well, quite," Nory agreed. They were flirting, and she was very into it. Not everyone would want to flirt with a woman who had rolled in a wheelbarrow full of manure. *Play it cool, Nory, you are in a sexy gardener's cottage with no bra on. This is the closest you've come to foreplay in months.*

"I've been developing a hybrid plant for the last couple of years. It's not something I would have expected a layman to recognize, though."

It was Nory's turn to give a quizzical look. "Have *you met* my family? I knew about perennials, annuals, and evergreens before I could say the alphabet!"

Isaac laughed. "I thought you said you weren't a flower nerd."

"I think we both know I am a total flower nerd."

"There we are similar, at least," he said.

They finished their cocoa to the gentle sounds of Lettuce snoring and the popping of logs on the fire.

"Do you miss it?" Isaac asked. "The quiet of the country-side?"

"The countryside isn't quiet! It's just a different set of noises. I guess you learn to tune them out. In London I'm used to the constant hum of traffic, and here I'm used to the incessant music of the wildlife. I find them both soothing in their own way. Although maybe not so much in the summer; London noise can feel oppressive at three a.m. when it's twenty-eight degrees."

"Ha, yeah, but the payoff is that you don't get eaten alive by midges the second you open a window!" said Isaac.

"This is true."

They were quiet for a long moment. After being so cold, warming up was making Nory's limbs feel soft and relaxed. She began to think about visiting home tomorrow.

"Do you ever see my brother?" she asked.

"Yeah, quite a bit. He's a good mate."

Nory mentally scrubbed out one of the ticks she'd given Isaac earlier for his bookshelf. If he was good friends with her brother, did that mean they shared the same attitude?

"How is he?" she asked.

"Don't you know?"

"We don't talk much. And I doubt I'd be the person he'd turn to if he ever wasn't okay. I thought maybe you could give me a heads-up before I go down there tomorrow. I like to know what I'm walking into."

"As your brother's friend, it wouldn't really be my place to divulge things he might have shared with me. But since I can think of nothing to cause you worry or to make me feel disloyal, I can tell you that he's fine. You probably know your dad is taking a bit of a step back at the nursery, and that seems to suit Thom. He likes being in charge."

"Don't I know it!"

Isaac laughed. "I mean, it suits him, the extra responsibility. I suppose we're alike in that way, both taking over where our fathers left off."

"I'd like to think I'll have someone to leave my bookshop to one day. Maybe I'll start training up my nephews now."

"Ha, good luck with that. Thom's already got them earmarked for the nursery."

*Of course he has.* Thom was like her dad, all about keeping the family business going. Nory couldn't help feeling that she had somehow betrayed them by not sticking around to play her part.

◦⌒◦

The clock on the fireplace read 1:00 a.m., and Nory could see Isaac struggling to stifle his yawns. If she didn't move soon, she was liable to nod off on his sofa.

"I'm going to head back up to the castle," she said, forcing herself to get up. "If they're not all in bed, they'll at least be too drunk to notice me."

Isaac stretched and stood. "I'll drive you round."

"There's no need, it's not that far."

"It's far enough in the cold and the pitch-dark. The castle staff will have turned off the outside lights by now. I'd rather not find you tomorrow frozen in the maze, like Jack Nicholson at the end of *The Shining*."

"Well, when you put it like that . . ." Nory smiled.

◦⌒◦

She was grateful that Isaac had ignored her polite protestations and even more grateful for the fur-lined Wellington boots he loaned her. The temperature seemed to have dropped even further, and the sky had the eerie yellow glow it got when it was holding on to snow. It only took five or six minutes in the car to get back to the castle, but Nory knew it would have taken her three times as long on foot in the dark. The old Range Rover was comfortable but definitely a working vehicle; the backseat was strewn with work gloves and jackets for varying weather. It smelled of earth after the rain with an undercurrent of damp dog.

Isaac pulled up at the back of the castle, beside a far less impressive door than the one she had entered upon her arrival. Here, a little porch light offered friendly sanctuary and lit a courtyard filled with old whiskey barrels, troughs filled with plants, and various brooms and other outside work tools leaned up against a wall, as though just left while the owner took a tea break. Isaac pulled out his phone and speed-dialed a number. Nory could hear a jovial voice on the other end of the line.

"How did you know I wouldn't be asleep?" came the voice.

"Because I know you. Who's winning?"

The voice laughed—a hoarse sound that suggested many cigarettes smoked and much alcohol consumed over countless years.

"I am, of course!"

"Well, put your chips down for a minute and come and open the back door. I've got a guest here who would appreciate being taken to her room via the back stairs."

"Be there in two," said the voice, and the line went dead.

The door opened a moment later, and a stocky man in braces and an undone tie strode out to the car.

"It was nice to meet you again, Elinor," said Isaac. "I think I like you better when you're not pelting me with mud."

Nory laughed. "Nory. Call me Nory. It was nice to meet you again too. Thanks for the cocoa and the clothes. I'll get them back to you tomorrow. And for the record, you started it."

Isaac smiled.

Nory climbed down out of the car, clutching her evening clothes in a carrier bag.

"Isaac," said the man, nodding. "Madam," he added, tipping an invisible hat toward Nory.

"Cheers, Andy, I owe you," said Isaac.

"I'm keeping score," Andy replied, and winked.

"Goodbye, Nory," said Isaac.

Nory waved at Isaac, smiling, then turned to follow Andy into the castle. She heard the gravel crunch as Isaac drove away.

Andy led Nory through a maze of narrow corridors; it wasn't exactly "upstairs downstairs" territory, but this area away from the guests definitely had a no-frills, business vibe about it. There were memos and timetables stuck to the walls with sticky tape, and the lights in the ceiling were the buzzy fluorescent tube variety—a far cry from the chandeliers dripping crystals in the public areas. They passed an enormous kitchen, a sea of stainless-steel humming appliances, and then a laundry room. The latter reminded Nory of the bag she was holding.

"Um, Andy, is there any chance I can have some washing powder?" She held up the bag in explanation. "I had a run-in with some manure."

"I can leave it here with a note for the morning staff if you like. They can do it for you."

"I'd rather not. It's not a nice job. I can wash it out in the sink."

She was pretty sure the dress was a lost cause anyway, but she needed the bra. Andy nodded and ducked into the laundry room, returning a moment later with a paper cup full of washing powder. Nory thanked him, and they continued on their way. Andy chitchatted without managing to say anything much at all, the polite nothingness that staff used with guests to fill the otherwise quiet air.

At last, they reached her door, having managed to avoid all

her friends—though she could hear Jenna shrieking with laughter from somewhere on the floor below. Nory thanked Andy and closed her door, grateful to be in her own company.

∽

While she rinsed out her bra and hung it over the towel radiator to dry, she thought about Isaac. He often used to call for her brother. Sometimes he'd even come upstairs to Thom's bedroom to listen to music and do whatever teenage boys did when they were together. She'd peek at him through the crack in her bedroom door as he climbed the stairs and watch from her window as they left for the park, swaggering in that way cocky lads do. Isaac had been out of her league, of course. Even aside from the verbal and actual mudslinging between Isaac and her friends from the posh school, there was the age difference. *And* he was also her big brother's mate—*so not* cool to have the nerdy baby sister simpering after you.

Nory climbed into the gloriously squishy four-poster bed and allowed herself to revel momentarily in living as the other half did. She wondered about the people who had slept in this room when the castle was a family home, before it became a wedding venue and a playhouse for the wealthy.

Her mind drifted back to Isaac, growing up here in the castle grounds, and then drawn back here again as an adult. *Does anyone ever truly leave the place where they grew up?* she wondered. Even if you never physically returned, a part of the place would always travel with you surely. Like an imprint, a tattoo on your psyche. At least that's how Nory felt about the village of Hartmead.

She felt comfortably displaced, like a ghost still walking the halls of its old home. She hadn't expected it to churn up so many emotions, feelings she thought she'd left behind her, that sense that she'd only ever half-belonged in either of the places she called home. She could feel herself reshaping to fit into an old skin. She sighed, opened *Good Omens* by Neil Gaiman at her bookmark, and read until she fell asleep with the book open on her chest.

# Nine

When Isaac's Range Rover pulled into the courtyard behind the castle the next morning, the rest of the house party had already headed off to a morning of archery. The sky was the color of lentil soup, heavy and brooding with either rain or snow. It wasn't common to have snow so early in winter—though it did sometimes happen this high up—but the weather forecasters had been warning of an extreme cold front closing in from the east. Nory—who had been sheltering from the cold wind in the porchway of the staff entrance—crossed to the car and climbed in, shivering as she pulled the door shut behind her.

"Good morning," Isaac said.

"Good morning to you," she replied, throwing a bag containing the clothes she'd borrowed onto the backseat.

Isaac was wearing a knitted hat and a different coat than the one she had borrowed last night. He smelled of soap and sandalwood and, she noticed, was even better-looking in the daylight. His skin was smooth, clean-shaven, his dark complexion a contrast to her own pale skin, which refused to tan and freckled instantly when the sun hit it.

"Did anyone notice you were missing last night?" he asked as they pulled out onto the long drive.

In the distance Nory could see two golf carts bumping over the grounds, delivering her friends to their morning activities.

"Ameerah asked me this morning where I'd got to. She checked in on me before she went to bed to make sure I hadn't been kidnapped. And Jeremy asked, but I don't think any of the others noticed. Or if they did, they assumed I'd gone to bed early."

"Are you known for going to bed early?"

"As a matter of fact, I am." Nory laughed. "Aside from a brief foray in my twenties, I've never been terribly into all-night parties. I like books and tea more than I like clubs and margaritas."

"Same," Isaac agreed. "But then there aren't too many night clubs in Hartmead."

They passed the tiny station, where one of her parents would usually meet Nory off the train and drive her back to her childhood home. Then her old primary school. Somewhere behind those walls, her nephews, Jackson and Lucas, were learning in the same classrooms she had.

"Would you like a lift back up to the castle later? It's no bother; I'll leave a space between the bedding plants for you."

"Thank you, that's kind, but I don't know how long I'll be. I'm sure I can get someone to drive me back later."

She would have liked to go back with Isaac, but it seemed selfish to make him wait around for her.

Isaac pulled into the Noel and Son Nursery car park. Nory's family home was separated from the nursery by a high fence, but there was a gate behind the dahlia greenhouse that led into the back garden.

"Would you like to come in for a cup of tea?"

"Thanks, but no," Isaac replied. "I need to catch up with Thom. He's been getting me some extra salad leaves started. Your friend wants her wedding banquet homegrown where possible. Two hundred salads is a lot of lettuce, and she's got competition from some pretty determined snails."

"She's an exacting personality."

"'Personality' being the operative word. Andy said the waitresses were giddy last night because she's in some soap opera?"

"Not just *any* soap opera—*Days and Nights*!"

Isaac looked at her blankly.

"Well, anyway, Jenna's a pretty big deal in the TV world. She's won awards."

Isaac nodded but looked unimpressed. It was a change for someone to be unimpressed with Jenna.

"So, you've got friends in high places. Anyone else in the group I should know about? No pop stars hiding in plain sight?"

"No. Ameerah's a barrister, and her date, Dev, is a model. Jeremy's an entomologist, and his wife, Katie, is in conservation, but she's not here yet. Pippa's—"

"Oh, I've had plenty of phone calls with Pippa Harrington," Isaac cut in.

That didn't sound good.

"She's the bossy wedding planner," Isaac continued. "I didn't realize she used to go to the school. Figures. She wanted me to rip up the front lawn to install the cables for thirty Parisian lampposts."

"I didn't notice any Parisian lampposts on the front lawn," Nory commented.

"No, you didn't."

"Oh," said Nory. That wouldn't have pleased Pippa. "Well," she said brightly. "Moving on, there's Guy, who's a journalist, and his interior designer wife, Camille. And last but not least is the groom, Charles. He's an investment banker."

Isaac sniggered. "Nobody with a normal job, then."

"Define 'normal.'"

"No waitresses or supermarket cashiers or farmers, you know what I mean, honest jobs. Jobs you graft at."

"Oh my god, you sound like my dad! *You* are an inverted snob, my friend," said Nory. "Let me just stop you in your bullshit tracks right now."

"I don't see that," Isaac blustered, clearly a little deflated at being called out on his workingman spiel. The old rough-diamond routine might work on the usual female guests at the castle, but it didn't wash with Nory. She'd been raised by Jake Noel; he'd practically written the inverted-snobs rulebook.

"You assume that because their labor isn't manual it doesn't count. That's inverted snobbery. I should know, I've been dealing with it on one side or the other for most of my life. Graft comes in many forms, you know. My friends work bloody hard, all of them. You don't get to belittle them because they don't go home with mud beneath their fingernails!"

"Okay, okay!" Isaac held his hands up in surrender but then added, "You were obviously brainwashed by the Braddon-Hartmead education system."

"I was not brainwashed! I can think perfectly well for myself, thank you very much, and I probably have a much more rounded view of things than someone who has spent their life nursing the giant chip on their shoulder."

Nory began to walk away. She had enough of this shit from Thomas, she didn't need it from Isaac as well. Maybe she was being oversensitive, but she didn't care. Start as you mean to go on was—after many failed relationships—her motto.

"Nory, wait. Please." He caught up with her beside a row of sprout trees. "I'm sorry. I was joking. Kind of. I guess old prejudices die hard. I don't really mean it."

Nory stopped.

"I don't think I mean it," he added.

Nory began walking again.

"All right, all right. I don't. It's just a reflex left over from an old habit. When you grow up in the shadow of people who look down on you, you learn to mirror back their casual disregard. But contrary to my statements of seconds ago, I am more worldly than I look. I was an academic, for god's sake. And I don't think anyone would stand a chance in hell of brainwashing you, Elinor Noel."

He smiled at her, and Nory felt her anger dissipate.

"But you *did* used to chuck mud at me." He grinned.

"You started it!" She laughed. "And I *may* be a bit touchy about the whole private-school thing. Being back here with everyone . . . trying to find my place in the dynamic. I guess you're right: Old habits do die hard."

They stood, appraising each other as the seconds ticked past. The look in his eyes told her that Isaac didn't see her as his mate's annoying kid sister anymore—not the kid part, at any rate.

"Nory!" Her mum's voice cut through the tension between them. She was standing at the garden gate. "Come on, my girl, I've crumpets under the grill. Get in here and let me squeeze you! Hi, Isaac, do you want to come in for a cuppa?"

"Hi, Sasha, no thanks, I've got to get on. Is Thom in the office?"

"Yes, love, number-crunching as usual. Go on over."

"Thanks." He looked down at Nory. "I'll see you later?"

"I expect you will."

"Maybe your admirer will chase you back into my cottage," he said, raising an eyebrow.

"Maybe I won't need to be chased."

"There's a mug of cocoa with your name on it if you find yourself in my neck of the woods."

"Good to know," said Nory, smiling.

"Your crumpets are burning!" her mum shouted.

Isaac laughed. "You'd better go."

"I'll see you," she said, and walked through the gate, turning once and feeling intensely pleased to find Isaac still looking after her.

# Ten

The kitchen was warm and cluttered, as always. It was the kitchen of a family who worked outside all day and didn't have the time or the patience for anything that wasn't functional and who needed a constant supply of good hearty food to keep them going, especially in winter. There was never much money when Thom and Nory were growing up, but they never went hungry.

The range pushed out heat, and already the smells of tonight's dinner—stew, unless she was mistaken—slow-cooking in the bottom oven were beginning to permeate the space. Nory threw her coat over the back of a dining chair and hung her scarf over the pot rack hanging from the ceiling above the range to warm it up.

"No Ameerah?" her mum asked, looking at the door as though she might be about to walk through it.

"Not this morning; she'll come down later in the week. She's brought a date with her, so she doesn't feel she can leave him until he's a bit more comfortable with everyone."

"That's fair. Did she say I've invited her for Christmas? She's just waiting to hear back from her parents. Such a shame, all that money and no time to spare for their only daughter."

"To be fair, I don't think they've got too much time for their only son either."

"Where is young Ahmed at the moment?"

"Last heard of residing in a private rehab in South Africa."

Her mum tsked. "Poor lamb."

Ameerah's elder brother, Ahmed, was a forty-six-year-old playboy. No one who had ever actually met him would call him a lamb. Nory had met him twice, and both times—high as a kite on cocaine—he had tried to seduce her. Nory had had no trouble resisting his charms because he looked uncannily like Ameerah and was smoother than a James Bond baddie.

"Your dad's just got an order pickup and then he'll be in for a cuppa. Poinsettias are very popular this year—the garden centers ordered twice as many as usual. They must be having a resurgence; they seemed to go out of fashion for a while. Are you seeing anyone at the moment?"

This is how her mum's side of conversations went, a stream of consciousness. Those who loved her best had learned to sift out the most salient points and leave the rest. It was her mum's way of dealing with the hundreds of things per day she was required to juggle. Her dad was a self-confessed workaholic, but her mum was the backbone of the business, quietly orchestrating and maintaining the life they had built.

"No, not just at the moment," Nory replied, though she thought about Isaac as she said it.

"That was nice of Isaac to bring you down here."

How did her mum do that?

"Well, it was on his way."

"I'm sure he doesn't usually offer lifts to guests."

"I'm sure most guests' parents don't live in Hartmead," said Nory, taking a bite of crumpet and slurping up the hot butter.

"Maybe." Which was her mum's stock response to anything she didn't agree with.

"I expect he's very popular with the guests." Nory was fishing for information. She could imagine the swanky hen parties, which the castle catered for, being all over the sexy gardener.

"Yes, I expect he is. But the marquis likes the staff to be very professional, so I doubt there's too much hanky-panky."

Nory didn't think the marquis's opinion would make much difference; she'd been to hen parties and some of those hens got pretty wild.

"He did have a girlfriend for a while," her mum went on. Nory's ears pricked up. "When he first moved back. I think they'd been together at the university, but after a while she stopped coming back. It's a very quiet place if you're used to city life."

"Hartmead is a quiet place *whatever* you're used to."

"Well, you say that, but you'll never guess which TV program wants to film here . . ."

"*Countryfile*?" asked Nory. "*Songs of Praise*?"

"*Midsomer Murders*!" said her mum, sitting back with her arms folded and a smug look on her face.

"I can see that," agreed Nory. "This is just the sort of picture-perfect place seething with underlying goings-on!"

"Precisely. They want to use the nursery. It's going to be the scene of a grisly murder. Can you imagine? How exciting! And they'll pay us a good fee. Your dad's saying no at the moment, you know how he feels about big corporations . . ."

"Oh, for god's sake. He needs to get off his high horse. How much money are they offering?"

"Five thousand pounds a day! They reckon they'll need three or four days."

"Mum, you've got to get Dad to agree. Offers like this don't come along every day. Think what you could do with that money. When was the last time you went on a holiday? You could get a new kitchen. A new sofa, you could get new carpets."

Trust her dad to put his *morals* before business sense. It annoyed her to no end that her dad was so stubborn. As if running a business wasn't hard enough, he had to be permanently on some kind of righteous crusade.

"Oh, don't you worry about Dad." Her mum chuckled. "I'll make him see things my way. We'll be having a murder in the nursery one way or another!" She winked at Nory.

"What does Thomas think?"

"He had his reservations, but now he thinks it's a good idea. Shelley is very sensible; he listens to her. To be honest I'd have the *Midsomer* people here for free just for the fun of it, but of course I won't; we need the cash. So you've still got a crush on our Isaac after all these years."

"I've not *still* got a crush on Isaac. I haven't thought about him since I was about fifteen." This was a small lie.

"But you're thinking about him now." Her mum smiled knowingly.

"Is it that obvious?"

"Only to me."

"How can you even tell? You literally saw us together for like two minutes."

"It's written all over your face. You used to get the same look when he'd call round for Thomas when you were a kid."

"Mum!"

"Oh, don't worry, I'm not going to do any matchmaking. Where is your father? I've got to get back to work; I can't be waiting around for him to choose what time elevenses is."

"I'll go and find him," said Nory, draining her mug of tea.

"You could do a lot worse than Isaac, Nory."

"I only just met him again last night, Mum. I think it's a little early to be marrying me off."

But her mum only raised her eyebrows and smiled. Nory grabbed her coat from the back of the chair.

"Tell your dad he's got ten minutes, and then I'm off; he'll have to toast his own crumpets. I've got a hundred hellebores being picked up by the Scotney Castle groundskeepers and I've got to make sure they're ready for travel."

Nory laughed as she stepped out of the warm kitchen and into the cold. Some things never changed; her dad would always think he was too busy to pay attention to time, and her mum would work to within a second of her carefully constructed schedule and woe betide anyone who didn't fall in.

She found her dad in a greenhouse full of ruby-red poinsettias, their striking petals and verdant leaves the epitome of Christmas, a vibrant splash of color against the gray weather outside.

"Hello, Nory, love," said her dad, pulling her into one of his bear hugs. "How's it going up at the castle with the high society?"

*Wow, record time for shoehorning in the politics.*

"My friends are fine, thank you, Dad. They're up there now formulating an elitism think tank to see how best they can monopolize the world's wealth. I've been tasked with coming down here to distract the working classes while they plan their evil scheme."

Her dad chuckled.

"Mum says elevenses are ready."

"Ooh, smashing. Crumpets or muffins?"

"Crumpets."

Dad licked his lips. Her parents were early risers, it was the nature of their business; you had to make the most of the daylight hours. Come rain or shine, they'd be out with the plants by 6:30 a.m., then back in at 8:30 a.m. for a quick cup of tea and some breakfast, back out again, and then home for elevenses. They had worked this way for Nory's whole life, so that her own body clock ran to the family business schedule. Nory had implemented elevenses at Serendipitous Seconds, and she secretly thought it was one of the reasons Andrew had remained with her so long.

"It's good to see you, love."

"You too. Mum says you've been offered some money for a murder in your greenhouse."

Her dad rubbed the back of his neck. "Well, I haven't agreed to it yet."

"Don't wait too long or they'll offer it to some big garden center chain instead, and do you really want to be responsible for growing their already obscene wealth? Surely that money is better going to the humble, hardworking everyman?"

"Have you ever thought about going into politics?"

"No, I'm too honest."

"That's my girl. How's the shop doing?"

"It's doing good. I've got a list of private collectors who will only buy through me, and having the online shop as well has made a big difference. And obviously Christmas helps."

"Can Andrew manage without you?"

"He's got Seb helping out as well. I think he's been looking forward to having the run of the place."

"How's parenthood treating them?"

"It's like they were born to it. If I ever have children, I'm paying them to childmind."

"What do you mean *if you ever*?"

"Well, I might not have children, it's not a given."

Her dad scoffed.

"You've got Jackson and Lucas to keep Noel and Son going, so you don't need to rely on me for future heirs."

"I'd just like to see you settled, Nory."

"I am settled, Dad. And besides, you've hated every one of my partners to date."

"Not all of them!"

"Name one."

"There was that one, you know, the taxi driver, came in and waited for the tow truck . . . Hitesh."

"He wasn't my boyfriend, Dad. He was an actual taxi driver. He crumpled his axle in a pothole driving me down from the station."

Her dad scratched his chin. "Oh yeah. Shame. I liked him."

Nory rolled her eyes.

There was a knock at the door, and Isaac's voice floated in.

"Jake, are you in here?"

Nory felt her cheeks get inexplicably hot. She looked up at her dad to find him looking at her curiously.

"In here, Isaac," her dad called, and they stepped out from behind the tall metal plant rack they'd been standing behind. "What can I do you for?"

"Sorry to disturb."

"Not at all, son, just catching up with my best girl," said her dad.

"Hello again, Nory," Isaac said casually.

"Isaac," she returned.

For a few seconds, the world seemed to stop as they stood looking at each other. She fought to keep a straight face, but her smile pushed through and she watched as it was mirrored in Isaac's expression.

"Ahem!" Her dad's rough voice broke through their private stare-off, and Nory busied herself with untangling two poinsettia plants whose flowers seemed locked in an embrace.

Isaac cleared his throat. "Yes, um, flowers, yes, right. I was wondering if you had any cyclamen plants. I want to put some in around the trees; I'm trying to put in winter color that the deer won't be tempted to munch on."

"Good luck with that, mate. How many do you need?"

"Forty-five? More if you've got them."

"I could give you sixty. Have you tried winter aconite? The little buggers will walk right past it. It'd work in your woodland area."

"Yeah, I've got quite a bit of that in already. I thought the cyclamen would make a nice color contrast. I've never known the deer to be such a menace; I mean, there's always a bit of damage, even though they're fed plenty through the season, but this year they seem ravenous."

"Yeah, you're not the first to say it. I think it means we're in for a hard winter. Nature's always the first to smell it coming."

"If that sky is anything to go by, it could be about to get going."

Nory's phone rang, and her mum's voice blared out through the speaker. She held it away from her ear so that her dad could hear it.

"Tell your father his tea's stewing in the pot and his crumpets are cold, I've got work to do."

"Roger that, O light of my life!" Her dad grinned into the phone. She heard her mum chuckle and ring off, the words *silly arse* just discernible before the line went dead.

"Well, that's me told," her dad muttered.

Nory excused herself while Isaac and her dad talked deer-proof plants and went off in search of her brother. He would be ambivalent to her presence but equally outraged if she didn't come to say hello. Thomas was like the Godfather; you had to pay your respects.

She found him in the office battling with the computer.

"No, I don't want to *delete files*, you bloody imbecile machine!"

"Arguing with insentient objects again, Thomas? One day she'll answer you back and then you'll be sorry."

Thomas looked up. "Nory. I wondered if you'd be down. Mum said you were lording it up at the castle with a bunch of your old toff friends."

*And here we go.*

"Nice to see you too, big brother."

Thomas grimaced. "Why is this a 'she'?" he asked, pointing to the computer screen.

"What?"

"When you came in, you said *she* would answer me back one day."

"Did I? Oh well, all the cleverest things are women."

Thomas screwed his face up and then smiled. "How are you?"

"I'm good. You?"

"I'd be better if I could get this spreadsheet to load."

"Need some help?"

Nory moved round to the desk without waiting for an answer. Thomas would never ask her for help out of principle—what principle exactly, Nory had never been able to fathom—so it was always best to just barge in and force help upon him. She reached over him and, with a few clicks, restored the spreadsheet and pulled it up onto the screen. Thomas grunted an approximation of a thank-you.

"How are the boys?"

At the mention of his children, Thomas's face split into a huge grin. "They're great. Literally counting down the days till Christmas now, of course. The excitement will crank up to ten when they wake up in the morning and find the advent calendars sent down by Aunty Nory."

Nory smiled. She remembered that feeling. Truth be told, she'd never really lost it. She sent her nephews advent calendars every year. Not a chocolate one, but one of the old-fashioned kinds, with beautiful Christmas scenes and proper pictures behind every door. Jackson and Lucas were two of the few things Nory and her brother could talk about without sniping at each other.

"I can't wait to see them, hopefully this week sometime."

"If you can break free of your busy schedule of quaffing champagne and devouring caviar."

*And the cease-fire is over.*

"I work too, you know, Thom, and I'm as entitled to a holiday as you are."

"*Entitled* being the operative word."

"I'm not entitled! How am I entitled?"

"Perhaps it's just reflecting off the company you keep."

"Since *your* business is benefitting handsomely from the *company I keep* this week, not to mention the wedding, maybe you could try to be a little more gracious toward my friends?"

Thomas's face darkened. *Sooo the wrong thing to say, Nory!*

"We are earning every penny of the money from this job."

"I didn't say you weren't."

"So, I'll treat *your friends* like any other customers."

"Oh, you mean you treat all your customers with disdain? Well, that's okay, then, so long as your sucky attitude isn't only limited to my friends."

The door opened, and Shelley walked in.

"I could hear you two all the way down by the cold frames! Hello, Nory, babe." Shelley pulled Nory into a hug. Nory could smell the cold on her. "How's it going up at the castle? Are you having a lovely time?"

Out of the corner of her eye, Nory could see Thomas shooting daggers at his wife. Shelley ignored him. She never rose to his bullshit, and her brother idolized her for it.

"It's lovely to be a guest," said Nory. "The food is amazing, and the bedrooms are lush! Your garlands look fantastic, by the way."

"Thanks, sugar. I'll be up in a day or so to take them down, and then I'll be up again Friday to do the ones for the wedding. I think Jenna wanted to make an impression on you when you arrived."

"They did that, all right. It was like something out of a film set!"

"She's so nice, she was chatting to me like she was a normal person."

Nory laughed. "She is a normal person, it's just that her job is on the TV."

Thomas snorted.

"What was that, babe? Did you say something?"

But Thomas only shuffled his chair in closer to the desk and squinted at the screen.

"It was lovely to meet her. And I got a lot of compliments from Pippa too. She was saying she could use me to help create some of her events."

"Over my dead body," muttered Thomas.

Without breaking her stride Shelley retorted: "If needs be, babe. So, obviously I said yes. It would be a great experience and the money wouldn't go amiss either, plus it would really get our name out there as a business. The floristry side of what we do has always been viewed as a bit of a sideline, really, but it's where the money is, and how many nurseries can say they offer the full service, right from seed to finished bouquet?"

"Oh my god, yes!" agreed Nory. "Especially with people being more aware about their carbon footprint and sustainability. You could really tap into that homegrown market. Pippa doesn't mince her words—if she says she likes your work she means it."

"Great, so you'll be swanning off to London and god knows where. What about the kids?" Thomas sulked.

"They have two parents and four willing grandparents," Shelley replied. "And London is an hour and a half away. Your mum and I have done weddings farther away than that."

"I don't think the *where* is the problem," said Nory. "I think it's the *who*."

"Stay out of it, Nory," Thomas snapped.

"If it was anyone else, you'd be biting their arm off for the work, but god forbid you should be on the payroll of one of my friends. Your self-righteousness is wearing thin. We're not at school anymore—there is no *them* and *us*. It's about time you grew up and got over yourself."

"No *them* and *us*? Do you watch the news? Have you seen the state of this country?"

"We're not talking about the state of the country, Thom, this is about your aggressive resentment of anyone you think has had an easier time of it than you, including me. It's playground stuff.

Let it go." Nory turned to Shelley. "Sorry, Shelley, same old same old. I'll see you later."

Nory left without saying goodbye to Thomas. She should've known better. Relations between them were only ever one misplaced word away from an argument. But her being a guest at the castle—with her old gang, which had caused so much animosity between them when they were kids—was bound to stir up old resentments. And Jenna using Noel and Son as her provider for the all the wedding flowers and floral arrangements just fed into all of Thomas's serf-and-master hang-ups. Something about her friends' money made him feel belittled, and Thomas was not a personality who did well with feeling small.

Her mum and dad were both busy somewhere in the maze of greenhouses, so Nory texted them both goodbye and promised to visit again soon. Then she called Ameerah.

"Hey, gorgeous, I just kicked everyone's arse at archery." There were sounds of loud disagreement in the background. "How'd it go with the fam?"

"Can you come and get me?"

"That good, huh?"

"Worse."

"I'll be there in twenty. Is that little coffee shop still going in the high street?"

"Yeah, I think so."

"Good. Go grab yourself a mocha, and I'll meet you there."

"Thanks, Ameerah."

"No problem."

༄

Twenty-five minutes later, Ameerah plonked herself down in the chair opposite Nory. Castle Coffee had gone full Christmas bonanza, complete with snow spray laying in heaps at the bottoms of the leaded windowpanes, and a festive scene of cuddly polar bears and penguins frolicking on a bed of cotton wool snow along the deep window ledge. Michael Bublé's voice crooned out of the speakers, beneath the hubbub of the busy café.

"I ordered us another coffee," said Ameerah. "Thought you might need to gather your wits before you come back up to the castle."

"Thanks, Ameerah. Sorry to drag you away from the fun."

"Oh god no, thank *you*! Guy's been insufferable all morning. I don't know how Camille puts up with him. Charles, of course, was in full competitive mode, which started Guy off. Camille, by the way, is like bloody Katniss Everdeen with a bow—properly blew us all out of the water."

"Good for her, I feel bad at how she's kind of in Guy's shadow all the time."

"Oh, I think she can hold her own in her real life; she's just a bit shy around us."

"It must be a bit intimidating coming into a group with so much history. Although it doesn't seem to bother Dev."

"I have to admit, I may have misjudged Dev."

"You don't say?" Nory mocked.

"It doesn't happen often, but when it does I own it."

"How gracious of you." Nory smiled across at her best friend.

"I'd put his happy-go-lucky demeanor down to a lack of brain cells. And I was fine with that; let's face it, it wasn't his mind I was drawn to."

"Bit unkind but go on."

"But it turns out, he's really intelligent!"

"I did try to tell you that."

"He has this inner confidence; it's like he doesn't care what anyone thinks of him because he has this quiet sense of his own worth."

"Admirable qualities," said Nory.

"I know," replied Ameerah, looking troubled. "I'm not sure what to do about it."

Nory laughed. "Why don't you give yourself a break from being a badass and let yourself fall in love? It's not anti-feminist to be in love, you know."

"I made a vow to myself."

"You made a vow when you were seventeen and had just gone through something horrible. You can't hold yourself to it forever. You're a different person now."

Ameerah's commitment to man-Barbies was self-defense. When she was seventeen, she'd been seduced by a grifter who had broken her heart and emptied her bank account. At the time, she hadn't yet grown into her long legs or out of her acne; she was an awkward teenager, grateful for the attentions of the handsome twenty-five-year-old and ripe for being hustled. From that moment, Ameerah had sworn off love forever.

"Or am I the person I am because of the vow?" Ameerah suggested.

"Then he's won."

"How has he won?"

"Well, you're never going to let yourself fall in love again because of him, so he's getting the last laugh."

Ameerah fixed Elinor with one of her steely glares, which worked wonders in the courtroom but had no effect on Nory at all. She huffed. "Love is overrated. I refuse to be a slave to it."

The waitress arrived with their coffees, and Ameerah took her chance to change the subject.

"So, what happened this time?"

"Oh, the usual. My brother still hates me for going to private school while he had to go to a state school."

"I don't think he hates you."

"No, you're right, he hates the privilege and prospects that it gave me, which amounts to the same thing."

"Pippa mentioned she'd approached Shelley about doing some events with her."

"Yes. Shelley's well up for it, which is another thing for Thomas to hold against me. It's as if he feels my very purpose in life is to affront him."

"And yet he's never been like that with me, and I'm rolling in it. My parents put the *A* in *affluence*, and he's never been anything other than kind to me. It's weird."

"I think he feels that you are a victim of circumstance, whereas I could have chosen not to take up my scholarship but didn't. They want to see you, by the way, my parents. Thom would have asked after you as well, but he was too busy shaming me."

Ameerah laughed. "I want to see them too. Maybe I'll have a word with Thom."

"God no! That would only make things worse. He'll feel ganged-up on and that'll be my fault too."

"Oh, to have a complicated family. I communicate with my mother via handbags, Instagram, and bank transfers."

"She's not that shallow." Nory laughed. "She's the CEO of one of the biggest fashion labels in Dubai; I'd say she's been a pretty good role model."

"Provided you don't mind viewing her from afar. My mother is like a unicorn: sparkly and completely unattainable."

"You heard from your parents?"

"An email, this morning. They would have loved to spend

Christmas with me, but unfortunately they completely forgot what time of year it was and are booked on a luxury cruise throughout the whole of December."

"I take it that means you'll be taking up my mum's offer of Christmas with the Noel family. Fights and dodgy cocktails guaranteed. You know it wouldn't be the same without you."

Ameerah smiled. "To be honest, I wasn't too sad my parents blew me off. I mean, it would be nice to see them, but it's only a proper Christmas with your family."

"It's just as well we bloody love you, then, isn't it?"

"You are lucky, you know. Even if Thomas does behave like a tit."

"I know."

"You ready to go back in a minute? I left Jenna screaming over the phone at an Italian pâtissier about ganache."

Nory raised her eyebrows. "I thought Pippa was in charge of all that sort of thing."

"She is. Pippa was threatening to gag Jenna when I left."

"I've only been gone a couple of hours and Jenna's become a bridezilla."

"I think she woke up this morning and realized this is actually happening; she's getting married on Saturday."

"Ahh, the reality check! Okay, let's go smooth some troubled waters."

t was decided that the best way to soothe the tensions beginning
to simmer within the group was to have some timeout. Guy took
Camille out for a walk in the grounds, and Charles and Jenna
went off to their room. Jeremy had calmed down after finally
being able to contact Katie. Thankfully today was her last day at
the monkey sanctuary, and tomorrow she would begin the ar-
duous journey back to England. Ameerah, Dev, and Nory had
ensconced themselves in the library, where a hearty fire crackled
in the hearth and the tartan sherpa blankets were plentiful.

This was the library where Nory would hide out when she
was little while her mum was working. It was where she first discovered her love of botanical art, in Lord Abercrombie's collection of old botany and horticulture books. She would leaf through
the pages, the musty, slightly vanilla scent of old paper filling her
nostrils. The edges of the pages were browning with age, yet the
plants seemed real, almost as though they'd been pressed into the
pages, breathed into life by the brushstrokes and ink-pen notes
from botanists long since dead. It was like falling into history.

In this library, too, Nory had discovered the works of artists
like Jan Davidsz. de Heem and Rachel Ruysch. Books too large

for her to carry filled with still lifes of twisting foliage, flowers curling around one another like lovers, and petals so lifelike you felt you could reach into the page and brush their velvety frills. If her natural interest in plants grew out of her family's business, then her love of art was born in this library. The botanical artist Serena De-Veer had once lived in this house. The family had rented it for a short time after they moved back from India, while they waited for their house in Surrey to be renovated. Nory wondered if that was how Isaac had come to have one of her prints in his sitting room. A retirement gift to his father from the marquis, perhaps.

She checked her watch. It was nearly six o'clock. Pulling the sherpa blanket around her shoulders, Nory slipped out into the entrance hall and called Andrew. The log fire was doing its best, but this was still the chilliest place in the house.

"You've been gone a day, Nory. One day. What do you think is going to have happened in one day?"

"All right, shirty! I'm just ringing to see how everything is. That's what good shopkeepers do; they check in with their staff."

"Everything is fine. We sold two of the books in the window . . ."

"Not *The Snow Queen*?"

"You really are the worst bookseller in London."

"But was it *The Snow Queen*? I really wanted one more look at the pictures before I had to part with it."

"You need to marry a rich man so that you can curate a library and never part with any books again."

"Obviously."

"*The Snow Queen* is safe . . . for now. It was the 1940s edition of *The Night Before Christmas* with illustrations by Leonard Weisgard and the vintage *How the Grinch Stole Christmas!*"

"Oh, come on! Not the Leonard Weisgard! That was one of my favorites."

"They're all your favorites, Nory."

"Yeah, but that was a proper classic."

"Which is why we sold it for such a good price."

Nory pouted.

"I can hear you pouting!"

"How can you *hear* me pouting?"

"You breathe differently when you're sulking. I recognize the post-sales brood breath."

"Well, that's really very rude, I may have to fire you."

"Go right ahead. Good luck getting another manager who puts up with you."

"Well, when you put it like that . . ."

"I thought as much."

"What else did you sell? A piece of my soul, perhaps?"

"The illustrated works of Shakespeare."

"Oh my god!"

"Would you like to hear what else we sold?"

"There's more? Hells bells, there'll be no books left at this rate!"

"Nory, we have walls made of books. *Actual* walls made of *actual* piled-up books. If we sold fifty books a day for a year, we would still have enough left to give the Bodleian Library a run for its money. When Matilda can walk, I'll have to attach a GPS signaling device to her nappy before letting her loose in the shop."

"God, you're dramatic."

"Said the pot to the kettle."

"Okay, tell me the rest."

"Can you handle it?"

"Just give it to me all in one go and don't stop even when you hear my screams of pain."

Andrew listed seven more books sold today—two of them online. She didn't really hate parting with her books, although she felt a little sad when a favorite left the building. In reality, she got a massive kick out of a book finding its new keeper, paying forward the book love.

Those were some good sales for a Monday. Andrew really was a remarkable bookseller, and she told him so.

"If you keep complimenting me, I shall have to ask for a raise," said Andrew.

"On second thought, you're nothing but a charlatan."

"A charlatan! How very lovable rogue; I rather like it."

Nory laughed. "What time is Seb's mum arriving?"

"She guestimates about nine p.m. She has asked that we don't make a fuss and just throw a few nibbles together, which is code for prepare something exquisite. Spare a thought for me when you're scoffing down your ten-course dinner at the castle tonight."

"I will. Text me the gossip."

"Oh, don't you worry, I will!"

"Love you."

"Love you more."

Nory was about to bury herself in the library once more when she heard her name being called. She followed the voice down the corridor to where the butler was systematically poking his head in at each door and asking if anyone had seen Miss Elinor.

"I'm here," she said timidly, so as not to frighten him.

"Ah, Miss Elinor, there you are. Excellent. There is someone for you at the back door."

Intrigued, Nory followed the butler down past the kitchens and through the boot room. Isaac was standing in the open doorway with his back to her, his face turned to the already dark sky. Nory felt a jolt of pleasure at seeing him.

"Hello," she said.

Isaac turned and smiled at her.

"Should I ask the marquis to turn the heating up?" he asked.

Looking down, she realized she was still draped in the huge sherpa blanket. "I was reading in the library. It felt like a curl-up-with-a-blanket kind of day."

"Quite right too," said Isaac. "Have you seen the sky this evening?"

Nory had not. Isaac moved aside, and she joined him out on the worn stone step, the cold seeping through her thick woolen socks. She looked up and sighed with delight. The navy-blue sky was peppered with silvery stars that seemed to stretch on to infinity without a single cloud to bar their way.

"It's going to be a cold night," said Isaac.

"Yes," Nory agreed. "I miss the stars when I'm in the city."

"I felt the same when I lived away from here."

"I like how small it makes me feel," she said, her face still tilted toward the stars. "There is something comforting in feeling there is so much more than just us and our silly lives." She turned to find Isaac looking at her. She smiled. "What?"

"It's nothing, it's just, I feel exactly the same way."

"Well, perhaps we are more alike than you imagined."

"Perhaps we are."

Nory could feel the crackle between them. She had an overwhelming urge to lean over and kiss him. But she resisted.

"I've got a telescope at the cottage. Maybe you'd like to come and look through it later." He smiled, suddenly shy, and shook his head, looking at the ground. "And I've just realized how incredibly lame that sounded."

Nory laughed. "Do you often ask women to come and look through your telescope?"

"Hardly ever."

"Well, I would love to look through your telescope, Isaac. Thank you."

He looked straight at her, the lamps behind her in the porch making his eyes glitter, and she felt that pull again, that almost irresistible urge to put her mouth on his.

"Did you call me out here to look at the stars?" she asked, trying to distract herself from his full lips. Oh my god, she wanted to bite them!

Isaac shook his head as if suddenly remembering why he was there. "Er, no, I didn't. That was an aside. I just came here to return this."

He handed Nory the scarf she'd left in her parents' kitchen this morning.

"Oh. Thank you, you didn't have to do that."

"I saw Thom in the White Hart pub earlier, and he asked me to give it to you with a message."

Nory was suddenly wary. "Yes?"

"He said, and I quote: 'I'm sorry for being a twat, Bugs.'"

Nory laughed, half out of relief.

"Why does he call you Bugs?"

"No reason, you know how nicknames are."

"Can I call you Bugs?"

"No, you cannot."

"He also asked me to give you this . . ."

Isaac leaned into her and kissed her cheek. Nory's breath caught. This was very confusing for her body; she did not want to be feeling the things that Isaac's warm lips on her cheek were making her feel when the kiss was a message from her brother!

She cleared her throat.

"Thank you." She didn't trust herself to send the same message back, and besides, she wasn't sure Isaac would kiss Thomas's cheek on her behalf.

Isaac pulled his collar up around his ears and stepped down onto the gravel. "Well, enjoy your evening," he said.

"Thank you, you too."

Isaac nodded once and began to walk away across the courtyard; the sound of his boots crunching on the gravel was audible long after the darkness had swallowed him from sight. Nory resisted the urge to sniff the scarf until she reached the bottom of the main staircase. It smelled of Isaac. Had he worn it, knowing that he would make it smell of him? Or had he worn it because it smelled of her? Did men do that?

"What are you doing?" Ameerah asked, coming out of the library with Dev in tow.

"Nothing. Just sniffing a scarf."

"I'm not even going to ask. Come on, weirdo, we've got to change for dinner."

I f anyone had still been on their best behavior before, the pretense had certainly been dropped by that evening's dinner. Nory marveled at how quickly they had all slipped back into their school roles.

Charles and Guy picked up where they had left off in their self-appointed capacity of alphas: general showing off and chest puffing, loudly reminiscing about daring exploits and mocking Jeremy just enough to keep him in his place of lovable, unthreatening nerd.

Camille was unimpressed, her mouth thinning into a line and her shoulders visibly tense beneath the shoestring straps of her evening dress, but for all the attention he paid her, Guy probably hadn't even noticed. Nory smiled apologetically at her every chance she got and tried to include her in their conversations. Dev and Ameerah were equally sensitive to the situation, and between them they tried their hardest to make sure Camille didn't feel like a complete spare part.

Jenna and Pippa—though thoughtful and generous of spirit— were always the badass girls at school: cool, immaculate, smartmouthed, and supremely confident in their sex appeal. They had carried elements of these traits into their adult lives, although they had matured over time, and what once could have been described as mean-girl mentality had deepened to become self-assurance. But in this environment, even they had regressed. They showed off and laughed too loudly, and though Nory didn't like to admit it, they could even be a little cliquey.

Ameerah had been the awkwardly gangly, spotty, desperate-to-fit-in girl at school. Though she was holding her own, Nory could see she was having to fight to prevent herself from falling—or being pushed—back into the role of pet minion. She had already stood her ground against two or three requests of "Ameerah, darling, could you just . . ." Nory was sure Pippa and Jenna weren't aware of what they were doing, and to be fair to them, they both inhabited worlds where they were used to people doing their bidding.

For Nory's part, she was the scholarship girl all over again, a beloved part of the group and yet ever so slightly on the outside. She was still less traveled and unpolished. She had been welcomed into their world at school, but through no fault of theirs, she had never quite belonged. And in a cruel twist, her acceptance into Braddon-Hartmead had made her belong a little less in her old world too. Now she found herself playing the part of the commoner once more, despite living a very middle-class lifestyle. She hammed up her working-class roots and played up to the old image they had of her in their minds: a sort of Eliza Doolittle character, the everywoman perspective of the group.

Nory supposed it was inevitable. This was the state in which they had known one another best. Though it pained her to think it, she wondered if some of them would have lost touch completely if Tristan hadn't died. But life was like that, wasn't it? A never-ending series of events, the ripples of which would either push you away from people or pull you toward them. Nory thought it made this second chance even more poignant.

After dinner they all filed back into the drawing room, before the men excused themselves to go to the billiards room—Camille looking distinctly like she wished to skewer Guy with a cue.

"What's with the men taking themselves off after dinner?" asked Pippa. "It's not 1902!"

"The men have to go off and talk about big-boy stuff like politics, and we women have to stay here and talk about kittens," said Jenna dryly.

"Fuck that shit! I'm off to kick some arse at billiards," Pippa announced, and scooping up the front of her gray waterfall gown, she marched out of the room.

"I might head off to bed and read," said Camille. "Reading is such a luxury for me these days. So is sleeping, for that matter."

"I don't blame you," said Nory. "My sister-in-law has two boys, and she says sometimes she locks herself in the toilet just for five minutes' peace."

Camille laughed. "Been there, done that!"

"What's Guy like as a father?" asked Jenna.

Camille bit her lip, wondering how much to say.

"I wouldn't say he's hands-on," she said diplomatically. "He loves them, but he finds them . . . challenging."

"They're children, they're meant to be challenging. If you ask me, Guy needs to grow a pair," said Ameerah.

Camille smiled.

"I think Charles will be a good father," Jenna mused, and the others made agreeing noises. Nory thought Charles would make a wonderful father; he was deeply kind-hearted underneath all his bluster—but even if they'd all thought he'd be a terrible father, they were hardly likely to voice it in front of his bride-to-be.

"Maybe I won't go the nanny route if I decide to have children," said Ameerah thoughtfully. "Maybe I'll surprise you all and go full-on smothering parenting. I'll become the chairwoman of the PTA, a school governor, a carpool legend, and the queen of the school bake sale."

"Oh my god," Nory laughed. "Your kids are going to hate you."

"Oh yeah." She smiled wickedly. "I will be all up in their grill. I will make attached parenting look slack."

"I wish Guy had some of your enthusiasm. He'd like the children to go to boarding school like he did."

"Charles and I have already agreed that there'll be no boarding school for our children. Depending on my work situation we'll probably have a nanny, but she won't live in."

"I will take my child into court with me and breastfeed while the prosecution makes its case," Ameerah announced.

"You're going to be popular with the white male septuagenarian judges," said Nory.

"Something happens when you have children," Camille said quietly, more to herself than the others. But there was something in her voice, something bordering on vacant or removed, that made the other women attentive. "I can't exactly explain it. I've continued to work at my business, and it's doing really well, thank god, but the bigger clients—magazines and stuff—suddenly seem to have less interest in me since I became a mother. They take me less seriously. As though I can't really be invested in my business or be investible if I have children."

"It doesn't surprise me," Ameerah began. "I talk the talk, but in truth, I dread what it will mean for my career. I've known women who have been completely unable to get back in once they're out."

"It isn't just work, though," Camille continued in that small voice. "I don't think people see me as whole anymore." She gave a little awkward half laugh. "My husband certainly doesn't. Maybe I'm not. Sometimes I catch him looking at me as if he's wondering what went wrong."

Nory felt the energy in the room change, and she knew Jenna and Ameerah were as concerned as she was. Camille's face was strained. For once, Nory was glad that straight-talking Pippa wasn't there. Nory rubbed Camille's arm tentatively, but it was Jenna who asked what they were all thinking. She knelt down in front of Camille and took her hands, forcing Camille to look at her.

"Are you okay, Camille? Like are you, really, okay?"

"I don't know," Camille replied. "I'm so tired. I'm not even sure I know enough about who I am anymore to know if I'm okay."

"Have you tried talking to Guy about how you feel?" Nory asked.

Camille gave another dry laugh. "Have you ever tried talking to Guy about feelings?" she asked.

"Fair point," Nory agreed. "But we're not married to him." *Thank god!* she thought. "You're supposed to be a partnership. You should be able to talk to him, and he needs to listen to what you have to say. Because despite what you feel about yourself, what you have to say is valid."

"And we all love Guy," said Jenna. "But equally, we're not blind to his faults."

"He needs to be more supportive," said Ameerah. "He needs to step up and stop being such a selfish man-baby."

Camille had tears in her eyes, but at this she actually giggled. "That's exactly what he is." She laughed, wiping her eyes on the back of her hand. "I'm sorry I blurted all that out at you," she added, embarrassed. "I didn't mean to, it just kind of came out."

"That's what happens when you bottle things up," said Nory. "Eventually the pressure gets too much, and you spring a leak, like a submarine that's gone too deep."

"Always one for a peculiar analogy, our Nory." Ameerah smiled.

"If you need to talk, then we're here for you," said Jenna sincerely, and the others agreed.

"Thank you." Camille sniffed, pushed her short, curly hair behind her ears, and stood. "Well, I'm going to go and lose myself in that book for a while."

"Why don't I ask the kitchen if they could send some cocoa up to your room?" Jenna suggested.

"That would be lovely, thank you. Thank you, to all of you, again. Good night."

Camille left the room, and Jenna went off to see about the cocoa.

"Do you think we should do something?" asked Nory.

"Like what?" asked Ameerah.

"I don't know."

"We'll keep an eye on her. We've got a few days yet."

"That sounds like a plan. I'll tell Jez too."

"I think she could use some counseling or something," said Ameerah.

"Something for sure," agreed Nory.

"I vote myself not to be the one to tell Guy." Ameerah grimaced.

"Oh, I think we'll leave that to Charles."

"And in the meantime, I think I might rescue Dev from the billiards room and see if he wants to get jiggy with me."

"Well, in that case, I might see if the gardener will let me peep through his telescope."

"Is that a euphemism?"

"Nope."

"Do you think Jenna will be pissed with us if we desert her?" Ameerah asked.

"I think Jenna will join Pippa in slaying the boys at pool. She won't miss us."

✐

In another twenty minutes, Nory had changed out of her evening dress and into jeans, boots, and an extra-thick jumper, and was knocking on Isaac's front door. It was just after 10:00 p.m., and Nory had wondered if it was maybe too late to call on him, but when she had stepped out from the trees, she had seen his lights were on and there was still smoke curling out of the chimney.

She could hear Lettuce snuffling at the door, but the old lurcher hadn't bothered to bark. Nory reasoned that she probably wasn't a great guard dog. The porch light flicked on as Isaac opened the door.

"Hello," she said, smiling hopefully. "Is your telescope available?"

Isaac cocked his head to one side, amused. "You're lucky," he said, stepping aside to let her through. "I was just about to close it down for the night."

Lettuce kept close to Nory's side, pushing her nose into Nory's palm.

"Have you had many customers this evening?" she asked.

"It's been steady," Isaac replied with a completely straight face. "I am known to have the best telescope in the village, so demand for my services tends to be high."

"I can well imagine."

"Would you like a drink before stargazing?"

"That would be lovely, thank you."

"I don't have much in the way of alcohol, I'm afraid, but I can offer you a beer or a brandy."

"Could I be terribly boring and ask for a cup of tea?"

"Tea is not in the least bit boring," said Isaac, smiling. "English breakfast, Earl Grey, green, rose, or peppermint?"

"Gosh, I didn't expect such a choice."

"My mum was a big tea fan; she swore by its health benefits. It didn't help her very much."

"I don't really remember seeing your mum often. Not as much as your dad anyway."

"My mum had MS. By the time I was in my teens, she wasn't getting out so much. She died when I was in my second year of uni."

"Oh, I'm sorry."

Isaac shrugged.

"So, what'll it be?" he asked.

"Um, peppermint, please. I think the chef is trying to induce gout in our party. I could do with something settling."

"Peppermint it is," he said, pulling out the box and filling the kettle.

⌘

They took their steaming mugs upstairs and into a room that was set up as a very comfortable study, with a large oak desk and chair, and a chaise longue pushed up against the far wall. The windows stretched from floor to ceiling, with two of them opening out like French windows onto a small balcony, where a rusting wrought iron chair was perfectly placed to admire the view.

The telescope—which was impressively larger than Nory had expected—was set up on a tripod, tilted up toward the sky in anticipation. Isaac took her mug and set it down on a coaster on the desk beside his own.

"You'll need to refocus it for your eyes, but it's in the right position," he said. "It won't take much; do it in tiny increments."

Nory took up her position at the telescope, and Isaac lifted her hand and placed it on the focus knobs on the underside of the optical tube. For a moment, all she could think about was his fingers touching hers. But then her eyes began to adjust to what she was seeing, and with another scant adjustment to the focuser, suddenly the cosmos seemed to explode in front of her. She gasped. It was as though someone had taken a loaded brush and flicked silver paint across a dark blue canvas.

"Can I see the Milky Way through this?" she asked.

She could hear the smile in his voice when he answered. "I'm afraid you've missed Milky Way season."

"There's a Milky Way season? Are you teasing me?"

Isaac laughed. "No, I'm not teasing you. The best time to see it in the UK is usually April to July. You could probably see Uranus, though."

"Oh, very funny!"

"No, I'm serious. It's a good time of year; it's a clear night, although it's before the full moon, which can make it a bit trickier."

Nory wasn't sure she would be able to pick out one planet from another among the mass of twinkles.

"That moon looks pretty full to me."

"Almost," he said.

"It's so beautiful."

"It is."

Nory kept watching the skies until her neck ached and she began to worry that Isaac might think her rude. When she finally stood back from the telescope, it took her eyes a moment or two to adjust; the room seemed darker than before, and she was literally seeing the imprints of stars before her eyes. She stumbled ever so slightly. Isaac was instantly by her side, steadying her.

"Whoops, sorry about that. Must have stood up too quickly," she said, feeling embarrassed.

"It can be a bit disorienting. Especially when you've been bent over there for a while."

Nory grinned sheepishly. "Sorry, I was being a bit of a telescope hog."

"Not at all. It was nice to watch you."

Nory raised her eyebrows at him.

"I mean, it was nice to see you enjoying the stars as much as I do. Stargazing isn't everyone's cup of tea."

"It should be." Talk of tea reminded her of her own abandoned mug on the desk. She took a swig. "Ugh, cold. I wasn't expecting that. I really was lost in the stars for a long time."

"Would you like another?"

Nory looked at her watch. "I ought to get back."

"Do you have a curfew?"

"No. But it's late, and I've got an early start tomorrow."

"Ah, yes. The pheasant shoot."

Nory grimaced.

"You're not keen?" he asked.

"I've been trying to get my head around it, and I know that we'll be eating what we shoot, but . . ."

"You prefer your meat vacuum-packed in the fridge section."

"Go on, tell me I'm a hypocrite. I'll own it."

"I'm not going to judge you because you don't have the heart to kill a living thing. Have a think about it, and if you still don't feel comfortable in the morning, then don't do it. It's not for everyone."

Nory appreciated his diplomacy. She didn't expect to get quite such an easy ride from the others if she decided to back out.

"Come on, then, I'll walk you back."

"You don't have to . . ."

"Yeah, yeah, I know. I'm old-fashioned. Humor me."

Nory smiled.

Isaac pulled the door shut behind him, Lettuce having vigorously declined the offer of a late-night walk. It had begun to snow. The white flakes tumbling down from the sky made it look as if the stars were dropping out of the heavens. Everything was quiet, muted by the snowfall, so that only the sounds of their boots crunching on the frozen ground broke the silence.

"It feels otherworldly," said Nory, her voice hushed. The quiet dark made her feel like she ought to whisper.

"It does," Isaac agreed. "This landscape brings a different kind of magic with every season."

"I suppose it does." Her mind was drifting back through her childhood growing up here; long, hot summers with crisp bleached grass, and grasshoppers jumping at her ankles. Spring with its yellow daffodils and Robins Wood a cerulean carpet of bluebells. Wading through the pumpkin patches in autumn and collecting chestnuts fallen from the trees down near the lake. And then the winters, sometimes so harsh she felt they would never end, numb fingers in frozen gloves as she helped her parents in the glasshouses. It hadn't felt like a charmed life at the time, but as she looked back on it now—perhaps with rose-tinted spectacles—she did so with more than a little nostalgia.

"I couldn't wait to leave here when I was a kid," said Isaac.

"Really? I'd always imagined it was just me who had itchy feet. You'd have thought the sky was falling when I announced I was applying for universities in Birmingham, Manchester, and London."

He laughed quietly and nodded. "Pretty much the same in my house. God, the quiet of this place used to drive me nuts!"

"Same. The only excitement was when the fair arrived each year; other than that it was dancing round the fricking maypole." Nory laughed.

"Ah, the fair. It still comes every year, and it's still full of overexcited, horny teenagers. I can remember the feeling of seeing all those flashing lights and the loud noises in contrast to the usual monotony. God, it felt like a theme park."

"You were all right, you had your motorbike," said Nory. "You could escape."

"How far away do you realistically think I could get in an evening? We made it out as far as Lamberhurst once. Saw two foxes having sex. Got refused a pint by the landlord in the only pub open. Rode home."

"At least you got out of Hartmead."

"You didn't seem stuck for entertainment over at Snob Towers."

"You've been reading too much *Harry Potter*. Boarding schools aren't all sneaking around the halls and midnight adventures."

Isaac made an agreeing sound that wasn't convincing.

"And during the holidays I was as stuck as you were, more so because unlike you and my brother, I didn't have a motorbike."

"Are we arguing about who was more bored growing up?"

Nory laughed. "I believe we are," she replied. "But to be honest, when I look back on it now, it wasn't that bad. And I would defy anyone not to be enthralled by this place in the snow, I mean, look at it."

"Enthralled?" Isaac drawled. "Who uses that in an ordinary sentence?"

"Someone who owns a bookshop," said Nory.

"Fair enough."

They walked on in companionable silence until they reached the Winter Garden. The little solar lights in the beds were making a stellar effort to remain lit, casting a yellowy illumination against the white snow. The heads of the hellebores nodded gently under the weight of the flakes landing on their bell tops, their spiky leaves almost black in the half-light. Once again Nory was drawn to the hybrid flower Isaac had been working on. In this light, the thick stripes at the base of the flower, which petered out to a thin ink line at the tips of the petals, looked blood red.

"What did you say this one was called?" she asked, stopping to bend down for a closer look, this time avoiding the near-invisible wire around the flower beds.

"I didn't. It's still a work in progress, so far as registering it goes. I haven't had the time, what with all the extra work needed on the gardens for the wedding. Then we've got to get the tree down to the village square for the ceremonial lighting. And then after that, the gardens are open to the public again up till Christmas. You remember the drill."

Nory did.

Christmas was always a busy time for both the castle and her family's business. On Friday, the garden team would drive a giant fir tree—freshly chopped from Robins Wood—down to the village and erect it in the village square. Then that evening the whole village would come out, and Lord Abercrombie, Marquis of Braddon, would turn the lights on, instigating carols and mulled wine and general merrymaking.

In the run-up to the tree lighting, there would be a rush to the nursery to pick up handmade wreaths for front doors all around the village—courtesy of her mum and Shelley—because nobody wanted to disappoint. It wasn't only about keeping up with the Joneses; lots of visitors would drive though the village to get to the castle, and if the village was picture-perfect, the visitors would stop to eat in the cafés and pubs and pick up last-minute gifts in the little independent shops that dotted the tiny high street. Noel and Son also supplied the garlands and fresh decorations for the castle's garden shop. Far from winding down, if anything, the nursery got busier as the weather got colder.

"You could call it the 'Robinwood Castle Hellebore,'" Nory suggested. "I'm sure gardeners would want to buy it. It really is lovely."

"Maybe," said Isaac. "Or maybe I don't want the castle to have a claim on it. Once it's called the 'Robinwood,' it won't be mine anymore. My family have a history of losing things to bigger powers."

Nory waited for him to elaborate but he didn't, so she said, "Call it the 'Isaac Malik,' then. Then everyone will know it's yours."

He didn't reply.

The snow began to ease up, and Nory couldn't help feeling a little sad. Snow was such an impractical thing and undoubtedly made everything more difficult, yet she loved the way it seemed to slow down time. She thought of her shop and wondered if it was snowing in London; the window display would look particularly lovely in the snow.

"Will you be coming down to the tree lighting on Friday?" Isaac asked.

"If I can get out of whatever Jenna has planned, I definitely will. Although by Friday I would imagine she'll be in full wedding mode, so with any luck I'll be able to slip away unnoticed. I might see if Ameerah and Dev want to come too."

"I guess it's been a while since you've been to one."

"Years," Nory agreed.

"It's not changed much."

"I'm glad to hear it. Some things shouldn't change. It's nice to have something solid to cling to. Something dependable."

"Is that what you're looking for in life? Something dependable?"

*Oh, great! Now I sound super boring. Oh well, better he finds out that I'm a square bear now, to avoid disappointment later.*

"Could be. I think fast and loose is overrated. When I first left Hartmead, I was drawn to everything that was its opposite. But it wasn't so long before I began to yearn for roots."

"So, you opened a bookshop."

"A *secondhand* bookshop! The least fast-lane kind of business in retail."

"Perhaps there's more Hartmead in you that you'd care to admit."

"There was more to it than that." Nory wondered how much she should say. How much Isaac already knew. "I lost a friend; we all lost a friend. His name was Tristan. It was a few years ago. You'd probably remember his face if you saw a picture; he was always with us, part of the gang. I was already feeling my own kind of lost when he died, and I realized that if I didn't find some way of anchoring myself, I'd just float away. Does that make any sense?"

Isaac nodded. It was hard to see his expression in the dark, but Nory felt like he understood.

"I remember Thom telling me he was worried about you for a while."

"Really? I can't imagine that."

"He didn't go into details, but he'd asked me if I'd help out at the nursery for a few days if he had to go to London."

"When was this? I don't remember him ever coming to see me."

"He didn't in the end. I think your mum talked him out of it. It was a few years ago—six years? Maybe seven?"

"And you remember that?"

Isaac shrugged and rubbed the back of his neck. "Well, I knew it must have been bad for Thom to think he might need to go and get you."

Nory thought back to that time. It was a sketchy period in her mind, blurred at the edges and laced with a kind of panic that even now made her chest constrict when she thought about it. She hadn't realized her family had known she was struggling; she especially wouldn't have expected her brother to notice.

"And what did he think he was going to do? Throw me over his shoulder and bring me back to Hartmead?"

"I honestly don't know. He's a good mate, but he's not known for his tact, so I imagine he would have been met with resistance from you."

"Yes, he probably would. But I didn't need to be rescued, not by him anyway."

Isaac laughed quietly. "At the risk of provoking your wrath, you are not as different from your brother as you'd like to think."

Nory conceded the point with grace since he was walking her back in the snow. "The Noel stubbornness runs deep," she admitted.

They reached the back door. The snow had stopped falling and begun to freeze in place. Alongside their own footprints in the gravel were those of Lord Abercrombie and his beagle, probably from their last walk of the night.

They were on the step now. A delicious tension hung between them. If Isaac moved to kiss her, she would definitely let him. They stood looking at each other. She could feel herself being pulled as though by gravity—or something more superlunary—toward him. She was so close to him that she could see the tick of the pulse in his neck. All her childish feelings of desire for him came flooding back, along with something darker and hotter. She heard his breath coming harder. *This is it! He's going to kiss me!*

Then Isaac stepped back. "Lord Abercrombie doesn't like the staff fraternizing with guests."

Nory stopped herself mid-pucker. Desire was replaced instantly with mortification and embarrassment, like a bucket of snow had been thrown over her.

"Really? Fraternizing?" she asked incredulously. "What century are we living in?"

Isaac looked pained. "I mean, he has asked that we avoid getting romantically entangled with guests. It's unprofessional. Takes the focus away from the job at hand. You know what hen dos can be like! And stag dos for that matter. All those horny drunken women and men . . ."

*What the hell is going on here?* thought Nory.

"Isaac, if I've been reading this all wrong, then please put me out of my misery. I like you and I thought you liked me."

"I do."

"Then what is the problem here? I'm clearly not a drunken horny hen!"

Nory's ardor was shriveling rapidly.

Isaac rubbed the back of his neck, looking at the iron mud scraper by the door as though it might give him the right answer.

"What I said is true, we are encouraged not to get involved with guests. Lord Abercrombie doesn't want the staff behaving like Ibiza holiday reps—his words, not mine. But I don't think that would apply to you and I."

"Then what?" Nory pressed.

"Thom," said Isaac.

"Thom," she repeated dully. "My brother is stopping you from pursuing whatever this is? How exactly?"

"He's asked me, as a friend, not to get involved with you."

"Wow!" She was going to kill Thomas. At the very least, maim him. And she was going to fill his desk drawers with slugs. And she was going to tell Shelley! "Can I ask why?"

"He wasn't specific. He just said he could tell that I liked you, and as a favor to him, could I refrain from pursuing anything with you. You're his little sister and I'm his mate, and he doesn't want things to get awkward. I guess he's protective of you."

Nory blew out a huff that was distinctly raspberry-ish. "Oh, protective my arse! The man's a megalomaniac."

Isaac laughed. "So, you see my predicament. I am trapped between honor and desire."

Isaac was moving closer to her again. Too close. Too close for someone who wasn't going to kiss her. She could feel the warmth of his breath as he moved his face near to hers, their cold noses touching, lips so tantalizingly close she could almost taste them. Arrrghhhh! She was so angry! But also very, very turned on. What cruel torture was this?

"Believe me, there is nothing I would like more at this moment than to kiss you." Isaac's voice was low, almost a whisper; their heads were still pressed together. "I have barely thought of anything else since hauling you out of that wheelbarrow. But Thomas is my friend."

"Right."

Isaac took her hand in his. "Nory, I am very attracted to you."

"Right."

"Say something other than 'right.'"

"Okay?"

Isaac smiled and leaned in to lay a single kiss on her neck, which Nory felt reverberate through every nerve in her body. *Damn stupid, horny body! You're supposed to be angry and aloof!*

"I promise you," he whispered into her neck, his breath a delightful warm agony on her skin. "I want to kiss you." He stood back and smiled at her. "I'll see you in the morning," he said, before turning and walking away.

Nory watched him go. When his figure had been consumed by the night, she texted her brother. **Stay out of my life!**

**You stay out of mine!** came the response.

She sighed and went up to bed. Propped up against multiple pillows on her four-poster, Nory cheered her soul by trawling through vintage-book websites, searching for the perfect midwinter books for her January displays. By 3:00 a.m., she'd sourced several first-edition classic crime novels set in large country houses and a vintage copy of *Murder on the Orient Express*, just the ticket to soothe the post-Christmas blues.

The book search had consumed her energies and she was now

too tired to be annoyed at Thomas. She liked Isaac. She really liked him. She hadn't felt this way about anyone in, well, she couldn't even remember in how long. Why was her brother being such a poo brain? She sighed. He was a poop head even when they were kids—except when he was being the best brother in the world, of course. And that was what made their relationship so complex.

She batted Thomas out of her thoughts and closed her eyes, letting Isaac fill her mind. Good grief he was gorgeous. All the promise of handsome he'd had about him when he was a teenager had been fulfilled and then some. She pictured his long, slender hands, imagining them on her body, and found herself biting her lip.

When sleep finally took her, her last enduring thought was that she wasn't prepared to back away from Isaac and whatever this spark was between them; she'd take her chances and hang the consequences.

The party traipsed out into the crisp morning air, their breath clouding above their heads, and last night's snow had all but gone. Still, the grass was silvered with frost and a misty shroud hung over the land as the winter sun warmed the frozen earth.

Charles and Guy of course wore traditional tweed coats and matching trousers tucked into Wellington boots and tweed flat-caps.

"Have you ever seen them look more *lord of the manor* than they do right now?" Ameerah asked as they followed them out to the waiting Land Rovers.

"I'd say I found it rather sexy if Charles didn't already fancy himself so much," Jenna added dryly.

Camille sniggered.

"How do you think Guy feels in his outfit, Camille?" Pippa asked.

"Like he is a man of might and consequence," Camille answered, raising a wry eyebrow.

The women dissolved into laughter.

"Charles wanted to have sex in his tweeds this morning. I

think it's the idea of being let loose with a gun; the power has gone to his head. I told him to take a cold shower."

"Guy kept strutting in front of the mirror. Thank god it's the right weather for woolly hats, I didn't have a hope of getting near any reflective surfaces to do my hair."

By contrast, Jeremy—whose family owned an estate big enough to warrant a gamekeeper and who had grown up shooting rabbits, deer, and grouse when the numbers required it—was dressed inconspicuously in jeans and a waxed jacket. He was chatting with Dev, who looked sublime in his outdoor clothing; never had an anorak and Wellington boots looked so erotic.

"There ought to be a law against looking that good," said Pippa, watching Dev with something like hunger in her eyes.

"Charles was complaining last night in bed that Dev was making the rest of them look bad."

"He is astonishingly handsome," Camille added dreamily.

"He's reading Tolstoy at the moment, I practically had to pry *Anna Karenina* out of his hands last night to get him to shag me," said Ameerah.

"For fuck's sake!" Pippa exploded. "Could he be any more perfect?"

"I didn't sign up for a man with a brain, he was supposed to be strictly brawn." Ameerah sulked.

"He's not even brawny, really," Camille mused. "More muscularly svelte." The other women sighed in hearty agreement.

Two Land Rovers clattered over the rise and down to meet them. Douglas, the head gamekeeper, climbed out of one and Isaac the other. Nory's stomach gave a clench of excitement at the sight of him that even her stupid brother's veto couldn't quash. Dev might be a vision of perfection, but there was something about Isaac's wiry frame and intense expression that made Nory's limbs go bendy. He smiled when he saw her and pushed his dark hair out of his eyes. Nory resisted the urge to flick her hair and giggle.

She was stuck somewhere between being annoyed that Isaac put his friendship with Thomas over her and being impressed that he was such an honorable friend. She was also more than a little thrilled at the idea of a clandestine affair behind her brother's back. Was that weird? Why was this so complicated? Perhaps she should follow Ameerah's lead and commit to man-Barbies only.

A cheer went up from Charles and Guy, with shouts of "Come on!" and "Get in there, my son!" as they punched the air, when Douglas showed them the guns they'd be using.

"God, it's like being with football hooligans," said Pippa.

"Do you think they'll be as competitive at shooting as they were at everything at school?" asked Ameerah.

"Shit, I hope not," said Jenna. "One of them will end up dead."

"Were they competitive with *each other* as well? I'd always thought it was just Guy being ambitious," Camille piped up.

"They were hideous," Pippa replied bluntly. "Those two could turn anything into a competition."

"They once held a contest to see who could hold the most popping candy in their mouths," Nory added.

"Remember that time they tried to see who could get the most detentions in a week?" said Pippa.

"Guy was almost expelled after that," Nory told Camille.

"I wonder what his father would have said about that," Camille pondered.

It was common knowledge that Guy's father, a military man,

expected great things from his children. Nothing could be worse in his eyes than a member of his family bringing embarrassment upon the family name. Guy and his father had the kind of relationship where Guy fought against his father while constantly seeking his approval. For his father's part—at least, this was how it appeared to Guy's friends—he wanted his son to be subservient, dominating, and respectable. And by *respectable* it was generally understood that this meant "behave appallingly, just don't get caught."

Three underkeepers had already left with a pack of short-haired pointers trotting at their heels. The pickers—the people who help with the retrieval of the shot birds—were already at the site.

Ameerah sidled up to Nory and maneuvered her away from the others.

"So, how did it go with the gardener? Did you get to play with his big hard telescope?"

Nory barked out a laugh before composing herself. "The one that looks at the stars, yes. If you're being euphemistic, then no, no such luck. Apparently, the marquis doesn't like the staff to *fraternize* with the guests, and my brother hath forbade him to pursue me romantically."

"What the fuck? It's not *Downton Abbey*."

"Tell Isaac that."

"He clearly fancies you."

"Maybe."

"And you definitely like him. I haven't seen you this doe-eyed about a man for a long time."

"It would be complicated, though," said Nory thoughtfully.

"Oh, I don't know. He's obviously forgiven you for the turd wars, and from the way he keeps looking at you, I'd say he's definitely looking for ways to defy Brother Thomas-Twatmonkey and have his wicked way with you."

Nory sniggered and gave Ameerah a shove. "What about you? Are you still pretending that it's just sex with Dev?"

Ameerah sighed and Nory caught the wistful note in her best friend's voice when she replied, "To echo your words, Nory darling, it would be complicated."

Nory linked arms with her. "Once again, we two are destined for a thorny road to true love," she said, grinning.

"Speak for yourself, Nory Noel, I have no intention of taking any roads to true love, thorny or otherwise."

Jenna and Camille joined them again. Pippa was across the yard snapping orders into her mobile phone.

"What are you witches cackling about?" Jenna asked.

"Just discussing ways Nory can get herself into Isaac's pants," said Ameerah, nodding toward Isaac, who was talking with Guy and Charles; their chests were pushed out so far they reminded Nory of pigeons.

Nory gasped. "Ameerah!"

Camille giggled.

"Really? You and the gardener?" Jenna grinned. "Well, well, well."

"There is no 'me and the gardener.' Isaac. There is no 'me and Isaac.'"

"Methinks the lady doth protest too much," said Camille, and the others sniggered.

"Who's Pippa yapping at?" Nory asked, trying to change the subject.

"One of her minions," Jenna replied. "Pip's got a client arriving back from Dubai today, and they expect their town house in

Kensington to be fully festive by the time they put the key in the lock."

"Isn't half the fun of Christmas decorating the house yourself?" asked Camille.

"Not once you get into the realms of silly money," Jenna replied. "It's all about appearances. It's theater, nothing more. Like dressing a film set."

"I'm with Camille on this one," said Nory. "I can't imagine having a team of strangers coming into my flat to decorate it with their idea of what my Christmas should look like."

"You can't get more than three people in your flat at a time, Nory," said Ameerah.

"True."

"I've never been to your flat," said Jenna.

"It's what you might call cozy chic." Nory smiled.

"But it's central," said Ameerah.

"Guy and I had to move out to Islington to be able to afford a house," Camille complained. "You have to be earning millions to buy in central London."

Nory found it hard to sympathize. She was approximately fifty years from having enough money for a deposit on a house, and it was unlikely to be a property in Islington.

"Oh god, tell me about it! We're renting one of Charles's parents' places in Kensington at the moment while the renovations are done on the Greenwich house. Charles wanted to be closer to town, but I'd rather forfeit nearness for a decent house with some land."

"Land?" Ameerah exclaimed. "That country-vet persona must be rubbing off on you."

"What can I say? I spend a lot of time filming on location

and most of the time it's in countryside like this. After a while, you begin to see the virtues of the country air. And you know, sooner or later we're going to want to have children . . ."

Pippa came striding back over, her phone call finished with an abruptness that she seemed to employ in all aspects of her life. "Christ on a bike, I've walked in on a conversation about kids again!"

"I thought you loved kids," Ameerah teased.

"I do! From a distance."

"You sound like the Grand High Witch in that Roald Dahl book," said Jenna.

"*The Witches*," added Camille.

"Try not to eat any of the children at the wedding," said Nory.

"There are going to be children at the wedding?" Camille asked. She wore a confused expression.

But the reply to her question was shelved by the gamekeeper, who called them all into a huddle to give them the safety guidelines.

Jenna could hold her own on a shoot, and Pippa, like Jeremy, had been brought up on an estate—though not as large as Jeremy's—so she was no stranger to a gun either. Ameerah was a crack shot; she had won awards for clay pigeon shooting. Everybody knew the only way to compete with old money was to do everything they had done for centuries but better.

Nory had grown up in the country, but her family couldn't afford to take part in pheasant shoots. The chest freezer in her parents' garage, however, was generally well stocked with plucked pheasants, thanks to the marquis's generosity. In the city, tips came in the form of cash; in the countryside, they more often took the shape of vegetable gluts and dead birds.

Lectures over, the group climbed into the Land Rovers. Nory made a beeline for Isaac's vehicle; "no fraternization" be damned! Jeremy made to get into the passenger seat but caught Nory's determined gaze and wisely held the door open for her to take it instead.

"I think you'll enjoy riding shotgun more than I will," he said quietly, pushing the door closed behind her and continuing their conversation through the window.

"Thanks, Jez. Any word from Katie?"

"She's packed and ready to leave. It's a day's journey to the nearest domestic airport, then a two-hour flight to the international terminal, and then she'll be on the homestretch—relatively speaking; she'll still have an eleven-and-a-half-hour flight ahead of her. She won't hit UK soil till Thursday."

"Crikey, all she'll want to do is sleep when she gets here!"

"Yes, I've had a word with Jenna and said she probably won't be partaking of much socializing before the wedding."

"Fair enough, I'd say."

Isaac climbed in behind the wheel.

"Ready?" he asked, as Jeremy climbed in the back and took his place in the seat behind Nory.

"I've thought long and hard about it and I don't think I'll be able to actually shoot a pheasant," said Nory. "I'm basically coming along to watch and grimace."

Isaac laughed softly. "Don't worry, I had a feeling you might come to that conclusion. I've got something you can do that requires no killing."

"Do you have many people like me coming on shoots?"

Isaac raised an eyebrow. "I've not had *anyone* like you on a shoot before."

Nory smiled. "I mean, do you have many people who won't shoot attending shoots?"

"It happens occasionally," he said, smiling while keeping his eyes on the track ahead. "They like the theory but the reality is a bit too real."

His hand brushed hers as he reached for the gearstick and Nory felt a delightful tingle along her skin.

⌒

While the rest of the gang went off to shoot birds—shouts of "Loser!" "Wimp!" and "If you won't shoot it, don't eat it!" ringing in her ears—Nory followed Isaac down a track to the next field, where the explosions from the shotguns were marginally less ear-piercing.

"Won't you be missed over there with the bloodthirsty bunch?" Nory asked.

"They have enough guides to keep them safe. And besides, it is our responsibility to make sure all our guests are catered for, and that includes you."

"Lucky me," she replied, licking her lips in a way that she hoped looked tantalizing and not just like she was hungry.

"Frank, one of the gamekeepers, was supposed to be entertaining any anti-shooters with nonlethal target practice, but since it was only you, I convinced him to let me do it." He grinned.

They stopped beside four wooden crates lined up in the long grass. Isaac swung the sack he'd been carrying off his shoulder and proceeded to pull from it several large swedes, a handful of pale pink turnips, and some beetroots. He placed the vegetables on top of the crates before leading Nory over to a grassy knoll some way away and handing her a rifle.

"This is an air gun," he said. "Your friends are dealing with the main course, and you are in charge of side dishes."

Nory laughed. "I hope those turnips are free range."

"Of course," said Isaac, managing to keep a completely straight face. "All our vegetables are free roaming." He laid the sack on the ground. "Lay on your stomach." He gestured for Nory to lie down on the sack and then he lay down next to her.

For the next forty-five minutes, Isaac taught Nory the subtle art of shooting root vegetables, otherwise known as target practice. This was usually done with tin cans, but as Isaac pointed out, Nory was an *unusual* kind of guest, which pleased her immensely. She accidentally exploded one of the turnips and sheared a beetroot in two, but by the end of her shooting lesson she had become rather good at it if she did say so herself. Most of the vegetables were still usable. Her final shot—at the smallest of the swedes—was a perfect bull's-eye and the swede remained intact.

"That is what we in the trade would call a clean kill," said Isaac, taking the gun from her and easing himself up onto his knees.

Nory had to admit she had very much enjoyed having Isaac sidled up close beside her, helping her to take aim, even though he had been consummately professional, much to her disappointment. But then, this was his livelihood. Who was she to ask him to put it on the line for a roll in the hay? Still, she felt the cold seep in where he'd left her side. She sat up and brushed the mud off her knees.

"What will the chef say about the shot in the vegetables?"

Isaac smiled. "Not much surprises the chef. We had a guest

in the summer who would only eat windfalls. And another who only ate raw or dehydrated foods."

"Am I the first guest to slay a swede?"

"I think you might well be."

Isaac reached his hand out and Nory took it, allowing herself to be pulled up to standing. They stood for a moment, very close to each other, her hand still in his. The tension between them was palpable. Nory was hardly breathing. She was so close to him, she could see the shadow of stubble along his throat, smell the lingering scent of pine and eucalyptus soap on his skin. He made no move to step away and neither did she. She let her eyes roam up over his chin, his ridiculously perfect Cupid's bow lips, and his equally perfect nose. Never mind kiss him, she wanted to eat him! Her gaze met his eyes, less dark in this light, flecks of amber in warm brown iris, framed by black lashes, which by rights should only have been possible with mascara.

"Elinor." He whispered her name and she wanted to melt into him. He tilted his head and his lips brushed hers, butterfly light, as though if they just remained in this tantalizing state of barely touching, they couldn't be accused of breaking any rules. Her heart was pounding. His lips found hers again, a whisper of touch, just enough to wake up every nerve ending in her body.

"Isaac, mate! Where are you? We're about done here!"

The shout from across the way caused them to spring apart. It was Frank; he couldn't see them down in the dip, but they could see him peering over the crest of the hill.

"Down here, Frank," Isaac called, stepping into view.

"Ah, there you are. You done with your target practice? They've hit about as much as they're ever going to. The birds have pretty much scattered."

"Yes, we're all done here too. Plenty of side dishes ready for prepping."

"Huh?" said Frank.

"Nothing," Isaac replied. "Start packing down, and I'll meet you there in a minute."

"Right-ho."

Frank's head disappeared back beyond the crest of the hill, and Isaac turned back to Nory, who had just about regained her composure. They looked at each other, quietly acknowledging that the moment had passed. But despite their idle conversations as they packed up Nory's "kills" of the day, there was an electrifying undercurrent of unfinished business passing unspoken between them.

# Fourteen

Everyone was relieved to get back into the warmth of the castle after the shoot, and nobody felt much like venturing out again for the rest of the afternoon.

Lunch was a generous buffet laid out in the dining room, but rather than eat together at the table, the group took themselves off to various different parts of the castle to eat. Charles, Guy, and Pippa ensconced themselves in the billiards room, while the rest of them retired to the snug, which was essentially a small cinema. There were several two-seater sofas and coffee tables scattered conveniently nearby, and a huge TV screen hung above a marble fireplace.

They settled themselves in, plates piled high with chicken drumsticks, salad, and hot potatoes. *Gremlins* won the vote against *It's a Wonderful Life* and *Die Hard*. Camille was asleep before the opening credits had finished.

When the movie ended, they left the snug, blinking against the light, yawning, and shivering slightly after the warm dark of the room. Camille, bleary eyed, went off to retrieve her husband from the billiards room. Charles was sitting on a brown leather chesterfield sofa in the hall, one leg crossed over the other while reading a book. He looked up as they emerged rumpled and relaxed from an afternoon of doing nothing. His expression at seeing Jenna was utter joy, as though he hadn't seen her for a month. Nory couldn't help feeling wistful.

"Who won?" Jenna asked.

"Pip, obviously."

"You didn't play for money, did you?"

"I couldn't help it, Guy wanted to 'make things more interesting'!"

"Oh, darling! You know you should never play against Pippa for money; she always wins—she always did. Don't you remember?"

Charles rubbed his chin and looked sheepish. "I thought I might have learned a few new tricks in the interim. Unfortunately, Pip's rather upped her game since school too."

Jenna tsked good-naturedly and passed her arm through his.

"Nory, I've been thinking, why don't you invite that gardener of yours to join us for dinner tonight?" Charles asked.

Nory flushed instantly. "He's not *my* gardener."

"You know what I mean," said Charles. "Guy reckons you've been sloping off to see him every chance you get."

"I'd hardly describe it as 'sloping off'." She almost added *and the first time I ended up at his house it was because I was trying to escape Guy*, but Camille might be in earshot.

"Well, whatever." Charles waved an arm dismissively. "Invite him up for dinner tonight, he'd be very welcome."

Nory wasn't sure it was a good idea. She wasn't even certain Isaac would want to come.

"I'll think about it," said Nory. "But if I do invite him, you're not to refer to him as 'the gardener.' His name is Isaac."

Jenna and Ameerah were grinning from ear to ear and Nory wondered if they'd had a hand in this.

⁓

Nory was hemming and hawing about whether to invite Isaac to dinner. She knew she would be crossing a boundary if she did, but if he accepted, then perhaps he was willing to cross it too. She spotted him out of her bedroom window, pushing a wheelbarrow through the formal gardens with Lettuce trotting along beside him. Before she could overthink it, she had grabbed her coat from the back of the chair and hurtled down the stairs, cursing briefly in the boot room as she fought to get her Wellies on, before dashing out into the frosty late afternoon.

The sun was low in the sky, and the peculiar pumpkin glow to the clouds hinted at more snow this evening. She found Isaac digging bulbs into the sleeping flower beds.

"What are they?" she asked, coming up behind him. Lettuce had left off sniffing around the borders when Nory had gotten near and trotted over to join her.

"Alliums, mostly. They'll give a nice height when the tulips begin to die back. I should have had them in by now, I didn't expect the weather to turn so fast. You out for a walk?"

"As a matter of fact, I was looking for you."

"I'm honored. How can I be of service?"

"I wanted to invite you to join us for dinner tonight, at the castle."

"Why?"

"Why not?"

"Whose idea was it?" he asked, and Nory noted more than a hint of suspicion in his voice.

"Charles suggested it, and I thought it might be a nice idea. You can meet everyone properly."

"Why do I need to meet them?"

Nory didn't have an answer for this. She felt suddenly foolish and annoyed with herself.

"I met them this morning at the shoot," he went on when she didn't answer. "And if you remember, I knew them before, when you were all at the Pomp." The Pomp was the local nickname for the private school; a sweeping generalization referring to the supposed air of grandiose pomposity given off by both the building and students who boarded there. "Didn't think much of them then, if I'm honest," Isaac went on, "and I'm not sure how much they'll have changed since. Aside from your friend Jeremy, I saw very little to convince me that they weren't still the same brats who used to shout offensive remarks at my dad over the garden fence."

Nory was embarrassed by how rude her friends could be back then, and hindsight also shamed her for her silence in the face of their rudeness. Her friends weren't bad people, they were just trying to navigate their way through puberty and pushing their boundaries like everyone else. And the kids at the Comp— the state comprehensive school that the local children attended— were no angels! Thom and his mates used to raise merry hell in Hartmead. But local bad behavior and outsiders' bad behavior were judged by different standards.

Frustration at finding herself in her mid-thirties and still dealing with the same old bullshit sparked her anger.

"Don't come, then. Forget I asked," she snapped, and began to stomp back the way she had come.

Lettuce trotted back and forth as the distance grew between them, as if not knowing which of them she ought to side with.

Nory felt Isaac's hand on her sleeve, but she shook it off and picked up her speed. Annoyingly, Isaac had no trouble matching it. Lettuce trotted happily along beside her, oblivious.

"I'm sorry," said Isaac.

Nory didn't answer. She was fuming. If she tried to speak, she might angry-cry, which was just the worst kind of cry because everyone assumed you were upset, when in fact you were so full of rage that if your tear ducts didn't let out some pressure your head would explode.

"Are you not going to speak to me now?"

Nory held her tongue and her tears in.

"Nory, please. I'm sorry. I would love to have dinner with you. But with your friends . . . old habits die hard. I had a lifetime of dealing with pompous little arseholes from that school. It wasn't only your friends; every year brought in a fresh wave of rich kids who thought they were better than everyone else."

"They weren't all like that," she snapped defensively. "And some of the kids from the Comp were right arseholes!"

*What the hell?* Were they still arguing over which school was better or worse?

"Granted," agreed Isaac. "Maybe I just remember your friends better because you were with them."

"Why would I have made them more memorable?"

"You mean aside from the fact that you used to throw manure at me and you were my mate's kid sister?"

"You were the one who started Turd Wars!" she said.

"Turd Wars?"

"That's what we called it."

"I see. Good name. However, I wasn't the one who started it."

"I think you were."

"I think I would remember."

"Clearly you don't."

"Are you always this stubborn?"

"Always."

"Is the offer for dinner still open?"

"Will it be classed as fraternizing?"

Isaac considered. "If a guest invites a member of staff to join their dinner party, the staff member is duty bound to attend."

"Duty bound?" queried Nory.

"The guest's will must *always* be done," said Isaac.

He was smiling at her and she felt powerless to resist returning it.

"That doesn't quite fit with the no-fraternizing rule," Nory countered.

"It's a gray area."

"And what about my brother?" she asked.

"Oh, I've never fraternized with Thom."

Nory swiped at him, and he ducked out of the way, laughing.

"Your brother is another gray area. I am leaning toward 'what he doesn't know won't hurt him.'"

"With regards to dinner, you mean."

"Precisely."

"We're meeting in the drawing room for cocktails at seven thirty p.m.," Nory said, moving out of his orbit and walking away. "Don't be late!" she called over her shoulder. She didn't look back after that, and she gave herself points for how cool she was.

# Fifteen

Nory was in a flap. She'd been in a flap ever since Isaac had agreed to come to dinner at the castle. Jenna had been delighted when she'd told her, and Pippa had gone ahead and spoken with the chef. She hoped her friends would make a good impression; she was feeling very anxious about it all.

"You need to calm down," said Ameerah, expertly pulling a straightener through Nory's hair and twisting to create lazy curls.

"What if Charles says something Charles-ish? You know what he's like. And Guy . . . oh my god, I can't even, I'm going to hyperventilate."

Ameerah passed her the empty hot-water bottle from the dressing table. "Breathe in and out of this," she said.

"It's supposed to be paper bags that help, not rubber bladders."

"Just do it."

Nory undid the stopper and began to breathe in and out through the water bottle neck. The rubber smell was so strong she could taste it, but weirdly it did seem to help.

"I think I need to tell Camille about Guy."

"What the actual fuck, Nory! Do you have a death wish or something?" They were talking in a loud hissy whisper that Nory was hoping would be absorbed by the thick walls and doors.

"She's a nice person, she deserves to know."

"I agree with you," said Ameerah. "But you can't tell her about Guy without confessing your part in it, and do you really want to do that? Do you really think you can look that woman in the eye and tell her that you had sex with her husband?"

"Oh my god, it sounds so much worse when you say it out loud. I'm a home-wrecker!" She started breathing into the hot-water bottle again.

"Look, Nory, you didn't know he was married. This is on Guy. And I do agree that Camille needs to know what kind of man she's married to, but you know the phrase 'Don't shoot the messenger'? Well, you'd be the messenger who slept with her husband."

Nory grimaced. "So do I simply not tell her? So much for female solidarity!"

"Let's just concentrate on having a peaceful and enjoyable dinner with Isaac for this evening, and we'll focus on being true to the sisterhood tomorrow. One more night isn't going to change anything."

"Okay," said Nory, laying the hot water bottle on her lap. "One crisis at a time."

"Try not to think about dinner with someone you fancy as a crisis."

"No, you're right. And Jeremy and Dev will be there; they're like an antidote to Charles and Guy."

"Just enjoy yourself, Nory." Ameerah laid the straightener down on the dressing table and ran her fingers through Nory's hair. "You look gorgeous."

Nory looked at herself in the mirror. Ameerah had done a good job, her usually beach-tousled hair had been transformed into smooth loose curls that bounced about her shoulders.

"Thanks, Ameerah, you're a star."

"I know." Ameerah grinned and blew a kiss to Nory's reflection in the mirror before leaving to ready herself for dinner.

Her dresses hung side by side in the wardrobe, and Nory bit her lip as she flicked through them, wondering which one would make her bottom look smaller and allow her to eat comfortably, while looking just the right amount of desirable. Isaac hadn't seen her dressed up—she wasn't counting the time she'd spent with a ripped dress in a wheelbarrow—and she wanted to impress him. She decided she would channel her inner Jessica Rabbit and wear the teal velvet. She shimmied into it and took a selfie in the full-length mirror, which she sent to Andrew. He messaged back immediately:

Gorgeous! Love the hair. Is that Ameerah's work?

Thanks 😊 Yes, she is a woman of many talents.
How is my shop?

Your shop is fine, sales are up. Had to re-stock the window.

Nory's stomach squeezed as she wondered which of her beloved vintage Christmas titles had left home. She hoped they'd be loved.

**Excellent!** Nory messaged back, trying to be brave. **And how are things at home? How's Mugwort?**

Mugwort is the least high-maintenance of my guests 😳
But Matilda is loving the attention from American

**Grandma. Tomorrow my parents are coming for dinner, so
I am expecting granny one-upmanship in the extreme!**

**Cripes! Will your dad intervene?**

**Absolutely not. He will watch it all with glee over the rim
of his brandy glass.**

Nory liked Andrew's dad. He was a quiet man, who came into the shop often to make use of the comfortable chairs and read while his granddaughter napped peacefully on his chest. Andrew's mum was not unlike her own, always busy and fiercely loving of her children. She most certainly wasn't going to like having competition from Seb's mum.

I'll expect updates, Nory messaged.

**If it all kicks off, I'll be driving to the castle to tell you
about it in person!**

**Ha ha. So, I may have met someone and tonight
might be kind of a date, but Thom's forbidden him
to get involved with me.**

Her phone rang instantly.

"What?" Andrew's voice trilled out of the phone. "You didn't think to tell me this part first?"

"I'm telling you now. Anyway, it might be nothing. I don't know."

"I must say, I'm impressed, this is quick work even for you!"

"Rude!"

"Tell me all about him."

"He's the gardener . . ."

"Oh, Lady Chatterley! I do say!"

"I knew you'd say that."

"And?"

"Weirdly I remember him from when I was at school. He was my brother's mate. And we used to have this kind of feud thing going on. Anyway, he moved away and then he came back, and now I'm back and he's coming to dinner tonight at the castle."

"And why exactly has Thomas forbidden him to date you?"

"I really don't know. I've been too angry to call him. Maybe he thinks I'm not good enough for his friend, or he just wants to be an arsehole. This is his way of asserting his big-brother dominance."

"Perhaps it's you he's looking out for?"

"Doubtful."

"Well, apart from the overbearing brother, it all sounds fabulous. I'm hearing the distant clanging of wedding bells already."

"Let's not jump the gun. That clanging could be a death knell."

"Don't be so dramatic. Tell me about your encounters thus far."

"So far all we've done is stargazing and vegetable shooting."

"That's not bad going, I never used to shoot vegetables until at least the sixth date."

"These weren't dates."

"But they were something!" Andrew said in a singsong voice. "Is he tall, dark, and handsome?"

"As a matter of fact, he is."

"I can practically hear you swooning."

"You cannot. Anyway, I've got to go. Wish me luck."

"Good luck. Love you."

"Love you too."

⌣

At 7:25 p.m. Nory was standing outside the drawing room, hugging herself against the chill in the entrance hall despite the giant log burning ferociously in the fireplace. She had been staring at the front door for the last five minutes, willing a knock to come. The sounds of her friends' chatter drifted out to her, and she felt the squeeze of nerves again.

A whisper in her ear.

"Boo!"

Nory jumped and turned to find Isaac smiling at her. He was dressed in smart jeans with a shirt, tie, and tweed jacket. His dark hair was brushed back off his face, which was clean-shaven, and his eyes sparkled with a mischief that made Nory feel suddenly warm despite the drafty hallway.

"Hello. I've been waiting for you."

"I came in through the staff entrance. Force of habit." He grinned at her. "You look ravishing, by the way," he said, and Nory allowed herself to bask in his gaze as his eyes roamed from her face, down her body, and back up again. Good grief, it wasn't going to be easy not to fraternize with him.

"Thank you, you scrub up rather well yourself."

He smiled. "Shall we?" he asked, extending his arm so that she could loop her own through it.

She took a deep breath.

"Yes," she replied, with more confidence than she felt.

Isaac turned the handle to the drawing room and pushed, and as the noise from inside became suddenly focused, Nory saw a look of apprehension cross Isaac's face, just for a second, before he fixed his expression into a smile and escorted her into the room.

They made it through cocktails without event, and Nory found herself relaxing a little. *Maybe it wouldn't be so bad after all. These are my friends, what am I worrying about?*

Charles seemed to feel the need to express his athletic prowess and extolled the virtues of triathlon and pentathlon training.

"Ever taken part in a pentathlon, Isaac?" he inquired.

"I haven't," Isaac admitted. "I'm not sure I've got the stamina."

This was of course the correct answer and instantly endeared him to Charles, even when Pippa protested that Isaac must have extraordinary stamina to work in such a physically demanding job all year round.

"Perhaps," Isaac replied diplomatically, "but mine is only one kind of physical; there's little call for swimming or fencing in my daily routine."

At dinner, Jeremy was his own sweet self and quickly engaged Isaac in a conversation about organic gardening and the use of one type of insect to naturally control the damage caused by another. Nory was glad that Pippa had shifted the table settings, so that Isaac was protected on either side by Ameerah and Pippa and sat opposite herself and Jeremy. Guy was thankfully at the other end of the table near Charles and opposite Camille. Camille had been quiet all evening and had a wan look about her, despite her exquisite dress and carefully pinned hair. Nory made a mental note to catch her after dinner and engage her in conversation, to try and gauge how she was. She felt protective of her and wanted Camille to know that she had allies here.

They all raised a glass to Nory's excellent vegetable slaying when the side dishes were brought to the table. The meat tonight was pork; the pheasants shot today would need to hang for twenty-four hours to be eaten at their best. Nory could only imagine the levels of testosterone at tomorrow night's dinner when Charles and Guy were presented with food they'd actually killed.

Dev had seemed delighted to have another new person in the group, and Nory could understand why. It was probably a relief to have the focus on someone else. With Isaac at the table, the space that had been left for Tristan was filled, and though nobody said it, Nory sensed that everybody felt it. But it would have been filled soon anyway, when Katie arrived, and Tristan was too much of a part of their shared history to be forgotten simply because his place was occupied.

"It must be nice taking over the role that your father had before you," Jenna said to Isaac when the plates from the main meal were being taken away.

"It is. I never expected to ever be working here, but now that I am, I'm glad."

"It's not something that happens so much these days, I suppose," said Dev. "Not like it used to be, where you'd follow your father down into the mines, or the factory, or the bank."

"Although my brother has gone into the family business," Nory put in.

"I think Jezzer's family were hoping he'd step up and take over the running of the family pile, but he prefers the creepy-crawlies to the landed gentry," said Charles.

"No, you're wrong there, Charles," said Jeremy amiably. "My sister always wanted to do it, and she's far better suited to estate management than me. I'm not equipped to take on that kind of responsibility."

"But surely you must have been your parents' first choice," Guy persisted. "Or one of your brothers?"

"Why?" Camille asked, and Nory realized it was the first time she had heard her speak all through dinner. "Why must they have preferred for one of their sons to take over?"

"Oh, don't get on your feminist soapbox, darling."

"But why?" Camille pushed. "Do you expect Theo to take over my business when I retire?"

"Oh, don't be daft. You do interior design."

The disdain with which Guy said the words *interior design* was enough to draw gasps from every person at the table.

"Guy!" Jenna declared.

"Interior design is far from a female-only space," Pippa chimed in. "If you won't take it from your wife, then take it from me. Having a good eye for design has nothing to do with whether you have a vagina or a penis."

"You can always count on Pippa to bring genitals into any conversation." Charles laughed.

"I work with an equal split of male and female designers and photographers," said Dev. "I think pigeonholing genders into particular fields of work is an outdated construct."

Ameerah raised her glass to Dev, who raised his own and clinked it against Ameerah's.

"Cheers to that!" Ameerah beamed.

"All right, all right," Guy conceded. "I admit defeat." He turned to Camille. "I'm sorry, darling, as usual I let my mouth speak without engaging my brain. Of course, I'd be happy for Theo, Emily, or Randall to take over your business." He looked sincerely into his wife's eyes and kissed her softly.

Camille smiled, and even from where she was sitting, Nory

could see the love in her eyes. She wondered if love alone would be enough to sustain her, with Guy for a husband.

"It takes all sorts, I suppose," Jeremy said quietly into Nory's ear, as though he had overheard her thoughts, and Nory nodded.

"Didn't your grandfather work here as well?" Pippa asked, steering the conversation neatly back to Isaac.

"He did, he was also head gardener. And his father was a gardener too. He moved to England with my great-great-grandmother, as part of the staff when the De-Veer family came back to England after living in India for some years."

"The De-Veers," Charles said thoughtfully, rubbing his chin.

"Oh, Charles darling, you big snob, you don't know every wealthy family in England," Jenna chided him playfully.

"No, but that name rings a bell."

"They owned Heron House in Surrey," said Isaac.

"That's it!" Charles slapped the table triumphantly, making the cutlery shiver. "Heron House. My parents took us there on a day trip. The wife was, oh what was her name, she was an artist, quite famous, my mother has a print of hers in the dining room . . ."

"Serena De-Veer," said Isaac in a flat voice.

"That's the one!"

"I've got a couple of her early editions; beautiful still lifes. Botanical drawings were one of the few forms of art women were encouraged to partake of at that time," said Nory. "Plants were considered a genteel enough subject for ladies." She rolled her eyes, looking at Isaac, but he seemed momentarily somewhere else; she wondered where.

"Like interior design," said Jenna slyly, and Camille laughed.

"So, gardening well and truly runs in your blood," said Ameerah.

Her question seemed to draw Isaac back to the present.

"It must be a very mindful job," said Camille.

"It is," Isaac agreed, his good humor returning as quickly as it had faded.

"Any job you don't have to think about is mindful," added Guy.

"As someone whose family business is growing plants, I can assure you that gardening takes a good deal of thought, especially with gardens the size of Robinwood," Nory retorted, rather more snappishly than she'd meant to.

"Really, Guy, you're too much sometimes," Jenna chided.

"I'm only joking, don't get your Bridget Jones pants in a twist!" Guy laughed and took another sip of his wine.

Camille looked suddenly tired again, the affection of moments ago having clearly worn off.

"Well, you can come and be mindful in our garden if you like," said Charles. "I've got more important things to do than titting about in the rhododendrons, and Jenna's on set from dawn till dusk most days. We just haven't got the time."

Isaac smiled graciously. "Thank you, but *I* don't have the time to tit about with your rhododendrons either; maintaining ten and a half acres of formal gardens is a full-time occupation."

Charles flushed instantly, and Jenna shot him a furious look. But at that moment the dessert course arrived, and the subject quickly changed to the trios of French patisseries laid before each guest.

Nory was mortified both for Isaac and Charles. Charles didn't mean to be a snob, it was just his way; he was thoughtless and buffoonish but ultimately well-meaning. And poor Isaac. Nory was used to being inadvertently made to feel like the lucky peasant at the party. She knew her friends didn't really mean anything by it. It wasn't anyone's fault; they were all the products of their upbringings, no matter which tax bracket they came from.

After dinner Isaac made a graceful exit, thanking his hosts while accepting humble apologies from them, especially Charles, who seemed genuinely mortified by what he termed his "giant boob."

"You're not leaving because of Guy and Charles, are you?" Nory asked as they stood in the courtyard. She had borrowed a heavy coat and a pair of Wellingtons from the boot room, which looked incongruous with her velvet evening dress.

"Not exactly. I do have to get back; I don't like to leave Lettuce too long. But I think there is something to be said for quitting while you're ahead."

"They're good people," said Nory, noting the sound of pleading in her voice.

"I'm sure they are."

Nory couldn't think of a response. She shifted from foot to foot, the pebbles crunching beneath her feet.

"You should go in," he said. Then leaning down and kissing her cheek, he whispered, "You are beautiful," before walking away from her.

Nory had hoped that her sexy dress might be enough to override her brother's romance embargo, but alas, Isaac had remained the perfect gentleman. Not even a closed-mouth kiss on the lips! Did that mean he wasn't into her as much as she was into him? Had she read this whole thing wrong? Maybe Charles's comments had sealed Isaac's decision not to get involved with her. It was so frustrating. You wait your whole life for an honorable man to show up and when he does, he's too virtuous by half! Why were the gods conspiring against her? Her final thought on the matter was the most mortifying of all: Maybe—and this would be a bitter pill indeed—he just wanted to be friends!

At first, Nory tried to ignore the person shoving her. She was wrapped in the thickest duvet she had ever slept in, and until a few seconds ago she had been in a blissful sleep.

"Nory!" the annoying shover hissed.

She kept her eyes closed and hoped they'd bugger off. It had to be the middle of the night; she could tell through her closed eyelids that it wasn't light yet.

"Stop pissing about and give her a shake!" said someone else.

"Drip water on her face," whispered another.

They were not going to leave her alone. And how many people were in her bedroom anyway?

Nory opened one eye. "If the castle isn't on fire, you can all fuck off," she grumbled.

"She never was a morning person," said Pippa.

"It's not morning!" Nory exclaimed. "And if you're trying to wake me up, why are you all whispering?"

"Because we know you're a miserable cow when you first wake up," said Jenna.

Nory laughed into her duvet. "All right, what do you want?" She pulled her head slightly out of the duvet and opened the other eye. Ameerah was perched on her bed while Pippa and

Jenna stood beside her; they were all three still in their pajamas, grinning.

"It's a full moon," said Ameerah, close to her face.

"Why do I need to know this?"

"It's a full moon . . . and it's snowing," said Pippa.

Nory was suddenly alert. She kicked the duvet off and sat up, scratching her head.

"No!" she said, grinning.

"Yes!" said Ameerah, jumping up off the bed.

Nory looked at her three friends and suddenly it was like she was a kid again.

"Snowball Croquet!" she yelled, punching the air as she scrabbled out of bed and joined the others in jumping about the room.

"The boys are already down there, come on!" Jenna yipped excitedly.

"Wait, how did you get in here?"

"We picked the lock, silly," said Ameerah.

"Braddon-Hartmead skills," Pippa winked.

Learning to pick locks had been a rite of passage at school; the whole place was locked down after lights-out and the only way to move about the quiet halls once the housemistress and master had retired to their quarters was to be an expert at breaking and entering.

Four sets of woolly socked feet careered down the staircases. Nobody got dressed; Snowball Croquet was always played in pajamas. They slipped and slid their way—laughing hysterically—along the polished floors to the boot room at the back of the castle. It was like they were sixteen again, sneaking through the darkened corridors of Braddon-Hartmead. The big moon smiled at them through every window as they ran.

In the boot room, they forced their bed-socked feet into Wellington boots and shrugged on heavy winter coats, not caring whose was whose. Ameerah pulled the door open, and the cold night burst in to greet them.

It was freezing and dark, but that didn't put them off. The moon was disappearing and reappearing behind the clouds, and the snow was drifting down like white rose petals being scattered from above. They made their way—boots crunching on the frosty grass—across to a gate hidden in the wall at the far end of the ornamental garden, which served as a shortcut to the farthest field of Braddon-Hartmead School.

The grounds closest to the school were set up with CCTV and motion-sensitive floodlights—much like a high-class prison—but this far from the main buildings there was no such security. These fields were only ever used for cross-country running and scavenger hunts; neither of which would be happening at one o'clock in the morning in below-freezing temperatures unless the school had employed a particularly sadistic PE teacher in the interim.

Nory held the phone torch while Jenna unlatched the gate, and they stumbled, giggling like schoolgirls, onto the far field. Jeremy handed them each a tumbler of pale-yellow snowball, while Guy knocked the croquet hoops into the ground with a stubby mallet. Nory noticed a plentiful supply of Advocaat and lemonade bottles leaned up against the wall and was relieved to see they were taking it seriously. She took a sip of the thick, custardy liquid and smiled, her spirits warm despite the cold.

"Where's Dev?" Nory asked, looking around the dark field. Someone had *borrowed* the hurricane lamps from the dining room and set them at the edges of the makeshift court. The flames danced on top of the pillar candles, making strange patterns on the ground.

"He gets up at sunrise to do yoga and meditation, he's not into late-night sports," Ameerah replied.

"Fair enough." Nory wished she was the kind of person who began the day with healthy life-affirming pursuits, but she wasn't. "Guy, where's Camille?"

Guy looked up from smacking a hoop. "She's making the most of not having to get up in the night with the kids. To be honest, she was glad to be rid of me. I think she likes having the four-poster to herself."

Nory could understand it.

"But wait, we're missing our eighth! We need an eighth."

Technically they didn't need an eighth at all; croquet was usually played with teams of two, four, or six, but they had always played as an eight. Tristan's absence left a hole in everything they'd done as a group.

"Worry not, Nory," said Jeremy, adding another splash of Advocaat to her glass. "Charles is on it."

There were sounds of twigs snapping and rustling undergrowth, and Charles emerged looking very pleased with himself, followed by a slightly bewildered Isaac. Nory's stomach flipped. Isaac saw her and smiled.

"Good man, Isaac," said Guy, standing to survey his handiwork. "Thanks for stepping up."

"I second that," Jeremy called as he hastily concocted a snowball for Isaac and handed him the glass.

Isaac nodded and came to stand by Nory.

"Old Bear Grylls here sleeps in the nude." Charles smirked, motioning toward Isaac, who shifted uncomfortably under the weight of six pairs of eyes suddenly turned his way. Nory felt a frisson of excitement zip through her at the idea. "I had to rummage around and find something suitably pajama-y for him to wear."

Nory looked down and saw he was wearing tartan fleecy trousers tucked into his Wellingtons.

"I'm sorry about this," said Nory quietly as she led him a little way from the others.

"What?" Isaac asked.

"Dragging you into our old traditions."

"I don't mind. To be honest, it's a bit of a dream come true."

Nory laughed. "How so?"

"Well . . ." Isaac shifted, scratching his head as though embarrassed. "My old bedroom was in the attic, and I could just see this field from it. You can't see it in the summer, but in the winter, when the trees are bare, there's a pretty good view. Anyway, I heard you guys out here one night and looked out and . . ." He waved an arm gesturing to the croquet court.

"You watched us playing Snowball Croquet?"

Isaac nodded sheepishly. "It's not as creepy as it sounds. I guess I was sort of fascinated."

"You should have come and joined us."

"Yeah, right!"

Nory suddenly felt bad. She knew the kind of reception he would have got back then.

"No, I suppose we wouldn't have welcomed you in," Nory said guiltily. "I'm sorry about that. We didn't think we were being arseholes at the time, but that's not really a defense."

"Don't worry about it." He smiled. "We were arseholes too. But we certainly wouldn't have been seen dead drinking snowballs," he added, clinking his glass to hers and taking a drink.

"I suppose you were all drinking tequila and riding around on motorbikes, like rebels without causes."

"Something like that." Isaac smiled. "Watching your lives was like climbing inside a book. Those kinds of things didn't happen in real life. Not in my life anyway."

"Isaac, you *literally* lived in a castle garden. You weren't exactly watching us from your inner-city tower-block window."

Isaac laughed softly. "Touché." He took another sip of his drink. "There's something I've always wanted to know . . ."

"Yes?"

"Why *did* you play croquet in the snow while drinking snowballs under a full moon?"

Nory felt a pang of something, not sharp like it used to be, more a lament, which sang a cavernous sorrow through her insides.

"Tristan," she replied. "At least, it started on Tristan's birthday. It was the night of his fifteenth birthday. It was April, just before Easter, and we were all due to go home for the holidays that Friday. And then weirdly, it started to snow—in April! It was so unexpected because it had been sunny all day. So then obviously we started drinking snowballs . . ."

"Obviously," said Isaac.

"And then someone, I can't remember who, said we should sneak out for a game of croquet in honor of the snow on Tristan's birthday."

"And you did."

"And then after that, if there was ever a full moon and snow, we played Snowball Croquet. Huh," she said, almost to herself, "funny how these things come about."

The court was set up, and after a brief explanation of the rules for Isaac's benefit, the game began. Isaac was on Nory's team with Jeremy and Pippa. Most of them were still a little drunk from earlier in the evening and the snowballs kept them topped up enough that they didn't feel the cold.

It was fun, even though the game had fairly quickly dissolved into anarchy. Nory liked having Isaac there with them. It felt as though the divide between them, which had seemed so prominent at dinner, was blurring, or maybe it was simply the alcohol blurring her powers of observation. Isaac seemed less guarded, but then it was easier to feel you were on a level playing field when everyone was wearing pajamas. Maybe, she mused, if all the attendees of the G8 summit came in their pj's they'd get more done.

"Isaac," Charles began, slinging a friendly arm around Isaac's shoulder. "Now that there's a few years' worth of water under the bridge, I feel we owe you an apology."

"Oh?" Isaac kept his voice light, but Nory could tell he was guarded. "What for?"

"We did you a disservice. We allowed you to take the blame for something."

"We never expected it to go as far as it did," said Guy.

"Oh god," said Jeremy, shaking his head, "I know where this is going."

"Can someone tell *me* where this is going?" asked Nory. She felt suddenly on edge; her friends could be boisterous and overbearing, which was unnerving to those who didn't know them well enough.

"It's like this," said Charles. "Isaac didn't start Turd Wars."

"What?" A laugh escaped her, nervous energy released into the night. "He threw manure at the back of my head!"

"Thing is, Nory," said Charles, biting back a laugh, "he didn't start it at all. It was Guy. Guy chucked a clod of manure at me, actually, I ducked, and it hit you square on. You were so incensed that we blamed it on the gardener's son."

Nory was speechless.

"That explains a lot," said Isaac, nodding slowly.

"You framed him!" said Ameerah.

"We did, Your Honor," said Guy. "To be fair, Nory was an awful beast when she was angry, and we thought that anger would be better aimed at someone who wasn't us. We never expected the feud to carry on as long as it did."

"Oh my god! Isaac, I'm so sorry." Nory tried to stifle her smile.

"I did tell you I wasn't the one who started it." Isaac laughed. "But since I may have inadvertently caused you to fall into a wheelbarrow full of manure the other night, I am prepared to be the one to call it quits." He held out his hand and Nory shook it.

"When did you fall in a wheelbarrow of manure?" Guy asked.

"Never you mind," said Nory.

∽

By half past two, the game had been abandoned and the snow had stopped falling. The sky had taken on an eerie amber glow, and the trees were spiky silhouettes lit from below by the snowy fields. They sat on the ground, wrapped in blankets, backs against the stone wall, looking out over land that stretched away to nothingness. Nory was sitting squeezed up against Isaac, resisting the temptation to rest her head on his shoulder.

"I always forget how big the sky is here," said Nory.

"It's pretty magnificent," Isaac agreed.

"When I'm here I feel like I could stay forever. But then I go back to the city and that feels like home too."

"I couldn't live in the country," said Pippa. "It's too quiet. I need the buzz of the city."

"I think what constitutes 'buzz' is different for everyone," added Jeremy. "For me, 'buzz' is being in the wild. I feel hemmed in in the city."

"I'm a city lad through and through," said Charles.

"You're a money man through and through," said Ameerah. "If your most lucrative deals were being brokered in the Outer Hebrides, then you'd be calling yourself a country guy."

"Did somebody say my name?" asked Guy drowsily.

"You make it sound like Charles is only driven by money," said Jenna.

"I don't think it's the money that drives him, Jen, I think it's the exhilaration of winning."

"Ameerah's right," said Charles. "It's never really been about the money, per se. It's the thrill of chasing down and sealing the deal."

"Only someone with money has the luxury of saying it's not about the money," said Isaac.

Nory's shoulders stiffened.

"Somebody needs to get Guy back to his wife. He's gone to sleep on my shoulder," said Ameerah.

"Not me," said Nory, and the others chuckled knowingly. She felt Isaac turn to look at her, but she didn't meet his gaze.

"I think we should probably all head back," said Jeremy. "Before we get frostbite."

They began to shift—stiffly—from their sitting positions, keeping their blankets wrapped around their shoulders.

The empty bottles, glasses, and croquet set had been stacked in a wheelbarrow, which Charles began to push toward the gate in the wall. Jeremy and Pippa each had an arm around Guy, holding him up. When they reached the point where Isaac would leave them to go back to his cottage, the others called their weary goodbyes, leaving Nory and Isaac alone on the path.

"Thank you for allowing yourself to be dragged into our weird traditions," said Nory.

"I had a good time," said Isaac, and then added, "I had a good time because you were there."

Nory's heart began to pick up speed. Was he going to kiss her properly this time and to hell with Thom? She wanted him to kiss her, but also, she hadn't brushed her teeth when she'd gotten up, and her tongue felt kind of furry from all the Advocaat. But if he made to kiss her, she definitely wasn't going to say no.

"I'd better go," said Isaac. "And you need to catch up with your friends so you don't get lost in the dark."

"Yes," said Nory, deflated. "Well, good night then. Or good morning."

Isaac smiled. "Maybe I'll see you tomorrow."

Nory nodded and tried to return his smile, but she knew it was halfhearted. *Maybe he'll see me tomorrow?* He couldn't even commit to seeing her.

Her disappointment must have been palpable, because Isaac moved in closer to her then.

"It's not that I don't want to kiss you," he said, letting the rest of his words hang in the air unspoken.

"I understand," she said, fixing her eyes on the ground.

Isaac touched her chin, tilting her head so that she was looking at him. He gently traced her jawline with his fingers and her breath hitched. He brushed her lips with the pad of his index finger and then closed his eyes, breathing deeply. Her skin tingled from his touch. Her desire for him was almost painful. He bent his head to hers so that their foreheads were pressed together, sliding one arm around her waist and pulling her body against his. With his free hand he twisted her hair and gently pulled her head back so that her throat was exposed. She gasped as the cold air hit her skin and then again as Isaac's warm mouth found the sensitive skin on her neck. She pressed herself to him.

A call rang out.

"Nory! Where are you?"

It was Ameerah's voice, some way off in the deep black night. The spell was broken. Isaac released her.

"You'd better go," he said, his voice husky.

Ameerah's figure came into view, appearing out of the shadows like a specter.

"There you are!" she said. "Where have you been?"

"I was just . . ." Nory turned, but Isaac was already gone.

"Come on," urged Ameerah, linking arms.

Nory looked ahead to the bobbing phone torches of her friends, and she and Ameerah hurried after them. She'd be glad to get back into her warm bed, but she couldn't help wishing it was Isaac's warm bed she'd be climbing into.

She was going to have to speak to Thomas, and she needed to do it soon.

# Seventeen

"You've got flower girls?" asked Camille.

Sitting in the morning room after breakfast, everyone was tired after last night's outdoor sport. Jenna had some final wedding arrangements to make with Pippa today, and so there wouldn't be any scheduled activities. Nory and Ameerah were planning to take advantage of their free time to go down and visit her family.

"Yes," Jenna replied. She had an overfilled A4 ring binder open on her lap, each page laminated and pertaining to some element of the wedding. "Four flower girls, two page boys, and two bridesmaids. I know it seems excessive, but you know what it's like, you can't have one without the other, and besides, Harry and Meghan had ten!"

"So, there *will* be children at the wedding." Camille's brow was furrowed. "When I asked you at the shoot, you didn't answer me."

"Didn't I? Sorry, I'm terrible for getting distracted at the moment. Bride brain!"

"But there will be. Children at the wedding, I mean," Camille pressed.

"Well, yes, quite a few actually, nieces and nephews and what not. We've both got big families. And quite a few of our friends have got kids."

"Then," Camille said, frowning questioningly, "why weren't our children invited? I mean, I understood that you might not want children around for the house party, it was really more of a grown-up affair and we're the only ones with kids. But Guy told me that the children weren't invited to the wedding either. I almost didn't come; I've never been away from them for that long. So"—she hesitated—"is it just my children who weren't invited?"

Jenna looked straight at Camille for a long moment, which seemed to stretch on uncomfortably. Her face was playing out different emotions. Finally, she said, "I'm sorry to be the one to tell you this, Camille, but you've been misinformed."

"What do you mean?" The color was rising in Camille's cheeks.

"Your children *were* invited to the wedding. They were invited to the house party, too. Guy asked us to change your invite so that it was just for you two."

Camille was stammering. "B-but—why would he do that?"

"It's really not for me to say."

"I really wish you would. I really wish someone would tell me what the fuck is going on because apparently my husband won't."

"Camille, I think he did it with the best intentions."

Camille raised an eyebrow. "Which were?"

It was clear she wasn't going to let it drop. Nory, Ameerah, and Pippa shared awkward looks.

"Look," Jenna began carefully. "Guy said that you two could do with some time alone. That things had been tough, with the children and"—she hesitated—"stuff, and he thought a break away would do you both good. He knew that you'd never agree to leave them behind if they were invited. So, he asked us not to."

Camille's eyes bored into Jenna's as she digested her words. "Does everyone know?" She glared at each of them in turn.

They all muttered a truthful no in response. Camille stood, smoothing her dress down over her stomach, and made to leave the room.

"Camille!" Jenna was standing too now. "I'm sorry. I didn't mean to upset you. We were only doing what Guy asked of us."

Camille smiled and nodded. "I know. I don't hold you responsible. You've all been lovely to me. Even though my husband behaves like a dick most of the time. I'm sorry."

She left the room, leaving the four friends looking after her.

"Shit!" said Jenna.

"What did Guy really say?" asked Ameerah.

Jenna bit her lip. "That Camille was too attached to the children."

"How can you be too attached to your children?" asked Nory.

"He also told Charles, though I'm not supposed to know, that Camille suspects him of having an affair."

Nory gulped.

"Is she right to?" asked Pippa.

"I don't know." Jenna was wringing her hands. "Charles wouldn't tell me, but I got the impression that something was going on. You know what they're like with their bloody boys' club. All the little secrets they keep."

"Jesus! They're not at school anymore, they can't keep covering for each other," Ameerah snapped.

"I don't think Jez knows anything about it," Jenna added.

"He hasn't been in the country much, and they aren't as close as they used to be."

"Jenna, I'm just going to come right out and say it," said Pippa. "Are you sure you want to marry the kind of man who covers for his friend's infidelity?"

"It's no different than when we keep each other's secrets," Jenna blurted. "Just because Charles keeps a confidence doesn't mean he condones it; he's simply being a good friend. So, if you're asking me if I want to marry the kind of man who has his friends' backs no matter what, without judging them, then yes. I do."

Ameerah touched Jenna's arm, and she flinched.

"Jen, as someone who prepares arguments for a living, I recognize a rehearsed speech when I hear one."

Jenna opened her mouth to argue, but Ameerah held up her hand.

"Pip's not questioning Charles's love for you. We all know he's loved you for years. But we'd like to feel that, along with his being an excellent friend, he will also be an excellent husband. You are too fierce to want to end up like Camille."

"You think he's going to cheat like Guy?"

"No," said Nory. "We want to be sure that *you* don't think he's going to cheat on you."

"I know he won't. We've talked about it. Charles knows that if he ever did, it would be over. He knows about my dad and what his actions did to me and my mum, and he has sworn on his mother's life that he will never cheat."

"Well," Pippa exclaimed, clapping her hands. "Why didn't you say so? That settles it. We all know what an abysmal mummy's boy Charles is, so if he's sworn on Mummy Montague-Smythe's life, that's good enough for me."

The tension in the room broke, and they all laughed, taking turns to smother Jenna with kisses. They were still messing about when the sound of glass shattering jolted them into silence.

"You are an arsehole!" Camille's scream reached down into the morning room and drew the four women out into the hall. The shouts were coming from upstairs.

"I did it for you!" Guy's voice was whiny.

"For me? How was any of this for my benefit? I didn't want to leave the children, you knew I didn't; all I've done all week is fret about them."

"That's exactly my point!" Guy was shouting now. "You're obsessed with the children. They're all you think about."

"They're my children, Guy! Of course I'm bloody obsessed with them."

"So where does that leave me? The children take up *all* your time. What's left for me?"

"What?"

"Don't look at me like that. It's not normal, Cam. And it's not only me; my mother thinks it's weird as well."

Nory winced.

"Should we be listening to this?" she whispered.

"Fuck yeah!" Pippa hissed back.

Camille's voice seemed to rise several octaves. "What the fuck would your mother know? You were brought up by nannies and then packed off to boarding school!"

"Now hold on just one second . . ."

"No, Guy, *you* hold on. Yes, *our* children take up all my time, and I'll tell you why. Because they are three and five and eight years old—they are physically and mentally incapable of looking after themselves because of the fact that they are three and five and eight fucking years old! If they aren't looked after, they will literally die!"

"I'm not an idiot, I know they need looking after. It's just that by the time you're done with them there's nothing left for me. We barely ever have sex, and when we do, I can tell you'd rather be sleeping."

"Wow!"

"I've offered to get you help . . ."

"I don't want a nanny!"

"Why not? Most women would kill for a nanny."

"I'm not most women."

"Don't I know it."

"Do you know why I don't want to have sex with you, Guy?"

There was no answer.

"Because I don't know where you've been!"

Nory felt the color drain out of her face.

Guy tried an approximation of a laugh of ridicule, but it came out like a frightened squeak. "What are you talking about? You're delusional, Cam. It's all in your head!"

The color flooded back into Nory's cheeks. Was he actually going to gaslight his wife? Ameerah put a steadying hand on Nory's arm.

"No, Guy, it isn't all in my head. It's mostly in your trousers. I was hoping you had enough decency to be honest with me, but apparently, you'd rather call me delusional than admit to it. Our problems have got nothing to do with the children. And nothing to do with my being tired. They have everything to do with you. I'll see you back in London. We can decide what we're going to do when you get back after the wedding."

And then everything went silent. Guy didn't protest or try to defend himself. Nory could imagine his expression: sullen yet resolute in his unwillingness to show any kind of vulnerability. A hangover from an outmoded upbringing where to be a man was to be indomitable.

～

Camille left an hour later. When the bedroom door had first slammed and they'd seen Guy striding across the lawn in the direction of the stables, Nory had felt that at least one of them should go and knock to see if Camille was okay. She felt strongly it ought not to be her, just in case.

Jenna had immediately fetched Charles and Jeremy to go after Guy. Guy might be a misogynist and a cheat, but he was also their friend. Losing Tristan had left them all afraid, unable to trust that the people they loved would stick around to wait for better days.

The women were still deciding who among them should check on Camille, when she came back into the morning room carrying a suitcase and a holdall.

"I suppose you heard all that?" she said.

They nodded awkwardly and tried and failed to start comforting sentences, but Camille cut them off.

"It doesn't matter," she said. "I just wanted to say goodbye. And thank you. You've all been very kind. Lovely, actually. Even though Guy is your friend and not me."

"We don't approve of his behavior," said Ameerah, and the others nodded emphatically.

"No. Well. Nothing's ever simple, is it? As much as I don't want to be the pathetic, pitied wife of a cheating husband, I still love him. I can't seem to turn it off."

"Maybe he'll change," said Nory.

Camille smiled at her. "Yes. Maybe he will. Or maybe I will. Anyway, I'll be off. I'm sorry not to see you get married, Jenna. I'm sure you'll be a beautiful bride. I know the meal and everything is already paid for, so feel free to bill my husband for my share."

"Oh my god, that's the last thing on my mind," said Jenna. "Honestly, don't worry about it. I completely understand. You need to get back to your babies." Jenna pulled Camille into a hug, and then the others each took a turn at hugging the poor, rich, beautiful wife of Guy Bailey, the stupidest man in England.

"Keep an eye on him," Camille said as she turned to leave. "He's not as tough as he makes out."

The butler, having brought the car round to the front of the castle, loaded her luggage into the boot, and Camille drove away. Nory, Jenna, Ameerah, and Pippa stood and waved on the stone steps until she was out of sight.

"Do you think she'll be all right?" Nory asked.

"She's close with her mum," Jenna replied. "She mentioned it when we were chatting last night."

"Good. She's going to need some support."

"You don't think it's an omen, do you?" Jenna was biting the corner of her mouth.

Nory put her arm around her friend. "Of course it isn't. Your wedding will be perfect. You're not embarking on a whirlwind marriage; you and Charles are meant to be."

Jenna laid her head on Nory's shoulder. "Thanks, Nory."

The friends turned back into the house and closed the door on the bitter morning. Nory couldn't help feeling grateful that she hadn't had to come clean about her fling with Guy. Luckily, he'd dug his own hole and she hadn't needed to join him in it.

With the others occupied with wedding planning and consolation, Nory and Ameerah drove down to Hartmead to visit Nory's parents. Dev had an online meeting with his agent and was then standing in as Charles's "stunt double," since he was on Guy duty, while Pippa, Jenna, and Christopher, the celebrity wedding photographer, decided where best to have the photographs taken on Saturday.

"Doesn't Dev mind being left behind?" Nory asked as they drove slowly along the narrow winding roads, which were caked on either side with frozen earth and frosted vegetation.

"Does the model mind being left with a professional photographer, you mean?" Ameerah smiled, honking the horn to get two magpies to leave their roadkill in the middle of the lane so that they could pass. "He's friends with Christopher. I think Dev was looking forward to being in the thick of the arrangements."

"What are you going to do about him?"

"What do you mean?"

"Now that you've broken your own cardinal rule and fallen for the no-strings-attached guy?"

"I keep telling you, I haven't fallen for him, Nory. Relationships are not for me. We just get on really well. I enjoy Dev's company, he makes me feel happy, like chocolate in human form."

"That sounds like a relationship."

"Well, it isn't. It's convenient, that's all. And when I'm old, I can look back on photos of the wedding and know that the hottest guy in the room was with me."

"I suppose it's good to have goals."

"He got on well with Isaac."

"Yeah, I noticed that too. It's not like they have anything in common."

"You don't know that. Maybe Isaac is a secret fashionista." Ameerah grinned.

"Or Dev's a closet horticulturalist."

"He could be, for all I know; he keeps surprising me. Last night he was talking with Pippa about playing bridge! I mean really, does Dev look the type who plays bridge?"

Nory shrugged. "Who knows. I've given up trying to fathom people. Who would have expected Isaac to have connections to Serena De-Veer, one of my most favorite artists of all time ever? Although, I seem to be a lot more excited about it than he is."

"Maybe he's not that into botanical art? Or maybe he was just trying to play it down?"

"I don't know why. If my family had worked for a famous artist, I'd be telling everyone!"

"Not everyone's a super-book-nerd like you, though, babe."

"Granted. But even so. I mean, he's got an original painting on his sitting room wall for heaven's sake."

"Yeah, but if it was his parents', then maybe he keeps it for its sentimental value rather than its artistic merit."

"I guess," Nory agreed halfheartedly.

They came to the bottom of the lane and Noel and Son came into view.

"God, I love this house!" said Ameerah when they'd parked.

She leaned forward over the steering wheel to look at Nory's childhood home. A compact, sturdy 1930s building, with big bay windows and pebble-dashed walls as protection against the harsh winds. It was a no-frills house, like the family who lived in it.

"Do you think we'll ever reach the stage where the places we *actually* live in feel like our homes, rather than the places our parents live?" Nory asked. "Why do I always think of this place as 'coming home' as opposed to my flat?"

"I don't think it's so much the places as the people," said Ameerah. "Maybe your parents are what signify home for you. It's different for me. I don't feel a particularly deep sense of connection to any place really, apart from this one, which isn't even my home."

Nory reached over and kissed her cheek.

"It's as much your home as it is mine," said Nory. "I think my parents prefer you to me anyway."

Ameerah sighed. "I think you're right."

They laughed as they made the chilly dash to the back door and let themselves in.

The kitchen was warm, with condensation running down the window over the sink, and something wholesome bubbled in the big saucepan on the stove; minestrone soup, possibly. A dozen rolls, freshly removed from the oven and still steaming, rested on a wire rack in the middle of the table, which was set for six. The extra two places must mean that Thomas and Shelley were joining them for lunch, and Nory groaned inwardly. She had hoped to corner her brother in private. At the moment, she wasn't sure she could keep a civil tongue in her head.

"You're here!" her mum trilled, walking in from the living room. "I didn't hear you come in."

She pulled first Nory and then Ameerah into a hug.

"Ameerah, you look gorgeous as always. How's work? Sit down, sit down. Jake will be in in a minute. Are those for me? Oh, Ameerah, you shouldn't have, but thank you; I won't be sharing these."

Nory's mum took the proffered box of Prestat chocolates and wisely shut them away in a drawer. It was pointless to buy flowers as a gift for a woman who grows flowers for a living. The house was always full of floral cast-offs dotted about in jugs and vases, but a box of chocolates from Prestat always did the trick, especially since her mum knew Ameerah would buy them from the actual shop in Piccadilly.

"Work's good, thanks," said Ameerah, taking a seat at the table.

"Are you seeing anyone special at the moment?" The work question was always her mum's opener to bring her round to the question that she really wanted to ask.

"You know me, Sasha," Ameerah said, smiling. "My work is the love of my life."

Nory's mum looked somewhere between proud and disappointed. "You can't live on work alone, love. Honestly, you and Nory, like peas in a pod. No wonder you get on so well. But what about the handsome model you've brought down with you?"

Ameerah shot Nory a look, but Nory shrugged. "It wasn't me! I didn't tell her."

"Oh, my goodness, if I waited for Nory to tell me anything,

I'd be waiting forever. The village is on fire with gossip about your house party. What with Jenna being a homegrown TV star—she won a national award for most-loved TV vet in the summer, did you know that? And then there's your model."

"He's not *my* model," Ameerah interjected, but she was instantly overruled by Sasha, who simply continued as though she hadn't spoken.

"Jilly at the newsagent recognized him first, when she was up at the castle delivering the papers, because of course she gets all the glossy magazines into the shop, you see, so she knew right away. And once she knew, everyone knew! Have you done something different to your hair?"

Ameerah shook her head, nonplussed.

Sasha scrutinized Ameerah's face and then slapped her hand on her thigh. "I know what it is," she declared triumphantly. "You're in love!"

Ameerah burst out a laugh. "I don't think I am."

"I know that look. Do you remember what she was like over that boy, Nory, oh what was his name? He spent that summer working at the farm, the year you had your arm in a plaster cast after you came off that ladder."

Nory was laughing too now. Ameerah squirmed and protested.

"Peter Leech," said Nory, watching delightedly as Ameerah buried her face in her arms.

"Peter Leech! That's it. Ran away with the carnival when it left. Old Dorian up at Pine Farm said right from the word *go* he wasn't suited to farm life; he was on work experience from a college up near Dewsbury. You were dotty for him, Ameerah. Soppy as a flannel on washday."

Ameerah groaned. "Thank you, Sasha, for reminding me about my terrible taste in men."

"He was too old for you anyway. What were you? Fourteen? Fifteen? He was nineteen if he was a day. The both of you were flushed as milkmaids all summer, you with your crush on Peter, and Nory hanging around the fair after that boy with spots and a Mohawk who ran the ghost train. Lord alive, I was glad when term started again. Your dad was this close to punching him on the nose, he was sure he was trying to get you to elope."

"Oh my god, really? I don't remember it being that serious. I know I fancied him, but I wasn't about to run away with the carnival like Peter Leech." Nory laughed.

"What was ghost-train boy's name again?" Ameerah asked.

"Thor," Nory replied.

"That was it. Did he give himself that name?"

"I don't think so, his brother was called Njord."

"Oh yeah, ran the bumper cars, looked like he'd had his face flattened with an iron."

"That's the one."

"Sometimes I wonder how I survived you girls," said Sasha. "Thomas was straightforward by comparison; even with all those motorbike hooligans he hung around with, and the wacky baccy, he still wasn't a pinch on you two."

The door flew open, and Thomas and Shelley walked in.

"Speak of the devil," said Ameerah, while the new arrivals divested themselves of boots and coats.

"Literally," Nory muttered, and received a frown from her mum.

"Amie!" said Thomas, ruffling the top of Ameerah's head like she was a dog, instantly ruining all her hard work with the hair straightener. "It's been a while. You home for Christmas? The boys were asking after you the other day." His gaze wandered lazily over to Nory, as though only just seeing her, and he swiftly gave her hair the same treatment. "All right, Bugs?"

Nory flushed instantly. "Get off, Thom!" she snapped.

"What's your problem?" he asked so innocently that Nory wanted to smoosh a crusty bread roll into his face.

"You!"

Before she could say more, Shelley cut in: "Hello, Ameerah, lovely to see you. Hi, Nory. Douglas had the drone out over the castle grounds the other night, and he caught you and Isaac taking a cozy moonlit walk. What's going on there, then, eh?" She nudged Nory and winked. Shelley couldn't possibly have known that this was exactly the wrong thing to say. Thomas scowled and Nory felt her cheeks flush with indignation.

Sasha clapped her hands delightedly. "I knew it! I could feel the sparks coming off you two the other day," she gushed.

"There's nothing to know, Mum," Nory said, looking square at Thomas. "And why is Douglas flying a drone over the castle?"

"It's poaching season," Thom answered. "It's easier to monitor the birds by drone than on foot. Oh, and leave Isaac alone, yeah? He's a mate, he doesn't deserve to be used for a fling."

"You are a megalomaniac," Nory blurted. "Concentrate on your own life and stop trying to dictate mine."

Ameerah studied her French manicure and stayed wisely quiet.

"What is going on here, you two?" Sasha scolded over their rising voices. "Thomas, what Nory and Isaac get up to is none of your business."

"It's my business if I have to pick up the pieces when she swans back off to London."

"Oh, shut up, Thom! Isaac isn't some helpless victim," snapped Nory.

"Why him? Why *my* friend? Can't you just leave him alone?" Thomas asked.

"Thom's asked Isaac not to get involved with me," Nory said to her mum. "Apparently I'm not good enough for his friend."

"Thomas!" Sasha looked shocked. "Is this true? Why on earth would you do that?"

Thomas visibly shrank as four angry women glared at him. Nory sat back and let him drown in the scorn.

"Thom, babe, that is a shitty thing to do, and you know it," said Shelley.

Thomas tried to avoid his wife's eye. "I'm just trying to stop people getting hurt," he said through gritted teeth.

"That's not for you to decide, is it?" said Shelley. "You can't control everything."

"I'm not controlling anyone."

"Not much," spluttered Nory.

"Enough!" Sasha's voice whipped the air.

Nory and Ameerah became suddenly interested in their place mats while Thomas and Shelley looked around the kitchen, anywhere but at Sasha.

"Can we have one family meal without you two at each other's throats? Thomas, stay out of Nory's business. Grow up, the pair of you! This subject is now closed. There will be no more cross words for the duration of lunch. Thomas, if you can't say anything nice, don't say anything at all. And, Nory, you should know better than to bite every time your brother tries to get a rise out of you; you're not five."

With all those assembled chastened, Shelley and Thomas took their places at the table, and Sasha passed over the butter dish and six bowls. Arguments in the Noel household blew up and blew out just as quickly. It was their way; they were a feisty bunch and cross words were usually quickly forgotten. The old animosities simmering below the surface were harder to reconcile.

Nory's dad came in and took his turn to say his hellos, completely oblivious to the ruckus of moments ago.

"Lovely to have you back where you belong, Ameerah," he said.

"Right, that's everybody in," Nory's mum called over the chatter. "Grub's up!"

Shelley and Thomas leaned left and right respectively to allow Sasha to maneuver the giant saucepan onto the waiting trivet, before taking her own seat. There proceeded to be a merry hubbub as bowls were passed around the table to be filled by Nory's dad, and a scramble for the butter dish as knives were hungrily dug into crispy rolls.

"Who's picking the boys up today?" Sasha asked.

"I'll get 'em," said Jake. "Is it swimming club tonight?"

"Nope, karate," Thomas replied. "Their kits are in the office."

"I'm going up to the castle after lunch," said Shelley. "I've got a last-minute meeting with Pippa and Jenna about the wedding garlands, and Pippa's got a job she wants to run by me for January."

"There isn't time for extracurricular work," said Thomas, ripping a chunk of bread with his teeth.

"It isn't extracurricular," Shelley replied, completely unperturbed by her husband's attitude. "Pippa will buy the stock and pay me through the business, just like any other job we take on."

"Only for twice the money," added Jake. "Don't be a hardhead over this, Thomas. It makes good financial sense. This is the kind of contact that could really grow the business."

"I don't think Thom would have such a problem with it, if it wasn't one of my friends," Nory remarked, staring at Thomas.

Thomas scowled back. "Shut up, Nory," he snapped.

Sasha slapped her hands down on the table before any more bickering could take hold.

"Thomas, you're being silly and stubborn. Whatever your problems are with Nory's friends—obviously not you, love." She rested her hand on Ameerah's. "You should be proud you've got such a talented wife. And it's talent that's got her noticed."

"I love Pippa, but she's a hard-nosed cow when it comes to business," Ameerah added. "And she's got a hell of a good name in the city. She was consulting for Fortnum and Mason last year on their food hall displays."

"Really?" Sasha exclaimed. "Oh, Shelley, this is such a great opportunity for you."

"For us," Shelley corrected. "I'm doing it all under Noel and Son. And if it takes off, I'll be needing your expertise, Sasha."

Sasha nodded, looking pleased.

Thomas huffed and tucked the hair that had loosed itself from Shelley's ponytail behind her ear.

"I'm being an arse," he said to his wife. "Ignore me."

"Already on it." She squinted her eyes at him and gave him a friendly elbow in the ribs.

"At this rate you'll have to change the facias to Noel and Family, Dad," Nory said, sneaking a sideways wink at Thomas, who glared back at her.

"Maybe we will," said her dad. "Credit where it's due. This family is built on good honest graft, and there's not many can say that."

"Jake, I really must protest," Ameerah cut in. "I'll have you know my father works damned hard; transferring one's money all around the globe to avoid paying tax must be exhausting."

They all laughed.

"And how is life in the murky world of the law?" Jake asked.

"Oh, you know, I'm just a gal fighting for the rights of the innocent and downtrodden, I don't like to brag."

Jake nodded. "And, Nory, how are you coping with being away from your books?"

"Better than I thought, actually," Nory replied.

"Don't be fooled, Jake, I keep catching her chasing books online," said Ameerah. "Nory can sniff out a rare book a hundred miles away."

"The day you got that business loan was one of the proudest days of my life," said her dad.

"Good," Nory replied. "Because I'll be paying it off for the rest of mine."

"But it's yours. You've built something. There's pride in that. No one can take that away from you."

"Apart from the bank if I don't keep up repayments," said Nory.

"Nothing worth having is free." Her dad chuckled.

Nory would have liked to disagree. She would have liked not to have spent nights lying awake with worry, wondering how she was going to find the money to renew her lease or pay the rent. Some free money would have been well worth having. But in her family, struggle was synonymous with pride.

"Having said that," said Sasha, "we've agreed to have a *Midsomer Murders* murder in the dahlia house in March."

Jake raised his tea mug and clinked it against his wife's.

"As always, my wife is the voice of reason. It'll help pay for new overhead misters for some of the greenhouses and a kitchen refurb for the camper van." He grinned.

"I'm so pleased you've agreed." Nory was delighted. "Noel and Son will be on TV!"

Even Thom smiled.

"Ameerah, love, any news from your parents?" Sasha asked.

"The suite on the cruise ship is the biggest my mum has ever seen, and they've signed up for every excursion available. They'll be spending Christmas Day on the Galápagos Islands."

"I hope giant tortoise isn't on the à la carte menu," said Thomas.

"Well, my love, I can't promise you an à la carte menu, but excessive noise, sherry, and Jake snoring from beneath a paper crown are all available if you decide to spend Christmas with us," said Sasha.

"Hear! Hear!" said Jake, before adding, "But I don't snore."

Cue many and varied impressions of Jake Noel snoring.

# Nineteen

Dinner at the castle had been a subdued affair. The chest-beating bravado that would have otherwise greeted dishes of kill-your-own-pheasant was absent due to the Guy-Camille fiasco; such visceral celebrations seemed in poor taste. Guy was drunk by the time Ameerah and Nory got back from lunch and seemed determined to remain that way. Pippa had rearranged the table to close the gaps made by missing friends, but the absences were apparent. Nobody quite knew what to say to Guy. What do you say to an old friend whose wife has just very publicly left him? Even if he did have it coming?

The group talked about the wedding, a little about politics—which they quickly had to abandon—and their various jobs. Dev got into a discussion about global warming with Charles, suggesting that someone with as much sway in the financial world as Charles was perfectly positioned to encourage investors to clean up their acts in terms of their carbon footprints. Guy butted in drunkenly to accuse Dev of having a higher carbon footprint than any of them because his modeling work took him all over the world on gas-guzzling airplanes.

In the end, the party disbanded early, some to their rooms, others to the snug, and Charles and Guy to the billiards room, where they ordered a bottle of whiskey and settled in for the night.

Truth be told, Nory was pleased to have her evening suddenly free. She left it a respectable amount of time before changing into jeans and a jumper and disappearing off to Isaac's cottage.

"Hello, I didn't expect to see you this evening." Isaac was smiling, looking at her with one eyebrow raised. He was dressed in the tartan fleece leisure trousers he'd worn to Snowball Croquet and a navy-blue sweatshirt. His hair was wet from the shower—slicked back—and Nory could still smell the fresh scent of soap on his skin.

She felt suddenly nervous. Was it such a good idea to just turn up? What if Isaac had someone with him? What if he didn't have company because he wanted to be by himself, without weird booksellers rocking up unannounced at his door?

"Is this a bad time?"

"No! No, not at all, you just took me by surprise. Come in."

He stepped aside, and Nory walked in past him and through the open door into the sitting room.

"Can I get you a drink?"

"Something hot, please, it's freezing out there."

"What about a glass of mulled wine? I had a hankering for some earlier, but it seemed excessive to make some up just for me." He looked at her and smiled. "But now you're here."

"Mulled wine would be wonderful. If it's not too much trouble."

"None at all. Come out to the kitchen, we can talk while I concoct."

Nory wanted to tell Isaac that she'd confronted her brother, but a part of her was holding back. She didn't want him to feel obliged to get with her simply because she'd cleared the path.

Lettuce had looked up lazily from her spot on the rug by the fire when Nory had come in, and then promptly let her head flop down again. Now she raised one ear inquisitively but decided she was too comfortable to move.

Isaac's kitchen was a generous size, covering the whole back of the house, with a battered farmhouse table at the far end, opposite a set of French doors that led out to the back garden.

"Take a seat." He gestured toward a tatty wingback chair tucked in beside a woodburning stove, and Nory sat down. The springs in the upholstery had well and truly sprung, but a small mountain of cushions made up for it.

"That was Dad's favorite chair," Isaac said. "I haven't got the heart to get rid of it."

"I know someone who could get it re-sprung, they've done a lot of work for me in the past. I brought in a load of old furniture when I opened the shop. I'd wondered why the chairs were so cheap when I bought them online and then discovered there wasn't a working spring among them when they arrived."

"Ah, the perils of the late-night eBay purchase."

"Ha, yes."

Isaac was busy at the worktop. He'd already glugged a bottle of red into a saucepan and was now busily slicing clementines, snapping cinnamon sticks, and throwing spices into the warming alcohol. Soon the kitchen was heady with the scents of orange and star anise. Nory let her eyes roam lazily around the space, feeling far too at home here with Isaac and far too relaxed to overthink it. Her gaze landed on an easel on one side of the table. She heaved herself out of the chair and wandered over.

"Did you paint this?" she asked.

It was a watercolor of the hellebore cultivar from the Winter

Garden. The confident brushstrokes of color over the curves of the petals and the movement in the leaves felt familiar. The flower head and its leaves were separated, as was its stem, so that this was not so much a still life as a botanical study.

"Oh, um. Yes, I did. I wanted to document the plant as I went along. I've done the same with every hybrid."

"Ever heard of a camera?"

Isaac laughed. "I guess it's kind of a hobby too. Art, painting . . ." Shades of embarrassment colored his voice, as though he needed to explain his work away. "My mum was a talented artist. She taught me how to look past what your brain is telling you you can see, and witness what's really there instead. You'd be surprised how much our brains try to fill in the gaps for us."

"You've clearly inherited your mum's gift."

Isaac handed her a glass mug of steaming wine and she thanked him.

"Do you have more?" she asked.

"Wouldn't you like to finish that glass first?" Isaac smiled.

"Not the wine! Do you have more paintings that I can look at?"

Isaac shrugged and rubbed the back of his neck. "Like show-and-tell?"

Nory pulled a face at him. "I'm interested. Stop being so coy. This is good, I'd like to see more."

"It feels a bit weird."

"Why?"

"I don't know. I do them for myself, I don't usually show them to other people."

"I'm not going to grade you! I'm just interested in art; that's *my* hobby."

Isaac stood cradling his mug for a moment while he deliberated and then finally said: "Okay. Come on. But if you give me any less than a C-plus, I'm taking the mulled wine back."

Nory followed him through another door, which led into what was once a dining room. The dark wood table was a depository for books, stacked boxes of paints, sketchbooks of varying sizes, and rows of plant pots with seedlings pushing their tiny green heads out of the soil.

A bay window looked out onto the front garden. A generous cushioned window seat had been built in, but for the most part this too was covered in books. The walls were made up of floor-to-ceiling bookshelves, leaving just two holes where shelves had been built around and above the doors to the kitchen and hallway.

"This room is pushing all my buttons," Nory exclaimed breathlessly.

"I know, it's a mess. I keep meaning to tidy it, but there's always something I need—"

"No, I mean my buttons are being pushed in a good way," Nory interrupted him. "It's almost a library. Wait, are those shelves double stacked?" She moved toward one of the cases and pulled out a book to reveal another row of books behind. "Oh, you, Isaac, are a man after my own heart. My god, I'd like a day in here to root around." She ran her fingers along old, cracked spines and faded leather bindings, occasionally pulling out a book and examining it briefly before carefully replacing it.

"When I said my parents could never bear to part with anything, that extended to books," said Isaac, watching Nory. "I got rid of most of the furniture, but I must have the same hoarder tendencies when it comes to these."

"Keeping books is not hoarding!" Nory said fiercely, clutching an aged copy of *Heidi* to her chest. "It's protecting history.

The written word is the key to the secrets of this world and all the worlds that live in our minds."

Isaac was smiling at her, and she felt suddenly self-conscious. This was the point where Andrew would normally tell her to rein in her inner book nerd or risk scaring passersby. But Andrew wasn't here.

"What I'm saying is, having a book collection is not the same as stockpiling bargains from discount stores or keeping your own urine in lemonade bottles . . ."

Isaac raised his eyebrows. She was making this worse. *Step away from the books, Nory*, she told herself.

"Well, thank you, it's good to know I'm not being lumped in with the body-fluid collectors." Isaac laughed.

Nory took a deep breath and reluctantly replaced *Heidi*, turning her back and hoping Isaac didn't see her give the book a little sniff before she pushed it gently back into its place. *Ahh, that old-paper smell.* She closed her eyes.

"I saw that," he said.

*Dammit!*

"I was checking for damp. Damp is the archenemy of books."

"Uh-huh."

"You are headed for a C-minus," she said haughtily. "Now, where are your paintings?"

Now it was Isaac's turn to look uncomfortable, as he sifted through the papers on the table and picked bound sketchbooks from a head-height shelf. Nory sipped her warm wine and waited as Isaac pulled his work together in some kind of order and stacked it, ready for her perusal. He stood back and gestured for Nory to come over.

The first book had the word *Spring* written in a scrawled hand across the cover. Inside were studies of purple crocus, pale yellow narcissus, bluebells, tulips, primroses, snowdrops, and other spring blooms, all dissected, painted, and labeled in the same scientific botanical style as the hellebore in the kitchen.

"These are just . . ." Nory whispered as she came to the end of *Spring* and immediately picked up *Summer*, forgetting to finish her sentence and almost forgetting where she was. She turned the pages slowly, consuming the paintings with her eyes, absorbing the colors, staring at the fluid lines and then closing her eyes in an attempt to collate the images in her mind, so that she could keep them to revisit later.

She laid *Summer* down and took a sip of her wine before reaching for *Autumn*. When she looked back up, Isaac was watching her, his face pensive, as though waiting for a blow to fall.

"Is it a C-minus?" he asked.

"Isaac, these are . . ." She fumbled for her words. "They're beautiful! I mean, really good. You've got a talent, Isaac. You could sell these, make prints, sell them framed or as cards, there's a market for these . . ."

"They're not for sale." Isaac smiled grimly.

"Why not? You're missing a trick here."

"Because they're mine."

"It won't stop being your work." Nory laughed at his vehemence.

"Are you sure about that?"

She looked at him. His expression was clouded, guarded even. "I don't understand," she said.

For a moment, Isaac seemed to be weighing something in his mind, and then he said: "I want to show you something."

"Okay." Nory was confused by the sudden change in atmosphere.

They made their way upstairs. Isaac pushed open the door to

the study and Nory went in. He fished around in a vase on one of the shelves for a set of keys, then crossed the room and knelt in front of a large traveling trunk in the far corner. The maroon leather on the trunk was flaking with age, and the iron studs had tarnished to a dirty gold. It had clearly seen some mileage. Peeling customs stickers from various countries had been haphazardly slapped onto the leather.

The locks clicked one after another, after another, until finally, Isaac pushed his thumbs against two rectangular brass buttons, and the top gave a jump as though surprised. Isaac pushed up the heavy domed lid.

Nory, who had been gingerly stepping closer and closer throughout the opening process, could no longer suppress her curiosity. She leaned over the trunk.

She saw a couple of yellowing parchments folded and secured with a wax seal, and some newer envelopes that looked as though they held bank statements and solicitors' letters. Isaac brushed them aside and carefully lifted out a set of A3 sketchbooks, which he placed gently down on the desk.

He turned to Nory, who was now practically hopping with curiosity, and gestured for her to take a look. At once she could see that they were very old. Most of the books had been handbound in cloth—calico, if she wasn't mistaken. Faded ribbons sewn into the edges of the discolored fabric were tied in loose bows to keep the books closed. Her heart was racing. It felt like finding treasure; just the bindings alone were enough to set her fingers tingling. She cast an inquiring look up at Isaac, who smiled and said quietly in answer: "Go on, take a look."

She picked up the first book and laid it flat on the desk, sitting herself on the chair in front of it. With utmost care and trembling fingers, she pulled one of the ribbon ties. The silk slipped out of its bow and spooled onto the desk. Nory opened the book to the first page.

It contained hand-painted botanical drawings, labeled in pen and ink in a spidery hand, as though the writer was unfamiliar with the words. The plants were unlike the common British varieties depicted in Isaac's books downstairs. These were tropical flowers, little stars of jasmine, voluptuous pink lotus flowers, and red tattered hibiscus petals with stamens lolling out of their centers like giant tongues. Nory turned the pages reverently, careful not to let any natural grease from her fingertips mark the delicate parchment pages.

It was strange. She had never seen these drawings before. How could she have? And yet they were so familiar. No, more than familiar. She recognized the hand that had painted them, as though she had looked at them a thousand times. She frowned as she reached for the next book. And when she unfastened the ribbons and turned to the first page, she knew these pages too. Not the plants themselves, though some were familiar to British gardens, but the brushstrokes, the way the colors had been leaked into one another, the careful and oh-so-delicate ink lines that outlined stems and petals.

"These are original Serena De-Veers," she almost yelped. "Oh my god! Some of these are from her time in India. I know these, Isaac. These are original sketchbooks. My god, do you have any idea how valuable these are? I mean. I can't even . . . each one of these would fetch thousands at auctions. Hundreds of thousands, Isaac, sitting in an old trunk in your study." She laughed then. A pure joyous laugh. This *was* treasure. "These are original Serena De-Veers!" she almost shouted, jumping up from the desk and skipping around to Isaac, grabbing him by the shoulders and shaking him. Isaac remained unmoved.

"Actually," he said coldly, "they're not."

Nory looked into his dark brown eyes, and they burned back into hers. "What?" Her voice faltered. "They are, I'm sure of it. I've studied her work . . ."

"You are half-right. The hand that painted these is the same hand that painted the picture in my sitting room and the books in the glass cabinet in your shop. But none of them were painted by Serena De-Veer."

Nory chuckled uncertainly, convinced that this must be some sort of joke that Isaac was playing on her. "But I don't understand, the provenance . . ."

"The provenance is wrong. Serena De-Veer"—he said her name through gritted teeth—"didn't paint anything; nothing that got published anyway. It was all my great-great-grandmother's work."

"W-what? But how?"

Isaac motioned for Nory to sit, and she settled herself down on the chaise longue. He remained standing and began to pace. He seemed both agitated and weary as he spoke.

"My great-great-grandparents worked for the De-Veer family when they lived in India. When they came back, my great-great-grandparents came with them. My great-great-grandmother Heba was a kind of lady's maid to Serena De-Veer. The De-Veers were very impressed with Heba's paintings and always very encouraging. Apparently, they had a friend who worked in publishing, and they offered to show him Heba's work. The publisher was very keen to go ahead, but it was decided that the books would carry more gravitas with booksellers if they were under Serena's name as opposed to that of an unknown Indian immigrant."

Nory watched his fists open and close in frustration. She'd never had to suffer the injustice of being discriminated against because of the color of her skin. She'd watched her best friend encounter a myriad of daily microaggressions during their friendship—many having nothing *micro* about them at all. She couldn't imagine the bitterness that Heba must have felt, a bitterness that had been passed down through the generations and now hung on Isaac's shoulders.

"They offered to pass the profits and any royalties on to Heba," Isaac continued. "And they'd promised that if the books were successful, they would come clean down the line, show people up for their prejudices."

"But they never did," Nory said, picturing Serena De-Veer's name on the covers of the books in her shop.

Isaac shook his head. "No."

"What about the money?" Nory asked.

"Not a penny."

"But how did they get away with it? I mean, surely Heba and your great-great-grandfather had proof? They could have gone to see a solicitor . . ."

"Heba signed a contract, handing over the rights of her paintings to the De-Veers. They told her it was the only way, and she trusted them. She thought she was making a better life for her family. The contract was written up by the De-Veers' solicitor. My great-great-grandparents didn't have the money to get their own solicitor. They didn't have a leg to stand on."

"That's so awful. It's wrong! So wrong. What about later on, your grandparents, or your parents?"

"Can you imagine how much money it would cost to contest a contract that old? To go up against the De-Veer family? They're still one of the wealthiest families in England."

"What about you? Have you looked into it? Times have changed, people would be more sympathetic now."

"The De-Veer family haven't gotten any less rich, Nory." He laughed humorlessly. "And my family haven't gotten any less brown. I did go to a solicitor once. He was very understanding but he made no bones about the cost. The De-Veers are still making money from Heba's books; they've been using her art to promote their business and bring tourists to Heron House for decades. They aren't going to let that go lightly. I was advised that they could drag the case out for years, bury it under a mountain of paperwork, and bury me financially in the process."

Nory's head was reeling. It seemed too preposterous that such an injustice could go uncontested.

"But. But. But." She was floundering for the words to express her feelings. "It's not fair!" Her petulant statement was a pin to Isaac's chagrin balloon, and he laughed, a genuine laugh this time, without the sharp edges.

"No, it isn't fair," he agreed.

"What if I try to do something?"

"Got a few hundred thousand quid to spare, have you?"

"Oh. No. Unfortunately very much not. Does the marquis know?"

"No."

"Then we should tell him." Nory jumped excitedly off the chaise longue.

"No."

"Why not? He's a good man. And he's got influence, which is just the sort of thing you need."

"Believe me, I considered it; I discussed it with my parents when they were alive, but it still comes down to money. We all agreed that we couldn't ask Lord Abercrombie to make that kind of commitment to one of his staff. I've thought of all the ways I could make it right over the years, but the stakes are just too high."

Nory went back to the desk and sat down. She gently leafed through the sketchbooks again. A life's work robbed.

"Poor Heba," she said quietly. "I can't imagine how betrayed and powerless she must have felt."

"These sketchbooks were her solace. The De-Veers thought they had all her artwork, but Heba had kept back some of her paintings from when she was in India because she didn't feel they were good enough—although of course, anyone looking at them can see that they are. And when she realized that she had been duped, she continued to paint in secret. She did some of her best work to spite her mistress. Of course, nobody knew about it, but that wasn't the point. It was a quiet rebellion."

"Sometimes they're the best kind," said Nory, marveling at the paintings before her.

Suddenly another idea flashed into her mind. She didn't like it, and at first, she pushed it away. But then she gave herself a talking-to: This wasn't about her; this was bigger than her. Heba deserved to have her name recognized.

"Guy is an investigative journalist," she said before she could talk herself out of it.

"Good for him."

"I know he's a thoughtless idiot. But he's a good journalist. He's broken some huge stories over the years, and he's nothing if not thorough."

Though she suspected the subjects of his stories might replace the word *thorough* with *single-minded arsehole*. Guy was forever bandying about phrases lifted from writers like George Orwell: "Journalism is printing what someone else does not want printed:

everything else is public relations." Isaac's was exactly the kind of story that would appeal to Guy's "avenger of truths" sensibilities. Nory was not blind to the paradox between his professional ideals and the way he conducted himself personally. Guy was, in every way, a better man on paper than in reality.

"I don't want my family's name dragged through the gutter press."

"Guy doesn't do gutter press!" *Dear god, I'm defending Guy!* "I mean, he's done some controversial exposés in his time, but they generally had it coming. Heba was the victim of exploitation. And Guy is bloody-minded enough and has enough of his own personal privilege not to be frightened by the De-Veers' legal team."

Isaac gave a long sigh as he looked out of the window at the starless night. "Look, I know you mean well. And thank you for caring and being outraged on Heba's behalf. But my family decided a long time ago that the most respectful thing would be to guard her secret and cherish her work privately."

"But people should know! Heba should be posthumously credited for her work. Your family should own the rights to it."

"It's too risky. This is all we have, Nory. These sketchbooks are more than money; they are my great-great-grandmother's honor. She already lost her art to the De-Veers. I will not have her name dragged through the mud in the papers when the De-Veers fight back—which they will. And what if it doesn't go in our favor? Heba signed away her rights to her work . . ."

"Yes, but under false pretenses. That's a crime!"

"And how will your friend Guy prove it? Heba's not here to defend herself. I can't take the risk of losing her art or having her sketchbooks impounded as evidence or something. All the while the De-Veers don't know about them, they're safe. If I go to the press, they won't be anymore. I am not about to hand over the rest of Heba's legacy because a hundred and fifty years ago a corrupt countess lawfully cheated my relative. The De-Veers have everything to gain by me going public, and I have everything to lose."

"Not if you win!"

"I don't want to fight with you, Nory. But if you're looking for a crusade, I'm not it."

"Then why did you show me?"

"Because I like you. And because you clearly love my great-great-grandmother's paintings. I wanted you to know who really filled the pages of the books you cherish so much. I'm trusting you with a great family secret." He looked at her intently. "Am I right to trust you?"

"It just seems so wrong to put them back in the trunk. The world should see—"

He cut her off before she could muster another argument.

"Can I trust you?" he asked again.

She sighed. What could she do? "Yes," she said at last. "Yes. You can trust me."

He smiled then. "Thank you."

Heba's sketchbooks were placed back in the trunk with loving care and the lid locked. But even though they were out of sight, they were definitely not out of Nory's mind, and she felt sure they were still on Isaac's mind too. Because despite the subject being changed for more lighthearted topics, the air was still heavy with the secret in the locked box.

Nory wanted to talk more about it. She had so deeply admired Serena's talent, but Serena De-Veer was a sham, a common crook. There was a hole in the provenance of her books that needed filling. She wanted to know about Heba: Who taught her to paint? What drove her passion? What was her life like, working in service for a wealthy family, the kind of family who could promise you a new life, only to betray you horribly and leave you powerless? But she could tell that Isaac didn't want to talk more about it. Not right now at least.

⮑

The moon and stars were covered over with cloud as Isaac walked her back to the castle. The sky and landscape one dark mass, as if someone had scribbled out the world with a black marker.

"Will you be helping out on the hack tomorrow? You seem to get roped into all sorts of non-gardening events."

"I'll be there to help get you all saddled up and then I'll go back to my actual job. I don't normally have to get involved in castle matters, but we're short-staffed and the marquis wants to make a good impression on your party. We get plenty of week-end parties throughout the summer, and weddings, of course. But not normally a weeklong house party plus wedding. Three or four gigs like yours a year would bring in some much-needed cash."

"The castle does all right, doesn't it?"

"The castle is a money pit. The maintenance alone would make your eyes water, and that's before any improvements are made. So, it's all hands on deck to impress the toffs in the hopes that they'll tell their toff friends, and then maybe I'll finally get a budget for the lost garden."

Nory tried not to be offended on her friends' behalf by the way he kept saying *toffs* and instead inquired: "The lost garden?"

"There's an old walled garden—one of several, actually—just

before you reach the dower house. It's been a dumping ground for as long as I've lived here. The Dower House is central operations for the castle office staff. I've been saying to the marquis for years that he should build the staff their own place; out past the east wing where it would be out of sight but close enough to be practical. Then turn the old Dower House into a holiday rental and let me work my magic on the old garden."

"It sounds like you've got it all worked out."

"I have a lot of time to think when I'm working."

"And what does the marquis think of your grand ideas?"

"He agrees with me. All he needs is a spare half a million to get things started."

"Yikes! No wonder he wants this week to go well. Can you take me there? To the lost garden, I mean?"

"Come find me when you get back from your ride tomorrow afternoon, and if it's not too dark, I'll take you on my tea break."

Nory couldn't help doing an inner yip at the idea of being *taken* by Isaac on his tea break.

"The marquis obviously thinks a lot of you if he takes your advice on how to run his castle," said Nory.

Isaac laughed. "I was born here, remember? I'm the only person who knows the castle the way he does. We're both a part of this place in our own way, and we both want what's best for it."

"But isn't he a *toff*?" Nory teased. "I thought you looked down your nose at toffs."

"But the marquis is different."

Nory opened her mouth to protest, but Isaac held his hands up.

"I know, I know, double standards. But Lord Abercrombie has never made me feel like I am less than him. Whereas some people . . ."

"Okay, point taken."

"It wasn't only your friends. I grew up being the punching bag for snotty-nosed Braddon-Hartmead kids who thought they were better than me. Those things take root."

"I know."

"My adult brain is over it. But there's a part of me . . ."

"You were bullied, Isaac, it leaves scars. You don't need to explain yourself to me."

She remembered Thomas coming home with a bloodied nose on more than one occasion after fighting with the kids from the Pomp. Her brother was argumentative for sure, but she'd lay odds that it wasn't always Thomas who started the fight.

"I spoke to Thomas," said Nory. "About his poking his nose into our business."

"You did? How did that go down?"

"Like a shit sandwich."

Isaac spluttered a laugh.

"He's worried I'll use you and leave you heartbroken," Nory continued.

"That's pretty much the vibe he gave me, although it was *your* heart he was concerned for rather than mine. I can understand a big brother feeling protective of his little sister."

Nory waved away his theory. She doubted Thomas's intentions were that noble.

"I think he's just afraid to cross the streams," said Nory.

"Cross the streams?"

"You know, like in *Ghostbusters*: 'Don't cross the streams!'"

"Are we the streams?"

"Yes. Thomas likes to compartmentalize; the prospect of having his best mate and his sister involved is blowing his tiny mind."

Isaac nodded sagely. "Crossing the streams," he said quietly. "And what do we do about that?"

"That, my friend, is up to you." Nory smiled.

They were back in the courtyard. She reached up and kissed his neck, lingering just a little longer than she needed to, feeling the hitch in his breathing. She stepped away from him, the porch light at her back.

"I'm ready to cross the streams when you are." She grinned before turning and walking purposefully into the castle and closing the door firmly behind her.

# Twenty

The horses milled about the stable yard, white steam pouring out of their nostrils. It was only half past eleven but already the light was dim. The weather was overcast, drizzly and bitterly cold. Nory hoped the ride would warm her up. The stables had been hung with fairy lights, and the water droplets on the cross beams glittered in their reflected twinkle. A Christmas tree decorated with wooden painted horses on strings and small silver horseshoes had been erected at one end of the yard.

Isaac saw her and smiled. She felt the secret he had shared with her tethering them like invisible twine. It had taken Nory ages to drop off to sleep last night after Isaac's revelations about Heba, not to mention the delightfully painful sexual tension that continued to fizz between them.

The party were due to hack across the castle farmland and down to the Mead and Medlar pub in the village—one of the few pubs that still kept a stable for peckish passing riders—for lunch. Since it got dark so early, the plan was to have the horses back safely in their warm stables by four o'clock.

Dev, looking long and lean in his riding gear, mounted his horse like he'd been riding since birth.

"Is there nothing he can't do?" asked Jenna.

Ameerah was shaking her head, mystified. At that moment Dev smiled at Ameerah, and Ameerah smiled back in a way that Nory could only describe as *goofy*. *Really, what was happening to everyone?*

Pippa appeared to be horse-whispering a determined, glossy-black Arabian into doing her bidding, while Charles was talking with one of the stable hands as they walked around the muscular form of a chestnut thoroughbred who knew precisely how amazing he looked.

"Need a hand getting on?" Jeremy asked Nory as Isaac brought a dappled, hardy-looking cob mare to stand near her. Katie was due to arrive this afternoon after a brief visit to her parents' house, and Jeremy had been as skittish as any wild stallion all morning.

Nory gulped at the size of her horse. They never seemed that big when they were frolicking in the fields, but up close, they were intimidatingly tall. She was a fairly good rider; she could certainly hold her own hacking across the fields, but she'd always struggled with mounting. Clearly Jeremy remembered her ungainly attempts from their school days. She wished sexy Isaac with his sexy eyes and ridiculously sexy smile wasn't here to watch her climb onto a horse. Every ounce of last night's allure was about to be obliterated.

She looked around: Ameerah, Pippa, and Charles were now sitting on their mounts, and Jenna gracefully swung one leg over hers and nestled her perfecto gym-bottom into the saddle.

"Come on," said Jeremy. "I'll give you a leg up."

"Thanks, Jez."

"I'll help too," said Isaac.

*Oh, fantastic, this isn't embarrassing at all.*

Nory lifted her leg to hook her foot into the stirrups. Why

were the stirrups always so high up? Clearly they were designed for people with longer, more flexible legs than hers. She sighed, resigned, and looked at Isaac.

"This isn't going to be pretty," she told him. Isaac raised an eyebrow but said nothing.

Using both hands beneath her thigh—cheeks blazing with embarrassment—she hoisted her leg up high while Jeremy, remembering the drill from their gymkhana events, held the stirrup firm and guided her boot into it.

"We'll head on down the lane to the meadow and wait for you there," said Ameerah. Nory felt a glow of gratitude to her friend; Ameerah knew Nory wouldn't want an audience. The others trotted off down the lane, their voices and the braying of the horses becoming fainter as they disappeared out of sight.

Nory threw both her arms over the saddle and pushed off the ground with the other leg. She felt two sets of hands on her backside propelling her upward. The heaving noises they made did nothing for her already disheveled ego. As she swung her other leg over and finally settled herself into the saddle, she wished that this wasn't Isaac's first experience of grabbing her bottom and wondered if he'd even *want* to grab it again after watching her ungainly performance. She ventured a look down and found Isaac smiling up at her.

"Sorry about that," she said.

"Don't be. I enjoyed it."

He was smiling in a devilish way, and Nory wondered if maybe she hadn't blown it after all.

"I'm actually very good in the saddle once I've mounted," she said.

Isaac's smile widened, one eyebrow lifted. "Good to know," he replied.

Jeremy had just mounted his own horse when a shout made them all stop in their tracks. Nory looked over to see Guy rounding the corner of the stables. He was stumbling, clearly drunk.

"Oh, good, I thought I might have missed you," he slurred. "Where's my horse?"

"You said you were going to give the ride a miss, remember?" said Jeremy, patting his horse.

"I changed my mind."

He zigzagged across the courtyard and came up beside Nory. Her horse snorted and stepped back.

"Guy, you're drunk," said Nory, leaning forward to stroke her horse to reassure her.

"How very astute of you, Ms. Noel." He grinned.

"I can't let you ride," said Isaac, holding the reins firm on Nory's horse, who seemed to want to retreat all the way back into her stall.

"Not sure it's down to you, *mate*." He managed to make the word *mate* sound anything but friendly.

The stable hand, Jimmy, came over and stood beside Isaac. "I'm afraid I can't let you ride, sir, not while you're under the influence of alcohol."

Guy leered at him. "I was riding horses when you were still in nappies."

"That may be so, sir, but I can't let you take one of the horses in my charge if you've been drinking."

"Just go back to the house, Guy," said Nory. She could feel her mare tensing beneath her, swinging her head from side to side in clear agitation.

"Don't tell me what to do" came the petulant reply.

"You can't ride in this state. How about I come back to the house with you? We'll get some coffee . . ."

"Oh, fuck off, Nory! Don't patronize me."

She saw Isaac bristle.

"Please don't speak to her like that," Isaac said, his voice even but for a slight tremor of anger.

"You can fuck off too!" said Guy, stumbling forward. Nory's horse snorted, tossing her head and sidestepping to get away from Guy.

"Guy, you're upsetting the horse," said Nory. Isaac held the reins tighter, but she could feel the mare's agitation. She wanted to get off before the horse threw her. Guy was trying to fasten the strap on his riding helmet but gave up and left the strap hanging.

Jeremy dismounted and came over, arms outstretched toward Guy placatingly, as though trying to calm a barking dog. "Come on, mate, let's take a walk."

"I don't want to walk, Jez, I want to ride. You know me, I can ride a horse backward and blindfolded."

"That may be, but you can't take a horse out in this state. For a start, no horse will have you, and I'm not sure the castle's insurance stretches to piss-artist riders." He smiled disarmingly. But today Jeremy's friendly demeanor didn't soothe; if anything it had the opposite effect.

"Come on, then, Nory, let's me and you go back to the castle, have some fun, now the old ball and chain's gone." He winked.

"I don't think so, Guy," said Nory coldly. She didn't want Isaac to think there was anything between her and Guy.

"I think you'd better take him back to the castle," Isaac said quietly to Jeremy.

Jeremy nodded and stepped forward, but Guy had overheard, and in a flash, he was up in Isaac's face, teeth bared, the anger that had been simmering under the surface since Camille had left suddenly breaking through.

"Who do you think you are?" he growled.

The horse whinnied, pulling at the reins.

"Step back," said Isaac firmly.

"You didn't answer my question."

"Guy, come on." Jeremy stood between them and reached for Guy's arm, but Guy shook him off and ducked round him, squaring back up to Isaac. Jimmy, a fresh-faced man in his early twenties, looked alarmed and out of his depth, his head snapping between the men like a tennis umpire.

"Come on, then, big man!" Guy goaded Isaac.

Isaac stood his ground, saying nothing.

"You think you're something? Big fish in a small pond, mate. You're just a fucking gardener!"

"Guy!" Nory snapped. She'd been trying to keep her cool so as not to unnerve the horse any more than she already was, but this was getting out of hand. "Go back to the house and sleep it off, you're being an idiot."

Guy looked up at her and laughed and then said to Isaac: "She always was a feisty one."

"Oh, shut the fuck up, Guy!" Nory said, exasperated.

Guy was still close enough to Isaac that Jeremy couldn't get between them, both men immovable; Isaac because he was trying to keep the horse calm and Guy because he was engaged in some sort of private standoff. His eyes were intent on Isaac. Nory recognized the stance, the angry drunk gunning for a fight.

"Let's go, Guy." Jeremy tried again, pulling him away more forcefully this time. But Guy yanked himself free and fell forward into Isaac. Isaac pushed him back up to standing with his elbow, while keeping hold of the reins. But Guy saw this as a move of aggression on Isaac's part and flew at him.

"You starting, mate?" He grimaced, shoving Isaac hard.

Isaac staggered backward but caught his balance. The horse whinnied and stamped her hooves. The groom hovered in the periphery, clearly wanting to take the reins from Isaac but wary of Guy, who looked wound up enough to lash out.

"Please don't push me," Isaac said with a quiet firmness.

"Jez, get him out of here!" Nory called, properly worried now. "Guy, pack it in."

"What was that, fella?" Guy had gone the kind of deaf that only a drunk man with his blood up can. His focus was solely on Isaac. "Don't push you? Is that what you said?"

He shoved Isaac hard with both hands. Isaac stumbled and lost his grip on the reins; the horse instantly began to rear back. Jeremy tried to grab Guy from behind, but Guy's adrenaline was pumping, and he swung round hard and fast. A crack sounded as his fist connected with Jeremy's jaw. Jeremy went down. Guy was temporarily shocked into inaction. Isaac had recovered his balance, while Jimmy rushed to the other side of the horse and grappled Nory quickly down off the horse's back before the frightened mare could throw her.

Nory's knees were shaking. Guy had always been belligerent when drunk, but she'd never known him to be violent. And Isaac was an unknown quantity.

As the groom helped Isaac get the mare back into her stall and calm her down, Nory rushed to help a dazed Jeremy. Guy was muttering halfhearted "sorrys" at Jeremy.

"Jez, are you all right?" Nory asked, crouching beside him and lifting his face with her hand to inspect him. His lip was split and bleeding freely. Nory rooted around in her pockets and found a clean tissue, which she pressed to his mouth. Katie was going to flip when she saw this.

"Yep," he said, taking over the tissue compression and rubbing his jaw with his free hand. "It's been a while since I've been in a brawl." He tried to smile, then winced. "I think I was probably about nine years old." He attempted a laugh, and blood splattered out onto Nory's coat sleeve. "Sorry, Nory, I'll pay to get it cleaned." His face had drained of color.

"Don't be silly," said Nory soothingly. "It'll wipe off. How do you feel?" She didn't like the sheen of sweat breaking out over his forehead.

"Fine," he said, grinning red. "I need to get cleaned up before Katie arrives." He went to get up and then slumped back to the ground. "Actually, I'm a bit dizzy, I might just stay down for a while."

"That's probably best. Did you hit your head when you fell? Might you be concussed?"

"No, I don't think so." Jeremy gingerly reached his hand to the back of his head. "No, I'm fairly sure I didn't. I think my blood sugar dropped at the shock of being in my first real fistfight."

"It doesn't really count as a fight if only one person throws a punch," said Nory, wrapping her arms around him and kissing the top of his head. He was bleeding on her jacket, but she didn't care. She was determined to send it to the best dry cleaner in London and send the bill to Guy.

"If anybody asks, I got in a few swings before I went down."

"Don't worry, Rocky, your secret's safe with me."

One of the stable hands proffered a wodge of paper towels, which Jeremy took gratefully.

"I feel like such a tit," he grumbled as the blood turned the green paper towels brown.

"Well, I'm hugely grateful that this will be the residual

memory of the morning rather than my ungainly climbing onto a horse." Nory smiled.

"I don't think Isaac minded," Jeremy whispered.

Satisfied that Jeremy was shaken and stirred but not broken, Nory stood and rounded on Guy, who had been hovering and swaying nearby, muttering incoherently. She was so angry with him, she felt as though her heart was pounding outside her chest.

"What are you doing?" she shouted.

"Oh, don't start, Nor, I'm not in the mood. Soz, Jezzer," he garbled.

"You started it by rocking up drunk!"

"Don't try to reason with him, Nory," said Jeremy with his head between his knees.

"You punched your friend in the face, don't you even feel a little bit remorseful, you selfish pig? You could have really hurt Jez."

But Guy wasn't listening. His eyes were fixed on Isaac, who had just emerged from the stables.

"Here he is!" Guy called, his arms outstretched as he stumbled crablike from left to right. "The man of the hour!"

Isaac ignored Guy, walking straight past him and taking Nory gently by the arm to move her a little way across the yard, out of Guy's reach.

"Wos up with you?" Guy jeered. "Strong silent type?"

"Are you okay?" Isaac asked Nory, helping her to unfasten her helmet and taking it from her. With his other hand, he tucked a strand of hair behind her ear. She smiled up at him reassuringly, while Guy swaggered nearby in her peripheral vision.

"I'm fine," she said. "Annoyed and a bit shaky but fine."

"Oy!" came Guy's voice. "Gardener!"

"Ignore him," Nory urged Isaac.

"I intend to," Isaac replied. "But we do need to get him out of here." He looked back at the stables; the remaining horses were braying and banging against their doors.

"I'm talking to you!" Guy shouted.

"Guy, for fuck's sake, go back to the castle and sleep it off!" came Jeremy's muffled voice from between his knees.

"Do you need a doctor?" Isaac asked, kneeling beside Jeremy.

"No, I'll be okay. My arse has gone numb with the cold, though."

Isaac looked at Nory. "If I handle the lager lout, do you think you can help Jeremy back to the castle? I'll get one of the stable hands to go with you."

"Yes, of course," said Nory. "I'm worried about you, though. I've never seen Guy like this. I don't know what he's capable of."

"Don't worry about me." He gestured back to where a small band of surly-looking estate workers had gathered. "I've got plenty of backup." He smiled, then kissed her cheek.

"Oy, oy!" Guy hollered.

Isaac and Nory turned to look at him, Guy pointed straight at Nory.

"Been there, mate! Done that and got the T-shirt!"

Nory barely had time to register her indignance before Isaac strode over to Guy and punched him squarely in the face. Guy went down like a sack of potatoes and lay spread-eagle in a pile of horse dung—just in time for the others to trot back into the courtyard to find two of their friends on the ground bleeding and the other snogging the gardener.

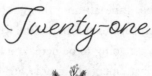

With two of their number incapacitated, the hack had been abandoned before it even began. Nory and Pippa helped Jeremy back to the castle. Guy was manhandled—while sobbing his remorse loudly—from the stables to his room by Charles and Isaac. Charles took his arms and Isaac his legs, while Jenna screeched that he was ruining her pre-wedding party, and Ameerah took photos on her mobile phone, presumably to be used as evidence against him later.

By the time they had gotten back to the castle, Jenna had wound herself up into such a frenzy that she was convinced Guy would be the ruination of her entire wedding, and was threatening loudly that she was going to disinvite him. Even Charles was unable to calm her down.

"Why did we think he would've changed?" she yelled. "He's always been like this; at school he was an argumentative twat and he's still the same now. Even his own wife can't stand him! And how will it look in the wedding album when two of the groomsmen are bloody black and blue? How do we explain that to our future children?"

"Jenna, honey, this will be one of those things we look back and laugh about," said Charles soothingly. "It'll be a great story to tell our children."

But Jenna's ninety-mile-an-hour thought processes had doubled back from their future children to the wedding day.

"*OK! Magazine* are going to be here, and my wedding party looks like they've just emerged from a bare-knuckle fight at a carnival! I need to call my PR and my PA and my agent, where's my fucking phone?"

"Baby, calm down. We can get the photographer to airbrush the bruises out," said Charles.

"I've got a better idea, let's just airbrush Guy right out of the wedding!" She leaned over the banister at the top of the first landing, sending petals and leaves from the garlands fluttering down the stairs as she yelled, "Guy Bailey, I hereby rescind your invitation to my wedding, you utter fuckwit!"

At this point, Dev ambled along the landing, a picture of innocence, his mobile phone held up in front of him at such an angle that it gave the impression he had simply bumped into Jenna screaming on the stairs by accident.

"Sorry to interrupt," he said, laying the kind of potent smile on Jenna that caused women all over the world to lick the pages of *Vogue*. "But I've just noticed that the Robinwood Hotel is running Christmas special spa afternoons. So, I gave them a call and told them we had a rather notable Christmas bride in our midst, in desperate need of some R & R, and they said they could fit us in this afternoon. The full works."

Jenna was beguiled both by the smile and the idea of a full spa.

"The full works?" she asked, smoothing her hair down.

Dev nodded. "They gave me some spiel about short notice at

first, and then I told them who you were, and suddenly they had the whole afternoon free."

Guy and his faults were instantly thrown over for the more pressing matter of being treated like the celebrity she was for the afternoon.

"Charles, I'm leaving shit-for-brains to you. I don't want to see his weasel face again until at least breakfast." Then she turned her attentions to Dev. "Quick!" she squealed delightedly. "Let's get our things and get over there."

Dev's smile was artless as he allowed himself to be led down the hall by Jenna.

Ameerah was watching him from their bedroom doorway, Nory beside her.

"God, he's good," Ameerah whispered. "It's like watching a demon in angel's clothing."

"Almost as sneaky as you at getting his own way," said Nory.

"Almost," agreed Ameerah. "He'd make a great barrister."

"Would you want to go up against him in court?"

"I'd put myself up against him anywhere," Ameerah swooned.

"Not quite what I meant, but okay. How long are you going to keep up this charade?" Nory asked her friend. "I know you like-like Dev."

"How long have you and Isaac been swapping saliva?" Ameerah countered.

"It was a heat-of-the-moment thing."

"And was it good?"

Nory remembered the way Isaac had swept her into his arms, the fire in his kiss, their breath coming hard . . . Nory shook herself, little spikes of pleasure shooting down through her stomach.

"I think it might have been the best kiss I've ever had," she mused.

"It looked pretty Fifty Shades from where I was standing."

"It came out of nowhere; I've never had an out-of-nowhere kiss before."

"The unexpected snogs are always the best. What now?"

"I don't know. We didn't exactly have time to discuss it."

✺

Ameerah, Dev, Jenna, and Pippa left for Robinwood Hotel within the hour. Nory waved them off from the gravel drive. Jenna was still spitting feathers about Guy's behavior, but already he'd been downgraded from Beelzebub to *typical bloody Guy*.

As much as Nory would have liked an afternoon at the spa, she equally wanted to check on Isaac and the horse, and make sure that Isaac wasn't in any trouble with the marquis for punching a guest in the face. Guy was sleeping off his liquid brunch, while Charles and Jeremy had retired to the drawing room with the day's papers.

The afternoon was colder even than the morning had been, the sun clearly having decided to stay home that day. The mist was hanging low over the land like a strip of gauze, smudging the lines of the trees and the fields as they dropped away down the hill, the village completely hidden from view.

Jimmy reassured her that the cob mare had calmed down quickly after a couple of apples and some fresh hay; Nory had a feeling Isaac would be less easy to placate. She went into the stables, which were soothingly warm and earthy smelling, and gave the horse a good brush, apologizing for the behavior of the stupid drunk man that morning.

As she left, a sheen of sparkling frost was beginning to form over the wet cobbles in the courtyard, and Nory was pleased she'd kept her warm clothes and boots on from this morning and not been tempted to change into something that a certain head gardener might find more enticing. Sexy came second to sensible every time. She'd had to swap her bloodstained coat for an old, padded hiking jacket she'd brought as a spare, but it was better suited to this weather so she didn't mind too much.

"Do you happen to know where Isaac went?" she called across to Jimmy, with as much nonchalance as she could muster.

Jimmy grinned at her as he cleaned the mud out of a pony's iron shoe. Who was she trying to kid? All her friends and half the stable hands had watched Isaac sweep her into a Hollywood-style embrace.

She'd never been kissed quite like that before. Certainly not in public. All her most favorite body parts had instantly stood to attention. Even Jenna's high-pitched wailing through the castle hadn't fully cooled her ardor.

"I think he said he had work to do on the cold frames, over near the potting sheds through the gate."

Jimmy winked at her, and Nory attempted a cool stare.

"Hey, you're not related to Thomas Noel, are you?" he asked suddenly.

Nory laughed. "He's my brother, why?"

"You looked just like him when you scowled."

‿͡ᵔ

Nory cut through a gap between the stables and crossed a field where heavy-coated sheep eyed her suspiciously. She climbed over a stile and let herself in through a wooden gate that led to a section of the gardens not open to the public. Here were glass-houses and polytunnels, and tool sheds both wooden and brick built. A network of vegetable patches and raised beds—where most of the produce for the castle was grown—ran along either side of a long path.

Most of Nory's serious relationships had been measured, sensible choices: men she'd thought her dad might approve of—though of course he never did. Even her throwaway flings tended to be disappointing on the passion front. Was she really so hard to please? Was it too much to ask to find a man who could give her better orgasms than she could give herself?

She was still thinking about orgasms when she caught sight of Isaac. He was piling garden trimmings into one of several large wooden compost bins. His discarded zip fleece hung on a fence post, and he worked in just a T-shirt, despite the cold. Nory slowed her pace so she could watch him before he caught sight of her. Lord, but he was good-looking! The muscles in his arms flexed as he reached down into a wheelbarrow and scooped up another load. *Andrew was right, I am turning into Lady Chatterley!* At that moment, Isaac looked up and saw her. Nory smiled and waved as though she'd only just arrived and had not been perving over him.

Isaac smiled at her, his dark eyes glinting as her cheeks flushed. There hadn't been time to discuss their impromptu kiss earlier. When Isaac had dropped Guy—somewhat roughly—into his room, he had left straightaway to speak to the marquis.

Suddenly Nory didn't know what to say.

"Are you okay?" Isaac asked.

"Yes. Yes, thank you, I'm fine. How about you?"

"Good."

"Good, then. Excellent."

"I'm sorry I left in such a hurry . . ."

"Gosh, no, don't be, I completely understand. I'm sorry about the things Guy said to you, about all of it, really."

Isaac frowned and cocked his head to one side. "Why are you apologizing for him?"

"I'm not. I'm just saying that *I'm* sorry on my own behalf, that you had a shitty morning."

"You didn't make it shitty."

Isaac turned his dark brown eyes on her, and her hand automatically went to her mouth. The pads of her fingers brushed her lips, remembering where his mouth had been earlier, the heat in his kiss, the way he had held her so tightly . . . She blinked and tried to bring herself back to the present.

"No, but Guy did. Make it shitty, I mean."

"I thought you weren't apologizing for him."

Nory was quiet for a moment. Was she apologizing for Guy? He certainly didn't deserve it. Maybe she was so used to having to excuse herself she didn't even realize she was doing it—apologizing to her family for her privileged friends and apologizing to her friends for her working-class family. It was exhausting. She'd spent her entire coming-of-age years trying to mediate between and reconcile the two parts of her life, and here she was in her thirties, still doing it. Isaac turned away from her.

"He thinks he's a cut above," said Isaac, steam rising from a compost pile as he turned it over with a pitchfork. "People like him are all the same. When it comes down to it, they think they're better than everyone else. The rest of us are just here to serve them."

"Guy's an idiot," agreed Nory.

"'Just a fucking gardener!' he said to me."

"Yes."

"*Just a fucking gardener?* How can you bear to be around these people?"

"They aren't all like that . . . and anyway Guy's a terrible drunk . . ."

"You're defending him."

"I'm not, I'm . . ."

"Being drunk is no excuse for behaving like an arsehole."

"You're absolutely right."

"All it means is that the alcohol has loosened his inhibitions and he's saying what he really means."

"Well, I . . . the thing is, his wife just left him . . ."

"Still no excuse."

"No."

"God. Now I'm being the arsehole!" Isaac rubbed a hand across his brow. "Sorry, none of this is your fault."

Nory smiled. "It's okay."

"I don't do so well with the whole 'the customer is always right' stuff. Never have done."

"You don't say."

Now Isaac smiled.

"Do you want me to talk to Lord Abercrombie? Confirm your version of events?" Nory asked.

"Nah, don't worry about it. Jimmy and a couple of the other stable hands saw what happened. And Jeremy's already spoken to him on my behalf, said I was acting in self-defense and defending your honor."

"See," said Nory, smiling. "They're not all bad."

She must remember to thank Jeremy. Isaac rested the pitchfork up against the compost heap.

"Come here," he said.

Nory narrowed her eyes. "You're muddy and sweaty," she said, smiling as she moved closer to him.

He returned her smile and hooked his arm around her back, pulling her to him. Nory let herself be pulled; a delightful fizz of excitement made her breath catch. He kissed her once, softly, pulling back just a fraction as though waiting to see if she would push him away. Nory kept her eyes closed, the taste of him still on her lips, hearing the sounds of his breathing, hard and fast, the air taut between them. He kissed her again, more deeply this time, and Nory's breath matched his for speed. She wondered how comfortable the potting shed floor would be. Isaac pressed himself against her and she let out a gasp of delight. *Screw the potting shed*, she thought, *that compost heap looks pretty soft . . .*

"Ahem!"

Nory and Isaac sprang apart like they had electrodes on their genitals.

"Sorry," said a young man, whose cheeks were flushed red in perfect pantomime dame circles. Nory recognized him as one of the groundsmen.

Isaac cleared his throat, grabbed his fleece jacket off the fence post and tied it around his waist. Nory tried to suppress her smile.

"Everything all right, Milo?" Isaac asked, running a hand through his hair.

Milo had the haunted look of a person who had just caught their parents heavy petting. "Er, a deer got into one of the greenhouses."

"Which one?"

Milo looked as though he didn't want to say.

"Not the kitchen garden," Isaac said, trying to read Milo's expression.

Milo nodded.

"Shit the bed." He looked at Nory, one hand rubbing his brow. "You think Jenna was pissed about missing her hack? Wait till she finds out a deer just ate the salad course of her wedding banquet."

Nory followed Isaac and Milo to the garden in question. The greenhouse was in complete disarray. Wooden potting benches had been overturned, pots lay scattered and smashed, and the planters that remained upright showcased the jagged green stubs of what had been salad leaves mere hours before.

"One deer did all of this?" Nory asked, righting one of the benches and bending to retrieve some seed trays from beneath it.

"There could have been more, but one hungry deer can pretty much devastate a veg patch given enough time. And with the threat of snow, they're stocking up on calories," Isaac replied, rescuing some planters that had slid down behind a trestle table out of the deer's reach.

"You don't seem that annoyed."

"You can't blame an animal for wanting to eat, it's just trying to survive."

"What will you do? About the salad course, I mean."

Isaac looked around. Milo was busily sweeping spilled compost and plant detritus into a pile at the far end of the greenhouse.

"There's a couple of nearby farms that supply the village farm shop. I'll ask Jake as well, see if Noel and Son can help us out. They top us up sometimes if we've got a shortfall."

"I'd say you've definitely got a shortfall situation."

Isaac nodded in grim agreement. "It won't completely satisfy the bride's wish for homegrown, but it'll be from within a five-mile radius, which isn't too bad."

"Oh, I wouldn't worry too much, she's having the wedding favors shipped over from a chocolatier in Switzerland, and her own personal wedding blend of coffee beans flown in from Ethiopia. Jenna's carbon footprint concerns are what you might call fickle."

"Maybe you'd like to be the one to tell her about the salad?"

"If you can guarantee me that the farms can provide, then I'll break it to her. But if we're looking at supermarket salad bags, you're on your own."

Isaac grinned and pulled out his phone. "I'll call them now."

"Do you need an extra pair of hands to clean up here?"

"No, thanks. We'll be fine. But I may have to take a rain check on showing you the lost garden later," he said, looking around.

"That's okay. I really ought to go and see how Jez's and Guy's bruises are coming along."

Isaac's expression darkened. "Did you and he used to be together?"

Nory chewed her lip as she considered that this question could be applied to almost *all* of the men in the house party. But she knew Isaac was referring to Guy and his comment at the stables.

"No," she answered honestly. "I made a mistake with him once, a long time ago, but we've never been together."

She could see Isaac processing this information and knew he was considering what form her *mistake* with Guy had taken. But she wasn't going to elaborate. She didn't need to. Her past was her own, and she was the only person allowed to judge her on it.

As if sensing her thoughts, Isaac said, "It's none of my business. I suppose what I was really asking is, do I have competition?"

Nory's smile seemed out of her control.

"No," she said. "You don't have any competition." And then she asked, "Just to clarify, does this mean we are ignoring my brother and the marquis?"

Isaac took her hand. "They're just going to have to lump it."

He leaned in and kissed her lips, just once, slowly, softly, making Nory's body thrill and ache at the same time.

"You're a very good kisser," Nory whispered, stumbling slightly as he moved away from her. She'd heard of people getting punch-drunk, but was snog-drunk a thing?

"You're rather good yourself." Isaac smiled. "I'm finding your lips very hard to resist."

Nory felt immensely pleased with herself and her lips. "Well, I'd better go, leave you to your salad search."

Isaac cast his eyes around and nodded grimly. "But I'll see you tomorrow?" he said, brightening.

"Yes, you will," she said.

She reached up and kissed him, resisting the urge to wrap herself around his body like a vine, and then stepped away from him as though not trusting herself. "Bye, then," she said. And she called, "Bye, Milo!" over to the young man, whose cheeks blotched again.

As she left Isaac and Milo to their damage-limitation exercise, there was one thing of which she was now absolutely sure: Isaac was as hot for her as she was for him, and the knowledge kept her grinning all the way back to the castle.

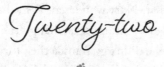

Nory found Jeremy and Charles in the library, where she had left them. They had been joined by Guy, who had taken a shower but looked like a man with one hell of a hangover. He and Jeremy sat on opposite wingback chairs, each intermittently applying ice packs to their swollen faces. Charles motioned for Nory to sit on the sofa next to him and poured her a cup of coffee from a large cafetiere on the side table. The three men were mid-conversation and continued on as Nory sipped her coffee.

"Couple's counseling?" snorted Guy. His voice was nasally from the nosebleed. "You weren't even married."

"You don't need to be married, Guy, you just need to be a couple. It was helpful, I'd recommend it," said Charles.

"What could you have possibly needed it for?"

"That's a bit personal, mate," said Jeremy.

"I'm a journalist, it's my job to be personal."

"Maybe I should go," said Nory. Though she was friends with both Charles and Jenna, her loyalties lay stronger in Jenna's favor. She didn't want to be put in a position where she knew things about her friend that Jenna might not want her to know.

"You don't have to go, Nory. It's nothing Jenna won't tell you herself. At the time, we'd been together for three years . . ."

Guy gave another derisive snort, as though three years didn't qualify as a serious relationship. Why did people in long-term relationships do that? Nory wondered. Why did they judge relationships by longevity rather than happiness? So far as Nory could make out, one didn't guarantee the other.

Charles fixed him with a glare, and Guy shifted in his chair and said, "Sorry. Go on."

"I knew I wanted to spend the rest of my life with Jen, and I knew she felt the same about me, but something was holding us back. Or rather, someone."

Nory suddenly knew where this was going, and she felt a rush of warmth toward her old friend.

"Tristan," said Jeremy, arriving at the same conclusion.

Charles nodded. "There was a part of me worrying that I was second best, that perhaps Jen had latched on to me because she was afraid of missing her chance at love. We all know how Jenna used to feel about Tristan," Charles went on. "I didn't know how I could compete with a ghost."

"But they were over years before you two got together. We were still kids, really, when they were sweethearts," said Nory.

"And you and Jen had been beating about the bush for years," added Jeremy.

"Oh my god, the flirting!" Nory laughed.

"I honestly considered locking the pair of you in a room together just so you could get it on and get it over with," admitted Jeremy.

Charles smiled, remembering, and then his expression clouded, and he said, "But when you've watched the love of your life be so in love with someone else, it makes you question whether you'll ever match up in her mind. First loves are pretty enduring, even after they've ended."

"And what about Jenna?" Guy asked. "Was she worrying about the same thing?"

Charles shook his head. "Not exactly. But that's not for me to say, not to you anyway." He looked pointedly at Guy. "My point in telling you this is that the counseling helped. We talked through all of our issues, and we made peace with them. There are no skeletons rattling their bones in our closets anymore, and it's . . . it's liberating, it honestly is. This is the healthiest relationship I've ever had with another human. We're from the same stock, you and I, Guy, both from families who would rather die than express an emotion . . ."

"You mean repressed as fuck," said Guy glibly.

"That's exactly what I mean. But we don't have to be like our parents."

Nory *wished* her family would adopt a little repression, instead of expressing every emotion they had the second they felt it. She'd been well into her teens before she realized that not everybody expressed themselves quite as openly as her family, and she'd had to work hard at remembering to keep some of her thoughts to herself.

"I get what you're saying," said Guy. "And I admire the way you've broken the mold, I do. It's just not for me. I am what I am. Camille knew what she married, and if she's decided that she can't handle it, then so be it."

"You really are the most conceited person I have ever met," Jeremy mused.

"It's not conceit. I'm accepting that she doesn't want to be with me."

"Do you really think that?" Nory asked. "Because I think Camille is still very much in love with you, even though you are a complete dickhead."

"She'll get over it. She's the most capable woman I've ever met. Nothing rattles her, which is probably why she's put up with me for as long as she has."

"Do you talk to your wife much?" Nory asked. "Genuine question."

"What the hell does that mean? Of course I talk to her."

"Guy, Camille is not okay."

Guy looked at her, confused. "She's fine," he said, brushing her off.

Nory's frustration was rising. "No, she isn't. And if you pulled your head out of your arse, you'd see it. She's struggling. I've known her for like five minutes and I can see it. I don't know if she's headed for a breakdown, but she's headed for something."

Genuine concern flickered across his face. "You don't even know her," he said, suddenly on the defensive.

"Exactly!" Nory retorted. "She had to share her pain with practical strangers because the person who should be listening to her is a narcissistic pig. What does that tell you about the state of your marriage? Or lack thereof, since she's all but left you."

"Don't lecture me on my marriage, little miss can't find a husband!"

"What's that supposed to mean?"

"All right!" Charles held up a hand. "Let's all just take a breath, shall we, before the fists start flying again."

"Nory's right," Jeremy added. "I wasn't going to bring it up because I thought you probably knew, being her husband and all. But Camille is going through something. We had quite a long chat after dinner the other night. I understand that you might have misgivings about couple's counseling, but maybe you should push Camille in the direction of some help."

"I don't want some shrink knowing my business" was Guy's response.

"You'd rather spend your days lifting the lids on other people's secrets than risk exposing your own," said Jeremy dryly.

Guy smiled sardonically. "I prefer to think of myself as a seeker of truth."

Nory had had enough.

"A complete wanker is what you are if you let Camille go," she exploded. "And an irresponsible, heartless bastard if you do nothing while your wife is clearly suffering. Are you really so selfish that you won't even *try* to be a better version of yourself for the sake of your marriage?"

Guy looked at her levelly. "I don't think I've heard so many insults come out of your mouth since the morning after Tristan's funeral."

"You're an arsehole!" said Nory. "I should have asked Isaac to punch you harder."

"I still haven't decided whether I ought to press charges," said Guy, touching the tips of his fingers to his swollen nose.

"Let me help to take your mind off the pain in your face," said Nory. She walked across to where Guy was sitting, leaned over him, and tipped the contents of the cafetiere in his lap. Guy jumped up, yelping and pulling at his crotch. She heard Charles gasp in horror but caught Jeremy's amused expression as she replaced the empty pot on the tray.

"Maybe some coffee will help you to sober up," she said sweetly, and left the library, pulling the heavy door shut with a bang behind her.

# Twenty-three

Nory was lying on her bed, staring at the canopy above. She'd called Andrew to ask about the shop, but also to tell him about the day's events.

"Urrgh!" Andrew made a disgusted noise down the phone. "Men like Guy make my skin crawl."

"There should be a place where people like Camille can go to build up an immunity to shit husbands," said Nory.

"Like an anti-bullshit bootcamp," suggested Andrew.

"Exactly."

"Camille obviously sees something in him that you can't."

"I don't know what!"

"Camille is an intelligent, articulate woman—I follow her on Insta, she's my style guru. Your personal knowledge of Guy has gaps that span years. You've seen him, what, twice in the last five years? She's lived with him day after day, she is privy to the parts of his personality that you don't know. And maybe those parts are the sides of her husband that she's in love with and doesn't want to give up on."

"God. I hate it when you're the voice of reason." Nory pulled a pillow over her face.

"Anyway, that's enough about boring bloody Guy. I want to know when you are going to see the handsome gardener again."

Nory couldn't stop her smile. Isaac seemed to have that effect on her.

"I'm not sure. I think he's going to take me to see a lost garden tomorrow."

"How romantic. Maybe you can get him to service your lost garden while he's at it!"

Nory laughed. "Bye. Kiss Matilda and Seb for me."

A knock at the door caused her to lose count of the roses in the fabric swirls of the canopy.

"Who is it?" she asked, not moving from the bed.

"It's Guy."

"Fuck off, Guy."

No sound of retreating footsteps. Another knock.

"Can we talk?"

"Nope. Fuck off."

"Nory, please. I need to talk to you. I'm going mad here. I don't know what to do."

Nory pulled the pillow back over her face and screamed into it. Like it or not, this was Tristan's legacy. She could never turn her back on a person who needed help, no matter how angry they made her. Suicide had left Nory forever in fear of the worst.

She pulled herself up off the bed and opened the door. Guy stood before her, contrite, in his third change of clothes of the day.

"Can I come in?"

"Into my room? Hell no!"

"That's fair. Somewhere quiet, then, just to talk."

Nory sighed. "Come on, then," she said, pulling the door closed behind her. "But if you try anything, I swear to god, I'll take a set of nutcrackers to your gonads."

As they came down the stairs, the bell for the front door rang. Jeremy shot down past them and skidded in front of the butler to get to the door. Katie stood in the porchway, wearing an oversized parka over baggy dungarees, tucked into a pair of green Dr. Martens boots. Her long box braids were pulled back into a thick ponytail, and she looked as tired as any pregnant woman Nory had ever seen. Husband and wife fell into each other's arms. Jeremy was sobbing and laughing at the same time, Katie was too exhausted to do much other than lean gratefully into her husband and let him hold her up. Nory felt like she and Guy were trespassing on an intimate and much-longed-for reunion, but Katie waved up at them, smiling, and beckoned them down to say hello.

Jeremy stood behind Katie, his arms wrapped protectively around her waist, hands splayed out across her stomach. They made a striking couple, he with his typically Celtic coloring: pale, freckled skin and strawberry blonde hair, and she with her dark skin and jet-black braids. When the greetings were done, Jeremy escorted his wife up the stairs to their room. Nory didn't expect to see either of them again today, but she hoped to get a chance to chat with Katie at some point, to hear about her adventure and her research.

The drawing room was empty. The others weren't back from the spa yet, and Charles had taken the opportunity to catch up on some work.

"I'm sorry," Guy began.

"I'm not interested in your sorrys, Guy; they don't mean anything."

"I felt trapped earlier in the library, like you were all ganging up on me. I reacted badly. I attack when I feel cornered. It's not ideal, it's just how I respond. But I am sorry, for all of it."

"It's not only me you need to apologize to. Your wife would be a good start. Isaac didn't deserve your vitriol either. And Charles was only trying to help. It took a lot for him to open up like that, and you belittled him."

"I know."

"Can't you see how amazing Camille is? Why do you not want to at least try and make things right?"

"That's the problem. She is amazing. She's too good for me."

"If you're looking for me to disagree with you, it's not going to happen." Nory leaned back on the sofa with her arms folded.

"I'm not. She'd be better off without me."

"That's just an excuse because you're too lazy to make the effort to be a better man."

"Maybe you're right. I don't have it in me to be good enough."

Nory frowned. He seemed genuine but she couldn't be sure.

"I'm a fuckup," he went on, his voice cracking. "I love her so much. I spend every waking hour in terror of the moment Camille gives up on me."

"But if you're so afraid of that happening, then why do you keep pushing her toward that conclusion?"

Guy rubbed his eyes and then winced. Gray-blue bruises were beginning to bloom in the sockets. He looked worn down. Without his cocksure bravado, he was just a sad, tired man who drank too much.

"I don't know how to explain it," he said, staring at his wedding ring. "If she leaves me, then I can stop worrying about it, it'll be done, and I can get on with my life."

"Guy, that makes absolutely no sense. You are perpetuating a behavior that will bring about something that you don't want to happen, just because you're tired of worrying that it *will* happen. Do you see the madness in that?"

"I didn't say it made sense. I'm explaining to you what is happening in my head. I have never been good enough. God knows my father's taken every opportunity to remind me that I never reached my *potential*. And then this amazing woman falls in love with me. And it's real. She really loves me—I couldn't believe it. I tried so hard to ignore the voice in my head. I even thought maybe I *could* be the man Camille thought I was. Then the kids came along, and all I could think was, I'm so lucky, I don't deserve to be this happy. But I knew I wasn't good enough for them, I knew I would let them down."

Nory didn't know what to say.

Tears pooled in Guy's eyes, and he blinked them away, rubbing at them roughly with his sleeve.

"It's agony to know you don't deserve the things that you love most in the world," he said, looking at Nory helplessly. "I just want it to be over. Camille is suffering, and it's all my fault."

"*Some* of it *is* your fault, but I think she's also going through some stuff that has nothing to do with you. I think you're both having these huge life crises and suffering in silence."

"Do you really think she's in danger of having a breakdown?"

"I don't know, Guy. I'm not a professional. All I know is she's hurting."

"I don't want her to hurt," Guy sobbed. "I can't stand it."

"I know you don't want to hear this, but Charles is right. You need counseling. You need counseling, and Camille needs counseling, and then you and Camille need counseling together."

"That's a lot of counseling for a man who doesn't like talking about his problems." Guy gave a halfhearted laugh.

"Yes, well, your lack of talking has messed you up and now you've got to unpick all the knots you've created."

"Thank you, Nory. I am genuinely sorry that I'm such a shit."

"Stop being a shit and I'll accept your apology."

～

Nory grabbed a coffee and went back to her room. She wondered if it was too late for Guy to change. Was there an age at which personalities became in stone? She hoped not. She'd like to think that redemption was always a possibility. She thought of her brother's innate ability to always jump to the worst possible conclusion where she was concerned. He surely loved her deep down, so what was it that kept them so at odds? Was it a habit so entrenched it had become subconscious? And if so, would they ever be able to break the cycle? She wondered how bad the fallout would be when he found out she and Isaac had decided to ignore his impolite requests not to get involved with each other. She wasn't looking forward to that conversation one bit!

"G ood morning, milady!"

"Woof! Somebody ate a lot of garlic last night, milady!"

"I am sorry to say that milady's morning breath stinks, milady!"

Nory pulled the duvet down to find Shelley and her mum dropped into low curtsies beside her bed.

"What the fuck?" She laughed hoarsely, rubbing the sleep from her eyes. "What time is it?"

"Seven fifteen, milady," said her mum.

"You're a lazy fecker, milady," added Shelley.

"How did you get in? I locked the door." She knew with certainty she had locked the door just in case Guy decided to come back.

"Andy lent us the skeleton key," said Shelley, climbing into bed beside her. "So, this is how the other half live."

*What is the point of locking doors around here?* Nory wondered.

"We thought we'd surprise you," said her mum. "It's all go today. We've brought up a load of flowers from the nursery, and we're expecting a big delivery up here in a bit. It's going to take us all day to get the castle dressed and ready for the wedding tomorrow."

"What time did you get here?" Nory asked.

"Half six," Shelley replied. "We wanted to get the old garlands down while it was quiet. We've just finished clearing down, ready to start all over again."

"Is anyone else up?"

"The bride's just gone out for a run, and your friend Pippa was already rearranging furniture when we arrived," said her mum. "She drinks a lot of coffee, doesn't she?"

*Jeez! Doesn't Pippa ever sleep?* She seemed to go to bed last and get up first.

"I really like her," said Shelley. "She's a powerhouse. I think I'm going to enjoy collaborating with her."

"Dad's already mapping out all the places we'll go once you're bringing in the London money."

"Are you going on holiday?" Nory asked, climbing out of bed and leaving Shelley to spread her limbs out into a starfish in her sheets.

"Holiday? We're retiring, my love."

Nory stopped mid-rummage through her toiletry bag. "Retiring?" she exclaimed.

"Semi-retiring. Your dad turns sixty-nine next birthday, and I'm not far behind him."

"No, I know that. It's just, I never thought you'd get Dad to retire."

"Oh, we'll still keep our hands in, you know your dad. But the business is doing well, and I said to him, 'You've spent every spare minute of the last twenty years working on that camper van in the yard, and if we don't make use of it soon, the only journey we'll be making in it will be in our coffins on the way to the chapel.'"

"Blunt," said Nory.

"Nothing short of sledgehammer sentiment makes it through Dad's thick skull. We're doing a European tour."

"Like the Rolling Stones," Nory added.

"Rolling Bones, more like," Shelley quipped from beneath the duvet.

"That's enough of your lip, Shelley Noel." Nory's mum waggled her finger in Shelley's direction. "You planning on staying in that bed all day, Lady Muck?"

"If you don't mind," said Shelley, rolling over and nestling into the pillows.

"I'll tell Thomas you were sleeping on the job," Nory teased, through a mouthful of toothpaste foam.

Shelley huffed and climbed out of the bed.

"Let's leave the countess to her ablutions!" said her mum.

"Laters, princess!" added Shelley.

Nory stuck two fingers up as the two women backed out of the room, curtseying and muttering, "Thank you, milady."

A waiter passed a piece of paper to Nory as she left the breakfast room. *We are go for salad! You may now tell the bride. P.S. I'll be in the Winter Garden at 11 a.m. if you'd like that tour around the lost garden. Isaac. x*

Nory grinned to herself and slipped the note into her pocket. The castle was ringing with the sounds of hammering, radios tuned to different channels in different rooms, and instructions being shouted. It had begun in earnest when the last guest was officially awake, and looked set to continue indefinitely. People ran up and down the stairs and darted in and out of rooms as the castle began its transformation from stately home to wedding venue. Nory felt uncomfortable being a guest in the castle while her sister-in-law and her mum worked on the flowers, and was glad of an excuse to slope off for a while later.

Katie and Jeremy had had their dinners sent up to their room last night and didn't make it down for breakfast either; Jenna was doing her level best not to pout about it. She had returned from the spa yesterday evening a calmer woman. But that serenity had dissipated this morning, with the arrival of Elsa, the PR woman for *OK! Magazine*, who wanted to "nail down" tomorrow's run of events, and an accompanying journalist who would be interviewing the bride and groom for the piece. Pippa and Elsa were already locking horns over who had seniority regarding the wedding.

"I'm glad not to be involved in this particular power play," said Ameerah as Jenna shrieked down the stairs: "I don't give a fuck who's in charge as long as someone gets me a goddamn double-shot cappuccino! And where the pissing hell is the sodding spray-tan woman, Pippa? I need time to develop."

"Maybe I'll tell her about the salad later," Nory mused.

"Oh, I'd get it over with now if I were you; this volcano's only going to get more volatile as the day goes on."

"I'd forgotten she could be like this."

"Had you? Lucky you."

"Are you and Dev coming down to the tree lighting later?"

"I wouldn't miss it."

"I hope the school tour is done by then."

"Christ, whose idea was this particular trip down memory lane?" Ameerah asked.

"Charles and Guy's. They wanted to relive the *glory* years.

Plus, I think it's a good excuse to get out of this madhouse for a couple of hours."

"Typical! They were the only ones who found those years glorious. The rest of us were just trying to get through it without PTSD."

"It wasn't that bad," said Nory.

"Not for you! You had a normal loving family to go home to at weekends and holidays."

"Define 'normal.' And anyway, you did all right, you spent most of the holidays at ours."

"When I wasn't summoned by my parents to be their trophy daughter, from wherever they had moored the yacht."

"Oh, you poor dear thing. It must be so tiresome being rich!"

Ameerah laughed and made to elbow her, but Nory sidestepped and she missed. Dev meandered up the corridor, whistling. He smiled when he saw them.

"It's all starting to get a bit explosive around here," he said.

"Don't you mean expletive?" Nory asked, just in time for Jenna's voice to ring down the hall: "Where the fuck is my fucking tiara?"

Dev winced. "I say we take a walk down to the village, grab a couple of papers, and hole up in the White Hart until the school tour," he suggested.

"That sounds perfect," said Ameerah. And again, Nory couldn't help noticing the way her eyes seemed to come alive when she was around Dev. She hoped her friend wouldn't wave goodbye to someone she really liked because of a silly pact she'd made with herself when she was a teenager.

"Fancy joining us, Nory?" he asked. "You're very welcome."

"Thanks, but I've got somewhere to be. You enjoy yourselves, and I'll see you later up at the school."

Nory left it as long as she could before she knocked on Charles and Jenna's bedroom door. Pippa opened it and arched an eyebrow. Jenna was sitting cross-legged on a four-poster that made the one in Nory's room look like a child's bed. She had the most enormous rollers Nory had ever seen in her hair and was verbally losing her shit down the phone to someone, who didn't appear to be answering back. Charles was standing next to the en suite, looking nervous.

"Welcome to the bridezilla suite," Pippa drawled serenely, as though she were not in charge of organizing an entire wedding and managing a medium-freaked Jenna. "I have to go downstairs and tell some people what to do. Don't mention Juliet Finnegan."

Nory was confused. "The one who plays the barmaid in *Days and Nights*?"

Pippa nodded infinitesimally and widened her eyes in a way that warned *Keep your voice down!*

Nory brought it down to a whisper. "Why would I be likely to mention her name?"

"Don't you read the gossip columns?"

Nory shrugged.

"Juliet Finnegan just announced her engagement!"

"So?"

"The day before Jenna's wedding! Talk about thunder stealing. The bride-to-be is not taking it well."

Nory was suddenly barged out of the way by a woman swinging a Gucci handbag, who strode into the room wearing stilettos so skinny they left dents in the carpet.

"This is a clear act of aggression on Juliet's part, darling," she snapped. "I've created merry hell with her agent. She's got *Prima* and *Heat* covering, but we've still got *Grazia*, *Cosmo*, and *Woman and Home*. Is *OK!* here yet?"

"That's Prue, Jenna's publicist," Pippa said quietly into Nory's ear.

Nory was barged for the second time in as many seconds by Elsa, the *OK!* rep, who materialized seemingly from nowhere, looking chic in a Chanel poncho, followed by a nervous waiter carrying a tray of coffees.

"Here!" said Elsa triumphantly.

"Thank god!" cried Prue, and the two women exchanged air-kisses before perching themselves on either side of Jenna's bed like two stone lion gate guardians.

"Right," said Pippa, seeing her opportunity, "I'm off." She slipped past Nory into the hall. "See you at the school tour, if I get time."

Charles was hot on Pip's heels. "Too much estrogen in here for me." He grimaced on his way past Nory.

Jenna finished with whoever it was she was roasting over the phone and allowed herself to be enthusiastically consoled by Elsa and Prue. Nory, who had been hovering while the trembling waiter took orders for egg white omelets and smoked salmon, stepped forward as he left.

"Ahem, Jenna?"

Elsa's and Prue's heads swiveled toward Nory and regarded her like two tawny owls eyeing up a mouse.

"This probably isn't a great time, but I said I'd tell you, although it's nothing to worry about and it's all in hand."

"Nory, what are you talking about?" Jenna asked, perplexed.

"It's about the salad . . ."

"The what?" asked Jenna. Her head was cocked to one side, her expression asking, *Why are you bothering me?*

Nory's palms felt clammy. She could feel disapproving glares coming from Elsa and Prue. "The wedding salad, the salad for the starter."

"Nory, why are you talking to me about salad leaves?"

"Well, the thing is, a deer ate them. But it's all okay; Isaac has managed to source enough locally for it not to be a problem. He just wanted to let you know because you'd asked for homegrown and it won't be homegrown, but it will be up-the-road-grown, which is equally as good. So, you don't need to worry, it's all good, the problem has been nipped in the proverbial bud." Nory smiled widely to illustrate that there was no cause for alarm.

Jenna blinked slowly like a cat. "A deer."

"Yes."

"Why would a deer want to eat my salad?"

"Maybe it was on a diet?" Nory suggested.

Nobody laughed. *Tough crowd!* she thought.

Quite suddenly and dramatically Jenna threw herself back onto the pillows and gave a sigh so sorrowful it was as though a tortured specter had just entered the room.

"This wedding is a disaster," she moaned. "Both the grooms-men have got double black eyes, I'm being eclipsed by bloody Juliet bloody Finnegan, and a deer ate my salad!"

Pippa walked back into the room and stood next to Nory as Jenna began punching a pillow and wailing, "I hate deer!"

"Congratulations," said Pippa. "You broke the bride."

Nory slipped out of the bedroom and pulled the door shut to the sound of Jenna's high-pitched whimpering: "Is it too much to ask that my wedding breakfast not be eaten by the pissing local wildlife?"

She decided it might be best to lie low for a few hours, and she knew just the place to do so.

# Twenty-five

It had snowed again in the night, and the ground had been cold and dry enough for it to stick. Nory found Isaac in the Winter Garden, as promised. He was busy with a pair of elongated clippers, pruning the branches of a large pear tree that hung over the wall. On her way over to him, she stopped to check the unnamed hellebore he had cultivated. Several more flowers had formed, which would last long into the winter months, adding a burst of much-needed color in the gray days to come. The open blooms were striped through with cerise slashes that bled like tiny veins into the pale rose-white petals. The buds resembled fat acorns of deep puce, the petals so tightly packed within that they looked as though they would burst if you squeezed them.

Nory heard Isaac's footsteps approaching, but she stayed where she was, crouched among the flower beds. He joined her in crouching.

"Checking out my handiwork?" he asked.

Nory smiled but didn't look at him. "Have you registered them yet?"

"It's on my list of things to do," he said.

"What else is on your list?"

She looked at him then and smiled.

He leaned forward and kissed her gently on the lips, and she almost overbalanced into the flower bed.

"Well, that was number one on the list," he said.

"Glad I could help you tick something off," she said, pulling herself up to standing and hoping she didn't look as flustered as she felt.

He stood too and took her gloved hand into his. "Shall we?" he said, motioning to the gate.

"Are we *officially* fraternizing now?" Nory asked.

Isaac looked coy. "I may have mentioned my intentions to Lord Abercrombie when I saw him last night."

"Your intentions being?"

"Copious fraternizing!"

A laugh burst out of her. "You did not say that to the marquis."

"No, I didn't. But I did tell him that I'd been enjoying spending time with you in an unofficial capacity."

"And?"

"And he said he was glad that we had finally put our mudslinging days behind us."

"He remembers that?"

"I guess so."

"Well, that's not embarrassing at all."

"At least you didn't live here; all my youthful misdemeanors were played out under the watchful gaze of the castle staff."

"Okay, you win."

The lost garden was not so much lost as abandoned. When Lord Abercrombie's father decided to open the castle to the public in the seventies, the old Dower House was *temporarily* taken over by the newly expanded office staff until more suitable accommodation could be found for them. They were still waiting. And the Dower gardens, tucked away—as was the dowager herself because historically, heirs who inherited country piles did not want their predecessor's widows hanging about—were out of sight and therefore easy to put out of mind. So they had fallen further and further down the priorities list, until Isaac had become their advocate.

Isaac shoved at a wooden gate in the wall, so perfectly devoured by ivy that only someone who knew the land well would know there was a gate there at all. The gate gave reluctantly, tearing a half-moon hole in a mat of old leaves as it opened. There was no discernible path, and trees had self-seeded and grown up in places the original gardeners would never have intended. Thorny brambles arched over everything like huge green coils of barbed wire. What might once have been topiary were now wild-haired giants blocking out the winter sun. Hollyhocks stooped, brown and withered above the green mounds of next spring's foxgloves and forget-me-nots. The gardens may have lacked human guidance, but Mother Nature had not sat idle.

"What do you think?" Isaac asked, leading her through an archway into another garden, equally as unkempt. A weeping willow stood at the center, its long, naked branches cascading down like tangled hair to brush the tops of the brambles, which rose up to meet them. The garden was alive with the tinkle of running water courtesy of a mossy gargoyle head on one wall, dribbling lazily into a green pool.

"I love it," said Nory, looking around. "What will you do with it if you get the go-ahead?"

"What would you do?"

"I'm not a gardener."

"But if you were given this space, what would you do with it? I am genuinely interested to know."

Nory looked around her. She could see through the overgrown archway into the next garden, which was as tangled and snarled up as its neighbors. "Do you have access to the original plans?"

"Yes."

"Hmmmm. You know, I can see the merit of restoring the gardens to what they would have been like. But equally, I kind of like the way they've been reclaimed by nature. Obviously, they need cutting back and some serious TLC for their own good, but is there a way that you could give a nod to the old gardens while keeping them a bit more free? Let them be wildly cultivated?"

"Wildly cultivated," Isaac repeated. "I like that."

"It feels magical here, and I think other people would feel it too."

Her eyes did another lap of the neglected garden before settling on Isaac. He was watching her.

"What?" she asked, smiling.

"I was hoping you would say that. The marquis is keen to do a precise restoration, but I want to keep the essence of what it's become. I needed another opinion, to see if my idea was too out there."

"And my idea matched yours?"

"Almost as if you'd read my mind. It's actually a bit unnerving."

Nory laughed. "Did I not mention I was psychic?"

"How would you feel if I sent you some designs? I know you've got the shop and everything, I'm not talking about a full collaboration or anything. But it would be nice to bounce some ideas off someone who feels the energy of the place."

"I'd love that," Nory replied.

She felt warm with satisfaction. And not only because Isaac valued her opinion; he was talking about keeping contact after she went back to London. She had tried not to think about her growing feelings for him. She had kept her hopeful little heart tightly bound to protect it from disappointment, telling herself that whatever this was would be a holiday fling, nothing more. But Isaac had just handed her a license to dream.

In the far corner stood a bony hawthorn tree, its thorny branches peppered with bright ruby berries, which were attracting a flock of hungry starlings.

"Is that . . . ?" Nory made her way over to the tree; some of the braver—or hungrier—starlings squawked indignantly at her but remained in the branches. Isaac followed her over. "It is!" she said, grinning.

Growing over one of the bigger branches in a matted ball of pea green leaves and small white berries was a large mistletoe plant. Isaac looked at it and he smiled too.

"Well, I'll be," he said.

Without stopping to think, Nory reached up and kissed him. Isaac responded, pulling her close to him, wrapping his arms around her. Every part of her felt alive, singing with pleasure in the places where he touched her and aching with want in the places he did not. They stumbled back against a wall, his mouth still on hers, her back against the cold stone as Isaac pressed hard against her. They explored each other as best they could through their arctic layers, giggling and fumbling like teenagers behind the bike sheds; gloves flung asunder, they gasped delightedly as cold fingers found warm skin. Eventually the cold won out and they stood, nose to nose, lips red and bee-stung, breath clouding fast between them.

"I wish we could go back to mine," Isaac said. His eyes were closed, and he was still pinning her to the wall. "But I have to work. It's the tree lighting tonight."

"And I have to go and look at my old school with Bridezilla."

Isaac laughed quietly. "Maybe you could come to the cottage this evening?"

"If I can get away, I would like that very much."

ꙮ

Nory snuck back into the castle via the trade's entrance, with ruddy cheeks, mussed hair, and the back of her jacket green with moss juice. It was lucky that she had thought to bring her smart fitted woolen coat with her, as she didn't think her soiled jacket would cut the mustard at Braddon-Hartmead. She was getting through jackets at a rate of knots this week. She had pulled off her boots and was consulting with Andy—who was beginning to feel like her personal handyman—in the laundry room about how best to get moss stains out of Gore-Tex, when a howling like a werewolf struck by a silver bullet rang out through the castle.

Andy, in his usual unharried fashion, raised one eyebrow and said, "The bride, I presume."

"I'd better go!" said Nory.

"Leave the jacket with me," he said, taking it from her. "I'll have it sent up to your room."

"Thanks, Andy, I owe you one," she said, before scooting off in search of Jenna, skidding along the stone floors in her haste.

From making out beneath the mistletoe to bride taming in under an hour. This week had felt like Nory was living two parallel lives. One steeped in old memories and allegiances, their historical tapestries tightly interwoven. The other new and un-charted, with needles threaded and canvas ready, but the design not yet fixed. Nory was no stranger to navigating more than one world at a time. The struggle was keeping true to herself as she slipped between them.

# Twenty-six

J enna was standing at the top of the stairs, hair wrapped in a muslin turban and a towel around her naked torso. She was hyperventilating while a group of women—one of them Prue and none of them Pippa—clucked around her ineffectually. Even from halfway up the stairs, Nory could see that Jenna was a most peculiar color. When she reached her friend, Jenna's eyes were so round that if she hadn't known better, she would have said she was on drugs.

"I'm the color of a pumpkin!" Jenna wailed before collapsing into Nory's arms. The other women saw their chance and made a quick exit, almost tripping over one another on the stairs in their haste to be gone.

Nory held her friend tightly as the sobs ripped through her.

"Okay, okay," Nory soothed. "Let's get you back into the bedroom, and we'll sort this out." Although she wasn't quite sure how.

Inside the bedroom, with the light spilling in through the large windows, the spray tan didn't look any better. If anything, it was worse—less pumpkin and more cheesy Wotsits.

Jenna collapsed onto the bed and sobbed into her pillow while a woman who looked as though she herself favored the tangerine shades on the color chart was feverishly stuffing a pop-up spray tent into its bag.

Nory addressed the woman. "Why are you leaving? You need to fix this. Can you respray her? Maybe with a darker color?"

"I will not have my work insulted like this!" spat the woman. "In ten years, I've never had anyone be as rude to me as her." She pointed at Jenna, who had curled into the fetal position.

"Was that before or after you turned her into a human carrot stick?"

The woman glared at Nory, and Nory stared levelly back at her.

"That is my own blend. It's called Miami Vibrance," the woman said unapologetically. "I've never had any complaints before. My other clients love it."

"Do your other clients live with Willy Wonka at the chocolate factory?"

The woman scowled, and Nory decided to try another tack.

"Look, I'm sorry to be rude. We're just not accustomed to Miami Vibrance, so it's come as a bit of a surprise. Is there anything you can suggest to tone it down a bit? My friend is getting married tomorrow. I understand accidents . . ."

"It's not an accident."

Jenna let out a heart-wrenching sob, and the woman seemed to relent.

"Her skin tone has reacted to the amount of DHA in the solution. She's paler than I expected; she already had a tan, and I assumed it was natural."

"Okay. What can we do?"

"Make up a scrub of brown sugar, coconut oil, and lemon juice. Rub it all over, then shower off. Then cover her in coconut oil again, let it soak in for a bit, and then stick her in a bath and leave her there for a while."

"Thank you," said Nory.

"Does this mean I'm not getting paid?" the woman asked grudgingly.

"At this point I wouldn't push your luck."

⟳

Twenty minutes later, having raided the chef's larder, Nory was slathering homemade body scrub all over her friend. Pippa sat on the edge of the bath pointing out the bits Nory had missed, in between texting and taking calls from people who were doing her bidding in varying parts of the castle.

"Do you think it'll work?" Jenna was looking down at Nory with pleading eyes. She was standing in the bath in nothing but a black thong. The bath looked as if it had been pebble-dashed, and Jenna smelled like a lemon drizzle cake. The encroaching bridezilla of the last few days was gone, and Nory's old friend was back.

"I really hope so. I don't want to have spent the last forty minutes rubbing coconut oil all over your tits for you to still be the color of a baked bean."

Jenna gave a small giggle. Nory had stripped off her jeans and socks and was kneeling in the bath scrubbing at Jenna's orange knees, in just her knickers and a T-shirt.

"Guy would literally come in his pants if he could see this," said Pippa dryly.

"Guy must never know of this," Nory stressed. "Okay, turn around and bend over, I need another go on the backs of your thighs. I don't know what that woman puts in her tanning solution, but parts of you are striped like a tiger."

Jenna groaned.

"Where did you even find her?" Pippa asked.

"On the internet. I just wanted a last-minute top-up."

"You got that, all right, you should have let me sort it." Her phone buzzed, and Pippa answered it straight away. "Yes. No. Put it in the fridge. I don't care, I've paid you to make me a croquembouche tower to feed a hundred, and that is what I expect to find when I come down there. Don't disappoint me." She hung up, and Nory was glad she didn't work for Pippa. "The left shoulder blade needs more work."

"I'm on thigh duty," said Nory. "You get the shoulder blade."

Pippa huffed, but after tapping out another lightning-fast message, she placed her phone on the side of the sink and scooped up a handful of scrub. All three of them were scrubbing and laughing—the atmosphere becoming less fraught with each glob of orange scrub flicked into the bath—when the bathroom door opened. Charles stood in the doorway with an expression on his face that was halfway between confusion and delight.

"I was t-told there was a p-problem," he stammered.

"All under control," said Pippa, as though finding two women massaging your naked fiancée in the bath was completely normal.

"Close your mouth, darling," added Jenna.

"But. What is happening?" he asked.

"You may have noticed that your wife-to-be is currently the color of Fanta," said Nory.

"Although, I'd say we've already faded her to a ripe apricot," added Pippa.

"It's not so easy to see at the moment because I'm covered in brown sugar," said Jenna. Even her face was caked in the brown lemony-scented crust. "But I was spray-tanned by a woman who thought being the color of marmalade was the height of sophistication. I was very sad earlier, but now I feel much better."

"She's had three-quarters of a bottle of wine," said Nory.

"And two old-fashioneds," added Pippa.

"She's more relaxed now."

"I don't think I'll be able to join you on the school tour, darling. Once I've showered this off, I've got to smother myself in coconut oil, leave it for an hour to soak in, and then wallow in the bath until I prune."

"But the end result should be that you don't marry Garfield," said Nory.

"Or Donald Trump," put in Pippa.

"Is my cleavage still luminous?"

Jenna turned around, and Nory stood up to look. "It could do with a bit more of a scrub," she said.

"I— I'm just going to— I need to, um, I have to go," said Charles, and he pulled the bathroom door shut behind him.

"I think we frightened him off," said Pippa.

"He wouldn't have lasted five minutes in the girls' dormitory," Jenna mused.

"Though it wasn't for the want of trying," Pippa quipped.

"Do you think it's weird that we've all slept with my husband-to-be?" Jenna asked.

Nory stopped to consider this, mid–cleavage scrub. They'd not spoken about it in their adult lives, the closeness they had shared as young adults, which had ultimately translated to bed-hopping.

"Maybe to an outsider," said Nory. "But we were always together; our friendship was pretty intense. And anyway, it's not like we were all sleeping with the same person at the same time;

it just happened that from the age of fifteen to nineteen we all kind of took it in turns to be boyfriend-girlfriend."

"Some of us were girlfriend-girlfriend," added Pippa.

"I wonder if any of them were boyfriend-boyfriend?" Nory mused.

"Oh, one hundred percent."

"The only one of us who didn't sleep with Charles back then was me!" Jenna laughed.

"You were mostly with Tristan," said Nory.

"Except when you were with Guy," Pippa reminded her, and they all made retching noises.

"Jeremy was always sweet," said Nory.

"Still is," agreed Pippa. "They all are, really." And then, quite out of character for Pip, she added: "Tristan would be so happy for you and Charles."

"He would, wouldn't he?" Jenna smiled.

"He knew Charles was in love with you, even back then. He told me once. He said he felt kind of bad that they both loved you but that Charles could only stand and watch."

"He's not standing on the sidelines anymore." Nory smiled at Jenna, whose eyes were glassy from more than just the lemon-juice fumes.

"He'd also be rather pleased to see you and the gardener's kid have finally laid your weapons down," said Pippa knowingly.

"I've been thinking about that," Jenna chimed in. "There's a meal going spare tomorrow. I had hoped Camille might have changed her mind and come back, but . . ."

"Can you blame her?" asked Pippa.

"So, anyway," Jenna continued, "I wondered if you'd like to bring Isaac as your date to the wedding."

"I'd love to. Thanks, Jenna, that's really lovely of you."

"It's the least I can do since you've spent the last hour trying to de-tangerine my crevices."

"What are friends for?" Nory smiled.

∽

They showered Jenna down, then smothered her all over with coconut oil and left her spread-eagled on a layer of towels on the bed with a book and a glass of red. Nory had set an alarm for an hour, after which Jenna was to transfer herself to a hot bath for a good long soak. This was the last stage in Project De-luminous Jenna's Skin.

"Better to miss the tour than look like one of the Muppets in a wedding gown tomorrow," Jenna had giggled. A member of the staff had laid a roaring fire in the hearth, and by the time they left, Nory was rather jealous of Jenna's afternoon ahead.

# Twenty-seven

The idea had been to walk across the castle grounds to get to Braddon-Hartmead, but it was bitterly cold. In the end, the party split itself between Ameerah's Mini Countryman and Jeremy's old Range Rover.

Even as an adult, Nory found the school building to be imposing. She wondered if it was still as drafty as it had been when she had boarded. A prefect met them on the steps and led them into the entrance hall, which had been decorated for Christmas, and disappeared off to tell the head teacher that they had arrived.

For a moment, the old pupils stood silently, awed by remembrance. Katie and Dev, who had not attended Braddon-Hartmead, were suitably impressed by its grandeur. The splendor of the public areas had always belied the more modest reality of student life: cold dormitories and even colder shared bathrooms, parquet floors sticky with a century of yacht varnish, classrooms with ancient desks and peeling plaster, and a food hall that more resembled a crumbling monastery than Hogwarts.

The headmistress was not much older than the gaggle of ex-pupils and their partners who stood before her. Ms. Strathmoore wore a long old-fashioned teaching gown, unfastened to reveal a 1940s-style trouser suit that may or may not have been, but probably was, Dior. The wireless earbud tucked discreetly into her left ear and the Apple Watch just visible below the gown sleeve, confirmed that there was nothing fusty about the current headmistress. When Nory had attended Braddon-Hartmead, the headmaster was well past retirement age. He had believed television was the devil's work, "the cause of an epidemic of slackened brains!" And he felt that the removal of corporal punishment in schools was a violation of his human rights; he kept his cane laid across his desk to remind him of happier times.

"It is always such a delight to be visited by our alumni." Ms. Strathmoore smiled, showing all her straight white teeth. "I was hoping that Ms. Baxter would be in attendance . . ." She craned her neck to look past Dev and Jeremy, who stood at the back, as though Jenna might be hiding behind them.

"Oh, she's tied up with wedding things, I'm afraid," said Charles. "Bride-to-be and all that."

Ms. Strathmoore's smile drooped, just for a second. "Of course," she agreed.

The tour took them through the old halls, omitting the shabbier corridors below stairs, and through the new science labs.

"These were completed in 2014. We are very lucky to receive continued donations from benefactors long after their children have left Braddon-Hartmead to make their way in the world."

With a wave of her hand, she directed their gaze to a plaque above the entrance to one of the laboratories, which read *Donated by Mr. Montague-Smythe, with thanks*. Charles flushed.

"And of course, we mustn't forget the generous and continued donations from the Bailey family," she went on. Now it was Guy's turn to look uncomfortable. "Mr. Bailey, I've been doing my homework, and I see that you are now the proud father of your own children; I hope that in the not-too-distant future we'll be able to welcome the next generation of Baileys through the doors of Braddon-Hartmead."

"Not if Camille has anything to do with it," Ameerah whispered.

Guy looked pained.

"She's like a marketing machine," Pippa added. "Has anyone checked to see if she's got a USB charging port at the back of her neck?"

They moved on past the English block and stopped at the library.

"This is our most popular place for donations. Benefactors old and new have been drawn to the idea of inspiring a passion for literature in future Braddon-Hartmead pupils. Mr. McIntosh and Ms. Hadid"—she looked first at Jeremy, then Ameerah—"your families have made generous donations to our beloved library over the years."

"She has really done her homework," Charles murmured.

"She won't mention my family," said Pippa through almost entirely closed lips as Ms. Strathmoore continued to gush about benefactors and pupils who had gone on to become famous. "My mother sued after my sister got addicted to cocaine during her GCSEs."

"I didn't know that." Nory struggled to keep her voice down.

"You are shitting me!" Ameerah hissed. "How did we not know this? I told you all about Ahmed, and you never said a thing."

Pippa shrugged, as if not telling the group had been a mere oversight. But Elinor knew it wasn't only Guy's family for whom "sharing" was considered the forte of hippies and weaklings. Nory suspected that one of the reasons Pippa had built up a business out of making people's houses and wedding venues gorgeously welcoming was because she was trying to create some of the comfort her own homelife had lacked. Pippa's mother was a woman so uptight she was almost Dickensian in her child-rearing and yet conversely an absolute socialite, famous for her soirees.

"You're such a closed book." Ameerah tutted.

"I'm sorry," hissed Pippa. "I didn't know my sister's drug abuse was so important to you."

"So not what I meant, Pip."

"Can we keep it down a bit?" Nory hushed them. "I don't want to get detention."

"But of course, Braddon-Hartmead's ethos isn't built on money. We are very proud to have our scholarship program, offering pupils from underprivileged areas the chance of an education that their families would never otherwise have been able to afford." Nory felt her cheeks burning, but to her surprise Ms. Strathmoore pointed straight at Katie. "Ms. Noel, I believe you were one of our scholarship pupils. I understand you run a bookshop now." She smiled.

Dev poked his head between Ameerah's and Nory's. "Racist much?" he asked sardonically.

"Actually, I'm not Ms. Noel. I didn't attend Braddon-Hartmead," Katie piped up, with a defiant smile. "I attended Wycombe Abbey private school for girls. My parents paid in full."

Ms. Strathmoore was momentarily ruffled.

"I was the scholarship kid," said Nory. "And I own a second-hand bookshop."

"Of course," said Ms. Strathmoore, recovering herself. "I must have got my wires crossed, how silly of me."

With the headmistress leading the way, Nory turned back to Katie and mouthed *Oh my god!*

Katie laughed quietly and rolled her eyes—of course this wasn't the first time someone had made an assumption about her because of the color of her skin, but everyone was a little stunned.

"Well, if we weren't sure before that junior wasn't going to be attending Braddon-Hartmead, we are now," Jeremy whispered, holding tightly on to his wife's hand.

The dining hall had been improved, although nothing could remove the claggy scent of decades' worth of mashed potatoes and pastry. And the assembly hall had lost none of its grandeur, and more names of pupils who had gone on to success in politics or other such worthy pursuits had been added to the large wooden plaque above the stage.

So many of the memories ignited by these surroundings contained Tristan, and once again Nory felt the familiar ache in her chest that he wasn't with them. His name was carried on all their lips as they roamed the halls of their childhood, his kind nature fondly remembered, and his mischievous antics whispered among them like folklore. They were happy memories, mostly, and it felt unfair that he wasn't here to share them. Suicide was greedy; it didn't just take your friend once—it kept coming back for more, taking and taking, so that your remembrances were always bittersweet.

They left Braddon-Hartmead in a reflective mood. Perhaps none of them had quite realized how it would feel to revisit the place. Nory was glad that Jenna's terrible tan had kept her away. Back in the car park, they hovered before climbing into Ameerah's and Jeremy's cars. They were only going back to the castle; they'd be apart for ten minutes and then be back together again in the warmth of Robinwood. But somehow it felt as though when they left, a spell would be broken.

"Was I an arsehole at school?" Charles asked.

"No!" said Ameerah.

"I don't mean on purpose. But would you say I ever bullied the younger kids?"

"No more than the rest of us, mate," said Guy. "And we were only doing what was done to us before."

"Doesn't make it right, though, does it?" Charles replied.

"I don't think you were ever cruel," added Jeremy.

"This isn't making me feel any better."

"What's on your mind, Charles?" Nory asked, giving his arm a friendly rub.

"I don't know. It's just being here. Remembering stuff. What if something I said to someone years ago, you know, like just a throwaway comment, I'm not even talking specifically. I can't recall specifics, if I'm honest. But what if I said something to someone and years later . . . You know Tristan was bullied."

"We were all bullied," Guy snapped. "Toughens you up."

"Bullshit!" said Ameerah. "Bullying doesn't toughen anyone up. It makes them miserable. It leaves scars."

"That's my point," said Charles. "I know we were all bullied to a certain extent, but what if the bullying that Tristan experienced stayed with him? And those kids who bullied him would have no idea that years later their words caused him to . . . well, you know."

Jeremy put an arm around Charles's shoulder. "Tristan had more issues than being bullied. I'm not dismissing it; I'm not saying that it didn't have a lasting effect, but Tristan had a lot of problems and not enough solutions."

"It eats me up." Charles's eyes were wet. "To think that someone somewhere, someone I don't even remember, might be hurting because of something I did when I was at school."

"We were all just trying to survive, mate," said Guy.

"That's no excuse!" Charles almost shouted at Guy.

"Charles," Jeremy's voice was soothing. "I was with you pretty much all the time at school. We got bullied together, remember? And I can promise you that I never saw you target any one kid or behave in any way like those kids who bullied us. I would have remembered. I would have flagged it with you if I had."

"Thanks, Jez."

"Jeremy's right," added Guy. "At worst, it was hijinks, nothing that would leave a mental mark. I always wondered why you didn't give as good as you got. When I told my father I was being bullied, he told me it was a rite of passage; it would make a man of me. And I paid it forward, just like he'd have wanted me to. I'm not proud of it, but I can't afford to analyze it. I'm hanging on by a thread as it is." He tried to laugh, but it came out strangled and he coughed instead.

"There's something else," said Charles. "Something that's been worrying me for a really long time and if I don't say it now, I might lose my nerve."

"Christ! It's like fucking *Oprah!*" Pippa muttered loudly.

"Easy there, tiger," said Nory.

"Ameerah, I was racist," Charles blurted. He had Ameerah by the forearms. Ameerah's eyes were wide. "Not on purpose, but I said things to you, Ameerah, and other kids . . . I would never say those things now. I'm sorry, Ameerah. I'm sorry I was racist."

There was a moment of silence as they all held their breath, wondering what would happen next. And then Ameerah leaned forward and kissed Charles on the cheek.

"Thank you for having the balls to apologize," she said. "You weren't by any stretch the worst offender, but thank you for acknowledging your part in it."

"This is all very touching," said Pippa. "But I'm telling you now, if this turns into some sort of teary, fucking kumbaya, rubbing-each-other's-chakras shit, me and my Manolo Blahniks are calling a taxi."

"Right, everyone in the cars!" Ameerah jumped in quickly before things escalated further. "Pippa, you're with me. Guy, you go with Jeremy. Sorry, Jez."

# Twenty-eight

They entered the castle to find that Jenna had toned down from brass to bronze.

"My skin has literally never been so soft," she exclaimed. "You two should go into business."

"I'll sign up," said Ameerah. "Got any of your magic scrub left? You can do me next."

"I've rubbed quite enough flesh for one day, thank you." Pippa's voice was clipped.

Charles was running his hands appreciatively up and down Jenna's arms. "Maybe we should go upstairs so I can see how soft the rest of you is?" he asked hopefully.

"Sorry, Charles, darling." Jenna kissed him lightly on the lips. "No nooky for you tonight, it's bad luck. You have to sleep in the room down the hall."

"It's only bad luck if I *see* the bride," Charles reasoned. "There is nothing in the rule book about *feeling* the bride before the wedding, so I'll just keep my eyes closed and we'll be all good."

"Nice try. I've already moved your clothes and toiletries into the other room."

Charles huffed, but was mollified with another kiss and Jenna's arms wrapped tightly around his waist.

Nory smiled at them. Their love for each other made her feel warm inside. Katie had her head resting on Jeremy's shoulder, his arm protectively around her; Nory didn't think they'd be living apart again. Whatever else was happening in the world, love was a constant.

After hot drinks in the drawing room, the party drifted off their separate ways. Katie and Jeremy went back to their room, Pippa and Jenna had their heads bowed together over the wedding binder, and Charles maneuvered Guy away from the whiskey bottle and into the billiards room. Nory had invited them all to the tree lighting down in the village, but it had begun to snow again as they arrived back at the castle, and they were reluctant to go out. And in fairness, the Hartmead tree lighting ceremony wasn't exactly Oxford Street.

"Just us, then," said Dev brightly, double wrapping his scarf about his neck before helping Ameerah with her coat.

"I guess so," said Nory.

"I'm pleased in a way, although I wouldn't tell the others. It's always been our thing, you know? My family aren't exactly big on traditions, so this was always special," added Ameerah.

"I feel rather honored that you're letting me tag along," said Dev.

"You should." Ameerah winked at him.

"What will you be doing for Christmas, Dev?" Nory asked.

"I'll go to my parents' place. It's not too far from here, actually. My sisters will be down with their kids, you know the drill—too much food, crap telly, noise, board games, and then one of my nieces or nephews will spew on the sofa. Perfect!" He smiled.

"You've just described hell," said Ameerah.

Nory laughed. "Don't pretend to be all Bah Humbug. He's

just basically described Christmas with my family, and you bloody love it."

Ameerah smiled. "All right, maybe I do. But not the spew on the sofa."

"That is admittedly one of the more unfortunate by-products of Christmas," Dev agreed. "I suppose your family Christmases are all caviar and polished silver?"

"Yes, they are. And my parents like to give me a slideshow of all the eligible men they know."

"How thoughtful," said Dev.

"It's all very professionally done," Ameerah continued. "There are companies you can hire to make discreet inquiries into potential partners from around the globe—what their ambitions are, what they were like at school, previous girlfriends, how much money they've got in the bank, how much they'll inherit. You know the sort of thing."

"Oh, absolutely," agreed Dev. "My mum's the same. Her net's not quite as wide as your parents', though; she usually focuses her searches within three streets of our house."

Nory laughed.

"And she doesn't need to hire a company to gather intel," he went on. "My sister calls her the aproned interrogator because she can winkle out all your secrets in the time it takes you to eat a slice of her coconut loaf cake."

"Your mum sounds like a force to be reckoned with," said Ameerah.

"She is. She's like Sherlock Holmes in a floral tea dress."

༺ྂ༻

They parked on Nory's parents' drive and followed the bustle of heads clad in hats, pulled like magnets toward the noise on the small village green. A brass band was playing Christmas carols, and the Hartmead gospel choir was doing its best to make its voices heard above them. The snow was still coming down, and Nory was glad that most of the wedding guests had traveled down early and booked into the Robinwood Hotel and the surrounding pubs; the roads tended to snarl up pretty quickly when the snows came.

The towering fir tree came into view before the green did. Nory looked about her as they drew near and spotted Jackson and Lucas waving wildly at her from the queue for hot chocolate that snaked out of Castle Coffee.

"Aunty Nory, Aunty Nory!" they called desperately, caught between wanting to run and greet her and not losing their spot in line.

The three of them made their way over, Nory leading the way. The boys hugged her and began speaking animatedly over each other in a rush, seemingly without gaps for breath, about what they had been doing at school and what they'd asked Father Christmas for, and a host of other things which made absolutely no sense amid the jumble of noise.

"Boys, calm down, give Aunty Nory a chance," said Thomas. He looked at Nory and said, "Nice that you found time to come down, sis."

Nory could never tell with Thomas whether his sentiments were friendly or barbed, but in this instance, he was smiling, so she returned his smile and hoped they could remain friends at least for this evening. Ameerah stepped forward, and the boys seemed to notice her for the first time.

"Amie!" they called in unison, and Ameerah was treated to the same jumping-hugging-shouting that Nory had been moments before.

Dev, smiling, reached across and held out his hand for Thomas to shake.

"Dev," said Dev.

"Thomas," said Thomas.

Nory rolled her eyes. Why were men always so minimal in their greetings to one another?

"Boys, this is my friend Dev," said Ameerah.

Dev smiled and bent down to shake each of their hands in turn.

"Are you a prince?" asked Lucas. "You look like a prince."

Dev laughed. "Far from it, I'm afraid," he replied.

"I think if you did fancy dress you could go as a prince," said Lucas, looking him up and down seriously.

"I'll bear it in mind for my next fancy-dress party," Dev replied with equal gravity.

"Can I get you guys anything while I'm in there?" asked Thomas as they neared the door to Castle Coffee. "Save you queuing up. The Mead and Medlar and White Hart are doing takeaways if you fancy something stronger."

Nory, Ameerah, and Dev all requested a hot chocolate.

"Here, let me get these," said Dev, reaching into his pocket.

"My treat," said Thomas tightly.

"We'll meet you over by the birdfeeder," Nory called as Thom and the boys disappeared inside.

"I get the feeling your brother doesn't like me," said Dev.

"Oh, he's like that with everyone. And anyone standing near me is collateral damage."

"Ah, the overprotective big brother." Dev nodded wisely.

"No, he's just difficult," Nory replied lightly. "He'll like you better when I tell him you went to state school."

"Would it help if I mentioned I grew up on a council estate?"

"He would probably make you a friend for life."

∾

They pushed through the crowd and hovered by the community birdfeeder, which stood on the edge of the green. The excitement was ramping up, and someone in the crowd had brought a set of jingle bells, which added another level of twee to the chocolate box scene, with its laughing children and Christmas music. Nory was always taken aback by how many people actually lived in the village; it seemed like such a tiny place until you squeezed everyone together on the small patch of grass.

Nory's mum and dad emerged from the White Hart, paper pints in hand, and joined them, signaling another round of hugs, kisses, and introductions. Her dad nearly keeled over laughing when Dev held out his hand and said, "Hello, Mr. Noel, good to meet you. I'm adopted, I was brought up on a council estate, I went to state school, and I am filthy rich of my own making."

"Well, then," said Jake, laughing, "I daresay you are good enough for our Amie in that case. Let me introduce you to some of the lads."

And with that, Dev was whisked off to the pub garden, where even the local farmers seemed starstruck by his handsomeness.

"Oh my god!" Ameerah exclaimed as they watched Jake clapping Dev on the back.

"What?" asked Nory.

"I've gone and fallen for man-Barbie, haven't I?"

"Yes, you have," Nory agreed.

"Now would probably be a good time to stop referring to him as 'man-Barbie,' then, my love," said Sasha. "I know you only say it in jest, but if Donald Trump has taught us anything, it's that locker-room banter is insidious; objectification works both ways."

"Sorry, Sasha," said Ameerah.

Nory's mum kissed Ameerah on the cheek. "Let yourself fall in love, my girl."

"Steady on, Sasha. At the moment I'm only committing to like-like him."

"Oh, pish!" Sasha waved her words away. "You're well on the way to love, I can see it in your eyes."

"But what if it doesn't work out?"

"Then we'll be here to pick up the pieces, won't we, Nory?"

"Every time," said Nory, feeling a rush of love for her amazing—slightly bananas—mum and her best friend.

"I'm not sure I'd be very good at being in love." Ameerah bit her lip.

"Nobody knows what they're doing, Amie, that's why they call it 'falling' in love. Now if we could just get someone to steal our Nory's heart, we'd have a full house."

At that moment, the crowd along the path parted, and Lord Abercrombie strode into view with Isaac beside him. Nory's heart sped up. Isaac stopped at the edge of the crowd while the marquis carried on to the center of the green to stand by the tree.

A hush fell over the gathering, and the marquis began to speak. It was an uplifting speech; he managed to acknowledge just about every element of Hartmead, from the farmers to the oral surgeons. Nory thought it no wonder the community remained so close, and so protective of Robinwood Castle, when the marquis kept the ties between them so strong. He might have made a good politician if he hadn't committed himself to keeping the family estate going.

Her ears may have been listening to Lord Abercrombie's rousing words, but she couldn't keep her eyes off Isaac. He in his turn seemed unable to break his gaze from hers.

The marquis's words became indistinct, as though he were underwater, and her vision seemed to tunnel so that the crowd was a blurry backdrop to Isaac's brilliance. Caught in his tractor-beam stare, Nory got the distinct sense that she would never be done looking at him, that she would never tire of this view. She'd found people attractive before, of course, but she'd never wanted to throw herself in and drown in them. This was new. And it wasn't just his aesthetics—though they were greatly appealing. She looked at Isaac and she saw hands that dug the earth but also held a paintbrush, eyes that studied the delicate science of plants in the ground and searched the stars far above them. She wanted to know what made him tick, to taste his thoughts, she wanted to consume him and be consumed by him. The urge to run to him at that moment was so great, she actually found herself grinding her boots into the ground to keep her in place.

A cheer went up around her, and Nory was dragged back to reality by the unified shouting of "One! Two! Three!" before the enormous fir tree spangled into life in an explosion of fairy lights. The air was filled with whoops and cheers, and beneath them the brass band struck up and the gospel choir began to sing "Deck the Halls." Nory cast her eyes sideways and saw Ameerah pulled in close to Dev, his arms around her waist as he whispered something in her ear that made her laugh softly. On the other side of her, her dad had one arm slung loosely across her mum's shoulders. The snow was falling harder, much to the joy of the children all around them, giving the tree the glittery, indistinct twinkle of a snow-globe tableau.

The pull toward Isaac grew too strong to ignore, and she found herself walking over to him in spite of herself. He watched her as though he had expected her, as if he had summoned her. She reached him and stopped, the toes of their boots almost touching. He hadn't taken his eyes off her, and they bore into her now, dark hickory irises and thick black lashes. Without a word, he reached his arms around her, closing the gap between them, and pressed his mouth to hers. In the far reaches of her mind, a thought that people would be watching tried to make itself heard, but the sensation of Isaac's lips on hers left no room for other considerations.

When they pulled apart, the crowd had thinned a little, drawn by the warmth offered by the pubs and café. The brass band had stopped playing to consume the trays of steaming mulled wine presented to them by one of the landladies, and the choir had the limelight to themselves as they belted out "The First Noel." Nory's senses returned, and she glanced about her. But if any of her family had noticed her and Isaac pashing on the green, they'd made themselves scarce now. Nory was relieved she wouldn't have to deal with their teasing right away.

"Um, would you like to come to the wedding tomorrow as my plus-one?" she asked, feeling a little nervous.

"And how would the celebrity bride feel about having the gardener at her wedding?"

"It was her idea," said Nory, and then added quickly, "but I'd really like you to come."

"In that case, yes." Isaac smiled. "It'll be nice to spend a whole day with you."

Nory felt so pleased she wanted to do a "Woo-hoo!" but she held it in.

"And now I'd like to ask you something," Isaac said, his eyes becoming hooded, his nostrils flaring ever so slightly.

"Yes?" she asked, her knees quivering in anticipation.

"Would you like to come back to my cottage right now?"

"Yes, please!" she gushed while thinking, *What's happening to me? My bosoms are actually heaving!*

He smiled and bent down, kissing her neck lightly and then gently grazing her skin with his teeth, so that she gasped. He grinned wickedly and said, "You've got five minutes to say your goodbyes and meet me by my car at Noel and Son's car park. And then you're mine."

*Good god!* At this rate she wouldn't make it as far as the cottage.

Her eyes scanned the clusters of revelers. Then suddenly a purple glitter hat pulled low over an elfin face rose above the crowd as Thomas lifted Lucas up and onto his shoulders. They were all together, *thank god!* Nory did a sort of half jog over to them and said her goodbyes.

"There's nothing wrong, is there?" asked her mum.

"No, no, just bride-to-be stuff, you know Jenna," Nory reassured her mum.

"I didn't get a call," said Ameerah, checking her phone.

"No, you wouldn't have, it's just for that thing, you know? The um, thing that I'd said I'd do and then I didn't . . ." *Fuck! Why am I such a shit liar?*

"Well, I can drop you up there," said Ameerah. "You don't mind leaving, do you, Dev?"

"No, of course not."

"Um, no it's fine, you guys stay and have fun, there's plenty more fun to be had! Fun, fun, fun!"

Ameerah was looking at her like she'd taken drugs.

"Are you all right, love?" asked her dad.

"Yes, god yes, I'm fine." She was wasting time! "I'm— Actually, do you know what, I've just remembered Isaac said he'd give me a lift. That's right, he totally offered me a lift, and then I forgot and now I'd better go, or I'll miss that blinking lift." She laughed too loudly and snorted like a pig and had no idea why she did it.

Realization plastered Ameerah's face, and her eyes widened.

"Oh gosh," she said, herding Nory away from her family. "You'd better get going. Jenna won't want to be kept waiting. You know what she's like. The bride is never wrong."

Nory could have kissed her friend, but she really didn't have the time. With blown kisses and goodbyes still lingering in the air, Nory hotfooted it through the throng and down the lane.

She made it to his car, moments before Isaac walked purposefully into the car park; the security light flicked on, flooding the scene. His jaw was set, his black hair glinting under the spotlight, and Nory had never wanted anyone more. She had only seconds before Isaac reached her and then kept going, pinning her body to the side of the car. He kissed her hungrily and she echoed his hunger. He unzipped her coat, and his hands found their way inside her jumper and then beneath her shirt. He let out a strangled moan as his hands met the rough lace of her bra and he ran them over the deep curves of her body.

"What are you doing to me," he groaned, his voice rough, and he pushed harder against her. Nory was thrilled in every way. The security light flicked off, and Nory fumbled through layers to the bare skin of Isaac's back beneath his jumper. Her hands were cold, and his breath hitched, his skin leaping to goose bumps beneath her touch. When she moved her hands up and down the muscular ridges of his torso and dug her nails into his back, he gasped.

"Take me to the cottage," she whispered. "Now!"

"Yes," he whispered hoarsely into her hair. "Yes."

# Twenty-nine

Nory was lying with her head on Isaac's chest. He was stroking her hair with one hand, the other resting on his stomach, fingers entwined with hers.

Two hours earlier, they had fallen through the front door of the cottage. A mess of boots and coats lay discarded on the hall floor in their haste to get up to the bedroom. From her position on Isaac's warm chest, Nory could see her clothes strewn across the floor. Her bra lay over a lamp, stiff and holding its shape like two lacy molehills.

"You could stay," Isaac said.

Nory sighed. "I wish I could, but I need to be on bridal duty in the morning."

"Would you like a cup of tea?" he asked.

*Oh my god, could he be any more perfect?*

"That would be lovely."

He lifted his arm, and Nory reluctantly rolled out from underneath. She watched him as he hunted the room for his boxer shorts, the moon shining in through the window illuminating the lines of his muscles. His was a body that was used to hard work, lean and athletic. By contrast, Nory's body was soft. She possessed no hard edges, only voluptuous curves, which Isaac had mapped with feverish precision.

"I used to fantasize about being seduced by you," said Nory, leaning up on one elbow. "When I was a teenager."

"Did I live up to expectation?" he asked, unhooking her knickers from the corner of a picture frame, where they had landed earlier, and throwing them at her.

She caught them and pulled them beneath the duvet to wriggle back into them.

"You exceeded all my expectations." She grinned. And it was absolutely true—no orgasm faking required!

"I'm relieved to hear it," he said, scooping his T-shirt off the bedpost and bending to kiss her.

"Of course, my knowledge of sex then was based solely on what I'd read in Judy Blume's *Forever*, so I couldn't have imagined all the naughty things that you'd *actually* do when you got me in your bed."

He was midway pulling on his jeans, smiling devilishly at her. "That was just for starters," he said, waggling his eyebrows at her. "I haven't even begun to get naughty with you yet."

Nory bit her lip and pressed her knees together. Oh, how she wished she didn't have to go back to the castle tonight. Although, it had been a while since she'd had sex, so she really ought to pace herself if she didn't want a dose of cystitis; they never mentioned that in the movies. Anastasia Steele never had to ask Mr. Fifty Shades for a night off because she was basically weeing fire.

"What are you thinking about?" he asked.

"Cystitis," she replied.

"Really?"

"Well, first of all I was thinking about how I'd like to stay here and have sex with you all night long, and then it occurred to me that that was just asking for a UTI."

Isaac nodded. "I see . . ."

"Sorry, was that too much information? It was, wasn't it? I really need to not express my every thought. Sorry." She searched Isaac's face, but he was smiling at her.

"To be honest," he said, "when I asked you to stay, I was thinking it would be nice to fall asleep with you. And you know, maybe have sex again in the morning, when we're all sleepy and relaxed. I probably couldn't manage to have sex all night long."

Nory's chest filled with warmth. "You wanted to fall asleep with me?"

"Yes," he said, sitting on the bed beside her. "I'd like to fall asleep beside you and wake beside you."

Nory leaned over and kissed him. That was possibly the nicest thing a man had ever said to her.

"What was that for?" he asked.

"For being better in real life than you were in my imagination."

"How was I in your imagination?"

"Perfect."

Isaac cupped her face in his hands and kissed her. "You are rocking my world, Nory Noel."

౿

The snow had stopped by the time they wandered back to the castle, in what was becoming a familiar routine. It was almost midnight, and she imagined most of her housemates had gotten an early night, ready for an early start in the morning. She couldn't quite believe she'd been here almost a week. And on

Sunday she would be heading back to London, back to the shop and Mugwort and meals for one.

"What are you thinking?" Isaac asked.

"I'll be going home on Sunday."

Neither of them spoke for a couple of minutes, letting that sink in. A hare bounded past them and disappeared into the herbaceous borders. Overhead, an owl hooted.

"It's only an hour or so away," Isaac said, breaking the silence between them. "Technically I get the weekends off; I only tend to work them because I'm here anyway. I could come to London . . ."

"And I could come down here. I don't work Sundays, and I've been saying for ages that I ought to take another day off in the week."

They reached the back door, and when they kissed goodnight, it wasn't with the urgency of a few hours ago, but with a tenderness that made Nory want to stay in his arms forever.

༄

The cotton sheets on her four-poster felt cold and stiff when she climbed into bed. She lay awake for some time, wondering if they could make it work from a distance and realized that she really did want to. She had fallen for Isaac. She had fallen hard.

When she imagined the kind of man she would fall in love with—and she'd had plenty of nights alone in her flat for such imaginings—it was always someone who would come into the shop; he would wander in looking for a vintage copy of H. E. Bates's *The Darling Buds of May* or a vintage copy of *Alice's Adventures in Wonderland* illustrated by Arthur Rackham for his niece. He would be bookish and would most likely wear a tweed jacket with leather patches on the elbows. He probably worked for a publisher or a museum. She had never imagined that the man to steal her heart would be the boy who used to throw mud at her head. But it was done; she had made a conscious effort to build a life away from Hartmead, only to fall for a man slap-bang in the middle of it.

Her phone buzzed and she reached over to the bedside table and opened the message: **You forgot something!**

Another buzz. This time it was a photograph of her bra, still resting on top of Isaac's bedside lampshade. Nory smiled in the dark and typed back:

> **I left it there on purpose, so that I have an excuse to come back.**

> **You don't need an excuse. I'm looking forward to being your date tomorrow.**

> **Me too. I had a great time tonight.**

> **Me too. Xxx**

# Thirty

The wedding was at one o'clock, which meant that the entire household had to be up and ready for action by 6:00 a.m.

Katie had padded down the stairs in sweatpants and bed socks, grabbed some food, and disappeared back up to her room. But there was no such luxury for Nory and Ameerah. Nory had woken at five to the sound of Pippa pounding on the door.

"Get showered, clothes on, and be ready for action," she had said when Nory answered the door, bleary-eyed and slightly achy from last night's fraternizing. Pippa looked immaculate, and her eyes were dancing in that way they did when she was high on the adrenaline of a mission; Nory wondered idly if her friend was actually a vampire.

"What's happening?" she asked, yawning.

"You know perfectly well what's happening."

"No, I mean what's happening that requires me to be up at five in the morning?"

"Bridal containment."

She said it as though this was a common term. Nory pushed the door closed while Pippa was still barking orders at her. Pippa continued, unperturbed by the wood between them.

"I won't take offense because I know that you are not a morning person, but know this, Nory Noel: If you are not in the dining room in one hour from now, I will set the dogs on you."

And so, at 6:00 a.m., Nory and Ameerah were picking at an enormous breakfast buffet laid out in the dining room. Continental options included Swiss cheese, ham, yogurts, fruit, various cereals, and a range of fresh breads from baguettes to sourdough loaves and crusty rolls. The scent of freshly baked croissants and pains au chocolat fought for priority over the wafts of bacon and sausages emanating from the covered hot plates. The buffet would be replenished over the course of the morning as more of the wedding party arrived.

"You look like a woman who got lucky last night." Ameerah grinned. Several pink rollers bobbed about her chin.

Nory couldn't suppress her smile. "I got very lucky indeed. Twice."

Ameerah made a squeak sound and bounced up and down on her chair. "I knew it. I just knew it! Is he coming to the wedding?"

"Yes." She was still smiling. She couldn't seem to turn it off.

"I haven't seen you this dizzy over a bloke in ages."

"I'm not dizzy over him."

"Yeah right! You're lit up like a Christmas tree."

Nory gave it up. "Oh, all right. Yes, I am dizzy and bananas and smitten and all other words that mean I have fallen for Isaac." She laughed.

Ameerah reached over and squeezed Nory's cheeks. "I love you, Nory Noel."

"I love you too."

"Yes, good, you both clearly got laid last night, but that's quite enough sentimentality for now. This is a wedding, not a lovefest," Pippa said, lifting the lid off the heat tray and ripping a slice of bacon in half with her teeth.

"Pip, I don't mean to question your authority, but if any occasion should be a lovefest, ought it not to be a wedding?" asked Nory.

"Not on my watch," she snapped back. Her eyes were glinting fire; this was Pippa's happy place. She was primed for charging into battle. "Bridezilla needs feeding, she's getting hangry, and I've got to go and make sure the orangery roof isn't leaking on my velour seat pads."

"Is it raining?" asked Ameerah.

"No, thank fuck. It snowed again in the night, and there's a crack in one of the glass ceiling panels. I got somebody to patch it yesterday. Go feed Jenna before she murders the manicurist."

As they got up to leave the dining room, the sound of heavy feet on the stairs drew them out into the hall. Charles, Guy, Jeremy, and Dev—who had been adopted as an honorary groomsman—were in the process of being banished from the house, still in their pj's. They carried their suits in large garment bags, and all of them, barring Dev, had the kind of hair that suggested they'd slept heavily after a hard night's drinking. Dev waved and smiled kind of goofily at Ameerah as they passed. He blew her a kiss, which, to Nory's astonishment, Ameerah made a show of catching.

The men were bundled into Andy's car, ready to be driven to one of the old coach houses, which had been turned into holiday lets. A full English breakfast was being laid out for them, and when they were wedding ready, they would be deposited in the Mead and Medlar until it was time for the wedding.

"How come men always get the easy jobs?" asked Ameerah, shivering against the chill of the early morning whisking into the entrance hall.

The courtyard glittered with a thick crystalline layer of ice, which had formed over last night's snow, a salt path melted through the middle. The sky was still dark but cloudless, and it didn't look like there would be any more snow today.

"Male privilege," Nory replied as the butler pushed the door closed.

"It's not fair. All they have to do is dress, eat, and go to the pub. While we've got to tame the bridal beast."

"Yeah, but imagine if we left Charles, Guy, and Jez in charge of organizing the wedding."

"I wouldn't trust them with organizing my sock drawer, let alone a wedding." Ameerah scoffed.

"Then you've answered your own question. They get the easy jobs because we don't trust them with anything else. It's a perpetuating cycle—we don't give them responsibility because we assume they can't handle it, and therefore they never learn to do the things we moan about them not being able to do."

"It's a bit early for that kind of radical feminism, isn't it?"

"I had three coffees with breakfast."

"Pace yourself, Noel, it's gonna be a long day!"

∽

"Hello, not-remotely-blushing bride," Ameerah said as they entered the bridal suite. Nory was carrying a plate laden with Jenna's favorite breakfast foods.

"Today is the day. Happy wedding day!" trilled Nory, who was feeling much more festive after two bacon rolls and a pain au chocolat.

Jenna gave them a look that said she was not feeling the joys right at that moment. Her skin was blotchy, and she kept looking back at the nail technician, who was making an inordinate amount of noise putting away the tools of her trade.

"Pip says you need to eat," said Ameerah, thrusting a bacon and sausage roll at Jenna.

"Nails!" was Jenna's response. She held up her hands, revealing a perfect French polish.

"Here, give it to me," said Nory, taking the roll from Ameerah and holding it in front of Jenna's face. Jenna leaned forward on her furry dressing-table stool and took a bite out of the roll, as though it was absolutely normal for her to be fed like a Roman empress.

"How are you feeling?" Ameerah asked.

"Ask me again when I've eaten," Jenna replied around a mouthful of sausage.

Nory took a tissue from the box on the dressing table and dabbed at a ketchup blob at the side of Jenna's mouth.

"Your nails look nice," said Nory.

"Toes too," said Jenna, munching. "I've been well and truly nailed."

"You're not the only one," said Ameerah under her breath.

"Huh?" Jenna exclaimed, biting into the croissant now being proffered by Nory, the roll having been polished off in two bites.

"Nothing," said Nory. "What's next?"

"Hair, then makeup. Photos in slinky dressing gown—made to look natural, as though I just woke up looking fabulous—then dress on, then . . ." She looked up, her eyes wide as if suddenly realizing a great truth. "Then I'm getting married!"

"Oh, yes you are!" Nory smiled.

"Oh my god, I'M GETTING MARRIED!"

Nory had barely enough time to replace the half-eaten croissant on the dressing table before Jenna jumped up and rushed forward, throwing her arms around them.

"Oh my god. It's actually happening!" she screamed.

"About time! Ouch, watch the curlers, Jen."

"Sorry," said Jenna, pulling away. "I'm just so happy you're both here for today. I'm the first of us girls to get married. How weird is that? I didn't think I was the marrying type."

"Oh, I always thought you were the marrying type," said Ameerah.

"If only your school self could see your grown-up self. Would you believe you'd be a successful actress and about to marry Charles." Nory laughed. "It's so perfect!"

"Elinor, stop gushing." Ameerah turned to Jenna. "She's overwrought because she actually had sex for the first time in forever." Ameerah rolled up a slice of Emmental cheese and bit into it.

"Oh my god! With Isaac?"

Nory laughed. "Yes, with Isaac. Who else would I be having sex with?"

Ameerah raised her eyebrows and said, "You really want us to answer that?"

Jenna grabbed hold of Ameerah and Nory again and began jump-hugging them just as Pippa walked in.

"You seem in a better mood than when I left you," she said wryly.

"We're all in love," cried Jenna dreamily. "Isn't it wonderful?"

"Technically I am still in like-like," said Ameerah. "And Pip is too busy ruling the world for love."

"I am in love," Pippa corrected her. "I am blissfully and

completely in love with myself. Don't underestimate self-love, it's a powerful force. Most nights I can't wait to get into bed with myself."

"Oh, come here, you big, beautiful Athena!" said Jenna, grabbing Pippa into the already crowded hug, and for a few seconds they could have been fourteen again, hopeful and untroubled by the future.

The manicurist clipped her vanity case closed with a snap and made to leave. Jenna caught her arm.

"I'm sorry about what I said, I didn't mean it," she said, giving the woman a look like a newborn lamb.

"It's all right, love." For her part, the woman looked resigned. "I've had worse than that from brides before now."

Jenna handed over a fifty-quid tip, and the woman inclined her head in thanks before leaving the room.

"What did you say to the manicurist?" Nory asked.

Jenna stopped midway through devouring another sausage and pulled a worried face. "She said nail technicians were like the fourth emergency service, and I said surely that was hairstylists, and then she said people always underestimated the training involved in becoming a nail technician, so then I said, 'Probably less training than being in the actual emergency services,' and then she said, 'Don't belittle me, you half-baked soap actress,' and then I said . . . well, it wasn't very nice and I'm not proud of it. I hope she doesn't go to the press. They love a celebs-behaving-badly story."

"Sounds like she started it," said Ameerah.

"I shouldn't have implied that her job was less important than a hairstylist's."

"Well, you're the bride, so you're allowed to behave outrageously on your big day," Nory soothed. "Have another sausage."

~

The bridesmaids, flower girls, and page boys, along with their parents and siblings, all arrived at eight o'clock sharp, as though their arrival had been coordinated with military precision, which of course, with Pippa in charge, it had. The upstairs became a beauty parlor with multiple hairstylists hovering possessively next to plug sockets, which were in surprisingly scant supply in the castle bedrooms.

The building was suddenly loud with the drone of hair dryers and people shouting over them, and the thunderous sound of children running from room to room. Katie emerged from her room, looking radiant in a maxi-dress that skimmed her baby bump.

"Hello, how are you feeling? You look much better," said Nory, who had almost run into her in her haste to get a flat white to Jenna.

"I think I've beaten the jet lag." Katie smiled. "Now I'm just back to the pregnancy lag."

"Oh, that's good, I think?"

"Yes." Katie laughed. "I feel human for the first time in days. I'm sorry I haven't been around very much. I was really looking forward to catching up with you. I hadn't anticipated how much the traveling would take out of me."

"You have nothing to apologize for. There'll be other times we can catch up. Especially now you're going to be back in the country for a while."

"Yes, I'm hanging my traveling hat up for the foreseeable."

"Jeremy must be pleased about that. I know he's missed you terribly."

Katie gave a little laugh. "Yes, Jeremy is ecstatic. It's been hard for him; he so wanted to be a part of the pregnancy, but our schedules wouldn't allow it. It's time we put us first for a while. You'll have to come and stay with us one weekend. I'd love it and I know Jeremy would."

"I'd like that very much." Nory smiled.

Jenna's voice cut through the cacophony like an angle grinder. "Is it too much to ask to get a pissing coffee round here?"

Katie winced.

"I'd better deliver this," said Nory.

It was midday before Jenna's parents arrived and took over bridal duties from Nory so that she could get herself ready. She had briefly seen her mum and Shelley making last-minute adjustments to the garlands on the banisters before they disappeared off to the orangery to add the final touches to the aisle flowers. The *OK!* magazine photographer had an uncanny gift of being everywhere, and Nory did her level best to avoid being caught in any shots. This became easier once the cast of *Days and Nights* began to arrive and he had more famous faces to play with.

For the first time since waking, Nory had a few spare minutes to get excited about spending the day with Isaac. This was essentially their first date. In truth, she was surprised he had agreed. She wondered how he'd feel being surrounded by soap opera glitterati. She herself was a bit freaked out at the idea of so many famous people in one room. And then she remembered that Isaac hadn't known what *Days and Nights* was anyway. And he probably didn't read gossip magazines—her own guilty pleasure—so he was unlikely to care.

It came time for any guests who weren't actually in the wedding to take their places in the orangery. Jenna had stopped swearing the moment her parents arrived, to the relief of all the parents and the disappointment of the children—they had most enjoyed listening to the potty-mouth bride and no doubt learned some excellent swears to take back to school in the new year. Dev had come to escort Ameerah to the rest of the wedding party.

"Do you want to come with us?" Ameerah asked.

"No, you go on, I've forgotten my phone. My mum will kill me if I don't send her pictures of the wedding."

"Isn't there an embargo on sharing photos before the magazine releases them, in case they end up on social media?" asked Dev.

"I dare you to tell my mum I can't show her any photos of the wedding," Nory replied wryly.

"We'll save you both a seat," called Ameerah as she and Dev clip-clopped across the entrance hall in Christian Louboutin stilettos and Savile Row derby shoes, respectively.

Nory headed back into her bedroom and found her phone beneath a damp hair towel. She noted four missed calls from her mum already and quickly switched her phone to silent just in case. She threw a fur-lined wrap around her shoulders and checked herself in the mirror. Her dress was 1950s-style: red velvet, with a sweetheart neckline, fitted to the waist and flaring into a full skirt. She never could stand up in high heels, so she teamed the outfit with a pair of black patent Mary Jane shoes. It suddenly occurred to her that with the cream furry wrap, she looked a bit like Mrs. Claus. She applied another layer of red lipstick and hoped nobody else would think the same thing.

After the constant noise all morning, the castle now felt

eerily quiet. As she made her way down the staircase the front door opened, and Isaac walked in. Nory gave a little gasp as she took him in. She was used to rugged, working Isaac. This was polished, sexy suit Isaac, and he wore it well.

"Hello. You look delicious." Isaac grinned up at her.

*Oh, be still my beating heart!*

"You look rather edible yourself. Are you here on Her Majesty's secret service?"

"As a matter of fact, I am. The word in MI5 is that there's a woman impersonating Mrs. Claus on the loose." He arched an eyebrow.

*Bollocks!*

The wedding was beautiful. Jenna looked absolutely stunning in a Vera Wang gown, and Charles looked as though he couldn't believe he was so lucky. Nory squashed the Austenesque heroine inside her chest who sighed as she imagined herself getting married one day. That was the thing about weddings: Those who were already married, reminisced (or perhaps lamented), and those who had never been, fantasized.

After the ceremony, in that period when people milled about getting hungry and drinking too much champagne, while the photographer corralled the different elements of the wedding party together for group shots, Nory and Isaac played "spot the snob." You could pick out Charles's close relatives by the way their expressions crinkled ever so slightly when being introduced to members of the *Days and Nights* cast, as though someone were holding a bottle of turned milk under their noses.

"That's old money for you," said Nory, as Charles's dad—a huge man who looked like a serial gout sufferer—said "Delighted" in a voice laden with apathy when introduced to the woman who played Dr. Emma Briggs in the show and had recently been papped falling knickerless out of a limo.

"And Jenna's family are new money?" asked Isaac.

"Yes."

"Which would you rather be?"

"I think new money. It comes with less baggage."

"But less history too."

"I disagree. It may not come with fourteenth-century bricks, but you can be rich in family history, and that's free. Everyone's entitled to history."

"That's your dad talking." Isaac smiled.

"Oh god! Really?"

"Come on, Mrs. Claus, I'll get you another drink."

Isaac had not been overly keen on being in the friends' group wedding photos, but his protestations were drowned out by everyone, especially Jeremy, who said he was part of the day and it needed to be documented—typical scientist.

When it came time—finally—to sit down to dinner, they were led through the orangery and into what had once been a coach house but had been transformed into a large formal ballroom-cum-banqueting-hall.

But first they had to process past the bride's and groom's parents. Jenna's mum hugged Nory warmly and her dad said, "Hello, Elinor, love, so nice to see all the old gang together again." Nory introduced Isaac as her "good friend" because terms had not yet been defined, although she secretly hoped they would be soon. The more time she spent with Isaac, the more she realized she very much wanted to continue seeing him after this week.

Charles's parents were friendly in a more formal way and greeted her like a business associate, even though Nory had spent many a long weekend at their country pile over the years, and she had drunk too much sherry with Charles's mother on more than one occasion.

At the table, Nory was flanked by Isaac on one side and

Jeremy on the other. Isaac had Ameerah on his other side. Guy was at the top table with the bride and groom; Jeremy was given the option as Charles's other best man but had chosen to stay with Katie, who looked relieved to be finally sitting down. In addition to the Swiss chocolatier chocolate favors, there were also little packets of sunflower seeds from the Mind mental health charity. The front read: *On the wedding of Charles and Jenna*, and the back: *In memory of Tristan.*

Isaac must have seen the ghost of melancholy cross Nory's face because he took her hand and said, "I'd like to come and see your bookshop."

"Really? That would be lovely."

"I'm curious to know if my vision of it is different from the reality."

"How do you imagine it?" she asked, curious.

"Haphazardly cozy."

"Would it surprise you if I told you it was white walled and minimalist, with floating shelves and Bauhaus chairs?"

"Really?" Isaac looked at her incredulously.

Nory laughed. "No, not really. You were right the first time; 'haphazardly cozy' just about sums it up. Andrew, my shop manager, says I'm the worst bookseller he's ever known because I fall hopelessly in love with all the books I'm supposed to be selling."

"Yes," said Isaac, "I can imagine," as though this confirmed all his suspicions about her.

⁓

The wedding dinner, complete with local un-nibbled-by-deer salad, went without a hitch and was delicious. Pippa was sitting at Nory's table but kept her wireless mic on to make sure everything ran smoothly, and, disarmingly, would suddenly begin speaking to someone else in the middle of a conversation. She sat bolt upright throughout the meal, head turning this way and that, like a meerkat on the lookout for predators.

"Who invited Madonna?" quipped Ameerah, nodding in Pip's direction.

Katie sniggered.

"Her tits aren't pointy enough," said Nory.

"She's very committed, isn't she?" added Dev.

"That's why they pay me the big bucks, sweet cheeks," Pippa replied dryly to Dev. "I don't give a fuck about your carpal tunnel. I ordered five hundred macarons and I expect five hundred macarons. I'll be counting."

"I don't think that last part was directed at me, was it?" Dev looked doubtfully at Ameerah.

"Pippa, try not to make eye contact with us when you're being the queen of bloody everything, it's very disconcerting," Ameerah admonished.

"Sorry," said Pippa. "It helps my focus if I'm looking at someone. Sorry, Dev, you're not expected to produce five hundred macarons. Put some bleach down it, then. Yep. Yep. Top up the perfume in the toilets while you're at it, would you. Someone's gone walkabout with the Marc Jacobs eau de toilette."

Guy had been looking increasingly relaxed throughout the meal. His was a face that wore the levels of drunkenness like a series of masks. His expression had taken on a familiar sardonic sneer, the one he wore when he had reached the belligerence level of inebriation.

"Aren't you two supposed to be doing the best man speech together?" Nory asked.

"Hmmm," Jeremy agreed grimly.

"I still owe Guy a sock in the jaw for punching you the other day," said Katie curtly. "I almost hope he does start, so I've got an excuse."

"To be fair, that punch was meant for me," said Isaac. "Jeremy got in the way of his swing."

"He shouldn't have been swinging for anyone. I work with primates who have more self-control than Guy." Katie's expression was dark. "He looks at Nory like he wants to eat her for dinner."

Nory flushed. She felt Isaac stiffen beside her.

Jenna's father finished his speech and handed over to the best men. Guy got to his feet and swayed as he took the microphone.

"Okay, I'm up." Jeremy dropped his napkin on the table and headed over to where Guy was standing.

Jeremy put Guy in charge of the PowerPoint presentation that beamed onto a white screen erected at the back of the banquet hall, and he took over the bulk of the speech delivery himself. Nory felt sick with nerves the whole time they were up there, and when she looked at Jenna, she saw the rigid smile plastered on her face and the tension around her eyes.

"It was Guy you were hiding from that first night, wasn't it?" Isaac asked.

Nory bit the inside of her lip. She was afraid that if she took her eyes off the two men at the front of the hall, something dreadful would happen, as though her overseeing things could influence the outcome. She sighed inwardly. She so didn't want to get into this.

"Yes," she said. They sat very close, close enough to speak quietly into each other's ears and not be overheard. The hall was in noisy rapture at the embarrassing photographs of Charles on the big screen, exploding into laughter as each excruciating story hit its punch line.

"You can tell me," said Isaac. "I'm not going to judge you on your past."

"You promise?"

Isaac took her hand and raised it to his lips, laying a kiss on her knuckles, which set little fireworks off in her stomach. "Promise."

Nory gave him the brief outline of the sordid events after Tristan's funeral. "I honestly had no idea he was married. We hadn't seen each other for years and it didn't come up."

"It wasn't your fault," said Isaac.

"It doesn't make me any less guilty."

"You can't be held accountable for something you didn't know about. Does his wife know? Is that why she left?"

"No. Camille left because she was tired of Guy's shit."

They stopped talking and joined in the applause as the best man speech came to an end with the toast "To shits and giggles!" and the microphone was handed to Charles. A cacophonous scraping of chairs filled the hall as everyone turned back to face the top table.

Charles cleared his throat. "Thank you, Jeremy and Guy, for that comprehensively embarrassing biopic. I am supremely grateful that my *wife*"—he stopped for the enthusiastic applause and foot stamping that the word *wife* induced—"was already privy to almost all of those revelations, or she may just have turned and run away." A ripple of laughter. "I have loved Jenna since I was eleven years old. Puppy love became teenage infatuation became adult love that just wouldn't quit, no matter how hard I tried to make my heart be quiet." Nory saw Jenna slip her hand into his. "My heart was lost to Jen from the moment I saw her giving a boy in the year above what for, for running in the corridor on our first day of school. I knew right then that I'd love her forever, even if she never loved me back as anything more than a friend." Jenna wiped a tear from her eye, and Nory was surprised to catch Ameerah surreptitiously doing the same. "I wish I could go back and tell sixteen-year-old me that one day, Jenna Baxter would do me the honor of being my wife." He turned to look at Jenna, who was looking back up at him with pure infatuation in her eyes. "I have loved you for so long. Everything that happened before I knew you was merely a prelude to loving you. Everything that has happened since has been the result of my loving you. And I promise that everything in my future will revolve around loving you."

Charles bent to kiss his new wife, and Nory could tell that they didn't notice the standing ovation or hear the whoops and shouts; all they could see was each other. And as Nory clapped, she hoped that no one saw her own tears fall—happy tears for friends and hopeful tears that maybe one day someone would feel like that about her.

Later, as they slow danced to George Michael's "Careless Whisper" (which Nory had always thought was something of an oxymoron), Isaac's hands were splayed out across her back, holding her close, he kissed her neck and whispered into her ear, "Would it be impertinent to ask if you'd like to come back to my place tonight?"

Nory shivered with delight. "It would be remiss of you not to ask me back to your place tonight," she replied, and she felt the low rumble of his laughter vibrate through her body.

"Thank you for asking me to be your date."

"Thank you for coming," she said.

Those with small children began to drift off first, back to

their rooms in the hotel and the pubs down in Hartmead. By eleven thirty, only the die-hards remained. To Nory's surprise, the cast of *Days and Nights* were not the party animals she'd expected at all, and most had been gone by half past ten, shortly followed by the *OK!* photographer.

Eventually only the shits-and-giggles gang remained. They had retired to the atrium, which had large, comfy sofas surrounding a crackling open fire, all except Guy, who had been hoofed up the stairs to bed by Jeremy and Charles.

Aside from Pippa, who sat closest to the fire, her long legs tucked neatly beneath her, they were all in couples. Katie rested her head on Jeremy's shoulder, his arm around her, an expression of deep peace on his face. Jenna had her head in Charles's lap, her tiara on the rug, her long gown spilling across the sofa in a waterfall of silk. Ameerah and Dev sat practically on top of each other, their legs in a comfortable tangle, each of them looking as though they had just won the top prize in a raffle. Isaac had his arm loosely around Nory's shoulder, by turns stroking her hair and running the tips of his fingers up and down the back of her neck. She could feel him smiling as he watched the goose bumps break out across her arms at his touch. His other hand held hers, and she idly brushed the work-roughened tips of his fingers as they talked. She loved this feeling of being close to him, of being *with* him.

"I'm so exhausted, I could sleep for a week," yawned Jenna.

"You're exhausted?" Pippa arched an eyebrow. "All you had to do was turn up, darling."

Jenna lifted her head and poked her tongue out at Pippa.

"Everyone knows you don't get tired, Pip, you're a machine," teased Charles.

"It is true. As humans go, I am very effective," Pippa replied.

"And modest," added Nory.

"Self-deprecating," Ameerah threw in.

"Society does quite enough of that for women over thirty," said Pippa. "Especially single women. I don't need to add to it."

"Hear, hear," agreed Katie. "In my profession, modesty about your expertise is taken to be weakness. If I want the same respect as men in the field, I have to adopt the same arrogance and self-confidence that men have."

"That's a bit unfair," said Charles. "I wouldn't describe myself as arrogant."

"It's not a personal attack," said Katie placatingly. "It's conditioning. Men are as much a victim of it as women. It starts in the nursery. Girls are conditioned to be self-deprecating . . ."

"Nobody likes a big-headed girl," Nory added.

"Exactly. And boys are taught to be *strong*." Katie did quotes in the air. "And self-confident. Historically, male and female personalities have been pigeonholed from birth. That's why we have men unable to express their emotions and women apologizing profusely on every step of the career ladder."

"We'll be changing history for our little miracle, won't we, darling?" said Jeremy, lovingly resting his hand on Katie's bump. "No girl- or boy-only traits; this child will be encouraged to embrace the full range of human idiosyncrasies."

Katie smiled at her husband and closed her eyes contentedly.

"You always were a goddamn hippie," said Charles, smiling fondly at his friend.

"I think you're absolutely right," Jenna said. "If we have sons, I don't want them growing up in fear of their emotions. And if we have girls, I'll be teaching them to kick arse!"

"I think your child is very lucky," said Isaac to Jeremy. Nory thought her heart would burst.

"Thanks, mate." Jeremy smiled.

"How about you two?" asked Charles, pointing at Isaac and then Dev. "Did you have to deal with the same macho bullshit we did as kids?"

"Charles, what kind of a question is that?" Jenna admonished.

"I'm curious. Guy and I were brought up in an almost Victorian environment in terms of the way men were supposed to behave."

"My dad was what you'd call a *man's man*," said Isaac. "We didn't talk about feelings, and they weren't encouraged. My mum handled all that stuff. He was a good man, don't get me wrong, a great father. But we didn't have the kind of relationship where I would go to him with my problems unless they were mechanical, or plant related."

Charles nodded in understanding.

"Mine was the opposite," said Dev. "We had to talk about *everything*!" He deepened his voice. "'Dev, my son, you must not bury things, it is bad for the soul. We were born with voices, so let us use them.'"

"Basically, the opposite of my family." Ameerah laughed.

"Your family sound like mine," said Nory to Dev. "Never repress what you could express," she said, wagging her finger.

Ameerah laughed again. "I don't think Jake Noel has ever repressed a thought in his life," she said, and Nory agreed.

The friends were quiet for a time, the warmth of the fire lulling them away from conversation. The only sounds were those of the flames licking the logs in the hearth and the faraway noises of Charles and Jenna's wedding day paraphernalia being dismantled by Pippa's power team.

"Well," said Jeremy, gently rousing Katie, who had dropped

off to sleep. "It's been shits and giggles, but I need to get my good lady wife up to bed."

Charles stretched and Jenna heaved herself up off his lap, her hair squashed on one side and the creases of Charles's trousers indented in one red cheek.

"Yup," said Charles. "I'd better get the old ball and chain upstairs." He grinned, and Jenna thumped him playfully.

"Good night, everyone," said Jenna, standing. "Thank you for making our day perfect."

Two by two, the little group unfolded themselves from the sofas and followed in a lazy crocodile out across the snowy courtyard and back into the warm castle. They all climbed the stairs and disappeared into their respective bedrooms, calling out cheery but tired good-nights as they went.

Nory, however, was suddenly wide-awake, not just from the arctic blast across the courtyard, but at the prospect of a night with Isaac. He waited for her downstairs while she quickly threw some clean clothes into a bag; changed into her boots; and layered a sweater, coat, and scarf over her wedding outfit. By the time she reached the bottom of the stairs, every part of her was tingling with excitement.

## Thirty-two

Nory was warm and relaxed, her limbs feeling loose as she basked in the afterglow of another round of excellent love-making, during which Isaac had pressed all her buttons and found some new ones. After a considerable dry spell, she really had hit the jackpot. It felt almost too good to be true that she was as fired up by his brain as she was by his body.

She was in danger of falling in love with Isaac and she didn't mind a bit. In fact, now that she thought about it, that danger had been and gone. Could you fall in love with someone after six days? Nory felt suddenly a little nervous of the big feelings she had for Isaac after such a short time. It felt reckless and yet right all at once. Maybe that was what love was: holding hands as you jumped off into an abyss and hoping that neither of you would let go in the fall. A beautiful, terrifying thing.

She could hear the steady rhythm of Isaac's heart, her head rising and falling with his breaths, and it occurred to her that she could do this forever, be by his side, talk with him, lay with him. He was worth risking her heart for. He was worth making the leap.

"I know you live in the city," Isaac began, "and it would be a commute . . ."

*Say it! Please just say it, don't make me be the one to ask . . .*

"But I'd like to see you, exclusively, see where this takes us. We touched on it briefly last night but I'd like to make it a solid understanding between us."

*Yes!*

"I'd like that too. Very much." Nory was smiling so hard she thought her mouth might be permanently stretched. She wondered if Isaac could hear it in her voice.

"I could come up some weekends, and obviously you could come here. I feel very strongly that we should pursue this, us. I don't want you to think I'm getting ahead of myself . . ." he carried on.

"You're not. I feel the same," said Nory. "I don't want this to end. I don't mean just this weekend. I mean us. I want to be with you. I wish we had more time."

Isaac stroked his finger lazily up and down her arm. "Me too. Do you need to rush off tomorrow?"

"I'll be getting a lift with Ameerah and Dev, but I don't think they'll be in any hurry."

"Good," he said, kissing the top of her head and holding her a little tighter.

They were quiet for a while and then he spoke again.

"So, tell me what you did before you owned a bookshop."

"Hmm, well after uni, I got a great job doing absolutely nothing to do with my degree whatsoever. It was fabulous pay with amazing prospects, and I absolutely hated it."

"What were you doing?"

"I was working in advertising. It was actually Ameerah's dad who got me the job. I knew it wasn't something I would enjoy."

"Then why did you do it?"

"It's complicated."

"Well, explain it to me and if I get confused, I'll stop you."

"I was never allowed to forget that I'd been given this brilliant opportunity that neither my parents nor my brother—especially my brother—had access to. And I had to make sure I'd deserved it, otherwise what would have been the point? Does that make sense?"

"You felt you owed them a debt of some kind because you'd had a private education."

"Exactly. I had to make it count or it would be unfair to someone who would have made better use of it but didn't get the chance. There were twenty kids in my primary school class and only I got chosen. That's a lot to live up to."

"I think you were being a bit hard on yourself," said Isaac, stroking her hair.

"You should have asked Thomas about it; he had very strong feelings on the subject."

"And that's why you felt lost? You mentioned feeling lost the other day."

"Partly." She raised herself up onto her elbows, so that she was facing him. "School was intense, you know? We were always together, twenty-four seven; for seven years we lived in each other's pockets. Then I went to uni and although I wasn't with *them* anymore, I was still a pack animal, always with people. And then suddenly it was just me. We'd all kind of drifted off: Jenna was running all over the country chasing acting jobs, Ameerah had her head down with pupilage. It sounds pathetic, but suddenly I was all alone, doing a job I hated, too proud to go home and too stuck to get out of the hole I'd created. I was drinking too much and . . ."

"And then your friend died."

"Yes. Nothing sobers you up to your own pathetic reality like your friend taking their own life," she said sardonically. "Tristan was dead, and there I was living a life that I hated in order to live up to other people's expectations. So, I cleaned up my act and started living the life *I* wanted, which involved a massive loan that I'll be paying until I'm one hundred and twenty-three, but I'm happy."

"I think Tristan would be pleased with your choices."

"I wish he were here to see them. I wish he'd known how much I loved him. Maybe if he did . . ."

"You carry a lot of guilt around," Isaac observed.

"I don't think so."

"You feel guilty about Camille, guilty about Tristan, guilty about Thomas," he said.

"Well, yes, but . . ."

"You aren't responsible for other people's actions, or their happiness. It isn't your job to make everyone feel better. Your altruism is to be commended but not at the expense of yourself."

Nory pulled the duvet up. It was chilly now.

"I'm bored of talking about me. Let's talk about you."

"What do you want to know? I'm an open book."

Nory turned on her side, flopping her arm across his torso.

"An open book? Ha! I don't think so, Mr. Hiding Historical Works of Art in a Locked Trunk!"

"Every man must have his secrets." He chuckled.

"Do you really not want to try and get Heba's work authenticated?"

He sighed. "The truth is, I'd love to. But I don't know where to begin, and the thought of losing them terrifies me. I don't know if I can take the risk. Maybe one day."

Nory wished he'd let her help. She decided not to push it.

"So, you were a horticultural lecturer in Cornwall. What came before that?"

"You want a complete résumé, do you?"

"If you don't mind. I like to know what I'm getting into."

Isaac laughed quietly. "I finished university and started as an undergardener at Chatsworth House."

"That's a bit fancy," said Nory, rubbing her feet against his.

"You ought to know there is nothing fancy about the actual act of gardening," he said, and she liked that she could hear the smile in his voice.

"True," she agreed. "What next?"

"Next came an estate in Cumbria. I stayed longer than I should."

"Why?"

Isaac sighed. "I met someone. She was older than me, and I relied on her more than I should have. It wasn't a healthy relationship for either of us. She felt undervalued, and I felt overpowered."

"How long were you together?"

"Two years. It ended when I took the job in Cornwall. How about you?"

"Oh, I wasn't with her at all."

Isaac gave her a playful squeeze. "*I mean*, relationships. Any significant others? Ex-husbands in the closet?"

"No, no ex-husbands. No great love affairs, just a series of unfulfilling relationships." She said it with a smile, but the truth of it was, she hadn't had any great love affairs. Nobody had ever really rocked her world, until now. Was that a terrible thing? To be in her thirties and to only have experienced skinny love?

"So, then." Isaac traced a line with his finger between her

breasts and down past her stomach. Nory's breath caught. "We have nobody in the past to live up to or to live down." He turned onto his side and began to kiss her neck, working his way slowly and delightfully down her body with excruciating slowness. "Only each other to discover and the future to write." But Nory didn't hear; she was already lost to the sensation of right now.

Nory lay awake while Isaac slept beside her. His breathing slow and steady. She felt happy. Happier than she'd felt in a really long time. She felt as if being with Isaac would be like signing up to be happy for life. She wanted to do something for him, something that would show him how much she cared. She wanted to help him. She lifted her phone from the bedside table and began to compose a message.

# Thirty-three

She was woken while it was still dark by Isaac kissing her cheek and stroking her arm.

"Mmm . . . what time is it?" she asked sleepily.

"It's half past six," he replied. "Lettuce needs to go out, so I'll take her for a walk. I've got a few bits of work to do, so I thought I'd get them done early and then we can have a lazy Sunday morning before you have to leave."

Nory stretched and tried not to breathe in Isaac's direction.

"It's not really a lazy morning if you've already done a day's work." She yawned.

"Ah, but it's so much more fulfilling knowing that you've done all your jobs and have nothing pending."

"Freak." She smiled, pulling the duvet up around her chin.

Isaac laughed quietly. He reached down and kissed her forehead. "I'll be back in a couple of hours and then I'll make us breakfast."

"That sounds perfect."

"I'm glad you stumbled into my life," he said, brushing the hair away from her face.

"So am I." She had never meant anything more.

She'd had all night to think about her feelings for Isaac, and they were far from skinny. They could make this work. She was ready for this; she was ready to do whatever it took to make this happen.

She was still smiling when she heard the front door close and the crunching sound of Isaac's boots in the snow growing fainter as the snowy castle gardens stole him for themselves. For a few moments, she lay contentedly beneath the duvet. She could just stay here. She didn't have to move. But then she shook herself and rubbed the sleep from her eyes and sent the text.

She showered quickly and slipped into the fresh jeans and jumper she'd grabbed last night before they left the castle. She pulled her hair into a topknot and padded across the landing in her socks to the study. After pushing open the door, she glanced quickly out the window. The coast was clear. With trembling fingers, she reached for the vase and tipped the key into the palm of her hand.

Nory took a deep breath. If she did this, there was no going back. But she was sure it was the right thing to do. She knew how much it hurt Isaac knowing that Heba would never have her rightful place in art history. She also understood, after such a personal betrayal, how he was paralyzed by the fear of losing what he had left of her. Nory could make this right for him; she could fix it and right the wrong that had been done to his family all those years ago.

She had to shake her fingers out to stop them from trembling as she undid the locks and opened the trunk containing Isaac's family treasures. With the sketchbooks gathered to her chest, she went back to the desk and began to lay the books out. Her phone buzzed.

**Here.**

Nory blew out a breath and ran down the stairs. She opened the door, and Guy grinned at her.

"How's your head?" she asked.

"Bloody awful. Where's the stuff?"

Nory motioned for him to come in. She poked her head outside the door and looked both ways before closing it.

Nory led him up the stairs. With each step she felt the road of return slip further away from her. She pushed open the study door and pointed Guy in the direction of the open sketchbooks. Guy immediately set to work with the electric fervor that made him such a good journalist.

"This is gold dust," said Guy, his phone camera capturing the images laid out on the desk.

"You think you can help?"

"Definitely. I did some searches into the De-Veers after you messaged me. This is a great story."

With steady hands, Guy turned page after page of Heba's sketchbooks, carefully documenting every single painting.

"You need to let me speak to Isaac before you go to print, okay?"

"I said yes already," he said, still snapping.

"I need you to promise me."

"I pinky-promise swear," he said sarcastically.

"Guy, this is important to me."

He lowered his phone momentarily. "I promise I won't break the story until you've spoken to Isaac and he's given me the okay."

"The reason he hasn't done it himself is because the family have been burned before. He can't afford a big legal battle," said Nory.

She was starting to have second thoughts. Guy was a brilliant investigative journalist, but he was also a giant arsehole. He wouldn't screw her over, would he?

"If this goes the way I think it will, he won't have any legal fees at all. The De-Veers won't want to be seen as condoning the actions of ancestors who stole the paintings of a poor immigrant woman for their own personal gain. Certainly not with Marcus De-Veer hoping for a place in the next Cabinet reshuffle. They don't need that kind of negative heat."

Nory bit her lip and picked at the skin on the side of her thumb. Guy leafed through the final sketchbook, snapping every page until he had a comprehensive gallery of Heba's secret artworks.

"Done," he said. "When is Isaac due back?"

"Not for a while, but I don't want to take any chances. I'll get these back in the trunk. Can you let yourself out?"

She began to gently close the sketchbooks and pile them up. Guy rustled about in his messenger bag. Suddenly she felt his hands at her waist.

"Guy!" She tried to shake him off, but he tightened his grip, spinning her around to face him. His legs were splayed on either side of hers so that she was trapped between him and the desk. "Guy, I'm serious, let me go." She shoved at his chest, but he only leaned closer, so that she was bending backward over the desk.

"Come on, Nory, you wouldn't have asked for my help if you didn't still want me on some level," he said huskily.

"I mean it, Guy, fuck off!"

Guy loosened his grip. He looked suddenly shamefaced, his face ashen.

"Sorry, Nory, I thought . . ." He was still leaning over her, horror in his eyes.

"What did you think?" she hissed at him. "For fuck's sake!"

"I'm sorry," he said again. "I'm so sorry." He reached his hand around to support her back and help her straighten up.

"What the fuck is this?"

They both jumped. Isaac stood in the doorway, his face contorted with a mixture of disbelief, hurt, and pure rage. Nory felt her blood pressure drop and she felt lightheaded. She swayed. Guy was still holding her up. With a sickening dread, she could see exactly how this looked in Isaac's eyes.

"Isaac," she gasped. She pushed Guy away, who looked as mortified as she felt. "It's not what it looks like," she began.

He cut her off. "Which part?" he asked. His voice was even and cold as a blade. "The part where you deceived me and stabbed me in the back, or the part where you were going to screw *him* on my father's desk?"

Nory was completely tongue-tied.

"Listen, mate." Guy held out his hands placatingly.

"You do not speak! You are not my mate."

Guy, for once, did as he was told.

"Isaac, if you'll just listen . . ."

"Get out."

"Isaac!" Nory pleaded.

Isaac looked away and said slowly, with a painful final enunciation on each word: "Get. Out. Of. My. House. Now."

# Thirty-four

The stairs seemed to stretch on and on before her as Nory made her way blindly down, her eyes filled with tears. This was a nightmare. It wasn't supposed to be like this. The cold air slapped her wet cheeks as she burst out of the house at a run and kept on running. She was crying like she hadn't cried since she was a child, big deep sobs that made her breath ragged and her nose run. She hadn't even stopped to retrieve her boots, and the snow was soaking through her socks and burning her feet.

The utter stupidity of her plan taunted her as she ran. Why had she ever thought it was a good idea? She had so wanted to help, to make it right for Isaac, and all she'd done was make a mess of everything. She kept seeing the hurt on his face, and she stumbled at the sheer agony of his expression.

"Nory, slow down!" Guy called, catching up to her. "I'm sorry," he panted. "I'll make it right."

Nory rounded on him.

"You ruin everything!" she screamed. "You destroy everything you touch! You are fucking poison. Don't talk to me, don't contact me. I am done with you!" She shouted this last bit so loudly that he recoiled and fell backward. She stood just long enough to watch his distraught expression, his face seeming to crack from the pain of it, and then she was running again.

She ran all the way back to the castle. The front door was open as the butler carried bags through to Jeremy's car. Nory didn't stop to wait and see her friends off. She ran straight up the stairs and into her room, slamming the door behind her and hurling herself onto the bed. In another moment, her sobs were interrupted by an urgent banging on the door.

"Nory! What's going on? Let me in!" shouted Ameerah.

Nory wrenched open the door and fell into her arms.

"Hey, come on now," soothed Ameerah. "Tell me what's happened. I saw you running across the lawn from my window. And where are your shoes?" She maneuvered Nory back into the bedroom, kicking the door closed with her foot, and sat them both down on the bed. "Okay, now tell me everything." She peeled off Nory's wet socks and covered her blue-tinged feet with a blanket.

"I've ruined everything." Nory sobbed out the words. "What have I done? I've ruined everything."

When she was a little calmer and the shaking from the violent cold had abated, Nory told her friend the whole sorry tale. From the first time she'd seen Heba's botanical paintings, to her brilliant, slightly wine-fueled 3 a.m. idea to surprise Isaac by asking Guy to help her get the sketchbooks authenticated. Then she lay back on the pillows and waited for Ameerah's verdict.

"Okay," Ameerah said, gingerly picking up several soggy, balled-up tissues between her fingernails and flicking them into the bin. "I'm not going to lie to you; it's a mess. I mean, Guy of all people!"

"He's such a good journalist. It's what he does. I thought he could help." As she said the words, the ludicrousness of her idea came back to slap her cheek.

"Unfortunately, he's not as good a person as he is a journalist," Ameerah said, her mouth a straight line.

Nory had reached the stage of crying where she was technically all cried out, but her breath kept hitching as her diaphragm spasmed. She covered her face with her arm and moaned, "It wasn't meant to be like this."

"No," agreed Ameerah. "Of course it wasn't. Do you think Isaac will talk to you?"

"I don't know. No, I don't think so."

"At the very least, he needs to know that you weren't getting it on with Guy."

Nory winced.

"Try messaging him," Ameerah encouraged. "Do you want me to go round there?"

"I don't know if that would help or make things worse."

"Well, we need to get your boots back if nothing else."

"And coat," said Nory weakly.

Ameerah nodded. "Maybe we could send Dev over, man to man and outsider to outsider."

"That could work." Nory sniffed. "Maybe I could write Isaac a letter."

Ameerah stroked the tear-wetted hair from Nory's face. "Okay. That's a plan. You get writing, and I'll speak to Dev and excuse you from breakfast."

"Oh god! Jenna and Charles will be expecting us all down at the hotel for breakfast with their families," Nory wailed.

"Jenna and Charles have had us at their beck and call for a whole week; the newlyweds can manage by themselves for one morning. And besides, Jez and Katie have already left, they're heading back to Katie's mum's for a few days."

"I didn't get to say goodbye," Nory lamented.

"They're grown-ups, drop them a message," Ameerah assured her.

There was a knock at the door.

"Yes?" Ameerah called.

A beat.

"It's Guy. I need to talk to Nory."

Nory rolled over so that her face was in the pillow, and screamed "Fuck off!" into the feathers.

"I'll handle him," said Ameerah. "You get writing." Ameerah kissed the top of her friend's head. "I love you."

"I love you too." Nory sniffed.

Nory never did find out exactly what Ameerah said to Guy that day, but Guy was politely cautious around Ameerah forever after.

*Isaac,*

*I am so sorry. I know that right now you feel like I betrayed you, but I promise you I didn't. I was only trying to help. Nothing happened or was going to happen with Guy, that's the god's honest truth. I asked him to help me, that's all. I didn't know he would try it on. Nothing would ever have happened.*

*It was supposed to be a good thing. I know how much Heba's work means to you, and I knew that you were too afraid of losing it all to challenge the De-Veers. I thought that if I could set the wheels in motion for you, take the leap that you couldn't, then it would set you on the path to getting*

*Heba's work back. Please believe I would never have risked
you losing her paintings. Guy was under strict instructions to
stop digging if he thought there was any risk at all and to
clear everything with both of us. I realize now how
irresponsible that sounds, especially given what you walked
in on. I put my faith in the wrong person, and I will always
be sorry for it. But most of all I am sorry that I hurt you.
Please forgive me. Please know that I did what I did for you
alone. Did I ruin everything? Please say we can get past this.
I am yours if you'll have me.*

*With all my heart,
Nory xxx*

❧

Dev had been unable to speak to Isaac because he wasn't at the
cottage, and neither, upon further investigation, did he appear
to be around the gardens. Nory's boots, coat, and scarf were
outside the front door on the mat. Dev had gathered up her
things, pushed Nory's note through the letter box, and left.

"I take it you've tried phoning him?" Jenna asked.

Nory held up her phone and scrolled through to show page
after page of Isaac's number having been called. "No response,"
she said, as though the evidence wasn't blindingly obvious. "I've
messaged a bunch of times as well. Nothing."

"I'm sorry, Nory," Jenna said. "I know you really liked Isaac.
Guy is such an arse."

"I'm not overly keen on Isaac right now either," said Pippa.

"It's not his fault." Nory leaped to his defense. "I've only got
myself to blame."

Ameerah and Jenna made soothing shushing noises.

"He didn't let you explain," Pippa continued. "Everyone has a right to a fair hearing, isn't that correct, Ameerah?"

"Innocent until proven guilty," Ameerah agreed.

"But I am guilty!" said Nory. "Not of doing anything with Guy, but for the whole secret investigation. Who the hell did I think I was? Nancy bloody Drew?"

"You were only trying to help," soothed Jenna. "And if he'd taken a second to listen to you, he would have realized."

"He took me into his confidence, and I betrayed him."

"'Betrayed' is a strong word," said Ameerah.

"But it's exactly what I did. I wanted to fix it and instead I broke it all to hell." Nory could see her friends exchanging worried glances. "I'll be fine," she assured them, wiping her eyes and sniffing hard. "I just need to get back to London. I need to be with my books."

"Chin up, old girl," said Charles.

"Why must all our group gatherings end with Guy causing a disaster?" asked Jenna. "I'm supposed to be the drama queen." She rolled her eyes, and they all laughed.

"It was a beautiful wedding," said Nory, holding a hand of both Charles and Jenna. "And an amazing week. Thank you for inviting us all, it's been lovely to be all together again."

"It's been shits and giggles for sure," said Pippa.

"Shits and giggles and then some," added Ameerah.

"We'll have to do it again soon. For no reason next time. I don't want us to be the kind of friends who only all get together in the same room for births, weddings, and funerals," said Jenna.

"Agreed." Pippa nodded.

"Although the next one probably will be for a birth," said Nory.

"Gosh, yes, Katie and Jez. It's not that long now," agreed Jenna.

"Well." Charles clapped his hands together. "We've got to get down to the hotel. It's been great." Nory saw him well up and quash it—blink and you'd have missed it. "Love you all, losers! Thanks for coming."

They exchanged hugs and kisses and then Ameerah, Pip, and Nory watched the happy couple cross the snowy drive, arms wrapped around each other.

"As you know, I don't believe in the concept of marriage," said Pippa, and Ameerah and Nory groaned dramatically. "But if any couple can make it, it's those two."

"Agreed," said Ameerah, kissing Pippa's cheek.

"Me too," added Nory, wrapping her arms around Pip's waist.

"I love you both with all my heart," said Pippa stiffly. "And if you ever tell anyone, I'll murder you both in your sleep."

The three friends stood quietly for a few moments in the grand hall decked with boughs of holly and let it wash over them one last time before they headed home.

Ameerah pulled away and out into the London traffic, leaving Nory on the curb. The city had never felt so loud, and Nory had never felt so small within it. If there had been any snow here at all, no evidence of it now remained, which made her time at Robinwood Castle feel even more like a dream. The pavements were wet and shining in the lights from shop windows. People rushed past, oblivious to the brokenhearted woman who wandered among them. It had always amazed Nory how one person's life could be irrevocably changed and yet the world kept on going regardless. She felt out of step with the present.

Nory looked across at Serendipitous Seconds. They were normally open on Sundays in December; it was prime shopping time, but they were closed today. She couldn't expect Andrew to work a seven-day week while she'd been swanning around a castle. She should never have gone. She should have trusted her instincts and stayed the hell away from Guy and Robinwood Castle and head gardeners who made you fall in love with them.

The Father Christmas in the window rocked in his chair, and the twinkle lights picked out the Christmas titles stacked up around him. She didn't need to go in. She could leave it closed and head to her flat and collapse in a heap on the sofa.

Her flat, cozy and warm, floated into her mind—did she really want to be alone with nothing to do right now? She stood for another moment in the busy square, halfway between her flat and the shop, and then she made her decision.

Nory flicked on the lamps and breathed in the comforting smell of old books and the lingering scent of cinnamon and spice candles. She turned the shop's sign to read *Open* and parked her case and bags in the kitchenette. Then she began to busy herself in the little shop, visually taking stock of what had been sold and moving books from one place to another to keep the view fresh for returning customers.

She stood in front of the glass display case, where Serena De-Veer's—Heba's—precious first editions lay on a bed of crimson silk. They shouldn't be displayed, not when the name on the cover was a lie. Nory unlocked the case and removed the books. She wrapped them carefully in a cotton sheet and locked them in the bottom of her filing cabinet.

It felt like she was dragging her limbs from one place to the next. The look of utter betrayal on Isaac's face kept replaying in her mind, making her breath catch every time. She wished she could unsee it, but her brain seemed hell-bent on torturing her over and over.

It was a blessed relief when the first customers came in and distracted her from her thoughts, and the shop was mercifully busy with Christmas shoppers for the whole afternoon. At times she had a queue for sales at the counter while several other people waited patiently around the shop for her attention. She was spread too thin, rushing from one person to the next, but it was all-encompassing, and she was grateful for more than simply the sales that day.

When Nory locked the door at half past four, she was exhausted but not ready to be alone with her thoughts just yet, so she set about hoovering the shop and tidying, getting everything ready for the morning. Andrew would be most impressed when he got in tomorrow to find all the morning jobs already done.

Two unopened boxes lay behind the counter, and she recognized the handwriting on the labels as one of her vintage book contacts. She opened them up and breathed in the perfume of age and possibilities that rose from well-loved pages. This was treasure in paper form, and she knew instinctively which of her customers the various titles would suit, as though their names were already written into the bindings, waiting to be reunited. She would call them tomorrow and tell them what she'd acquired.

Eventually she had to go home. She thought about going out for dinner, but she would only be putting off the inevitable; sooner or later she was going to have to be alone, without the bolster of other people forcing her to keep her shit together.

Pepe's was open, every table full, the smell of garlic and caramelized onions bursting into the air every time the door was opened. Nory thought about her empty fridge and barren cupboards and considered going in and ordering a takeaway, but she couldn't face Anthony's friendly greeting; she suspected that if anybody paid her the slightest kindness she would collapse into floods of tears. Instead, she ducked into the corner shop—where the staff only spoke to tell you the cost of your items—and bought herself two KitKat Chunkys and a Pot Noodle. It was a far cry from the gourmet pleasures she'd enjoyed for the last seven days, but given her mood, it felt fitting that her dinner should be crap too.

∽

Her mum called as Nory was drinking the dregs of the salty broth straight out of the Pot Noodle tub.

"Hello, love, Ameerah called me. She's filled me in on what's happened."

*Of course she did.*

"Right."

"How are you doing?"

"Not so good, but I'll be okay."

"I can't believe Isaac wouldn't let you explain yourself. I'd expected more from him; he always seems like such a nice boy, but I suppose you never can tell."

"It's not Isaac's fault, Mum. It's mine and Guy's. Whichever way you look at it, I betrayed Isaac's trust."

"I don't like the sound of this Guy at all. Ameerah said you went to school together. And he's married too!"

"Yes. All of the above."

"Can't you just talk to Isaac?"

"Mum, he doesn't want to talk to me, and I don't blame him."

"Maybe Thom, or your dad could?"

"Oh god, Mum, no!"

"They might be able to help. Thom and Isaac go way back, and I think Isaac's always looked up to your dad . . ."

"Mum, do not get Thom or Dad to talk to Isaac. That is the worst possible course of action you could take. In fact, please don't tell Thom about Heba's books. Isaac never wanted anyone to know, and I've already told too many people."

"I only want to help, love. That's a mother's job. When our babies are hurt, we fix it."

"I appreciate the offer and I understand that it comes from a good place, but you can't fix this, Mum."

She didn't want to, but she began to cry down the phone. Once the sobs came, they came thick and fast, and she didn't seem to be able to stop them. She wished at that moment she was snuggled up in the sitting room at her parents' house, the TV on in the background, her mum chatting regardless of whether anyone was listening or not. Her dad would keep her topped up with an endless stream of mugs of tea because that was the only way he knew how to deal with his daughter's boyfriend issues: to drown the problems in an ocean of tea in the hopes they would float away—and to be fair, it had always been pretty effective.

"Oh, my darling girl." Her mum sniffed. "You know I cry if you cry!"

"I know." Sniff. "I'm sorry."

"Don't you be sorry—I'm sorry! I didn't realize you liked Isaac so much."

"Neither did I at first." More sobs. "Mum?"

"Yes, love?"

"Do you think it's possible to fall in love with someone in six days?"

"*Do* you love him?"

"Yes."

"Then it's possible. The phrase 'love at first sight' had to come from somewhere."

"Should it hurt this much, though? Shouldn't I still be in the shallow end of love after so short a time?"

"Love is love, my darling girl. Time is no measure for the depth of it. Do you want Dad to come and get you?"

Nory managed a weak laugh. "No, Mum, I'm a big girl, I'll be fine. But if you do see Isaac, can you tell him . . . can you tell him that I'm sorry?"

"I'll tell him."

"Thanks, Mum."

Nory climbed into bed and messaged Andrew while watching *Antiques Roadshow*, the BBC's most soothing Sunday program. She began her message with *Please don't reply tonight, I'll see you in the morning* because she couldn't face another phone call this evening.

She sent one more message before putting her phone on silent and trying to concentrate very hard on the television program in which people brought old heirlooms from their attics to show experts.

> I don't know if you got my note, or any of my
> other messages. But I'll say it again just in case:
> I'm sorry. My intentions were good, if misguided.
> Guy means nothing to me. But you mean
> everything. My heart belongs only to you. xxx

Nory pressed Send, not knowing if Isaac would bother to read it; for all she knew he may have already blocked her number—she probably would have if the roles were reversed.

∼

She hadn't expected to sleep. She had imagined that she'd be tossing and turning and pacing the floor of her tiny flat all night long in despair. Instead, she had fallen into an almost coma-like sleep the moment her head had touched the pillow and had woken up to the voices of the peppy broadcasters on BBC *Breakfast*; she must have left the TV on all night. As the events of the previous day came back to her, Nory was overwhelmed by a sudden urge to turn over and go right back to sleep. Apparently, heartbreak was soporific. But sleeping all day wasn't an option. She had a shop to run and a grumpy cat to reinstate.

Andrew knocked on her door at 8:15 a.m. He was red-faced and panting and holding a scowling Mugwort in a cat basket.

"I hate those stairs," he said, leaning in to kiss her cheek. "How are you, my little heartbroken shopkeeper? I would have brought coffee, but your cat weighs a ton; he was a two-handed job most of the way here. I got some very strange looks on the tube."

"Thanks, Andrew, you're a star."

"Yes, I am."

Nory was glad he wasn't being overly tender, even though it was absolutely in his nature to be so. She was still very much in danger of bursting into tears at the first sign of sympathy.

Mugwort slinked out of his basket and shook himself. He gave the corners of the sofa and the chair legs a good sniff and then, as though satisfied that everything was in order, he jumped up onto the sofa and began to snore almost instantly.

"Let's get a coffee before work," said Andrew, pulling her into a hug. "And don't you dare weep on my shoulder. This jacket is suede, and everyone knows salt stains are a nightmare."

# Thirty-six

The Christmas rush in the shop continued, as did the radio silence from Isaac. Nory had tried to call him, but it went straight to voice mail, which Ameerah agreed most likely meant he had blocked her. Nevertheless, she persevered with two more WhatsApp messages in the following days, which remained "delivered" but not "read."

She felt as though she was living in her own peculiar montage, faking happy for her customers during the working days and throwing herself into paperwork in the evenings, with take-away meals from Pepe's and too much wine before falling gratefully into sleep: a blissful respite from thinking about Isaac and lamenting what might have been.

"If you keep being this efficient, I will be out of a job," Andrew commented, having gone to check the stock and finding it completely up to date. "I think I preferred you when you were hopeful and haphazard rather than crestfallen but competent."

"I'm sorry my shattered love life is making you feel redundant."

"What are you wearing to our Christmas do?"

"I'm not sure yet."

"Well, you haven't got long to decide." He looked at her pointedly. "You do know it's tonight, don't you?"

Nory stopped what she was doing, a book hugged against her chest.

"Tonight? It can't be. Are you sure?"

"Yes, Nory, of course I am sure. It's been booked for months."

"But. So today is Saturday? Saturday the twelfth?"

"Correct."

"How did I lose track of the time like that?"

"You've been in a wormhole of woe."

"Oh god, that's pathetic!"

"I'm surprised Ameerah hasn't been on at you about outfits; the only thing that woman likes more than the law is clothes."

"Don't forget Dev."

"As if we could! Who knew that under that hard-nosed barrister lay a hopelessly romantic Marianne Dashwood?"

Ameerah always joined them on their Christmas work dos, partly because she bopped into the shop so often she was practically an honorary employee, and partly to add to the numbers; only Andrew and herself actually worked at Serendipitous Seconds, and if she didn't rustle up a date that year, it would just be Andrew, Seb, and Nory out on the town.

"Now I think about it, the last few times I've spoken to her, Ameerah has mentioned the work do," Nory mused. "I'd just assumed she was talking about it for, you know, sometime in the future, sort of getting ahead of the curve, you know how organized she is."

"Yes, well, the future, as they say, is now. So, you'd better start thinking Christmas pudding and drunken bankers; these venues love to pack in the work parties. I hope they don't deconstruct my food. I hate that. Just put the bloody meal together. Don't hand me a plate of separate ingredients and call it deconstructed, it's just laziness. If I wanted to make my own dinner, I'd have stayed home."

Nory made a mental note to check the menu before tonight. If Andrew's Christmas pudding came out as separate piles of brandy-infused dried fruits on a plate, there could be trouble. He already had an aversion to foods served to him on pieces of slate and/or tiles.

"And don't get me started on slate tiles!" he said, as though reading her mind. "Slate is for roofing, not for eating your dinner off of. The only people who should be eating from slate tiles are roofers on their lunch breaks."

Nory thought she'd better change the subject. They were skirting dangerously close to the subject of Jenga chips: the restaurateur art of building a structure of precisely cut rectangle chips in the style of the Jenga game—another foodie foible that drove Andrew to distraction.

"Is Seb's mum babysitting Matilda?"

Andrew pulled a face. "Yes. It'll be her first time alone with her. I had hoped to get my mum round as well—I was selling it as a sort of granny-bonding movie night—but *that* won't be happening. Grandma jealousy is real! They compete over *everything* to do with Matilda. It's the battle of the babushkas in our house every time my mum crosses the threshold."

"But your mum is so calm and lovely," Nory reasoned. "She makes Miss Marple look like Cruella De Vil."

"Or so we all thought." Andrew snorted. "Throw in an interloper grandma from America, and she's a completely different woman. She keeps trying to prove her seniority. It's all 'Glenda darling, that's not how Matilda likes it at all!' Or 'You wouldn't know, Glenda dear, you don't have the same bond with Matilda that I do, I've been here from the start!'"

Nory was trying and failing not to laugh. "I just can't imagine it. Quiet little Nina with her embroidery club and volunteering in the cat café," she said.

"It's all been a facade—she's a power-hungry diva granny! I'm surprised she hasn't been scenting the baby's things."

Nory pulled a face.

"At least with my mum there, Glenda's eccentricities don't have the chance to take hold. We'll probably come home to find Matilda and American Grandma wearing matching pearls and twinsets."

"But it's nice that they're both so enthusiastic?" Nory ventured.

Andrew huffed. "I'd prepared myself for the challenges of raising a tiny human, but nobody told me about the perils of trying to contain two competitive grandmas."

Nory was trying to get herself into the party zone, but it wasn't easy. She had booked the work do at Brasserie Zédel, a rather marvelous Art Deco restaurant in Piccadilly. She'd told Ameerah she would meet them there, but her best friend and Dev—recently upgraded from man-Barbie to actual boyfriend—insisted on coming to call for her. Nory suspected this was so that she couldn't feign an illness at the last minute, which she had considered. It was annoying when your friends knew you so well.

She had given up messaging Isaac. As desperate as she felt, she refused to torture herself further by watching the unread messages pile up. Whatever had begun to bloom between them had been most assuredly stamped out of existence, and she would just have to face it.

The green velvet swing dress was suitably festive and flattered her body shape in all the right ways. Her hair was pulled into a loose chignon and her makeup was done, the thick liquid eyeliner accentuating her hooded eyes. To an outsider, she would look like a whole person and not the empty decorated shell she felt.

Her phone pinged with a message just as she was about to join Ameerah and Dev downstairs. Her heart leaped and then dropped like a stone when she saw who it was from.

Guy: I don't blame you for ignoring my messages. I promise you I hate me more than you do. Camille knows everything—including about us. She's thrown me out, and I don't blame her. I'm getting counseling. I'm going to make it right, Nory. I'm going to make it right for everyone I've hurt, I promise. I'm sorry.

Nory looked up at the ceiling and took slow deep breaths. What did he expect from her? Forgiveness? She didn't have enough emotional energy at the moment to spare any for Guy. She put her phone in her bag and pulled open the door to find Ameerah wild-eyed and slightly breathless.

"Hello, where's Dev?" Nory asked, looking out into the hall.

"Downstairs. I told him I needed the toilet."

"Oh, okay." Nory stepped aside for her friend to pass into the flat.

Instead, Ameerah grabbed her by the shoulders, pushed her into the flat, and kicked the door shut with a Louboutin-booted foot. She forced Nory down onto the sofa and, still holding onto her shoulders, as though she might float away if she didn't, she knelt before her friend, eyes wide, her breath coming in shallow little gasps.

"What the hell, Amie? Are you on the run or something? You haven't been framed for a crime you didn't commit, have you?"

"It's worse than that."

"What could be worse than that?"

"I'm in love with Dev!"

Nory laughed. "Oh, thank god you've finally realized. I thought I was going to have to perform an intervention."

"This is not okay, Nory."

"Why not?"

"Because I don't know how to be in love! I'd only just gotten used to being in like-like. I've spent years training myself not to fall in love. I don't know how I'm supposed to act. I can't relax around him anymore. How am I supposed to behave?"

"Just behave like yourself."

"That's no help!"

Ameerah was becoming frantic.

"Does he know you're in love with him?"

Ameerah's eyes bulged with horror. "Of course he doesn't know."

"Well, don't you think you should tell him? You might be able to relax a bit more if you tell him. Because I'm pretty sure he's been in love with you for quite a while. It'll be a relief to Dev that you feel the same way."

"This wasn't supposed to happen."

"Well, love is rarely planned. You can't help who you fall in love with."

Nory could feel the dull ache in her chest that had taken up residence since she'd left Hartmead.

"Oh, sorry, Nory, this is shit for you. I'm so thoughtless. I just didn't know where to turn. It happened so suddenly, like BAM!"

Nory jumped, but Ameerah carried on regardless.

"One minute we're walking out of my apartment perfectly normally, and the next Dev hails a cab, and love wallops me right in the solar plexus. I've been trying to act casual all the way here, it's exhausting."

Nory smiled as she unfastened Ameerah's grip on her shoulders one finger at a time and then pulled her into a hug. "Don't ever be sorry for falling in love. You will be fine. You battle miscarriages of justice every day, you can handle being in love. And I will be here every step of the way."

"Thanks, Nory. I'm not going to tell Dev yet. I need to get my own head round it first."

"You do it when you feel ready. I don't think Dev's going anywhere."

Ameerah nodded and took a deep breath. "Okay, I feel better now, let's go and meet the others."

The brasserie was packed, mostly with rowdy Christmas parties. The Serendipitous Seconds party seemed dwarfed by comparison, but they had been given a table a little away from the bulk of the frivolity and Nory was glad of it. The restaurant and cocktail bar were underground, reached by a sweeping staircase down from the café above. The vibe was the elegant Art Deco era: gold leaf, marble columns, and table lamps in the brasserie and dark wood, leather, and intimate low lighting in the bar. As you descended, it felt like walking into a more glamourous age, where the bright young things had once ruled the night.

While spirits were rising all about them, both emotional and alcoholic, the meal at the Serendipitous Seconds table had turned into a conference about Nory and Isaac, and the villainous Guy.

"So, how do you feel about Guy's wife knowing about what happened between you?" asked Seb.

"Actually, strangely relieved. She should know. It felt wrong to lie to her."

"You didn't lie," pointed out Dev. "You just didn't tell her. Guy is the only liar in this scene."

"Quite right," said Ameerah, resting her hand on Dev's and then glancing at Nory, who gave a tiny nod of approval. Ameerah relaxed.

Dev smiled. He was so obviously in love with Ameerah. Nory hoped they'd be able to tell each other what everyone else already knew sooner rather than later.

"If I were Camille, I wouldn't take him back." Andrew waved his knife in the air as he spoke. "All the counseling in the world isn't going to change him."

"Maybe it will," said Nory. "He might sort himself out properly and become a decent human."

"You are too good," Andrew protested. "Even after all this, you still see the best in him."

"Oh, I assure you I don't, but it's not about me. I'm remaining hopeful for Camille's sake. He's too good for her, but she loves him, and if she's going to love him either way, then he ought to be the best version of himself that he can be to deserve her."

"And what about you?" asked Ameerah.

"The way I feel at the moment, I will never forgive him. But I'll never forgive myself either."

"Oh, Nory, that's not fair. You thought you'd found a way to help Isaac. If he'd had access to an investigative journalist, he might have done it himself," Ameerah protested.

"But I broke Isaac's trust. I thought I was making this grand gesture and imagined him being so grateful and falling instantly in love with me. I guess I got carried away by the fairy tale of it all, the castle and everything."

"I know what you mean. It felt surreal being all together again, and in a castle for god's sake! Talk about suspended reality. But I don't think you're being fair to yourself. Your motives were good, don't lose sight of that. What you did wasn't some kind of ego trip, or because you were enthralled by the scenery. That's not who you are."

"I second that," said Andrew. "You are terrible at parting with books, but you are good at being a lovely human."

"Can I quote you on that? Maybe I'll record it and send it to Isaac."

"Say the word, Nory, and I'll pay him a personal visit," offered Seb.

Andrew's eyes widened. "I am very attracted to you right now, Husband."

Seb looked over at Andrew and smiled. "Even though I'm a tired and grumpy, harassed parent?"

"Especially because of those things."

"You guys are actually relationship goals," said Dev.

Nory was never more grateful for her friends, but being surrounded by two such loved-up couples was a bittersweet experience.

❧

When they spilled outside—replete with fine French cuisine and house wine—the night air felt ice-sharp against their warm cheeks. But the Christmas lights glittering above their heads below the thick black sky, and the city pulsing with energy, the thrum of cars and the wild melody of a million voices, soothed the sting.

Andrew and Seb hailed a cab.

"Don't you want to get more drinks?" asked Ameerah.

"This is the most excitement we've had in months," said Andrew. "I think we'll quit while we're ahead."

"In bed with a sleep tea by midnight is our idea of how to end a perfect evening," Seb added. "Our daughter will be awake and ready to play at six thirty a.m., and there is nothing, and I mean nothing, worse than toys that light up and sing when you have a hangover."

Ameerah grimaced. "Fair play."

They waved Seb and Andrew off, Nory wrapping her arms around herself against the cold.

"What about you, Nory? Fancy another drink?"

"Not really. I've got to open the shop tomorrow—only two Sundays left till Christmas! But you two go on."

Ameerah puffed out her cheeks. "To be honest, I'm trying to kid my body into thinking it's still twenty, but it isn't working. It's taken me all this week to recover from last week. When did we get so old?"

Despite being bitterly cold, it was a clear and lovely night, and the three of them decided to walk back to Mayfair and soak up the atmosphere. Central London was never quiet, but it was never so alive as at Christmas. High above the shops and the offices, Christmas trees twinkled in the windows of studio flats and apartments.

When Nory was little, she had dreamed of a life in London, of living practically in the sky, like the roof scene in *Mary Poppins*. Well, she had done it. And for the most part, it had lived up to expectation—though she was yet to meet a handsome singing chimney sweep named Bert. What she couldn't have anticipated in her fantasies of escape was that, once she was ensconced in the big city, Hartmead would forever tug at her soul.

# Thirty-seven

Sunday became Monday, and Monday became Tuesday. Nory's days were busy, and her nights were long. Her mum texted, multiple times a day, with banal anecdotes or queries, which Nory knew was her way of being supportive and keeping an eye on her daughter without actually raising the subject that they both knew was on Nory's mind.

She didn't hear from Thomas, and she was grateful for it; he'd asked her to stay away from his friend and she hadn't, and look what had happened. She half wanted to message Thomas to give her side of things, but what would be the point? He was always poised to think the worst of her and now she had given him a carte blanche.

"What does Thom say?" she asked her mum on Tuesday night's phone call. "I'm guessing by now he knows that something went down."

"Don't you worry about your brother, you know he loves you," said her mum diplomatically.

"Does he?"

Her mum blustered. "What kind of a question is that? Of course he loves you. You're his sister, we're a family. I do not want to hear any more of this nonsense from you, young lady. Your brother would throw himself in front of a bus for you."

"Only so that he could haunt me for eternity."

Her mum tsked. "I give up."

The conversation moved back to safer territory—who had been seen smooching who in the White Hart and how Aunty Jada was recovering after her disastrous hysterectomy and so forth—until Nory heard her dad come in.

"Is that Nory?" she heard him ask.

"Yes, love, I was just telling her about Jada's hematoma."

"Tell her Isaac looks like hell. Every time he came down last week, he looked worse."

"Jake!" her mum hissed. But her dad was unrelenting.

"Those two want their heads banging together. You haven't been on the phone to her this much since she first went up to that school up the hill. With all that's going on in the world . . ."

Her dad was about to go into a rant. This happened sometimes; Nory would be on the phone with her mum, and her parents would suddenly begin a whole discussion about what was happening on the TV or in the news, and Nory would be left sitting on the phone, quietly waiting for her mum to remember she was still on the end of the line.

"Don't belittle people's feelings, Jake. You always do this. You compare every problem to world hunger, and you can't do that! Just because a person isn't experiencing a global tragedy doesn't mean they aren't suffering . . ."

"Mum, I'm probably going to go . . ."

"I'm not belittling anyone, Sasha. I'm merely trying to give a little perspective; they've got roofs over their heads and food in their bellies . . ."

"Well, if that isn't patronizing, I don't know what is. You are a Neanderthal when it comes to mental health . . ."

"Mum, can you hear me? I'm going to go now, leave you two to it. Say hi to Dad for me . . ."

"I know plenty about mental health. My grandfather had shell shock after the war . . ."

Nory gave up and ended the call.

꒰꒱

The books in the Christmas window had been selling out almost faster than they could refill it. Nory had reached the stage where she was having to place some of her most favorite vintage titles in the display—titles that she had surreptitiously held back because she couldn't quite bear to part with them. Of course, Andrew had been onto her from the start.

"Here, this would go nicely near the front, propped up by Santa's boot," he said on Wednesday morning, handing a book through to Nory, who was kneeling inside the deep bay window with her back to him. She took it and sucked in a sharp intake of breath.

"This is a 1955 edition of *Pookie Believes in Santa Claus.*"

"I know, that's why I handed it to you."

"I can't sell this!"

"You absolutely can, and you must. You are a bookseller, it's literally what you do."

"God, you're mean." Nory opened the book and looked at each illustration in turn, trying to imprint them onto her brain, then she closed it, lovingly gave the cover a stroke, and placed it in the window, nestled in a fake snow drift.

"And don't put it where nobody can see it."

Nory harrumphed and sat the book up straighter. Almost immediately two women stopped at the window and one of them pointed delightedly at Pookie.

*Dammit!*

Andrew passed her a 1970s copy of *'Twas the Night Before Christmas*, with a very Coca-Cola Santa on the front. She sighed and leaned it up against one of a pair of kitsch fawn bookends that held a row of classic Christmas titles between them, including a tattered copy of *The Nutcracker*, which Nory was hoping would slip under the radar, sandwiched as it was between the two bright intact spines of *How the Grinch Stole Christmas!* and Raymond Briggs's *The Snowman*.

Andrew handed her another book, but the moment Nory touched it, she knew it wasn't for the window. It was faded from red to burned orange with tinges of its original brilliance hidden on the inside cover. A picture of a Victorian Christmas tree sat in the center of the cover, which had been worn shiny.

"Ah, no, not this one. Magdalene will want this," she said.

"It's not on the list," Andrew mused. He knew the names in Nory's little book.

"No, I only just realized that it's for her," Nory replied thoughtfully.

Andrew laughed quietly. "The book whisperer strikes again."

It was wet and cold outside, and despite the fearful draft from the ancient windows, Nory felt deeply cozy as she looked out through rain-mottled panes onto the busy street beyond. She wondered for the ninetieth time that day what Isaac was doing. She could never have imagined that her short time spent with Isaac would have such a profound effect on her thought processes, but there it was: Her brain was now tuned to think about Isaac whether she wanted to or not.

"Come along, madam. Get your bottom out of the window, and I'll make you a nice hot cup of tea," said Andrew.

Nory shuffled backward out of the bay.

"Ooh, lovely," she replied, shivering.

Andrew went into the kitchenette to make tea, and Nory busied herself with a box of vintage books she'd bought at an online auction after half a bottle of wine. She could feel her fingertips tingle as they brushed against sepia pages. The faces of customers who were—whether they knew it yet or not—destined to love these books bloomed into her mind's eye. She grabbed her notebook and began to make a list.

The door tinkled, and Nory looked up to see Guy looking apprehensive. She froze. Guy gave her a tentative smile and held a leather satchel up, as though this should indicate something to her.

"What part of 'leave me alone' are you having trouble with?" Nory crossed her arms defensively across her chest.

Guy shifted from foot to foot. He seemed reluctant to leave the welcome mat.

"It's finished. My investigation. It would benefit Isaac greatly if he would let me interview him for the piece, but I understand he may have strong feelings about that." He had the decency to look shamefaced. "If he's happy to go ahead, I could get someone else to do the interview with my questions."

"Why are you telling me?"

"I promised you I wouldn't go to print without your go-ahead."

"It's not like you to keep a promise."

Guy looked down at his shoes. "I found an expert willing to look at the pictures I took of Heba's paintings. He was happy to go on record and go up against the De-Veers. He's worked on similar cases, repatriating artworks stolen during the Second World War. He would need to see them in the flesh, as it were, to properly authenticate Heba's work, but he thinks the case has legs. I think we've got something here, Nory. It's a huge story. If it goes the way I think it will, I believe I can help Isaac prove the authenticity of his great-great-grandmother's work without a costly legal case. My guy says he'll work pro bono, and I've found a solicitor who will do the same; the publicity is worth more to them than the cash."

He finished speaking and took a deep breath, like he'd been building himself up for it and was relieved it was over.

"May I come in?" he asked when she didn't speak.

"You're already in."

He nodded to himself and stepped gingerly off the mat as though the floor might be made of lava. He undid the straps on his satchel as he crossed the shop floor, pulling out a thick manila folder, which he laid on the book-strewn desk.

"It's all here. The expert's initial report, my investigation into Serena De-Veer. According to the archives, she had never shown any aptitude for art before she took those first paintings to the publisher. Her old governess was pretty scathing about her disappointing efforts in the feminine arts. I've tracked down the family of an officer who was serving in India at the time the De-Veers lived there. He had paid Heba for some of her botanical paintings and brought them back for his wife. They've stayed in the family, I've seen them. They want to help in any way they can. There were others too; Heba gifted one soldier a painting for his new daughter and another to an army chef."

Guy flicked through page after page of handwritten and typed notes, photographs, and various photocopied forms. He closed the folder and rested his hand on it as though it was hard for him to part with it.

"And now it's up to you," he said, looking her in the eyes with none of his usual bravado. Instead, his expression was pleading, as though if Nory didn't give him this lifeline, he would fall into an abyss.

"You've done all this in ten days? You've been busy," she said.

"I checked myself into the Priory clinic. As an outpatient. I go every day for counseling and then I work; it's like double therapy. I'd probably go completely mad without Camille if I didn't have my work. I'm sorting myself out, Nory."

A tear escaped and ran down his cheek, and he let it. No joke about being a crybaby. He didn't even try to wipe it away, he just let it fall and be chased immediately by another.

"I love Camille and I want her back. I'll do whatever it takes. I'll be a better man; I'll be the man she deserves."

"Words are easy," said Nory.

Guy nodded. "That's why I'm putting them into action."

Nory looked at him properly. There was an earnestness about him that she hadn't seen in a really long time, maybe never. She could cut him out of her life forever; it would be no more than he deserved. But despite it all, she believed he was trying.

"Wouldn't it be better for you to send it to Isaac directly?" Nory asked, looking back down at the folder.

"No, I don't think so. I've taken enough liberties with your life. This one's all yours—you get to make an informed choice about what happens next. If you don't send it on, that's your decision. I won't publish without consent. If you send it on and Isaac agrees, we'll take it from there."

Nory's stomach was writhing. "Do you really think Isaac has a chance to get Heba recognized as the artist?" She searched Guy's face.

"I do. I wouldn't put my name on the line if I wasn't confident. You of all people know that I don't like to lose."

A laugh escaped her, in spite of herself. Anger was such a draining emotion and it had certainly been taking its toll on Nory's well-being. She wasn't ready to forgive Guy. But as much as she wanted to shoot fire out of her fingertips and banish him to the underworld for all eternity, she knew she couldn't hate him forever.

"Okay." She sighed. "Leave it here. I'll have a think." She rubbed her temples, the urge to lie down and sleep overwhelming her once more.

"You'll make the right decision," said Guy. "You always do."

She nodded but didn't answer, and Guy began to walk away.

He stopped on the mat and turned. "I know it doesn't mean much now, but I am sorry. Not my usual bullshit sorry. This one's real. I'll prove it to you."

"Camille needs it more than I do."

Guy nodded. "She's top of my list."

He opened the door and pulled his collar up against the cold, and soon he was lost in the mass of Christmas shoppers.

Andrew came back into the shop bearing mugs of hot tea.

"Who was that?" he asked, glancing at the folder on the desk.

"Guy," said Nory absently.

Andrew sucked in a breath. "What did he want?"

"To give me his investigation into Heba."

"Why did he give it to you?"

"He says it's my choice whether I pass it on to Isaac or not."

Andrew looked at the folder as though it contained explosives. "Which way are you leaning?"

"I don't know."

Nory was on the sofa, Mugwort half off her lap, as though to let her know that he could take her or leave her. He had sulked for the last nine days, though she wasn't sure if he was punishing her because she had gone away or because she had returned and taken him away from his beloved Matilda.

The tastefully decorated artificial Christmas tree managed to look huge in Nory's apartment even though it was only four feet tall. Each year she liked to meander around Fortnum & Mason and take inspiration from their decorations. This year she had splashed out on a gold stag to sit on the mantel above the skinny Victorian fireplace. Of course, the fireplace itself was long since defunct, but it made a lovely feature . . .

The plain-looking manila folder that was the cause of so much internal conflict sat on the coffee table, next to a tin foil tray of Pepe's spaghetti puttanesca, a side of garlic bread with mozzarella and parmesan, and a tiramisu; Nory was *not* one of those people who forgot to eat when they were heartsick.

Her initial thought was that maybe she should catch the train down to Hartmead and present Isaac with the folder face-to-face. But given their last encounter, she felt that her presence might make him dismiss the contents out of hand without giving it a fair look.

Another idea had been to bury the folder in the bottom of her wardrobe and forget about it. And then maybe in twenty years time she would send it on, and everything between them would be water under the bridge and they might even renew their friendship. The flaws with this idea were, firstly, that he might be married with children by then; secondly, she didn't want that folder beating its presence in her wardrobe like the Jumanji game until she was fifty; and thirdly, twenty years was far too long to be living on tenterhooks.

"Oh, Mugwort! What shall I do?"

Mugwort pricked up one ear and gave her a disdainful side-eye before tucking his head under his paws.

"Unfortunately, not all of us have the luxury of burying our heads in our paws."

Mugwort would not be drawn into an argument and began to snore.

Nory nudged the folder with her foot as though the answer might float out from between the pages. She thought about Tristan and the decision he had made that could never be undone. When held up against that, whichever choice she made would be less final; there was a way back from anything but death. Perhaps it was a macabre way to think, but for Nory, it was a way to not forget, a way to put things into perspective. Because however desperate she might feel at times in her life, she would—God willing—never feel as desperate as her dear friend must have felt.

She took a deep breath in and let it out slowly. She knew what she would do. Deep down she had known all along. She would post the folder to Isaac and let him have the choice. It was, after all, his family legacy and therefore rightfully his decision. Of course, it would likely be the final death knell of their short-lived relationship. But if Isaac decided to go ahead and let Guy publish, and Heba got her name rightfully restored to her work, then maybe she could live with the mess she'd made of everything. One good thing would have come of it. Maybe justice for Heba would be enough to sustain her through the heartbreak of losing Isaac.

⁓

Nory got up early the next morning to get to the post office before work. She handed the parcel, wrapped in thick brown paper, over the counter and paid extra for express delivery. The clerk took the package and tossed it casually into a sack behind the counter, as though her whole heart wasn't held within. Nory sent out a silent prayer to the universe that Isaac would see that her motives were pure, even if her execution had been clumsy.

*Dear Isaac,*

*Please don't dismiss this package out of hand. It contains Guy's full investigation, and he believes that you have a strong case against the De-Veers. It's all in there. Please read it. I know that I went against your wishes. There aren't enough sorrys in the world to express my remorse that I betrayed your trust. I ruined something that I think could have been wonderful and I'll have to live with that.*

*Guy has given me his word that he won't take this to print without your consent. It is your choice. If I can make just one thing good out of this mess, then maybe I can live with the thought of never seeing you again.*

*I want you to know that nothing happened between Guy and me, I promise you. It never would have. He took me by surprise, and I was dealing with the situation when you found us. The truth is, that from the moment we met, there could never be anyone else but you.*

*Please don't let your anger at me color your judgment when it comes to Heba's legacy. Everything you need to*

*right the wrong that was done to your family is within
these pages.*

*I hope that one day you can forgive me.*

*With all my love, always,*
*Nory xxx*

# Thirty-eight

Today was Friday, the last Friday before Christmas. At this time of year, time worked in terms of "lasts": the last Friday, the last weekend, the last day for post, the last shopping day. The countdown was palpable in every aspect of daily life. For Nory, this Friday was its own countdown. Isaac's folder would be delivered today. She didn't know if he would open it, or if he would read her letter or toss it aside, or whether the whole folder would be cast into the fire.

"I think you should take the weekend off." Ameerah was bouncing Matilda on her knee. Matilda was looking straight past Ameerah, mesmerized by the twinkling lights in the window. Ameerah's case had been adjourned until 3:00 p.m., and she had hopped into an Uber and come across town.

"It's the last weekend before Christmas; it'll be wildly busy."

"Why don't you see if your mum can come up here?" Andrew suggested. "She can mooch about town and see the sights while you're working and then be there in the evenings for, you know, mum stuff."

"That's an excellent compromise," said Ameerah. "You need your mum to fuss around you and make you eat soup. She's batty as hell, but by god she's good in a crisis."

"I don't need my mum. I'm not five!"

"Everyone needs a mum occasionally," said Andrew. "It doesn't even have to be your own mum, just a mum or a mum figure."

"I mean, I wouldn't go to *my* mum if I needed soothing, because she has the maternal instincts of a dustpan. But I'd go to yours," Ameerah added.

"Do I really look that bad?" Nory asked.

"Worse," said Andrew, squinting at her. "I've seen more color on a peeled parsnip."

"Has my mum been on the phone with you?"

"Yes!" They shouted in unison. Matilda, thinking it must be screechy time at Serendipitous Seconds, let out a piecing scream of delight and clapped her hands.

"Relentlessly," said Andrew.

"I'm afraid to check my phone between court sessions because I know I'll have thirty-six voice mails from Mama Sash," Ameerah added.

Nory pulled a face. "Sorry about that. She overly worries."

"I'm not sure she'll be able to hold out until we head down for Christmas on the twenty-third," said Ameerah. "Jake may have to start tranquilizing her."

"I'm still not sure about being closed on Christmas Eve. It feels like shopkeeper sacrilege." Nory was worrying at a thread on her jumper.

"That's your dad talking," Andrew chimed in. "We both agreed back in the summer that we would have Christmas Eve off this year. I honestly don't think we're going to make a killing, saleswise, the day before Christmas. All the offices around here will be shut already; this is Shepherd Market, not Oxford

Street. The kinds of people who want to buy vintage books as gifts will already have done so, trust me."

Her friends were looking at her with pained expressions. Nory surmised this was probably a fifty-fifty split between worry for her and being worn down by her mum's incessant phone calls. She should have known better than to sob down the phone to her mum; sobbing was guaranteed to fire up her mum's fix-it receptors. And when Sasha Noel was on a mission, she made the Terminator's efforts look half-arsed.

"You're right, of course you're right." Nory threw her arms into the air in surrender. "We'll close for Christmas Eve, and I'll call my mum and try to calm her down. Now hand over my goddaughter, you baby hogger."

Nory hugged Matilda close, and when the baby rested her head against Nory's chest, she bent her head to sniff her hot little neck. Why did babies smell so good? Matilda looked up and made a noise that sounded distinctly like a meow.

They all looked from one to another, stunned.

"Did she just meow?" Ameerah asked.

"It sounded like it," Nory replied.

"My daughter's first word can't be 'meow'!" cried Andrew. "It should be 'dada'! This is all Mugwort's fault."

"I think Matilda's a bit young for first words yet, to be fair," said Nory.

"Not if she's a child prodigy, she's not. She could be, you know. Seb agrees; she's uncannily clever. We think she might be gifted."

"But would a child prodigy's first word be 'meow'?" Ameerah asked.

Andrew gave Ameerah the kind of bone-shriveling look he

usually reserved for drunk men on the tube. Nory's phone tinged with a message.

**GREAT NEWS! YOUR PARCEL HAS BEEN SUCCESFULLY DELIVERED.**

*Well,* she thought. *It's in the lap of the gods now.* If she had expected to feel some sense of relief, she'd been mistaken.

‿ᴖᴐ

Charles and Jenna wandered into Serendipitous Seconds on Sunday afternoon just as a family of German tourists were leaving, having purchased a rare and rightly expensive 1882 edition of *Grimm's Fairy Tales.* Several other customers still milled about the shop. Nory directed a fair-haired woman in a green blazer toward a vintage copy of P. G. Wodehouse's *Blandings.*

"Oh my god!" said the woman, her hand flying to her mouth. "My dad had a copy just like this, and I never could find it after he died. How did you know?"

"Just a little bookseller's intuition." She smiled.

The woman held the book to her chest and continued to browse. She would be buying a lot more books this afternoon.

Andrew was having a well-earned day off, though from the tone of his messages, not necessarily a relaxed one. Andrew, Seb, Matilda, and Glenda were all invited to Andrew's parents' house for Sunday lunch. From what Nory could gather, Nina was behaving like the Queen, and Glenda's comment on every room of the house was "So tiny, how British!"

"I didn't expect you to be so busy on a Sunday," said Jenna, air-kissing Nory before seeming to remember that she was an actual friend and pulling her into a hug.

"Oh, well, you know, last Sunday before Christmas and all that. What brings you to this neck of the woods?"

"We've just been for lunch around the corner, and I was saying to Jen that I've never been to your shop before. So here we are," Charles said.

"What do you think?" Nory asked, smiling as she looked around at the piles of books and fairy lights. All the random armchairs were occupied by readers, one or two looking as though they were settled in for the afternoon. A girl of about nine years old was perched on the old milking stool reading a vintage copy of *Little Grey Rabbit's Christmas* by Alison Uttley while her dad browsed the shelves.

"It's sweet," said Charles. "I like it, it has a good feeling about it."

"Thank you," said Nory, imagining this must be what Andrew felt like when people compliment him on Matilda. "How is married life treating you?"

"It's wonderful!" Jenna gushed. "I love being a Mrs."

"Though not enough to take my name," added Charles.

"I'm an actress, my name is my calling card. You could take my name if you're that worried—you don't need yours for publicity."

"I'm not sure my father would approve of that." Charles laughed.

"Have you heard anything from Isaac?" Jenna asked.

Nory shook her head. She didn't want to talk about it. There was nothing to discuss.

"Pippa saw him," said Jenna.

"What? When?"

"She stayed on at the castle for an extra couple of days. She had business meetings with Lord Abercrombie or something. I think he's keen to get her on board for castle events. And I think she needed to see your sister-in-law too. She's really taken with Shelley. If it wasn't for your brother and the children, I think Pip would whisk her away to work in Pip Land."

"Did Pippa talk to Isaac?" There was absolutely no point in trying to appear nonchalant about her feelings for Isaac; Jenna had seen her snot-crying, after all.

"Well, you know Pip. Ever to the point. She apparently called him a fuckwit and told him if he let you go over some old paintings and a compromising position, he had manure for brains, and she'd expected better from a horticulturalist."

Nory laughed in spite of herself.

"Good old Pip," said Charles. "Ever the oversimplifier."

"And what did Isaac say?" Nory was on tenterhooks. Her organs seemed to quiver with anticipation.

"Not much, apparently. He seems to be the strong, silent type. He said thank you and he'd bear it in mind."

Nory balked. "That's it? He'll *bear it in mind*? I'm crying my bloody heart out over him, and he'll *bear it in mind*?"

"Men show their emotions differently from women," Jenna soothed. "And you said yourself he's a very private person, and proud too. For all we know he might well be crying his bloody heart out on the inside."

"Oh, god! It's such a mess." Nory covered her face with both palms.

"We saw Guy," said Charles. "That is to say, we helped him move into an apartment. He's hell-bent on winning Camille back. It seems that after more than a decade of marriage he's finally realized he's in love with his wife."

"Let's hope Camille doesn't discover she feels the opposite!" said Jenna.

"Or maybe let's hope for her sake she does," added Nory.

Charles shot her a look.

"It's not that I want Guy to be unhappy. I just don't want him to be happy at Camille's expense," she explained.

"But Guy is our friend," said Charles, as though unable to comprehend anything other than absolute loyalty no matter what. "We have history."

"He is and we do. But I don't think we should ignore behavior that hurts people out of loyalty. That's how bad things are allowed to happen," said Nory.

Charles scoffed.

"If friends don't hold each other accountable, then maybe they're not really friends," Jenna ventured.

"I don't believe this," said Charles, running his hand through his hair as though he'd just lost big at the races. "Guy did you a real solid in putting together that investigation for Isaac."

"I know. And I'm grateful for it. But it doesn't negate what's already past. I don't want to argue with you, Charles, you know I love you. We all want what's best for Guy, that's not in question. I wish him all the best, I really do. I hope he's able to be the person he wants to be."

Charles nodded. "I get it," he said, rubbing wearily at his forehead. "I do. It's just. You know."

Nory rubbed his arm. "I do. Guy will be okay."

"And what about you?" asked Jenna. "Will you be okay?"

Nory shrugged. "What other choice do I have?"

"Is Isaac worth it?" asked Charles. "Worth all this angst?"

Nory didn't need to think. "Yes. He is. Every bit of it."

Charles nodded. "Well, as someone who spent half his life in the unrequited-love club, all I can say is, don't give up hope."

Jenna rested her head on Charles's shoulder.

"Thanks, Charles." Nory smiled. "I'll try."

∽

Charles and Jenna left with hugs and kisses and calls of "Merry Christmas!" Friendship groups like theirs were like a family in lots of ways; complicated and simple all at once. Sometimes they fought, sometimes they drifted, but the knots that bound their lives were too intricately tied to ever untangle truly.

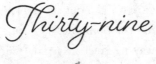

Nory's mum had called just as she was closing the shop, and instead of heading straight home, she found herself walking and talking. It was dark but the streets were busy, and Nory made sure she kept to well-lit areas and dropped her location into conversation frequently, as was the unfortunate necessity of any woman walking alone after sundown.

By the time she had assured her mum that she was not crying herself to sleep every night (she was) and that she was eating well (she wasn't), she had wandered off Park Lane and was about to turn toward the direction of Shepherd Market.

"You're sure you don't want to come home now—right now? You could jump on a train and be here by suppertime."

Nory's parents were the only people she knew who still ate supper. Mealtimes in the Noel household went: breakfast, elevenses, lunch, afternoon tea, dinner, supper.

"Mum, I'm fine. Please don't worry about me."

"Don't worry? Pah! You wait till you're a parent and then you'll know."

"I'll be home on the twenty-third, it's only three days away."

The call ended with her mum somewhat mollified, although Nory fully expected her to begin a WhatsApp conversation later.

Nory was just passing by Le Gavroche, a very fancy restaurant that she could never in her wildest dreams afford to eat at, when a familiar figure walked out the door.

"Pippa? What are you doing here?"

"That's a fine way to greet a friend," said Pippa, who was dressed like a young Princess Anne taking the dogs out for a walk in Balmoral.

"Sorry. Obviously, I'm delighted to see you. I'm just *surprised* to see you."

"I've got business."

"On a Sunday night?"

Pippa licked her lips and one eye twitched.

"You're lying!" Nory smiled with mischief. "I know when you're being cagey."

Pippa exhaled and pulled her shoulders back. "If you must know, I was having dinner with someone."

"Duh, I would never have guessed. Who?" Nory asked. "Don't make me drag it out of you."

"I should like to see you try."

"I know where your ticklish spot is, remember?"

"Lord Abercrombie. There, I've said it. Now you know. I'd appreciate your discretion in this matter."

Nory clapped her hands to her mouth to squash the squeal that wanted to escape. "What, like, dinner, dinner?"

"Yes."

"How old . . . ?"

"He's only fifty-two."

"Oh yes, of course he is. I suppose he just seems older to me because he was already a proper adult when I was a child."

"Don't make it icky."

"Sorry. It's not icky at all. In fact, you two make perfect

sense. I don't know why I didn't see it before. He is very hand-some in that rugged landowner sort of way."

"Yes, well, it's early days."

"But you like him."

Pippa smiled. "I do."

"Where is he?" Nory asked, exaggeratedly peering around Pippa's shoulders as though Lord Abercrombie might be hiding behind her tall friend.

"He's talking with the chef. He chats to everyone, he's much friendlier than I am. I needed some air."

"I think you're friendly." Nory grinned.

"You are one of the few."

"So, did you go Dutch, or did you actually let a date pay for you?"

"I paid for dinner; Mitch is paying for the hotel."

Nory giggled.

"What?" asked Pippa.

"Sorry, it's just, you called the marquis by his first name."

"Well, I can't exactly call him 'Your Lordship,' can I? I'm not a serving wench!"

"No, sorry. I suppose not." Then she giggled again.

"What now?" asked Pip lazily.

"Are you having sex with a lord?"

Pip merely eyed her coolly. "It wouldn't be the first time."

Nory could feel her eyes bugging out in spite of herself. At that moment, Lord Abercrombie emerged from the res-taurant.

"Elinor!" he said jovially. "Fancy seeing you here."

To her astonishment, the marquis slipped his arm around the waist of Pip "I'm Not a Hugger," Harrington and she didn't so much as flinch.

*Blimey!* thought Nory. *The world's gone mad. First Guy gets counseling and now this!*

"I heard there's been a bit of a bust-up between you and Isaac," said the marquis. "I don't know what it's about, it's none of my business, but I'm sorry to hear it. Isaac's not been the same since you left."

Nory wondered if Isaac was sobbing into his pillow nightly like she was. Probably not.

"I told Isaac he was a fuckwit, by the way," added Pip.

"So I heard," Nory replied.

"Do you want my advice?"

"Always."

"Don't lose hope."

This advice was so incongruous coming from Pippa's mouth that Nory had to force herself not to rear back in surprise.

"Give him time," Pip continued. "When things have calmed down a bit, he'll realize that you had his best interests at heart. And stop sniveling, it makes your eyes unappealingly red."

"Is this something I ought to know about?" Lord Abercrombie asked.

He didn't know about Heba's paintings, and as much as Nory would have liked to tell him what had happened, she was in no position to break Isaac's confidence again.

"No," she said, smiling reassuringly. "Just something Isaac and I have to work out for ourselves."

Despite her protestations, Mitch—as she was apparently now expected to call him—called her a cab to take her the short distance home. She was secretly grateful. The streets had quietened down now, and though she was well used to holding her keys in her fist, it made a nice change not to have to.

Monday's trading was even busier than Sunday's had been. Luckily, Seb had come in with Matilda at lunchtime, because it meant Andrew had help in the shop while Nory was leaned against the worktop in the kitchenette, listening as her brother slammed her over the phone.

"You don't have all the facts, Thom," Nory said wearily.

"I knew something like this would happen."

"Something like what, Thom, what did you know would happen?"

"That you would screw him over. He's a mess, Nory."

Nory massaged her temples. "What's he said?"

"Nothing. That's just it. I can't get anything out of him. Whatever went down with you two has messed him up proper. You always do this; you swoop in like a whirlwind and then you leave."

"Why am I always the bad guy? You only ever think the worst of me. Maybe it was Isaac's fault."

"Was it?"

Nory sighed. "No," she said quietly. "None of this was Isaac's doing. I messed everything up."

"Like I said." Thomas sounded triumphant.

"I'm hurting too, you know." Her voice broke.

"You'll come up smelling of roses. You always do."

"What did I do to you, Thom?" Her voice was brittle, rusty even to her own ears. "Why do you hate me?"

There was a pause.

"I don't hate you!" He sounded hurt.

*He was offended?* She raised her eyes to where a damp patch bloomed shades of sepia and brown across the ceiling, something else she needed to find a budget for.

"You've been carrying a me-shaped chip on your shoulder for the last twenty years!" The exasperation in her voice rang out in the small room. "You hated me when I went to Braddon-Hartmead, because you thought I was getting an advantage that you were denied, and then when I didn't use my advantage to make millions, you hated me for that too. I can't win with you."

"That's not— I never hated you for it, Nory, I just . . . Everything's so easy for you. I've had to struggle for everything I've achieved."

"And you don't think I have? I had a private education, but it didn't magic me into an easier life."

"Yeah, well."

This was Thomas's stock phrase for when he didn't have an answer.

"I know I was lucky in lots of ways. But it's not fair for you to keep punishing me for it."

Nory remained silent then, waiting for the final barb.

But instead he said, "I'm sorry. I don't mean to . . . I guess I'm just used to us being this way with each other. It's how we are. It doesn't mean . . ."

"I don't want this to be the way we communicate anymore, Thom. I'm tired of it. I'll see you at Christmas, yeah?"

"Yeah," Thom agreed. "See you at Christmas."

❧

Nory was thankful that business continued to be unrelenting in the shop. It meant she didn't have time to think about Thom or Isaac, or her broken heart. For now, it was enough that she could throw herself into her work, seeking out perfect matches for her customers, sending them on their way with the Christmas presents they'd come in for but also a gift for themselves: a book they hadn't known they'd needed or missed until Nory had placed it in their hands and they'd felt the rightness of it. Some books wrote themselves into people's hearts as children and lived there, all but forgotten, until a bookseller recognized the spark and reunited them. Other books held their words close, waiting on the shelf to ignite a passion in someone who hadn't even known they were wanting, until a bookseller introduced them. Booksellers were matchmakers of sorts. Too bad Nory wasn't as good at reconciling herself with the people she loved as she was at rehoming books.

# Forty

It was two days before Christmas, and after a morning so busy (Nory hadn't even had time to lament the selling of a vintage edition of Shirley Hughes's *Alfie Stories*), Serendipitous Seconds was quiet. Most of the offices in the surrounding area had closed at lunchtime and wouldn't be open again until January 4. The last of the online sales had been express delivered yesterday morning, and now it was time to take stock and batten down the hatches before they closed for the holidays.

"Should we take the decorations down now? So we don't have to come back to it in January?" Andrew asked.

"No," said Nory, looking lovingly around her shop. She loved her shop all year round, but never so well as when the days were dark and every shelf glittered with frosted leaves, red glitter berries, and fairy lights. "Let's leave them up. Let's keep the magic going for a little longer."

Nory remembered when she was a child and her dad would bring her and Thomas up to London on one of the dead days between Christmas and New Year's to look at the shop window displays. It had felt magical, like the Christmas picture books she read. For those hours in the quiet city with the sparkling windows, it had felt like she was living inside one of her books. Now, she liked to think of someone else's child out for a cold afternoon walk, stumbling across her little shop with the jolly Father Christmas in the window and the twinkling lights within.

"Did the nanas decide who would be cooking the turkey yet?" she asked Andrew.

"Seb is going to do it. It all got rather out of control, and we very nearly had another trifle incident on our hands."

Nory winced.

"Seb's printed off a spreadsheet and given each of them specific jobs. Nina and Glenda may each shine in their own right."

"Who gets to cook the roast potatoes, though? Roast potatoes can be a contentious issue."

"Yes, so it would seem. I will therefore be doing the roast potatoes." Andrew pulled his phone out of his pocket and scrolled down the screen. "Yes, here we are. Nina is on roast parsnips. Glenda is on glazed carrots and minted peas; now she gets two vegetables because I am reliably informed—by Glenda herself—that roast parsnips counts as two vegetables in terms of importance."

"It's like vegetable Top Trumps!"

"It is exactly like that. Glenda gets to do braised red cabbage in spiced red wine, while Nina will be making panfried Brussels sprouts with chestnuts and crispy bacon lardons."

"Wait, doesn't that count as three things?"

"You would think, but no. The braised cabbage in red wine is apparently a higher skill level than the panfried sprouts and therefore it's allowed."

"Who's doing the gravy? That's surely a pistols-at-dawn situation."

"Yes. Which is why we handed over the gravy making to Marks and Spencer, because no nana would argue with M&S."

∽

They closed the shop at four o'clock because the only customers they were getting were the post-work Christmas-lunch kind, and Nory didn't want beer hands on her books. And they weren't buying anyway; they only wanted somewhere warm to wait until the pub queues quieted down a bit.

Nory locked the door for Serendipitous Seconds for the final time that year. Andrew was holding a small sack over his shoulder like a well-groomed robber. They were Nory's gifts to her goddaughter.

"You spoil her," said Andrew kindly.

"Only with love."

"These are *things*!" he said, rattling the sack slightly and smiling.

"Things given with *love*," Nory corrected him.

Andrew pulled her into a hug with his free arm.

"Happy Christmas, darling Nory," he said into her hair.

"Happy Christmas to you too, my lovely friend."

They pulled apart from each other.

"Oh my god, it's your first Christmas together as a family." Nory was suddenly welling up. "It's so wonderful! You've waited so long."

"Now don't start," said Andrew, wiping at his eyes. "Because you'll start me off."

"I love you."

"I love you too. Now go on, off with you. I don't want you to see me cry."

Nory laughed and crossed the square toward her flat. She turned and called, "Say merry Christmas to Seb and give Matilda a big kiss from me!"

"Consider it done!" Andrew called back as he rounded the corner and disappeared.

*~*

Ameerah called for Nory and her cat at six o'clock, and after settling a grouchy Mugwort in his basket on the backseat, they began the slow drive out of London along with the thousands of other people leaving the city for the holidays. At one point the traffic was so still that Nory jumped out of the car, ran to the garage across the road, grabbed two coffees and a bag full of snacks, and made it back before Ameerah had moved two car lengths.

"Jackson and Lucas will be in bed by the time we get to Hartmead," Nory lamented.

"You'll see them in the morning."

"It's probably for the best. I'm not sure I can take another fight with Thom just yet."

"We should still have time for Jake Noel's annual Christmas cocktail hour, though."

Nory groaned. Every Christmas when she and Ameerah arrived home, her dad would prepare them a "London-style" cocktail, the recipe for which he would find on the internet before adding his own personal touch. These cocktails were generally lethal with alcohol and often peculiar. Last year's concoction had been a New Fashioned Old-Fashioned. Nory was fairly certain her dad had obtained some moonshine from one of the farmers on the Robinwood estate; she had almost slept through Christmas. She congratulated herself now on buying them a host of filthy car snacks to line their stomachs before they reached home.

"Are you coming back to the city for New Year's?" Nory asked.

Ameerah developed a sheepish look, like she was trying and failing to stop the corners of her mouth turning up into a smile.

"What?" asked Nory, grinning at her friend.

"It only just happened."

"What only just happened?"

"Dev's taking me to meet his parents, and we're staying with them for New Year's."

"Oh my god. Ameerah! Oh my god. This is huge!"

"I know," Ameerah squealed, and it was for the best that they were stationary in gridlocked traffic because neither one of them was fit for anything for a good five minutes.

"And . . ." Ameerah began.

"There's an and?"

"I told him I love him!" Ameerah clapped her hands to her mouth as though she couldn't quite believe the words had come from it. Further screaming from both women, of course.

"Congratulations! Oh my god, this is the best thing ever. What did he say?"

"That he loves me too." If Ameerah's smile got any wider her lips might have looped around her ears. "He said he knew he was in love with me after our second date. We hadn't even shagged yet."

"I've never seen you like this."

"Oh! I love him, Nory, I really do. I absolutely love him. I didn't even know I *could* love someone this much."

"Oh, Amie." Nory welled up for the second time that day.

"I didn't want to tell you because you're so sad about Isaac and I didn't want it to seem like I was gloating or rubbing your face in it . . ." Now Ameerah was crying too.

"I would never think that! I am so happy for you. You deserve to be in love and to be loved, Amie. This is so amazing. And Dev is just bloody wonderful."

"He is, isn't he," said Ameerah dreamily.

"Are you nervous about meeting his parents?"

"I was, but then his mum rang me up and told me she'd heard so much about me and she was so proud that her son was in love with a barrister, and that she couldn't wait to meet me." Ameerah was now bawling her eyes out, as was Nory.

"That's so lovely," Nory sobbed.

"I know, right!" Ameerah cried. "I love him so much!"

"And I love you!"

"And I love you more!"

There was a knocking at the window, and a worried-looking man with gray bushy eyebrows peered in.

"Is everything all right, ladies?" he asked. "My wife and I, we couldn't help hearing a lot of screaming and crying coming from your car."

"Oh, everything's fine, sir, thank you," Ameerah hiccupped through her tears. "It's actually better than fine. It's brilliant. I'm in love, you see."

"We never thought it would happen." Nory sniffed. "But it has, and he loves her back."

"And my front," added Ameerah.

"Yes. All of her, in fact."

"Well, that is wonderful." The bushy-eyebrowed man beamed at them. "Angelina!" he called to his wife in the car behind. "It's okay. There's no problem. She's crazy in love is all!"

Nory turned in her seat to see a round woman climb out of the car and walk toward them.

"Who's this in love, Eric?" she asked as she reached the car. By now, other people were also getting out of their cars and coming over to see the curious goings-on beside the Mini Countryman.

"I am," said Ameerah.

"Are you the lucky woman?" Angelina nodded at Nory.

"Oh, no . . . not me, she's in love with a man." Nory beamed back at her.

"And he loves you too?" Angelina confirmed.

"Yes," Ameerah gushed.

"Front and back," added Eric.

Angelina clapped her hands together and laughed the kind of laugh that dares you not to feel instantly joyous.

"You just found out you love each other at Christmas! Well, if that's not a miracle, I don't know what is. Get out here, child, and let me hug you. You too." She pointed at Nory. "I got love to go around."

And that was how, in the middle of gridlocked traffic on the Blackfriars Underpass, a small group of people left their cars to congratulate a barrister who had recently fallen in love with a model, and her very happy best friend.

# Forty-one

"RRRRRRAAAHHHHHH!"

The noise jolted her from sleep, and the two boys jumping on her, yelling "Aunty Nory! It's Christmas Eve!" made sure she was very definitely wide-awake. They'd arrived late, due to a mixture of London traffic and heavy snow when they were about forty minutes outside Hartmead. Nory had slept like the dead last night, after her dad's potent variation on a Moscow mule, and now she had a stonking hangover.

"Hello, my gorgeous boys!" Nory put on her bravest smile and gave it her best children's presenter delivery, despite the evil elves in her head attacking her brain with an ice pick. "So does Christmas Eve mean one more *month* till Father Christmas comes?"

"No!" they yelled delightedly.

"One more *week*, then?"

"No, Aunty Nory, not one more week!"

"Well, I'm sure I don't understand it. How long is it, then, till Father Christmas comes?"

"One more day!" they yelled in unison.

"Oh my goodness! Are you ready for him?"

"Yes!"

"Okay, let's do a checklist and see. Have you got your stockings ready?"

"Yes!" They were rolling around her bed now, giggling.

"Mine's got snowflakes and squirrels on," said Jackson.

"And mine's got . . . What has mine got, Jackson?"

"Yours has got snowflakes and reindeer."

"Yes," agreed Lucas, nodding vigorously.

"Phew, well that's the stockings sorted," said Nory, smooshing her pillows against the headboard and sitting up. "Now, did you remember to send your letters to the North Pole?"

"Yes. I put two stamps on mine," Lucas said seriously.

"Okay, we can check letters off our list. Now the final thing: Have you been good this year?"

Both boys stopped suddenly. This was serious stuff. Nory could see them calculating their misdemeanors.

"They've both been very good this year," said Thomas, who was standing in the doorway. At this, Jackson and Lucas whooped with joy and relief. "Boys, did you know Aunty Amie is in the bedroom next door? I'm sure she'd love to see you."

Nory was sure she would too, but possibly not at seven o'clock in the morning after Jake Noel's Christmas cocktails.

"Hey, Thom," she said. *Keep it light and friendly*, she thought, since this was the first time they'd spoken since their argument.

"Listen, I'm gonna need your help today. We're snowed under and the kids are home. Shelley's doing a wreath-making session at the hotel, and I've got last-minute orders to drop off."

"Oh. Okay. Sure, do you need me to mind the boys for you?"

"No, I'll take them with me on my rounds. I need you to take a load of table centers up to the castle for me. The marquis has got family arriving for Christmas and he needs them this morning."

"Oh, Thomas, come on!" Nory flopped back against the pillows. Typical that her brother would punish her by making her go up to the one place she needed to avoid like Krampus! "Can't you take them, and I'll take the other orders?"

"No. There's too many. I'll have to take the van and you haven't driven the van before."

Nory shrugged sulkily. "Can't be that hard." She pouted.

Thomas held the bridge of his nose between his thumb and forefinger, a reaction to stress he'd inherited from their dad.

"Look, the gears are a bit sticky, and I haven't got time to take you out for a practice run. You can fit the table centers in the back of the Audi if you push the seats down. I've already put the snow chains on for you."

Nory closed her eyes and puffed out her breath. She could hear Ameerah being bounced on in the room next door.

"Is there any way, at all, that we can rearrange things so that I don't have to go up to the castle? Like *any* way at all. I am open to *all* possibilities."

Thomas looked at her for a long moment. There was something in his face, something he was trying hard to fight back. *Maybe he's biting his tongue because it's Christmas, the season of goodwill to all men and sisters?* she thought hopefully.

"None," said Thomas blankly, and left the room.

Nory puffed out the breath she'd been holding. "Fine!" she shouted after him. What could she do? This was a family business, and she was family.

She grabbed her stuff and headed for the bathroom, bumping into Ameerah on the landing, who was also holding a towel and wash bag—no second-bathroom luxury in this homestead.

"Shit the bed, you look like I feel!" said Ameerah. "Do you think your dad's cocktails have gotten more potent over the years?"

"I just don't think we handle hangovers in our thirties as well as we did in our twenties."

"I don't even remember having hangovers in my twenties," said Ameerah. A sheen of sweat glistened on her top lip and forehead.

"Do you fancy doing some deliveries to the castle with me this morning?"

"I would, but Dev's coming down. We're meeting in the Mead and Medlar." She raised her towel to her mouth and swallowed hard. "For lunch," she finished weakly.

"Fair enough. Since I've got to be on my way before you, do you mind if I go in the bathroom first?"

"Not at all. Do you mind if I just vomit in there before you go in?"

"Not at all."

∽

Her parents were already out when Nory came downstairs feeling very much like she'd done twenty minutes in a tumble dryer on the super-dry cycle. Mugwort was sat in a cushioned cat bed next to the range, repeatedly licking his nose, an empty food bowl beside him. He gave her a smug look. A large frying pan with a lid sat on the hot plate, and Nory felt instantly better when she discovered it was full of sausages. In the pan behind it was bacon. Her mum's homemade baked beans blipped gently in a saucepan, and in the oven there was tray of potato rostis. Nory smiled. "Thanks, Mama," she said out loud. This was the perfect hangover cure.

She sat alone at the table eating her breakfast of kings and thinking about Isaac. The pain still spiked when she conjured up his face, but she had learned not to wince on the outside. She was caught between hoping to see him and hoping not to see him. She wished she'd never meddled. If only she hadn't been cursed with the need to fix things, she would never have ruined things with Isaac. They might even be spending Christmas together, instead of her being down here with a brother who could barely stand her, and Isaac up there alone . . . or not; maybe he'd moved on already. The thought winded her.

Why did love have to be so painful? Surely this was love; nothing else would hurt this much. Nory briefly considered leaving the rest of her breakfast for dramatic effect but then thought, *Who am I kidding!* and finished her plate, wiping the last bits of bean sauce up with a thick slice of buttery toast.

## Forty-two

Last night's snow made the village look like a Christmas card. Thom had parked his car, and Nory began to carefully transport the fresh floral table centers to the boot. The color scheme was the same for all—red, gold, green, and burned orange, with touches of gold and glitter in the ribbons and delicate porcelain fruits. But each arrangement was slightly different. Some were arranged in stubby clay pots, like vases of flowers, while others were more traditional with candles and hurricane lamps at their centers.

She could see the outline of her mum working in the hothouse, but her dad remained hidden so far, probably out back somewhere turning compost, she thought. The plants would all be given an extra good watering and some TLC, and then work would stop at 2:00 p.m. and the nursery would have to look after itself until the twenty-seventh.

Nory pushed a large arrangement to one side—pricking herself on a particularly spiteful holly sprig and swearing loudly—to make room for a rather grand centerpiece. Swags of ivy, holly, and bendy pine sprigs cascaded down from a long-necked gold punch bowl. Deep burgundy hydrangea heads exploded up from the center alongside fuchsia pink heathers, impossibly fat cream roses, eucalyptus, and rose hips. It was bloody heavy; she knew that much, and she wondered idly if the punch bowl was made of actual gold. She pushed it gingerly into place and tested the boot lid to make sure it wouldn't crush the arrangement, before carefully pulling the lid down and locking it.

She was just about to climb into the car when Thomas came striding across the car park toward her from the direction of the village. *Now what?* she thought grumpily.

"I thought you might have left already," he said breathlessly.

"Just about to. What do you need?"

"I wanted to give you this," he said, thrusting a copy of the *Observer* into her hand.

"Okay." Nory looked down at the newspaper, nonplussed. "Do you want me to deliver this to Lord Abercrombie? Are we offering a postal service now?"

Thomas held up his hands. "Nory, can you just . . . can you just listen to me for a minute?"

Nory closed her mouth and made a locking motion at her lips before throwing away the imaginary key.

Thomas's face cracked momentarily into a smile before becoming serious again. He looked uncomfortable. "About your feelings for Isaac. I didn't realize. And what you wanted to do for him, well, that was . . ."

Nory opened her mouth to speak, but Thomas held his hand up for her to be quiet.

"You were right, I've been hanging on to old stuff for so long, that I got stuck in a kind of rut. I couldn't seem to let it go. I know it wasn't always easy for you. But it was easier for me to blame you than face my own failings. The thing is, Nory, no matter what, you're my baby sister, and I love you. Despite what it often looks like, I only ever want you to be happy."

He bent down and kissed her cheek then straightened.

"Anyway, that's it. That's what I wanted to say." He nodded to the paper in Nory's hand. "Center spread," he said. "Read it before you go. I'll see you at supper." And with that he strode away into the maze of greenhouses and polytunnels.

Nory watched him go. *Brothers!* she thought. *Complicated creatures.* Laying the paper out flat on the bonnet of the car, she flicked to the middle pages.

### Revered Botanical Artist Found To Be Plagiarist

read the headline. Nory couldn't quite believe what she was reading. There was a picture of Isaac looking uncomfortable holding Heba's sketchbooks and, below it, a personal interview. She could hardly take it in. Aside from Isaac's own evidence, there were testimonials from the families of officers and soldiers who had served in India, diary entries, appraisals from experts, and a statement from a solicitor's firm in London that specialized in art law. The De-Veer family were quoted as being shocked and saddened by the wrong that had been done to Heba and her family. And they were cooperating fully with the Scotland Yard art fraud department to have Heba's name restored to her work and the books repatriated to Heba's great-great-grandson.

Snow was coming down in flurries, dusting onto the newsprint like confetti. Nory shook it off and folded the paper. This had thrown her. The butterflies in her stomach didn't know whether to make her jump up and down or faint. Isaac had given an interview to Guy! Was there a chance that Isaac had forgiven her?

"Nory!"

Nory jumped and saw her dad over by the dahlia sheds. He tapped his watch and made a shooing motion at her.

"Right! Yes, sorry! On it now," she called.

The snow was fast enough to warrant the windscreen wipers. The farmers had been out salting the roads, so the lanes up to the castle were pretty clear, but she was still glad of the snow chains. She hugged the steering wheel as she drove—she only ever drove when she was home, and not very often at that.

She decided that she would seek Isaac out when she got to the castle, and once she had made the decision, she couldn't get there fast enough. It was frustrating, therefore, when a group of pheasants took to sauntering along the middle of the lane like it was their own private highway. She beeped at them impatiently, but they only panicked, rose into the air, and landed back down on the road rather than seeking the safety of the fields beyond the hedgerows.

"You really are the stupidest of all birds," she called out the window at them. "Get out of the road! No wonder so many of you get killed." But they only ran faster three feet in front of the car, looking back at it every few seconds as though wondering why it was still chasing them.

Eventually she passed a farm entrance, and the pheasants ducked beneath the gate and took flight into the adjacent field. She shook her head in annoyance.

When Nory turned the car onto the long castle drive, her stomach was a jumping mass of nerves and excitement, which rose up into her chest and forced her to take deep breaths. She drove round to the back of the castle, her eyes wide and wild, hoping to catch a glimpse of Isaac, her heart quickening at being back here, where so much had happened.

Andy opened the staff entrance door as she pulled in.

"Hi, Andy!" she called as she headed round to the boot.

"Hello, young Elinor, good to see you again. I trust you're still getting up to mischief! Ruined any more outfits recently?"

"Oh, absolutely." She smiled, glancing around the courtyard as though Isaac might be hiding behind a barrel. "Although there are fewer manure-filled wheelbarrows to fall into in the city."

"Pity," he said. "They don't know what they're missing."

Andy helped her in with the table centers, calling for reinforcements from a couple of housekeepers loitering by the bins on a cigarette break. Still no sign of Isaac.

"Are you working throughout Christmas?" Nory asked.

"Only until after dinner is served tomorrow and then we're off till the twenty-ninth."

"Wouldn't you like to get away? Visit family?"

"There's no place I'd rather be than here, and I don't have much family. It's just me and my sister. She came down the other day and she'll stay for the holidays."

"Oh, that's nice. I expect she loves staying in the castle, doesn't she?"

"That she does. It's a lot of fun here at Christmas. Lord Abercrombie and his guests cook for all the staff on Boxing Day and cater to their every whim; it's one of the old traditions that he likes to keep up."

"That must be funny!"

"Oh, it is. It's hilarious."

They laid the last arrangement on the cold larder floor. The shelves above were laden with enough food to see the marquis and his guests into the following Christmas.

"Would you mind if I left the car in the courtyard for a short while?" Nory asked. "I thought I might—" *What did you think,*

*Nory? What are you planning to do, hunt him down?* "—have one last look at the gardens," she finished lamely.

Andy smiled. "I've been asked to give you this." He handed Nory a folded note.

Her hands trembled. Her heart stuttered. She didn't want to open it here in front of Andy; suppose it was a "never darken my door again" note.

"Um, thanks," she said. "Merry Christmas!" she called, hurriedly making for the door.

"Merry Christmas to you too, Elinor Noel!" he called after her.

With heart pounding and fumbling fingers, she unfolded the piece of paper.

*Meet me under the mistletoe.*
*Isaac xxx*

Nory gasped, then she jumped—she actually jumped for joy—before taking off at a run. If she had taken a moment to look back, she would have seen Andy smiling after her from the porchway.

It was a long time since Nory had run for anything that wasn't the Tube. By the time she reached the secret gate to the lost garden, she was sweating alarmingly, and her breath was coming in ragged wheezes. She leaned against the wall for a few seconds, hands resting on her knees until she had recovered enough to be able to speak.

With her hand on the gate latch, she sent up a silent wish to the spirit of Christmas and then shoved the gate hard. Her eyes scanned the overgrown garden. Freshly pulled brambles lay in tall piles beside areas of cleared land. The snow lent an extra air of magic to the enchanted garden. Her eyes settled on the old hawthorn with the mistletoe bough. Isaac stood below it, leaning on his spade. He smiled at her, and her nerves disappeared. As she walked toward him, he pulled off his gardening gloves and flung them aside.

They collided in an embrace under the mistletoe, with the snow falling silently all around them. Cold lips were made warm with hot desperate kisses, and even when they stopped for breath, they remained wrapped in each other's arms. Isaac's embrace was tight, as though Nory might float away from him if he were to let go. He whispered, "I'm sorry, I'm so sorry," into her hair.

She breathed him in, realizing only now that she was back in his arms how utterly lost she'd been without him. She was home.

"I'm sorry," he said again.

"I'm sorry too."

"You have nothing to apologize for. I was too stubborn and stupid to see that all you wanted to do was help."

"I could have gone about it better." Nory laughed quietly against his chest.

"You couldn't have done it any other way. I was paralyzed by the responsibility of it. I needed to be pushed. I can see that now. Although I could have done without walking in on you and Guy."

Nory looked up at him. "You know nothing happened, don't you?"

"I do."

"What made you decide to let Guy run the story?"

"A lot of things," he said, nosing her scarf to one side to kiss her neck.

"Like?" She was trying to keep her head, but the brush of his lips against her throat was making it difficult.

Isaac stopped nuzzling her neck and looked at her. "Okay,

well, for starters I regretted my reaction almost immediately. But I was so jealous and angry," Isaac began.

"You were jealous?"

"I couldn't bear it, seeing the woman I love in another man's arms, even if you hadn't wanted to be there. It just kept playing over and over in my mind. And it frightened me how much I couldn't stand it. I've never felt that before . . ."

The rest of his words slid out of existence, leaving just one.

"You love me?" she asked, looking into his dark brown eyes.

"I must do," he said, raising one eyebrow. "Only love could wreak this much havoc in my nice, ordered world."

"You make me sound like a hurricane." She laughed.

"You kind of are." Isaac smiled.

"I love you too, by the way."

"Good," he said, putting his mouth on hers to seal their confession with a kiss.

When the snow had begun to form an actual layer on their heads and shoulders, they decided to abandon kissing beneath the mistletoe in favor of hot chocolate beside the woodstove in Isaac's gardener's hut.

"It was Pippa who yanked me out of my own head," Isaac explained. "She's not a woman who minces her words."

"Yes, she did mention that she'd spoken to you."

"Scolded me, more like. Do you know she and Lord Abercrombie . . ."

"I do."

"In all the years I've been here, I've never seen him so smitten with anyone."

"I should think not. Pippa is a most excellent woman; there's no one else like her."

"You really love your friends, don't you?"

"They're like family. Some of them are harder to like than others, but I suppose that's like family too," she said.

Isaac nodded in understanding.

"We've got Thomas to thank for pushing me toward the interview."

"My Thomas?" Nory asked in surprise.

"You could say that Pippa threw the first punch and then Thomas came along and finished the job."

Nory could feel her eyes widening above the rim of her hot chocolate mug. "He didn't actually hit you, though, did he?"

Isaac laughed. "No, only a good metaphorical punching to snap me out of my self-pity. He said it was against your programming ever to do anything purposely unkind or immoral."

"Blimey!"

"He told me you had only ever wanted to fix things for me, and that if I broke your heart, I'd have him to deal with."

"Oh dear." Nory sighed.

"What?"

"This means I have my brother to thank for making things right. You have no idea how much he likes to gloat."

Isaac gave her hand a squeeze and smiled. "I think he was just being brotherly. If I had siblings, I'd want someone like Thomas looking out for me."

"Ugh, I suppose you're right," she said, pulling a face. A physical memory woke in Nory's chest, spreading its warmth through her in a way she'd almost forgotten, it had been so long. The unquestioning certainty she'd felt when she was a child that her big brother would always be there for her.

"You're not here because you're scared of my big brother, are you?"

Isaac laughed. "No. The only thing that scares me is not being with you. I think I fell in love with you the moment I hauled you out of my wheelbarrow."

Nory felt her cheeks flush.

"Which reminds me," he said, standing up and slipping an envelope into his pocket. "I've something to show you."

"You've got a new wheelbarrow?"

He shook his head, smiling. "Come on," he said, taking her hand and pulling her up off the upturned terra-cotta pot she'd been sitting on.

All around them, the gardens were an undulating mass of feathery white snow, and in the gaps between the naked trees, the view of the valley below was a patchwork eiderdown of mis-shaped chalky squares.

They held hands as they walked. Nory had borrowed a pair of Isaac's gloves and her fingers didn't reach the ends.

Isaac pushed open the gate in the wall to the Winter Garden. The sight of it was otherworldly, as though the garden existed entirely separate from the rest of the world, untroubled by time or the problems of human beings. It was fully embracing its name this morning. The pale silver birch trunks stood like ghostly sentries behind the crimson stems of the dogwood, which rose up out of the snow like a tangle of blood vessels. The coral quince blooms shone out from snow-laden branches, and in the beds, spots of color speckled the white as determined flowers poked their heads triumphantly above their frosted blanket. It was so quiet. Even the wildlife seemed to have decided to stay home today.

Theirs would be the first feet to walk the Winter Garden that day, and Nory held back, pulling on Isaac's hand, not wanting to sully the ethereal scene with footprints. But Isaac only smiled back at her and motioned that she should follow him. As though reading her mind he said, "There's more snow forecast. Our footprints will be reclaimed soon enough, don't worry."

They wandered through the garden, the first place where they had set eyes on each other as adults. It seemed like no time ago at all and yet also an age. Perhaps, Nory mused, that was part of the garden's magic: You could live a lifetime in here and outside not a moment would have passed.

Isaac stopped by the hellebores, their bonnets straining under the weight of the snow.

"This is where it all started," he said.

Nory smiled. "With your new hellebore," she agreed. She crouched next to the bed. With gentle fingers, she brushed the snow from the pink petals. "Perhaps you should name it Heba," she said, marveling again at the unusual markings on the hybrid plant.

As she moved her attention to dusting the snowflakes off the leaves, she noticed a wooden plant label poking out of the snow next to it. Without thinking, she cleared the snow that had banked against it and then she stopped. She looked again and then she glanced up to see Isaac watching, amusement and mischief dancing in his eyes. She looked back at the label and blinked the tears out of her eyes. The words *Nory Noel* were printed above the Latin name.

"Is this for real?" she asked, gazing up at him again.

Isaac nodded. "It is."

He helped her to her feet and pulled an envelope from his pocket, which he handed to her. Dazed, Nory took it from him and found herself looking at an official authentication form with registration stamp: *HELLEBORUS. HELLEBORE. "NORY NOEL"*

"You named your hellebore after me!"

She felt like a girl again, just tall enough to peek over the potting tables, playing the strange sounds of the Latin and Greek plant names in her mouth, letting them roll around on her tongue. And now she had her very own: *Helleborus* Nory Noel.

"I knew as soon as I found you here that night that I couldn't call it anything else. Do you know how many people have walked through this garden and never even glanced at it twice? But you saw it, straightaway. And you saw me. You saw me in a way I didn't even know myself. I would never have done anything with Heba's books; they would have stayed a bitter secret forever. But you saw what I couldn't see myself and you did it for me."

"Some people might call that meddling," she said, her voice sounding hoarse around the lump in her throat.

"Not me." Isaac smiled. "You, Nory Noel, are now a part of horticultural history."

Nory laughed and dashed away the tears that didn't seem to want to stop falling.

Isaac smiled. "And now that we've sorted out your history, I wonder if you would agree to be very much a part of my future? Because ever since you stampeded into my life, I can't imagine a future without you in it."

"I think I can manage that," she whispered.

Isaac bent and kissed away her tears, while the Winter Garden watched on in quiet majesty.

# Epilogue

I t was a small wedding, certainly by Robinwood Castle standards, but small did not mean quiet. Jackson and Lucas had become instant and firm friends with Camille and Guy's children. They ran laughing and shouting around tables and between chairs inside the well-heated marquee, which stood in the lost garden—which were now *lost* only by name since being completely restored to their former Arts and Crafts glory earlier in the year.

In the weeks and months after the story about Heba's paintings broke, Guy helped Isaac navigate the media interest and kept pressure on the legal teams to see the case through to its successful end. Guy had given up drinking, and most recently, had given up his flat to move back in with Camille and the children.

Jeremy and Katie's baby, Audrey, was making herself heard, while Matilda took great delight in toddling toward her and declaring "Baby!" as though she herself was not just months older. Andrew and Seb watched on proudly and told anyone who asked, as well as everyone who didn't, how clever their daughter was, and how she had amazed the health visitor at her last developmental checkup.

Charles didn't leave Jenna's side throughout the entire day, and she seemed perfectly happy to have him there. If he had been entranced by his wife before, he was even more awed now that she sported a rather fetching baby bump, which she frequently and lovingly ran her hands over. When the sonographer had announced that they were expecting a boy, they had looked at each other and said at the same time, "Tristan."

Pippa proved once and for all that she really did "fucking love children" by organizing winter scavenger hunts for the underage guests and then proceeding to lead them on their quests. Thomas, who had warmed significantly to her since last year, named her the Pied Pippa of Robinwood, a nickname that would be used for years to come. Jackson and Lucas fell completely in love with her, although they were not nearly as smitten as Lord Abercrombie. Pippa had not only transformed the castle's financial fortunes but also succeeded in transforming the famously commitment-shy marquis into a very committed boyfriend.

It didn't take long for the buzz surrounding Shelley—the hottest new name in London floral design—to be felt in Hartmead. Thomas, who had always been in love with his wife but perhaps took her contributions to the family business a little for granted, had seen Shelley in a new light since her collaboration with Pippa. He'd since had all their business signs repainted to read *Noel & Family*. He was Shelley's biggest fan on Instagram, and her biggest advocate in life.

Jake and Sasha had semi-retired and spent most weekends traveling around in the camper van that had waited so patiently to be used. In January they planned to start their European tour. But they would be back every school holiday to help out with the grandchildren and the business.

Ameerah, looking sublime in her best woman outfit and faux-fur stole, was outshone only by the dazzler of an emerald on her ring finger and by the smile of her handsome fiancé. Dev's family had instantly welcomed Ameerah into their hearts. Her own parents remained distant both physically and emotionally, but between the Noels and the Chakrabartis, Ameerah had all the family she needed. And when she'd earned a big promotion in the summer, both families were in attendance for her very noisy celebration dinner.

Dev and Thomas had hit it off when they'd met again in the pub last Christmas Eve, and Dev was now firmly ensconced in the Mead and Medlar pub quiz team with Thom, Isaac, Jake, Sasha, and Shelley. And when Jake and Sasha were away in the camper van, Nory and Ameerah filled in on the team.

After splitting her time between London and Hartmead, Nory had finally moved in with Isaac in November. Lettuce and Mugwort were still working out their differences—though to be fair, the problems were mostly Mugwort's. He was still suspicious of the outside world, but he certainly enjoyed telling off the birds from the windowsill.

Nory found that she enjoyed the commute to London; it felt like having her cake and eating it, being ensconced both in the country and the city. It had taken her a while to train up Imelda, her newest member of staff, but finally she was ready and Nory could stop working six-day weeks. She felt that Imelda was a little gung-ho in her bookselling technique, but Andrew assured her that Imelda was exactly the right amount of gung-ho, and that Nory would have to increase her searches for vintage books to keep up with demand. This was music to Nory's ears.

Isaac had set his horticulture students from Hart's College to work with him on the lost garden, using the original plans from the 1860s. His case against the De-Veers was settled out of court. The evidence was so overwhelmingly stacked in Heba's favor that they simply agreed to all terms and signed over ownership. Heba's name had been posthumously added to all her works. And Isaac had received a very generous compensation payout, a portion of which he used to buy the freehold on Serendipitous Seconds for Nory.

The wedding ceremony took place in the Winter Garden on the last Saturday before Christmas. Warm winter coats and fur-lined Wellingtons were worn over the more traditional wedding outfits. Isaac looked devasting in a black sherwani, and as Nory walked down the path, her arm looped through her dad's, she couldn't imagine what good deed she must have done in a past life to be allowed to marry Isaac in this one. By chance, Nory had seen an evening gown in the exact pink of the Nory Noel hellebore, and knew she'd found her wedding dress.

Nory and Isaac said "I do" beneath a pergola laced with ivy, holly, and mistletoe, surrounded by the people they loved most in the world. Everyone clapped as loudly as they could while wearing thick mittens. And then, led by the happy couple, they made their way hastily along snowy paths to the marquee in the lost garden.

As a wedding gift, Lord Abercrombie had very kindly offered a night in the castle free of charge to all the guests; Jackson and Lucas were beyond excited at the prospect.

A full moon had been paramount in their choosing of a date for the wedding. It had started snowing a couple of days ago and had begun in earnest again now. At the stroke of midnight, with the children tucked up in bed and sleeping soundly, a group of old friends, along with some new ones, crept out onto the lawn just in front of the castle. They wore pajamas beneath winter coats, and some of them hugged baby monitors. Some carried the sporting equipment and others the components for the traditional toast. And there beneath the full moon and the falling snow, they played croquet and drank Snowballs, in honor and remembrance of their friend who hadn't been able to stay in the world.

Surrounded by fresh snowfall and love, Isaac took Nory in his arms and kissed her, and the rightness within her warmed her bones. She hoped Tristan had found peace, and she hoped he knew that he would never be forgotten. Because sometimes life is too short, but love lasts forever.

# Acknowledgments

Firstly, I would like to thank you, dear reader, from the bottom of my heart for reading my book. It still feels like a dream that I not only get to write books but that people read them. I will never stop being gratefully amazed.

There are so many good people involved in getting a book published. Behind the face of the author there are a host of dedicated book heroes making the magic happen, and they deserve some serious thanks. If there is someone I don't mention here, I apologize for my scatterbrain, but please know that you are appreciated.

A huge thank-you goes to my agent, Hayley Steed at Madeleine Milburn, without whom I wouldn't be a published author at all. Thank you for always having my back. You are wise and strong-willed, and you are deeply appreciated. I can't tell you how much it meant to me to have you and Jayne Osborne by my side at the Romantic Novelist Awards. Thank you to the whole team at MM. From working tirelessly to get my books out into other countries to talking me through my foreign tax panics, you are all lovely. Thank you, Elinor Davies, Liane-Louise Smith, Georgina Simmonds, Valentina Paulmichl, and Hannah Ladds.

Thank you to my editors, Kate Dresser and Jayne Osborne, at

Putman and Pan Macmillan, respectively. I love working with you both. Thank you for your enthusiasm and patience and your gentle guiding hands when I go off on a tangent. Left to my own devices, every character would have their family tree traced back to the Middle Ages. Simply put, you make my stories better, and I have learned so much from you both. At the time of the writing of these acknowledgments, Kate had just recently given birth, so huge congratulations to you, Kate! And an extra thank-you, Kate, for having a meeting with me just days before you had your baby and letting me throw plotlines at you, even though you had much more pressing things on your mind!

On the Putnam dream team, I would like to thank copy-editor Kathleen Go, for—among other things—her excellent timeline-error busting skills and for highlighting all the idioms and phrases that totally don't translate from the UK to the US; it's both fascinating and fun. Thank you, Sanny Chiu, for another beautiful book jacket; this one actually made me yip with joy when I saw it. To Alexis Welby and Elora Weil, thank you for being fabulous at getting me and my book seen in the world and for helping me through it when I am a jittery Jenni! My thanks to Hannah Dragone, Tiffany Estreicher, Anthony Ramondo, Maija Baldauf, Emily Mileham, Shina Patel, Sally Kim, and Ashley McClay, for all your hard work in making this book actually happen. And to Tarini Sipahimalani, editorial assistant and so much more, whom I speak with over email so often it's like chatting with a friend, thank you for your constant support and input.

To the kind people on Instagram, Twitter, and BookTok who take the time to share their thoughts and review my books, I thank you, and I hope you enjoy this one. Many of you have become friends over this last couple of years, thank you for making my social media a safe and joyful space.

Thank you to my sister, Linzi, for letting me write much of this book in your dining room, while you sat at your easel painting and randomly bursting into song. And to my brother, Simon, who stands next to me at book launches and reminds me to breathe. I got lucky when they dished out siblings.

Thank you to my dear friends for putting up with my long absences while I write, I am lucky to have you. Aileen, Jo, Adele, Daniella, Beth, and Victoria, I owe you all cake!

I am blessed with parents who are joyful to be around and marvelously bananas! Thank you, mum and dad, for early-morning beach coffees and for rocking up on my doorstep with cough medicine when I have a cold, even though I'm forty-eight years old.

To my friend Jayne, thank you for regaling me with your hilarious dating exploits down the years. Nory and Isaac's root vegetable shooting is shamelessly plucked from one such anecdote. You, Bev, and Helen have been my constant friends since we met at sixteen, when I transferred schools. We've seen one another through a lot in the last thirty-two years. Thanks for being there!

To my sons, Jack and Will, you are my world.

And last but not at all least, thank you to my husband, Dom, for allowing me to hijack our holiday last year and turn it into a research road trip of castles and gardens around the south coast. Thank you for being my filler-in of all forms because you know that forms make me flop about dramatically. And thank you for listening when I moan relentlessly about the perimenopause! You are too good.

# Discussion Guide

1. Nory resides in London, where she's "used to the constant hum of traffic," a big contrast to her quieter, plant-loving personality. What stops Nory from pursuing her same day-to-day routine back home?

2. Nory owns a bookshop in London and loves making connections between books and their owners. In what ways does this preliminary backdrop—the way Nory makes a living—foreshadow how she navigates differences among the people she loves?

3. Nory and Isaac meet again after fifteen years, in the castle's intertwining gardens. How does their reunion differ from Nory's reunion with her friends? Discuss the symbolism of the mazelike gardens and how it might reflect their romantic journey.

4. Nory and Ameerah manage to stay close friends long after their school years. How does Ameerah's character influence your experience of their other posh friends?

5. We learn early in the story that Nory recently lost one of her dear friends, Tristan. Discuss how this loss influenced your reading of each character's struggles. In what ways can grief impact the dynamic of a friend group?

6. *Meet Me Under the Mistletoe* pays tribute to the winter magic of the Christmas season. With the hustle and bustle of a big, lively wedding that is set in the English countryside, full of fresh-cut winter greenery and an air of nostalgia, the story elicits both a sense of exuberance and calm. How do the story's quieter, more solemn moments speak to the holiday spirit?

7. Nory's scholarship opened for her many doors but closed some others. Did you find yourself relating to any aspects of Nory's family dynamic? Using examples from the story, what set roles do you think Nory might have wished her family fulfilled? Discuss your perceived position in your own family, and whether your parents and/or siblings would agree.

8. "Nory had once harbored a fancy that she might be the sort of person who made sourdough bread after work; she often fantasized about being a domestic goddess. . . . if she was being honest, it frightened her a bit. . . . Nory decided to leave sourdough to the professional and went back to buying it from Pepe's." (pg. 59). Dissect what this quote reveals about Nory and her desires. How does this relate to her passion for books and botanicals?

9. Isaac and Nory's brother, Thomas, are close friends and mutual confidantes. How would you feel if your crush knew more about your sibling than you did?

10. Nory and Isaac make a few references early on to their mudslinging days. What did you think of these nostalgic moments? In what ways if any did this dynamic carry over into their adult relationship?

11. In navigating a more mature relationship together, Isaac and Nory must face a few hurdles. At the end, how does

Isaac come to terms with their missteps and learn to trust Nory again? Conversely, how does Nory believe Isaac is ready to leave the past behind? Discuss the fragility of trust in a relationship and how it manifests in Isaac and Nory's relationship.

# About the Author

*Photograph of the author © Dominic Jennings*

A former professional cake baker, **Jenny Bayliss** lives in a small seaside town in the UK with her husband, their children having left home for big adventures. She is also the author of *The Twelve Dates of Christmas* and *A Season for Second Chances*.